BEST SERVED COLD

Published by Red Kimba Press

Paperback ISBN-13: 978-1-7398510-0-2
eBook ISBN-13: 978-1-7398510-1-9

Printed in the United Kingdom

Cover design and layout by www.spiffingcovers.com

BEST SERVED COLD

GABRIEL GALLETTI

CHAPTER 1

"You know why they caught me, Mr Hilton?"

Chad rubbed his knee under the table. Right now, he thought, I couldn't give a shit. I don't care if they used a clairvoyant or a fucking Ouija board, you mad, murdering bastard. The throbbing was getting worse and the pain screeched up his leg, hung a left into the spine and hurtled on to the brain, hammering and pleading for relief. The source of relief – Fentanyl – was gone. The empty silver strip of tablets nestled in his jacket from when he popped the last one three hours before, and there was time. Now the intervals were getting shorter. Concentrate, he thought and stared across the table. But please make it end.

The room was concrete, painted white, and roughly three metres by two. The ceiling lights released an unremitting glare. Everything in here was bleak, he thought. One table, two chairs, two occupants. The difference between the two – a pair of handcuffs, prison sweats and the fact that one of them was a killer.

"You see, Mister Hilton, they only caught me because I allowed them to. Simple as that. The police don't get it, but you do. Don't you?"

"Get what, Jim?" Thank God there was a time limit, or he'd have to kill him to shut him up. That would take some explaining. "What do I get?"

"It's obvious, Mister Hilton. They caught me because I decided that I wanted them to see me for who I am. But I had to give them some clues because they couldn't see me otherwise. They could only see the mask I let them see. Because we all wear masks, Mister Hilton, don't we? You do, I do, we all do. But I wanted them to see the real Jim Dunn."

Piss off, you mad old twat. Classic delusion. Jim Dunn was a sadistic killer who took pleasure in his work. He'd been caught because he got carried away, and in his frenzy left DNA on his final victim. Then I get lumbered with determining if the guy was mad or bad. Both is the right answer. But for the purposes of due process and in my professional opinion, Jim Dunn was as sane as the next guy. He just loved the slaughter.

The door opened and a prison guard entered. "Time's up."

Chad eased the chair back and held on to the table to help him stand. He looked across the table for the last time, to find Jim Dunn staring at him.

"You want to get that leg seen to," said the killer. "It looks painful."

Chad watched as the prisoner edged towards the door.

He stopped and turned to Chad. "Been a pleasure talking to you, Mister Hilton. I'll look forward to our next chat."

The phone in Chad's pocket vibrated. A text from DI Lee Wallace. *'Mate, call me - urgent. On my way to Leeds Infirmary'*

He'd have to wait, thought Chad and leaned on the table to take the weight off his knee. He had an appointment of his own with Freddie Jackson. And that was fucking urgent.

CHAPTER 2

Lee peered through the glass panel in the door. The woman lay waif-like in the bed, black hair splayed across the pillow. One side of her face was swollen and angry, purple bruises contrasting with the brash white of the bed linen. Her knuckles were split open. Either side of the bed, two female detectives stood holding her hands. He saw the girl's lips move. At least there was dialogue, he thought. In his experience it went one of two ways. Either the victim was too shocked to recall and articulate what had happened, or they had an almost photographic memory of the event. Let's see.

He typed into his phone. *Chad, need you now buddy. I'm at the hospital. Think we've got a fifth victim.*

Seconds elapsed, then his phone pinged.

Shit. Okay, no probs. Let me know what she says, I'll text you with any questions.

The rap of his knuckle on the glass broke the stillness in the corridor and he saw the thumbs up to enter. God, she's so tiny, he thought, she makes the bed look too large for the room. There was grazing on her neck as well as to her face, but he knew that would fade long before the mental scars.

He pushed the door open and said, "Hi Emily, I'm Lee, am I okay to come in?"

She nodded.

His skin prickled with the oppressive heat in the room and the smell was an instant reminder of countless previous visits to other rooms on other cases. Keep a low profile, he thought, a man in the room of a rape victim can cause triggers.

Detective Sergeant Jas Carter spoke first. "Emily, I know this is difficult but, if you could, try and tell us what happened. Take your time, there's no rush, and stop if it gets too much for you, okay?"

The girl nodded.

"Just start from when you finished work," said Jas.

The girl in the bed blinked away a tear and looked past Jas, out the window and to the night sky over Leeds. After a few seconds, she began to speak. "I was grumpy with my boss 'cos he always does this. Leaves me and the other girls to make our own way home late at night while he sorts himself out. He makes sure he has a few drinks with the punters so he can't drive, then gets himself a taxi home on expenses. And we're left to our own devices." Her voice was trailing off. The hiss of the drip discharging its contents broke the silence. She took a breath and started again. "So, I'd walked down to the taxi rank outside Leeds Station. I reckoned there must have been a game on 'cos the queue was full of blokes wearing Leeds United shirts. All I could smell was beer and cigarette smoke." She paused. "I didn't fancy standing with that lot. It was drizzling and I reckoned there was no chance of getting a cab for at least a twenty-minutes. I could walk home in that time."

"Go on," said Jas, "you're doing great."

"I thought about calling dad to pick me up, but I decided it wasn't worth the argument and if Leeds had won, he'd probably have had a couple of beers so wouldn't drive anyway."

Lee saw Emily look up to the ceiling. Silence hung over the room. There was no movement, no shifting in chairs and a stillness in the bed. She took another deep breath and continued.

"I walked about fifty yards past the queue, silly boys singing their songs and one or two whistling at me then went down that flight of steps, you know, opposite the station entrance that lead down to Granary Wharf. It stank of wee and chips and at the bottom there was a young guy wrapped in a sleeping bag and clutching a dog. He asked me for change but I had none."

Lee watched as Jas, squeezing Emily's hand, gently stroked her arm.

"It was cold and I pulled the collar on my coat up. It's only a short walk if I cut through Granary Wharf and pick up the tow path along the canal. It takes about ten minutes. The cobbles were shiny from the rain and I told myself to be careful and not to slip. There was no-one around. It was quiet." She paused again. Tears tumbled down her cheeks and Jas wiped them away with a tissue.

"There's lampposts every twenty or thirty metres along the path and it looked deserted so I just thought, come on, get on with it." The words started to tumble out. "I started to walk as fast as I could, but the wind was biting. I was getting scared because the lights from the buildings on the opposite bank reflected weird shapes off the water. The canal was dead quiet and I dunno, it was black and seemed to slither beside me."

Lee looked up as Emily paused again. He saw her look at Jas and receive an encouraging nod in return. "I kept thinking I'd have a nice cuppa when I got home. And maybe some toast. I started to go a bit faster but then… I thought I'd seen a shadow beside a lamppost so I stopped walking. I think I shouted, "Who's there?" a couple of times, but no-one answered. There was nowt, just the water. I set off again and then…" She stared at Jas. "And then, it was like, I could smell something."

Lee stiffened, alert. This was new. He sensed his detectives thought the same and caught Jas' eye. Emily was still talking. "I was thinking what is that smell? It was familiar but… Then I thought, where's it coming from? And that was it. I felt an arm lock around my neck and lift me off my feet. I thought I should scream, but I just couldn't. I felt one of my ballet pumps fall off but then I saw his hand in front of my face holding this massive knife. I felt the material he had on his face move a bit and he said, "Scream and I'll kill you." And then he said it again. "Scream and I'll kill you." I couldn't scream, even if I'd wanted to. I couldn't do anything."

Lee saw the resolve and the tension fall away from her tiny frame in the bed. Exhaustion and shock setting in.

Jas kept her voice low. "What can you remember about him, could you see what he looked like, or what he was wearing?"

"No, there was nothing to see. When he was…" she paused again and a sob escaped. "When he was on top of me all I could see was this balaclava, it had slits for eyes. That was it. Nothing else."

"What about his accent, Emily, was it local?" asked Sally. Emily nodded.

"Could you tell anything about his age?"

"Well, he was strong, and his body felt, you know muscly, so I'd say he was younger rather than older."

Lee put his phone onto silent mode, so the messaging wouldn't disturb her, but the room illuminated as the screen lit up. *Chad, she remembers a smell just before the attack but can't describe it.*

The reply was instant. *Ask her if it's pleasant or unpleasant? Toast versus toilets.*

"Emily," said Lee, "you mentioned that you could smell something a few seconds before the attack, can you tell us anymore about it, was it an everyday smell? A kitchen? Food, perhaps? Or was it unpleasant, toilets for example?"

"Oh," said Emily. "It wasn't horrible, but it wasn't nice either. I'm good at being able to remember a place, or a memory, from the smell, but I just can't tonight." Her voice died to a whisper.

Neither pleasant nor unpleasant but can't remember where she's smelled it before.

Chad replied. *Probs the trauma that's caused the disassociation,*

I need a session with her to bring it out. Time for you to take the plunge, Lee. Hire me. Let me help you catch the bastard. Mates' rates.

"Emily, do you think you'd recognise the odour again?"

"Yes, I think so. I know I've smelled it somewhere, defo." She sank deeper back into her pillows, grief and exhaustion etched on her face.

Jas signposted towards the door with her eyes, then said, "Emily, we'll come to see you tomorrow, if that's okay? Go to sleep now and maybe there'll be something else you remember when you've rested, but don't worry, you've been brilliant."

* * *

Lee closed the door behind him and glanced back through the glass. Her eyes were closed, face pained. Her life changed in an instant, he thought.

Jas said, "Wow, how well did she do? She's a tough one. Her recall was fantastic, especially as she's still in shock. Same MO as the others, Boss, Emily's the fifth for certain, and still no frigging clues. Although, unless she's got it mixed up, we at least have a smell. We'll go back through the notes, tomorrow, and see if any of the other girls mention a peculiar whiff. Any thoughts, Boss?"

"I think I know someone who can help her identify that smell. If we can find out what that is, it'll take us a damn sight further than we are now."

"Great, let's hope so. Night, Boss, see you tomorrow."

Lee watched them go then dialled the number.

"Hi, this is Chad, please leave a message and I'll get back to you."

"Fuck," he gripped the phone tight in his hand, to stop himself from hurling it down the corridor.

CHAPTER 3

Chad's phone vibrated in his hand. He clicked off the call and sent it to voicemail. No point having that conversation until the morning.

At 1:00 a.m. Vicar Lane was empty, from the Victoria Gate shopping centre to his left to the old Kirkgate Market on his right there were only a few punters, crab walking, looking for another bar and another drink. The grey metal fire exit door in front of him was cold to the touch. It looked like any other, but that was the point. There was a keypad on the wall. He checked the text from Freddie, then keyed in the number. The buzz of the lock opening wasn't loud enough to attract the attention of the crab-walkers.

Holding tight to the stair-rail, using his left leg as lead, he took the metal stairs one at a time. He could hear the soft beat of the music. The staircase fell from street level to the basement in which the original large stone flags led through an archway, beyond which two fire doors protected a low-ceilinged, brick-walled bar. Chad peered through the safety glass. It had the look and feel of a 1930s Philadelphia speakeasy. A three-piece band with a singer in a red sequined dress and crimped blonde hair was belting out Jessie J's *Price Tag* at the far end of the room. In front of the band, a small dance floor heaved. The music throbbed behind a swell of conversations. A hatch to his right gave a view of a kitchen, where four guys in chefs' whites hurried between stainless steels tables and piles of food. On four TV screens around the bar, incongruous given the setting, Sky Sports was showing. Typical Freddie. He'd probably got *Freddie Jackson's Best Leeds United Goals of the Nineties* on a loop. Chad could see a barman in a white wing-collared shirt with a red bow tie and leather apron leaning over and rearranging the beer mats. He looked like he'd won a moustache-growing competition. The punters were a crush of steroid-laden bodies that looked like a bouncers' convention, each suited and booted for the occasion. Chad did as he'd been instructed and sent Freddie a text.

In the fire escape.

He leaned against the wall taking the weight off his leg and waited. On the other side of the doors the muscle in suits began parting. Moses couldn't have done a better job, and somewhere in California, Chad reckoned, they'd be measuring a small tremor on the Richter scale. He saw Freddie's head first. Towering over them all, his shiny black skull gleamed in the lights. He had the frame of a 49ers Line-backer and the face of a film star. As Freddie moved through the throng Chad saw that he wore a double-breasted blue suit, with glistening silver pinstripes, complemented by a white satin shirt which shimmered against his ebony skin.

Chad heard the bar on the other side being pushed and the fire doors swung open. Freddie walked through and closed them behind him leaving three of his henchmen standing guard on the other side.

"Freddie, how are you buddy? So, I'm your best mate but you make me use the tradesman's entrance. Nice. Very nice."

"You know very well why," said Freddie as he released Chad from a hug. "Given why you're here it's better not to be seen. Anyway, I couldn't have you out the front dressed like that. You look like a bloody geography teacher and that's not the vibe we're looking for in here."

Chad laughed, "Fair enough. How's this place doing? I saw you had the glitterati at the opening a couple of weeks ago."

Freddie leaned his back against the doors blocking out the lights within. "Can't complain, buddy, can't complain. We've been open two weeks and it's been heaving every night and busier on Saturdays." Freddie reached inside his jacket pocket. "Chad, bro, you know I love you, man, so take this as it's meant."

Chad knew what was coming.

"You're doing too many of these."

Chad saw he held six foil strips in his hand.

"My guy was telling me that Fentanyl is uber strong. They're frigging dangerous. We need to get some help to get you off them, buddy, I mean look what happened to Prince. And Michael Jackson, bro. Prescription drugs killed 'em. I won't let you go the same way."

"Stop worrying, you sound like Angie. I know what I'm doing. They help me to function, that's all, without feeling like someone has taken an electric drill to my knee. And what I get on prescription is nowhere near enough."

"That's shit, man, and you know it. You get hooked on these, buddy, and the pain in your knee will be the least of your fucking worries."

"Yeah, I know, but that isn't going to happen. I promise."

"And how is the lovely Angie, I haven't seen her for ages? You should be at home snuggling up with her, not doing this shit."

"All good, my friend, same old. She's fine. No news."

Freddie's smile remained, but the raised eyebrow asked the question.

Chad ignored it. "We'll have to get a dinner arranged, you could bring Grace, maybe, or is Jocelyn still on the scene? Or maybe Charlotte? Look, Freddie, thanks for these, and I promise I'll get some help. I can't stay, I've got a bit of work to do for Lee tomorrow, and I need to call him early doors."

"Jesus, you've got to get a real job. I've told you before, getting in the head of psychos will twist your brain. Whatever the Feds pay, it's not enough for that shit. You know I'm not Lee's favourite person, right?"

"I know, but they need some help, and it's an earner so, hey, who am I to say no? Stay safe, Freddie, and thanks for these. Let's do that dinner soon, yeah?"

"Stay cool bro, call if you need me."

Left leg first, he could feel Freddie's eyes follow him out.

* * *

Emerging from the underground cavern onto a deserted Vicar Lane, Chad's breath disappeared in swirls into the night and his skin stung with the cold. The sweat on his back dried and his nostrils puckered at the smell of late-night kebabs, making his mouth water. Shit, I could just eat one of those, he thought, remembering that he hadn't eaten since a tuna and mayo at lunchtime. No time now. The taxi-stand opposite had two black-and-white cabs at the rank, one of which was going to be lucky and get his £40 fare back to Harrogate. His phone found a signal and vibrated in his pocket.

Be at my office tomorrow at 08.30. Don't be late. Meeting with my Chief Super at 08:00 to tell him I'm bringing you in. The lady we interviewed tonight confirmed as the fifth victim.

CHAPTER 4

The clock on the dashboard read 8.15 a.m. Plenty of time. Traffic was thinning near Leeds United's ground on Elland Road, and the statue of Billy Bremner outside the East Stand was draped with scarves. That had been the case for as long as Chad could remember. He may have only stood five feet four but to the people of Leeds, Billy was a colossus. "Morning, Billy," said Chad. "Where the hell is Police Headquarters? I'm sure it's down here on the left somewhere."

A news report on the radio blared through the speakers.

"Police have confirmed that an attack on a twenty-one-year-old woman in the Armley area of Leeds last night was carried out by the same attacker responsible for four previous assaults. No details of this latest victim have been released, but West Yorkshire Police will be holding a press conference later this morning. We'll bring that to you live from Police Headquarters."

The new Headquarters of West Yorkshire Constabulary appeared on his left. Opened in 2014, it was a modern design; white and mainly glass, à la mode. He followed the signs to the car park and found three at the rear of the building, all bordered with manicured flower beds. Bloody hell, he thought, no expense spared here. His knee was complaining from being in the car for so long. The muscles in his leg spasmed as he rubbed and massaged above and below the swelling. Holding onto the door for support he hauled himself upright. "Let's get moving," he murmured. "Come on, don't give way on me, let's just try and limp for fuck's sake."

By the time he'd reached the steps leading to the reception at the front of the building, the knee had turned up the volume on its complaint and was now delivering the grievance more formally.

"Crime seems to pay then?" said Chad, standing before the policeman on duty at the front desk.

"How do you mean?" the copper asked. He was well over six feet and hefty to boot. Exactly the sort of bloke Chad didn't want to rub up the wrong way.

"It's a very nice place you've got here. Expensive. Crime pays, get it?"

The desk duty copper gazed back at him. The lips didn't move but the expression said *do one, knobhead.*

Good start, thought Chad. "Okay, we'll leave it. I'm here for a meeting with DI Lee Wallace."

The officer checked the calendar on his desktop. "That's right, sir, you're in Room 106 on the first floor. But you'll have to wait here and I'll get a constable to escort you. I'll let DI Wallace know you're here."

"Okay, thanks."

Chad took in his surroundings while he waited. The atrium was high-ceilinged glass, and massive potted plants formed the central decorative piece. More Deloittes than detectives, he thought. A policeman in uniform arrived and Chad followed him up the escalator to the first floor. Room 106 was at the far end of a wide, airy corridor, down which Chad limped several paces behind his escort. The constable knocked and pushed the door open then poked his head inside.

"We can wait in here, sir, I'm sure DI Wallace won't be long," he said as Chad reached him.

"Thanks," said Chad and stepped inside. The copper took up a discreet stance to the side of the door next to a ubiquitous hand sanitiser, a reminder were one needed of the recent pandemic. Chad looked around. Six desks formed a rectangle around the perimeter of the room, all facing inwards towards a central desk at the front, behind which were state-of-the-art wipe boards on a wall. Photos of the five victims were stuck to the boards with brief details written below. The windows at the back of the room gave an impressive view of the stadium to his right. Chad turned as the squeak of hinges heralded an arrival.

The door inched open and a black polished shoe forced it wider. Lee sidestepped into the room carrying two cups of coffee and put them on the desk nearest the door.

"Hey, Chad good to see you, you found us okay then?"

"Yeah, no probs. How're things with you, big fella, come on and hug me, or is that not allowed in here?" Chad took a step back and said, "Now, let me look at you. Bloody hell, you've had a haircut and a pay rise by the look of that suit. Hugo Boss, if I'm not mistaken. Things must be looking up in the law enforcement game and I hope one of those is a black Americano?"

"Yes, black Americano, or at least, the coffee machine's version of that," said Lee, staring at a black sludge in a thin plastic cup. "Black, I reckon it can do, but not sure about the Americano. And you're not looking too bad yourself, for a washed-up footballer."

"Ha, thanks, you prat. By the way, tell the bloke downstairs on reception to get a sense of humour."

Lee picked up the vending machine's attempt at a latte as Chad's escort exited the room. "Have you been cracking funnies again? Doesn't it bother you that no-one ever laughs?"

"Nah, you get used to it. So, what did the Boss say? Delighted to welcome me on board, I bet?"

Lee looked over his shoulder and made sure the door was fully closed. "Now you are being funny. He's not keen on profilers in the first place, let alone ex-footballers taking up a second career. The two together don't do much for his heartburn. He's worried that having you involved in this will only increase the press coverage for all the wrong reasons. We don't need them giving this the 'celebrity' treatment. He also has concerns that they'll rake up your friendships and go digging into Freddie bloody Jackson's dodgy businesses. Again, we don't need that. So, I want your involvement kept hush-hush. Can you live with that?"

"He who pays the piper, et cetera. You're paying me, so I'll do as I'm told."

"Good, glad that's clear, and I need you to stay away from Freddie while you're involved. Okay?"

"Yes, mate, no problem." Fingers crossed so it didn't count. "By the way how come you got involved in this case. I thought you were too far up the ladder to have to get into the muck and bullets?"

"Chance would be a fine thing." Said Lee. "Any time there's a shit storm brewing the Chief Super "parachutes" me in as he likes to say. I got put onto this a couple of days ago. Can't say I'm massively inspired by the team yet but it's early days. I've had my say to them on what I think of their investigation so far, but I'm interested to hear your thoughts when you've met them. Joe Schmidt was the Senior Investigating Officer so as you can imagine his nose has been put out of joint. And don't expect red carpet treatment from them. They're struggling with the fact that they haven't caught this guy and that I've been brought in. Adding a profiler to the team won't brighten their mood. They mean well and they're not scared of hard work but…well see what you think but try not to be at your dogmatic worst please."

"No offence taken."

Lee smiled. "None intended. Oh, before I forget," he perched on the end of a desk. "I've arranged for you to meet our latest victim, Emily Barrett at her parents' home in Wortley as soon as we're done here. DS Carter will take you. Let's see if you can get anywhere on that smell."

They heard the door open.

"Come in, guys, come in," said Lee as a posse of five coppers stepped in and took up positions around the room. "Guys, this is Chad Hilton, he's a profiler and I've brought him in to help us build a picture of the guy we're after. He'll start today by visiting Emily, our latest victim, with you, Jas. Emily is being released home from Leeds General Infirmary later this morning. Chad, this is Joe Schmidt, don't be fooled by the surname, he's more Yorkshire than Tetley's, and this is Luke Deakin. And over here are Sally Plunkett, Jas Carter and Debbie Granger."

Chad nodded a general hello as he made some first glance assessments. Schmidt was old school he thought. His body language was crap and he couldn't hold eye contact. Deakin was younger and looked to Schmidt to check his reaction before he committed himself. Of the women, the smiled "hello" of Plunkett and Granger seemed to give him the benefit of the doubt but DS Carter was another matter altogether. Mid-thirties he guessed, raven black hair, skin the colour of caramel chocolate and a smile to die for.

Lee beckoned to Schmidt. "Okay, Joe, bring us up to speed and, for Chad's benefit, do a recap on what we have on all the attacks so far."

The detective slouched to the front desk and looked at Chad.

Chad recognised the words behind the look. Years of playing against hard-knock defenders had taught him the language. It said don't be a cocky little shit or you'll get a slap.

Chad listened as Schmidt spoke in a low monotone, detailing from thread to needle the activities of the team. His growling Yorkshire accent made it harder to concentrate on what was said as oppose to how he said it. Not exactly Churchillian leadership, thought Chad. Even the team looked bored, maybe they'd heard it too many times. The nub of it, came down to five victims all attacked near their place of work between 11:00 p.m. and 01:00 a.m. All worked in the hospitality industry and from what Schmidt said everyone they had contact with was alibied. No DNA or forensics. Schmidt continued to drone for nearly half an hour. Chad looked at Lee and his knee throbbed. He needed to move, he thought before it seized up. But for Christ's sake having listened to this it was no surprise they hadn't caught this guy.

Schmidt seemed to be concluding. "We've put thousands of man hours into this, we've done over three hundred interviews and we've checked and verified every alibi. Everything is documented and labelled. It's like we said, he attacks at random so someone needs to come to us with information or he needs to make a mistake."

Chad looked around the room as the team emerged from its stupor.

"First thoughts, Chad?" asked Jas.

Chad ran his hand through his hair. First thoughts, he mused. What a fucking shitshow. How's that for first thoughts? If he said what he wanted to this was going to be the shortest project on record. But how could he not say what he was thinking? Chad rubbed his knee and scanned the faces in front of him. He was about as welcome here as a fart in a space suit that much was obvious. He looked across the room and caught Lee's eye. Might as well deal with this now. "Lee, can we have a quick word in private?"

Lee stared at Chad then stood and opened the door. Chad shuffled off the desk and walked out of the room, the glares of the coppers following him out.

"What?" demanded Lee. Then he raised his hands palms facing Chad. "Okay, okay, I know what you're going to say. It's hardly an advert for progressive innovative police detection is it? I've told them it's a pile of shit."

"Look, Lee you're the new SIO so why don't I play bad cop? Excuse the pun. That way it's to me they'll direct their anger, not you. I'm listening to Schmidt and thinking, what the fuck? All I've heard is police procedure. I's dotted and t's crossed but that isn't going to catch this guy. And this random attacker stuff is just fucking nonsense. Now I can't just sit here and nod. I want to help but first I need to rattle your guys' cage. Make them think. Make them see things differently. And I can't do that diplomatically and worrying about their feelings. I need to be blunt. I wanted to check you're okay with that before I say anything. If not, we may as well call it a day now and not waste each other's time." Chad watched the conflict on Lee's face. Trying to decide if this is worth it, Chad thought.

"Okay," said Lee, "we've got to try something, so carry on. I'll jump in if it gets too confrontational."

Chad followed Lee back into room 106. Entering, he could almost feel the scepticism. He understood it, profilers faced it every day. But scepticism wasn't his problem, it was theirs. They'd have to deal with it. It just made their acceptance of him that much harder. Right, in for a penny, he thought.

"So, Jas, you asked for my first thoughts." He paused and saw five faces staring at him with varying degrees of hostility. Lee looked at the floor he knows what's coming, thought Chad. "Look, guys, time is against us so I'm going to be blunt. A sixth victim isn't far away unless we stop this perp." Chad watched the heads turn towards him. "And there's no easy way to say this, but my summary is that you haven't got a clue who this guy is, where he is or how you're going to catch him."

Schmidt muttered something under his breath that Chad couldn't hear. "What you've just said was like some police procedure check list." Chad mimicked crossing things off a list, "*We've done this, tick. Interviewed that, tick. Dotted that I and crossed that T,* but you're no closer to catching this guy than when you started. This reminds me of the Ripper investigation." Schmidt shoved back his chair and stood. The alpha male was clearly riled, Chad thought.

"Fuck off," snarled Schmidt. "What the fuck do you know? It's nothing like that."

"Oh, no?" said Chad. "Thousands of interviews, rooms full of statements, hundreds of thousands of man hours spent on it.

And not a fucking clue. What's different? If you don't get a result soon that's how your investigation will be seen. Only worse, 'cos back in the seventies they didn't have the software that you have to analyse and identify links or trends." Chad looked at Lee who inclined his head and then nodded. Carry on.

"In the Ripper case the coppers couldn't see the wood for the trees. They interviewed the Ripper nine times. Nine times, for fuck's sake. I bet that somewhere in all the work you've done is the clue to breaking this, but you're too close, you can't see it. And to cover your arses you've opted for the random attacker theory which is basically saying *we've done all we can, the public have to help.*" Chad paused for breath and surveyed the wreckage of his profiling assignment. Fuck it, he thought, they need to hear this. He checked out the body language. Only Jas seemed open to listening, the rest displayed a collective scowl.

"This rapist is not an opportunist. That theory is utter bollocks." Chad saw Lee stiffen by the door, but continued. "He can't account for passers-by interrupting him, or the girls being met by a boyfriend, or family waiting to take them home. The chances of him being caught doing it once are massive, but getting away with it five times? Seriously, you must be kidding. Propagating that theory, or even convincing yourselves of it, will mean you miss the clues that are available. There's loads of people in Yorkshire who remember the police cock-ups that came out after the Ripper was caught. They won't forgive you if they find the same again."

Chad took a sip of coffee. "I'll tell you why the attacks aren't random. Because there are 402,000 women in Leeds and 10% are aged twenty to twenty-five. 40,200 potential targets, for fuck's sake. So, if you're one of the five victims you are either fucking unlucky – your random theory – or you've been selected. Guys, the victims all work in the hospitality industry, that links them for a start. So, begin again. This perp somehow has access to these women, and their work is the most obvious connector. Find out how." Chad saw the team shuffle and exchange looks. "Before I finish, remember this. Your perp carries a massive knife. He's got lucky so far and nothing has gone wrong, but what if it does?" The team were staring at him. "For now, you've got a rapist to find." Chad paused and looked back at them, "But you're one mistake away from having a murder on your hands."

No-one spoke. There was nothing left to say.

CHAPTER 5

That went well, Chad thought, following Jas out of the building and into the car park. "Are we going in yours?"

"Yep," said Jas, "unless you've got somewhere to go afterwards, in which case follow me. If not, I'll drop you back here."

Flashing sidelights on an electric blue BMW 3 series saved him asking. Chad opened the passenger door. "Bugger me," he said, "don't you have waste bins at home?" He stared at the seat then looked across the roof of the car at Jas. "Where the hell do you want me to sit 'cos it looks like these crisp packets, those receipts and this parking ticket have shoved a big fat reserved sign on this one."

"Very funny. When do I get time to clean up? Never," she said, leaning over and grabbing an Adidas holdall from the footwell. She moved some dry cleaning hanging up behind the driver's seat and shoved the bag on the back seat. "Just shove that other stuff on the floor, I'll sort it later."

"I see you have an eclectic taste in crisps. You'll do salt and vinegar or cheese and onion. I like plain. Nice car, is it leased or does it come with the job?"

"Come with the job? You must be kidding." Rain kicked the automatic wipers into action. "How do you know DI Wallace, have you worked with him before?" she asked, turning onto

Elland Road.

"We go way back. We've been friends for, Christ, it must be twenty-odd years. After I qualified, he sometimes used me as a sounding board, but this is the first time he's hired me. Might be the last, judging by that meeting."

"Oh, don't let Joe bother you. He's a grumpy bastard at the best of times, and his professional pride is hurt because the Boss has had to bring you in to help. How long have you been a profiler?"

'I did a psychology degree after I finished playing, and enjoyed the profiling part most, so I specialised in it for my PhD. It's weird, I don't know many other professions which polarise opinion as much as this one. Some people think profiling a perp is a great crime-solving tool, others, like Joe and your Chief Super, think it's a load of bollocks. Where do you stand?"

"Oh, I don't give a shit. Anything that helps us catch the bad guys works for me. What did you mean about when you finished playing? Playing what?"

"I was a footballer. Played for the guys we've just driven past."

"Oh, wow, is that right?" she said. "My nephew's a massive Leeds fan, will he know you?"

"Depends how old he is. I played in the nineties, and retired in ninety-eight when the surgeons got pissed off with operating on my legs."

'Well, he's only eight, so I don't suppose he will, but he'll be super-impressed that you played for Leeds. His dad was a season ticket holder for years, so I can check you out. Were you any good?"

"Not bad, so I'm told."

"So, how come you didn't become one of those ex-footballers who spend all their time talking shit on Sky Sports?"

"I couldn't think of anything worse. Playing football was fantastic, and I could imagine why some go into coaching or managing when they finish playing, but waffling on about nothing, just to be on the telly? Nah, not for me." He looked out of the window. Ange wouldn't agree with that, he thought. Not being on the telly was high on her bone-of-contention list.

Jas turned and smiled, then said, "How do you want to play it with Emily? She only got home this morning, so we need to be mindful that her mental health will be fragile."

"Yeah, I know and, to be fair, I reckon it's going to be a bit weird. I want her to test everyday household items. I'm assuming she'll have smelled whatever it is either at home or work, the two places she spends most of her time. But according to my mate Google, humans are crap at identifying smells. Let's hope she spots it, but even if she doesn't, we'll be able to eliminate lots of items from the possible list. That will narrow things down."

The small oval tablet eased from the foil into his hand. Smooth like a jelly bean. Chad coughed and popped it in his mouth.

"Sounds like a plan," said Jas. "A weird one, but a plan nonetheless."

"Yeah, well, I can't think of a better one, but if you can, fine let's hear it."

"No, we'll stick with yours."

"What's up, why the frown?"

"Oh, nothing. That bloody prison gives me the creeps every time I drive past it. It's like a medieval castle," she said, looking ahead to the ominous turrets of HMP Armley.

"Me too," said Chad, "but when we catch the bastard who's been doing this, it'll be good to know he'll end up in there."

Number twenty-one was a small two-up, two-down in a row of terraces that looked like they'd been built in the seventies to house the prison officers. Grey pebble-dashing and some UPVC windows were the only more recent additions. To the left, the road ran towards Wortley and, to the right, the prison was the next-door neighbour. Chad looked up and down the soulless street. They'd been spotted for coppers before the engine was off, he thought.

* * *

The door was answered by a man in his fifties with hunched shoulders, three days of stubble and a face demanding a fight. Chad smiled.

"Come in," he said putting a fat hand on Chad's shoulder and ushering him into a cramped porch while peering outside to ward off prying eyes. "Her mum has had to go to the doctors' and Emily's upstairs. I'll get her."

"Shit," Chad muttered as he stumbled over a pair of ladies Doc Martins that were on the mat.

"Mind yourself there, lad, I keep bloody telling 'em to take their shoes upstairs but you know what lasses are like. She's got more shoes than Imelda Marcos, my wife, and Emily's not much better. Now find yourself a seat."

"This is a lot bigger than you'd think from the outside," said Jas.

In the centre of the lounge a wooden coffee table took up most of the floor space, and a substantial leather three-seater settee occupied the length of one wall. A matching armchair was the seat of choice for Emily's dad, who sat down and picked up the remote control indicating, Chad thought, that he felt his role in the proceedings was over. Both settee and armchair faced a mammoth, wall-hung TV. Chad felt the Fentanyl beginning to hit. Shit, he thought, get control and sit the fuck down. The drug surged through his veins. It was yellow, like car headlights at night. And the pain eased. Breathe, just breathe.

A creak on the stairs interrupted Lorraine Kelly. A young woman clutching a hot water bottle and swamped by a large dressing gown was coming down. She managed a thin smile, then sat down at the end of the settee.

"Hi Emily, I bet you're glad to be home, aren't you? Did you get much rest?" said Jas.

"Not really, no. But I feel a lot better being at home, and in my bed."

"Emily, this is Chad Hilton, he's not a policeman, he's a specialist, helping us try and build a clearer picture of the man who attacked you. You mentioned yesterday that he had a smell about him, so Chad wants to try and help you remember what that was. Is that okay?"

"Yeah, if it will help."

She sounds subdued. Not surprising, Chad thought. "Hi Emily," he began, "as Jas said, I want to try and place the odour that clung to the guy. So, what we'll do is work our way through a list of possibilities, and see if any triggers a recognition. Okay?"

"Okay," said Emily, looking at her dad, who, realising something was required of him, gave a confirmatory nod.

"Fine. Well, I suggest we just walk room to room and pick the household items. Most of these will have a chemical base. We may get lucky, we may not. So, can you lead the way?"

An archway led into the kitchen, which was similar in size to the lounge. The windows looked out onto a small, well-maintained lawn. On the worktops were an assortment of countertop electricals, an empty fruit bowl and a vase of fresh flowers that looked like a recent addition. There were five floor cupboards with vivid red doors and three matching wall units. A fridge freezer, washer dryer and a dishwasher completed the white goods. The detergents and washing-up products were in the cupboard under the sink. Emily picked them up one by one and put her nose to each, with an expression of hope which faded on each sniff.

As she put the last detergent bottle back, she said, "It's weird, I can sort of smell it around me now, it's like on the tip of my tongue, and I know it's common, so why can't I remember it?"

Poor kid, Chad thought, attacked, badly hurt and now she thinks she's going nuts. "Well, you've undergone a dreadful, traumatic incident, and sometimes the memory shuts down to block things out. I think your brain is acting as a protection mechanism. Does that make sense?" Chad said.

"So, you think that when I do smell it again, I'll recognise it? And what happens if I don't?"

"Yes, I'm certain you'll recognise it, but if none of the household products triggers the memory, then we'll know it's connected to his work, which narrows things down. Shall we go upstairs?"

Emily nodded and led them back into the lounge. Chad looked at the steep incline of the staircase and gave thanks that the Fentanyl had kicked in. At the top was a small bathroom and a landing with two further doors, both closed. In the bathroom, the shampoos, and conditioners were arrayed along the side of the bath. A yellow plastic duck with Elvis hair and sunglasses had pride of place behind the taps.

Emily worked her way through the products. "Nope, it wasn't any of these. It wasn't beauty or hair." She led the way along the landing.

"Okay, well that's cool, we are beginning to rule out certain smells. That's important," said Chad.

"This is my mum and dad's room." She said, hesitating by the door. Chad understood her reluctance to allow strangers into her parents' bedroom but pushed the door open and entered.

A double bed took up the bulk of the available space, allowing room for a small bedside table on either side. One with an alarm clock, the other with a pair of glasses and a book, Gone Girl, open face down. The curtains were open, and Jas' Beemer was attracting the attention of a bunch of kids outside. There was a built-in wardrobe, running the length of the wall opposite the bedhead. "Don't think there'll be anything in here," said Emily, opening the sliding doors. "Wait, though, that's a bit like it."

"What is?" asked Jas.

"Well, that first smell, as I opened the door. Not quite the same, but similar."

Clothes hung on hangers, across the length of the wardrobe, beneath which were shelves, with a range of ladies' shoes.

"Clothes, or shoes?" asked Chad.

"I'm not sure."

"Could be several things. There are your mum's work clothes, going out gear, and by the look of it, some sports stuff. What made your nose prickle? Perfume maybe?"

"I dunno, I'm sorry. I thought I could smell it but now it's gone."

"Okay, no worries, let's keep going."

* * *

Twenty minutes later, Jas, opened the front door and said, "Thanks very much, Mr Barrett, I hope Emily gets some rest and we'll keep you up to speed with any developments. Chad, don't fall over the shoes this time."

"Thanks for coming, and we'll call you if she remembers anything else," said Emily's dad.

Chad's phone vibrated. Ange. He clicked it off. No time for that right now.

The rain was coming down faster as Jas pinged the car open. "How do you think that went? Don't think it's taken us much further forward, do you?"

"Fuck, I'm getting soaked here, remember I can't go as fast as you," Chad shouted. He splashed to the car and opening the door sat at right angles to the dash then swung his legs in. "Maybe," he said "she'll remember it as the trauma reduces, and I do think we have moved on a bit. Whatever that odour is, we now know that it isn't a household item, don't we?"

"Yeah, we haven't covered all household items, but I suppose, yes, the ones Emily is familiar with."

"If it's not household, it's related to his work. I think that's important. Anyway, something in her mum's wardrobe triggered a response. Mothballs, maybe? Do people still have mothballs? I don't know, but we need to remember that."

Jas was staring at him.

"What? What have I said?"

"Nah, nothing. I was thinking, that maybe you're not as green as you are cabbage looking."

"As backhanded compliments go that's up there, but I'll take it."

CHAPTER 6

The walk from Jas' car to his own was thirty metres but took enough time for the rain to plaster his hair to his forehead. By the time he'd contorted himself into the driver's seat, icy little streams ran down the back of his neck and steam formed a foggy blur on the windscreen. The back of his trousers squelched against his skin. "Fuck, I'd better call." Rumblings from his stomach added to his apprehension. "Shit, I've got butterflies," He stared at his mobile, then dialled.

Angie answered, "Hey babe, thanks for calling me back, how are you?"

"I'm okay, I suppose. Hanging on in. How's things with you?"

"Yeah, likewise. I'm still staying at the Hotel du Vin which is fine but not a long-term solution. Look Chad," she paused "we need to talk, we can't continue like this"

"I'm ringing you, aren't I?"

"Don't be childish, you know what I mean. Have you given any more thought to us going to see a counsellor maybe, someone who can help us, someone who can mediate? Please Chad, I want to make amends and work it through with you. I do. Or, if you won't see a counsellor can I come home and we'll talk?"

"Look, Angie, I don't know if I'm ready yet. I'm still trying to get my head around it."

"I know, babe, and I understand, but we need to do it together. Being on your own and not talking isn't going to help. It'll only make things fester inside you and we'll never sort it. Let's try and have a conversation. Don't twenty-one years of marriage warrant that?"

"Hey, don't come that with me," he knew he was shouting. "Twenty-one years meant a fuck sight more to me than it seems to have meant to you. Ange, I don't even know if you've stopped seeing him, let alone who he is. Let's make a start there. Cut this, '*you don't need to know, what does it matter?*' bullshit. Tell me his name and where you met him and we'll have something to talk about. A starting point."

"I told you I've stopped seeing him. Come on, Chad, don't be a prick. Let's discuss this like two adults. You're meant to be the one who can rationalise things. Let's be grown-up about this."

"For fuck's sake Ange, what's grown-up about what you did?" He paused. This was getting nowhere. "Look, I haven't got the headspace right now," he said. "I'm working with Lee on this rapist case and I can't do that and sort this mess out."

"So, that's more important, is it? Helping Lee is more important than getting your marriage back together?" Her voice ratcheted up a few notches.

"Maybe if you hadn't started shagging someone else, I wouldn't have to try and do both." He shifted in his seat, angry at himself. Why the fuck had he said that? He had to get better at managing these conversations.

"Fuck you, Chad! Maybe you should ask yourself why I started seeing someone else. Maybe then we'd get somewhere. You're quick to point out everyone else's shortcomings, but you're a fucking hypocrite. Have a look in the mirror." The mobile's screen went from light to black. Mute condemnation.

Chad listened to the rain on the windscreen. What did she mean? She couldn't think he'd been having an affair as well, so was she talking about the drugs? He knew they consumed him and made him oblivious to everyone and everything else? But had she seen it? Was that it, had his behaviour driven her to this other guy, or was she heading there anyway and his drug use was the excuse? Which came first? Who knew?

Pressing the ignition, the engine fired and the radio blared. The Stones. Paint it Black. "You couldn't make this shit up."

CHAPTER 7

The clock said 5:50 p.m. Elland Rd for the second time in the day. It was a different copper on the reception desk but Chad decided not to waste his one-liners this time. Taking his Security card, he followed another constable up the escalator to room 106.

The team was already assembled. "Not late, am I?"

"No, Chad, you're fine, bang on time. Right, thanks everyone, let's make a start," said Lee. "Jas, how did you and Chad get on with Emily Barrett, any joy with tracing the source of this smell?"

From his vantage point on the desk by the window, Chad saw their fatigue and felt their frustration. How could he help? Not by being a prick like this morning. Not by antagonising them. There was less hostility than earlier, at least that's if a couple of nods and a smile meant anything but they needed a break.

Jas was answering Lee, "Yes and no, boss. We can rule out household products, bleach, hairspray that sort of thing as none of those triggered any sort of response. But as Chad pointed out, that means the smell must be related to the perp's work."

"Well, that's a step in the right direction, but we're going to need a lot more than that. Joe and the rest of you guys, how did you go reviewing the victims' statements about their work? Anything leaping out?"

Chad shifted on the desk, rubbed his thigh muscles and listened to what Joe had to say.

"Nothing. We've re-read the victims' accounts, and we've gone through the witness statements of their colleagues, but there's nothing to link any of them to these crimes. All the male co-workers have alibis and we can't find evidence that points to any of them as the perp. We've taken another look at the punters at the bars, restaurants and regulars at the hotels where the girls worked. Drew a blank there as well."

Chad frowned as Schmidt detailed the routine procedures they'd carried out. It was clear that the team were bogged down, unable to find their way through the mass of detail, he thought. He had to try and assist without being a dick. He heard Lee's words from earlier that day. "*Don't be dogmatic.*" "Lee, may I?" All eyes turned towards Chad.

"Yes, by all means, jump in."

"Thanks. Look, guys, I'm convinced that the smell that clings to our perp is from his work. And I stick by what I said this morning, our guy is not an opportunist. He's planned the attacks. He's detailed and cautious. We know the girls work in hospitality, so how has he met them?"

"Well, as Joe's just said, he's not a punter, we've checked all those. And he's not a colleague 'cos all their alibis stack up. So, I don't know, maybe he's a..." Luke Deakin ran out of ideas.

Chad looked up as Jas slid from the adjoining desk, her eyes gleaming. He felt a sudden energy in the room. Go, girl, he thought.

"I know we've checked the main suppliers to their workplaces, but maybe there's others we haven't checked? To me it seems that the perp would be someone who's had contact with all the victims, but not someone they'd notice if you know what I mean? So, a supplier fits that bill"

"Yes, Jas, I think you could be right." Said Chad. "Someone that blends into the surroundings, a person who the victims know, but don't know if you get me. Unremarkable, comes and goes, but has access to them. It wouldn't be difficult for our bloke to find out times the girls finish work, where they go, how they get home and therefore where they might be vulnerable."

"There must be hundreds of bloody businesses that supply to all these bars, hotels and restaurants, we need to find a way to narrow that down," said Joe.

Lee turned to Joe. "Yes, but Emily Barrett said he had a Leeds accent so we can make a start with checking which local firms deliver or collect from all the victims' workplaces. Right, let's crack on, meet back here at 10:00 p.m. for a final debrief. I'll get us a pizza."

CHAPTER 8

Puddles from the afternoon's rain lingered on the pavement, and the chill in the wind made his knee throb. There was a matching throb at the front of his head. Stress. How to deal with his situation with Ange? He checked his mobile. No missed calls and no messages. She wasn't going to make a move, so he'd have to if he wanted to get this sorted. Chad looked at the clouds scudding overhead. What did he want to sort? Reconciliation? Was that it? But how the fuck could you trust someone that had betrayed you? A puddle's icy contents spilt over his shoe into his sock. Shit. He tapped the screen and Angie's name illuminated.

"Hi, this is Angie, leave a message and I'll call you back."

"Angie, it's me. Look, I'm sorry we ended up shouting, I know that isn't going to help. Can we meet for coffee? Maybe tomorrow? I'll be in Leeds so if you can nip out from work for half an hour that would be good. Let me know," he paused "Night, babe." He ended the call and stared again at the black screen. "Twenty-one years and this is where we are" he whispered.

He rubbed the metal strip of Fentanyl between his fingers. Were these just a comfort-blanket, or was he hooked? Was that what she'd meant about looking in the mirror, she thought he was a junkie? The football stadium across the road was shrouded in darkness and loomed over him. The scene of all his triumphs. But what now? Was he like a has-been gladiator with no future, living on past glories? He leaned against a wall. "Pull yourself together" he said "You're better off than ninety-nine percent of people, you dick. Get a grip, and stop feeling sorry for yourself." He checked the foil, should he take one now? Nah, but they're there if he needed to. He felt his breath quicken. Maybe just one to keep him going, before the pain kicked in? No, he was okay, he was doing fine. Just when he needed to.

He popped out a tablet. Yeah, when he needed to, fucking clown. His marriage was on the rocks, he'd only got two mates, one a copper and one a crook. Brilliant. And now he was turning into a fucking junkie. Yeah, doing fine. He looked down at the tablet. Okay, big boy, no more until bedtime. His hand trembled as he pushed the pill back into the foil.

"Clumsy bastard," he said as the tablet slipped from his grasp. He scrambled to catch it as it fell from his hand then, averting disaster, he held it tight between his fingers. It would get lost in his pocket. Can't have that. He dropped it onto his tongue. Last one until bed.

A pub called The Old Peacock was set back from the road. He'd seen it countless times from the team coach on match days. That'll do, he thought. Food required. The interior was warm and bright, but empty. Not surprising. Tuesday, winter, no game on across the road. The barmaid seemed pleased to see him. "I'll get a Diet Coke please and a look at the food menu as well."

"Of course, love, go and sit down and I'll bring those across for you."

"Where are all the team photos and shirts?" he smiled, looking at the unadorned walls. "I thought the place would be full of them given you're across the road from the Ground?"

"They get nicked, love. We used to have loads of signed photos but every home game we'd end up with faded patches on the wall. Looked awful, so Eric decided to re-decorate and not bother with the photos."

"Fair enough, makes sense."

The bar had benches around the walls in brown faux leather. He sat at a table adjacent to the front door and opened his iPhone, clicked on the "Notes" app and began to type. Q. *Local or Out of town? A. Local. Q. Why local? A. He must have the ability to be in Leeds at different times of the day and night. Q. What's he delivering?????* A shadow blocked the light from over his head, a man was standing in front of him leaning on the table. He was over six feet tall, portly, well into his fifties and, if he'd been wearing a tee-shirt proclaiming 'Landlord' his status could not have been more obvious.

"Now then," said the proprietor, "don't I know you?"

This must be Eric. "No, I don't think so. First time I've ever been in here, mate." Chad scrutinised the menu. He couldn't be arsed with chit chat tonight.

"You haven't aged much," Eric went on, undeterred. "Must be the hair, you've kept it the same style as when you played. Good footballer in your day, I reckon with advances in the medical world, if you'd been playing now, those injuries wouldn't have ended your career."

"I'm impressed," said Chad. "Recognising a has-been footballer from years ago, you must know your stuff."

"We don't get the players coming in any more. They used to, years ago. Big Jack Charlton sometimes had a pint before a bloody match let alone after." The landlord chuckled at his joke. "Too much money now, don't want to mix with the punters. Can't say as I blame 'em given some of our clientele. So, what brings you into the Old Peacock?"

"Old times sake maybe. I used to see this place from the team coach but never came in. I just had to nip somewhere down the road so thought, why not? What's worth eating?"

"Well, there's only one place down the road and that's the cop shop, you doing work with them now?"

"No, not really, just some research that's all." A thought

occurred to him. "Maybe there's something you can help me with though?"

"If I can I will. What do you want to know?"

"I'm looking at the hospitality industry and trying to work out what gets delivered by local firms compared to what the big nationals deliver. I'm thinking you get your beer and spirits supplied on contract from the brewers, so what stuff do the local boys deliver?"

Eric looked past Chad out of the windows towards Billy's Bar in the South Stand.

"Maybe eggs, milk that sort of thing. There's a company called Westwoods that deliver all over Yorkshire. Based in Ripon. Other than that," he paused "laundry may be a better bet if it's specifically Leeds. Several firms do laundry for the hospitality trades. Towels, table cloths, napkins, sheets all that sort of thing. One's in Armley not far from here called Leeds Laundry Services, we use them."

"Laundry," Chad repeated and typed the word into his phone with several exclamation marks after it.

"Aye, we get a good service, only use them for towels and covers but they're reliable and cheap. A guy called Tom does the collections and deliveries. Bit of a Jack the lad and likes to have some banter with Becky." He pointed over his shoulder to the girl behind the bar. "Have a word if you like, she knows them better than me." He turned to the bar. "Becky, here a second, love," he called.

Becky sauntered from behind the bar. "What's up Eric?" she asked, smiling. "This fella doesn't look like trouble to me."

"Silly bugger," said Eric. "He's not trouble, he's Chad Hilton, played for Leeds before your time, back in the nineties."

Becky aimed for the demure look but missed. She smiled. "A bit old for me, but beggars can't be choosers. Are you married, sweetheart?"

"Yes," said Chad, "sorry about that." He smiled.

"Anyway," said Eric, "that bloke, Tom, does deliveries for Leeds laundry. That's right, isn't it?"

"Yeah, twice a week they come here. Why?"

"Oh, I'm doing some research," said Chad, "we're trying to get a handle on the types of firms that supply the hospitality industry locally, that's all. Where else does Tom collect from apart from here, do you know?"

"No, sorry love, we just banter with each other. All harmless stuff, but I know he's busy. Told me he has a few collections and deliveries every day in Leeds so he must be doing some of the bars."

"What's he like, this Tom guy?" asked Chad

"Oh, he's a nice lad, mid-twenties I'd say, funny and a bit of a charmer but harmless. He has this gormless mate that helps him though who always looks a bit weird. Can't remember his name. Ben, maybe?"

"Well, thanks that's been very helpful. I'd better be getting back."

"Aren't you going to have a bite to eat?" asked Eric. "Haddock and chips with mushy peas are lovely."

"Nah, thanks, I need to get off, there's something I need to do," said Chad.

* * *

"Come on, come on, answer the bloody phone."

"Hi Chad, what's up?" said Jas.

"Jas, answer this. That suit you wore this morning, had it been to the dry cleaners recently?"

"Yeah, I'd just picked it up , it was with some other stuff that's in the car. Why?"

"Do you remember this morning, downstairs in the kitchen Emily said the smell was all around her?

"Yeah."

"I'm certain that what she was smelling was the chemicals

from your suit and the same in her mum's wardrobe when we first opened the door. Call Emily Barrett's house and tell them we're coming over now."

"Chad, are you sure? If we go barging in and you're wrong, the police complaints department are going to have a field day."

"I'm right, and we have to test this. Look Jas, just do it, I'm calling Lee now, get there, I'll be there in fifteen minutes."

CHAPTER 9

Chad looked up and down the street and knew their arrival would have the curtains twitching again. Jas hit the doorbell and the chimes reverberated inside the house. Lee had still not replied to his voicemail, and it looked like Angie was avoiding him. Shit.

It was raining again, the light from the street lamps creating kaleidoscopic patterns of colour in the puddles on the pavement. As icy rivulets ran down his head, Chad turned up the collar on his jacket then shoved his hands in his pockets, hunching to keep the water from trickling down his neck again. He wondered, not for the first time, why he never had a fucking umbrella? The light in the porch flickered on, and footsteps approached. The door opened a few inches and a small, timid-looking woman peered around it.

"Hello, you must be D S Carter?" she said. "And is this Mr Hilton?"

"Yes, that's right, Mrs Barrett, and we wouldn't disturb you if it wasn't important, so thank you for agreeing to see us," said Jas.

"You'd better come in," said Emily's mum, "Emily's in bed but she's awake. She's very anxious and not in the best place. The doctor has given her some tablets to help her sleep but she hasn't taken any yet."

The shoes had been moved from the porch, for which Chad said a silent *Thanks* as there was now less danger of an embarrassing fall. They congregated in the lounge which seemed full with four people in it.

"I don't want my girl upset, do you understand?" Said Emily's father.

Chad wondered whether the dad's change in tone was for his wife's benefit.

As they trooped into the kitchen Chad said, "We understand, and that's not the intention. But if we can identify the smell, we are much closer to catching whoever did this to her before he does it to someone else."

"Can I get you a cup of tea or anything?" Emily's mum asked as he joined them in the kitchen.

"No, thanks, we're fine," replied Jas. "Chad, do you want to explain to Emily's mum what we want to do?"

"She smelled something in your wardrobe this morning, Mrs Barrett, and I think I know what it was. From what I can recall, hanging to the left were your everyday clothes and in the middle of the hanging rail were your work clothes. Is that right?"

"Yes, it is."

"To the right of the rail, are the going-out clothes, the stuff you wear every so often and then get cleaned. Do you hang those with the polythene covers supplied by the dry-cleaning shop still on?"

"Yes, I do, it keeps them fresh."

"And of those do you know which is most recent?"

"I think it must be my black sequined dress, I wore it to the Christmas party at work."

"Okay, thanks. When you go upstairs, I want you to sit with Emily, and ask her to close her eyes then place that dress in its polythene cover under her nose. If it's the correct smell it will trigger a reaction from her and, I'm afraid, Mrs Barrett, that she might get flashbacks to last night's trauma."

"Do we have to do this now? can't we wait a few days till she's more herself?" said Emily's mum, the concern was etched on her face.

Not surprising. "Mrs Barrett, I'm very sorry but the longer we leave it the more likely it is that there'll be another attack. Also, the less time that elapses, the speedier her recovery process can begin."

Jas nodded her encouragement to the frightened mother. Looking out of the kitchen window into the night Emily's mum seemed to make up her mind.

"Okay then, let's go and try this. I hope you're right Mr Hilton."

The diminutive figure led Jas out of the kitchen and across the lounge towards the stairs. Chad massaged his knee, more out of habit than need, and counted the stairs in his head. They'll be at the top now. His stomach churned. Turn right past the bathroom, four or five steps to mum and dad's room. Please, please let this be okay. Through the door, open the wardrobe, shuffle a few of the garments along the rail, now pull out the black dress. Turn and take a couple of steps, then down the landing to Emily's room. He took a deep breath. Her mum will go in first, she'll hold her hand and have a whispered conversation, Emily will be scared, but she's tough, she'll agree. He crossed his fingers. Jas goes into the room with the dress. Now what?

Emily's screech penetrated every part of the house. "That's it. That's the smell. Oh my God, that's it."

Her father leapt from his seat shouting, "What the hell have you done?"

Chad didn't reply but stood and waited for the noise upstairs to subside. Even from the kitchen, he could hear the sobs and cries of anguish as Emily relived the horror of the previous night. Being right was not all it was cracked up to be, he thought.

Five minutes passed before Jas came down the stairs, she looked to Emily's father. "Mr Barrett, Emily is calm now and your wife has given her a sleeping tablet which I'm sure will help. I'm going to arrange for a family liaison officer to come here first thing tomorrow and she'll be able to offer support and arrange any help that Emily may need. Thank you very much for allowing us here tonight, this will help us catch the man who attacked Emily. We'll see ourselves out. Thanks again."

Chad held out his hand to Emily's dad. The man's shoulders had collapsed inwards and the fight had left him. What remained was the worried, forlorn despair of a shell-shocked father. He shook Chad's outstretched hand.

CHAPTER 10

10:00 p.m. and the team were ranged out in front of Chad in Room 106. Looking at Jas was the only thing that took his mind off the bloody pain, he thought. Holding the Fentanyl strip in his pocket he counted the number of empty spaces. Five. Jesus. Four was the max prescribed limit. The problem was he needed one right now. It had been three hours since the last outside the pub, and the effects had all but worn off. One more now and another before bed. Shit, seven. What the fuck would happen? Was he in overdose territory? But in the competition between overdose later and dealing with the agony now, only one winner. He released a tablet and checked that no-one was watching him before swallowing it.

The door opened and Lee bristled in.

Chad marvelled at Lee's energy levels. The man was still raring to go like it was first thing in the morning. Hats off to you buddy.

"Joe, how far have you got on narrowing down the list of laundry service companies?"

"The five places that employed our victims used two laundry suppliers. Leeds Laundry Services based in Armley and Eco-Laundry based in Hunslet. But there are several others that we might need to check if we need to widen the search. That's if we're sure it's laundry."

"We're sure," said Lee. "Jas bring the team up to speed with tonight's developments."

Jas stood and walked to the front of the room.

Chad thought he'd never tire of watching her move.

"I got a call from Chad around seven-ish demanding that I meet him at Barrett's house, he said he was onto something. Boss, let Chad explain and I'll take up the running when we get to the bit with Emily."

Chad bought some time and rubbed the area around his knee. Shit. He'd thought Jas would have done the update otherwise he'd have held off taking the Fentanyl.

"Okay Chad, fill us in."

Chad took a deep breath. Control, breathe, stay focused. He managed to smile at Joe who had been unable to keep his annoyance at this latest turn of events, from finding its way to his face. He'd be a crap poker player thought Chad

"After our meeting earlier this evening, I went to find a bite to eat and ended up in the Old Peacock. I was chatting along to the landlord and asked him what sort of goods were delivered or serviced by local contractors rather than the nationals. He talked about various products and then blurted out that the most local service was laundry and mentioned Leeds Laundry Services and the delivery guys who work for them. That's when I remembered Emily catching a whiff of something when she opened the wardrobe door this morning and wondered if it could have been dry cleaning. I rang Jas and left a message for Lee and flew over to the Barrett's. That's about it, Jas did the rest."

"How did you check whether it was laundry?" asked Deakin.

"When we got there," said Jas, "Chad asked her mum if the posh going-out clothes in the wardrobe were still in the polythene that the dry cleaners put on them. She said yes. We told her we wanted Emily to smell one of them and see if that was the odour that clung to her attacker. Her mum wasn't keen but agreed to do it, so she and I went upstairs, found the dress and asked Emily to close her eyes and smell it."

"What happened?" asked Sally.

"The poor girl nearly leapt out of her skin. She howled and sobbed and clung to her mum. It was awful. She'd recognised it straight away, the mixture of chemicals and plastics."

"Bless her, poor thing. You weren't in there, were you Chad?"

"Hell no, that's all she'd have needed, a strange bloke in her bedroom. I stayed downstairs with her dad. He's a surly sod, but I felt for him."

Lee nodded. "It may not be our usual methodology, rocking up at a victim's house at night so soon after her assault, but it's done the trick. We are now as certain as we can be that the last attack was carried out by a laundry worker. The other victims didn't mention this smell, but the MO on all five is the same, so if we can nail him for Emily's attack, we'll link the others to him. Joe and Luke, take Leeds Laundry Services, Sally and Deb, you take Eco-Laundry, get there as soon as they open and check the delivery schedules, places, times, frequency and the names and addresses of all delivery drivers, drivers' mates and names of any temps or agency staff they've used. I want them interviewed tomorrow. Let me know if you need any extra resource. Jas, I want you to contact all the bars, restaurants and hotels that are serviced by these two laundries and identify any female staff that know them. Everyone get that?"

Chad continued the massage on his knee as he heard a rumbling of consent. The Fentanyl was taking hold, but he needed to share something before he started to slur his speech, or worse. Six was too many, his brain was slowing, God alone knew what seven would do. "It's called a Proustian Moment," he said.

"What is?" asked Lee. "Are you getting weird on us, mate?"

"No, sorry, but it's important. What Emily had tonight is called a Proustian Moment. It's when a smell recalls a specific event and memory. Not a good one in her case, but it gives you a huge advantage because the perp won't know how you've found out it's a laundry worker. That'll lead him to think he's made a mistake, which will panic him because he believes he's infallible. He'll be desperate to find out how you know, and his behaviour will become more erratic as his anxiety grows. Also, a smell noticeable to us will not be noticeable to the laundry workers themselves, like a smoker doesn't know they stink of fags, so the perp will not suspect this is what's betrayed him. Don't fucking mention it."

"Well, bugger me you learn something new every day. Thanks, Chad, good advice. No one mentions the smell. We let our perp think he's fucked up which may lead him to make a mistake. Great, that's been a very productive day, guys."

The door to room 106 pushed open and with it the smell of pizza.

"Pizza's here," said Lee, "so tuck in."

The screen on Chad's phone lit up. Angie, had finally replied to the message he'd sent hours ago. Why did she do that? Why leave it hours? Just to wind him up?

"*Yeah, got a busy day tomorrow but call me when you're in Leeds and we'll grab a coffee. Thanks for leaving me the voicemail, meant a lot. Night babe xx.*"

"Well, it's a start," he murmured.

"What is?" Lee had overheard him.

"Oh, nothing, mate, just glad this is moving along. By the way, you don't need me in the morning, do you? Thought I'd start to draw up the profile of the perp ahead of any interviews you'll be doing with suspects. Is that okay?"

"That'd be great, Chad. And thanks for today. You've moved this investigation further than we've got in six weeks of hard slog."

"No problem, fresh eyes sometimes help and I got lucky going to the pub. I'm going to get off, buddy. Enjoy the pizza and call me if you need me. Oh, and let me know how it goes at the laundry places tomorrow."

"Yeah, will do, buddy. Thanks again. Night, mate."

"Night all, have a good day tomorrow, I'm off," Chad shouted to the team.

They called out their goodnights. His stock was high. He pulled the door open and as he walked out, he heard Jaz behind him.

"As I said, you're not as green as you're cabbage looking."

He didn't turn, just smiled and walked.

* * *

Chad caressed the glass in front of him which glowed with the honey tones of his favourite Highland Park 12-year-old. The Fentanyl strip lay on the table next to the bottle. His two best friends together. They say it's your friends that can hurt you the most, he thought, but that's not true. Angie was way out in front of that race. He sipped his drink and looked through the windows to the blackness outside. Stop feeling sorry for yourself again, you prick, think what Emily Barrett's going through.

He put the smooth tablet on his tongue and took a long pull on his whisky. Seven today, what the fuck, but on the upside, there was no pain in his knee. A drunken chuckle made his shoulders shake, "I can't feel any of my limbs for that matter."

He closed his eyes. Lights in the distance, the yellow beams were coming. Surging. His brain was trying to flag danger, he knew his pulse was slowing, his breath shortening. As he slowed, the room spun and raced past him. Yellow everywhere. Then black.

CHAPTER 11

Katie Archer thought things had gone well. Filling in at short notice wasn't easy when you weren't used to where everything was. And the punters were nice, a better class of clientele than the bar she worked in at Uni in Newcastle. Mind you, it was the Roundhay Fox in a posh part of Leeds, not the student bar in Jesmond. Nice of them to offer her a taxi home as well, but that would have been silly. It was only a five-minute walk across Roundhay Park and she could see mum and dad's house from here. The Bar Manager was happy, and Katie could have a ciggy before she got home.

The rain had stopped but there were puddles everywhere so she picked her steps carefully. "Never walked across here in heels," she chuckled.

A shadow seemed to flit across the path, she stopped and looked around. No one. She could see her house two hundred metres away at the end of the path. Better have another before she got home, she thought. She pulled a pack of Marlboro out of her bag and lit a cigarette, taking a deep drag of the smoke. Her eye caught something on the edge of her sightline. It glinted.

A whispered voice right in her ear. "Scream and I'll kill you." She felt an arm around her neck crushing her throat. As the cigarette fell from her mouth in a cluster of sparks, she saw a large knife in front of her face.

He said it again. "Scream and I'll kill you."
What else could she do?
She screamed.

CHAPTER 12

"Right, Lee, you'd better fill me in damn sharp." Chief Superintendent Tony Jones sat behind his desk like an angry Buddha.

"The girl's name is Katie Archer, and she was found by a passer-by at 23:45 last night." Lee began. "She was heading home after a shift behind the bar at the Roundhay Fox and was two hundred yards from her parents' house when she was attacked and left behind a tree just off the path in Roundhay Park. She has multiple stab wounds to the neck and torso. Forensics are still at the scene but their preliminary findings suggest she had been dead less than a few hours when she was found. We'll do the leg work, of course, but I think it's too much of a coincidence for this attack to be the work of anyone other than our rapist. We know he carries a knife, and we know he's threatened to kill. Looks to me like he's carried out his threat. I think our perp has added murder to the charge sheet."

"For God's sake, Lee, how has this happened? It was only last night that you told me Chad Hilton had identified our perp as a laundry worker and that you were confident of identifying suspects this morning. Now, this. We've gone from nailing a rapist to having a fucking murder on our hands." Tony Jones blew out a long breath. "So, what now? What's the plan from here?"

"Sir, I've sent Jas Carter to lead the team at the scene, she'll be back later and I'll get a full report to you. The Roundhay Fox has CCTV so we'll be reviewing that as well. I pulled the guys off visiting the laundries to work on this, we'll get to Armley and Hunslet later today of first thing in the morning."

"Okay, keep me close on this, I'm going to have the press baying for blood. Talking of baying for blood, have you met Jed Forrest?"

"Jed Forrest, as in the new MP that got elected in December? No, never met him. But isn't he the guy everyone thinks will be a future PM?"

"The very same. Well, I've had him on my case asking why West Yorkshire Police are so unresponsive when it comes to missing persons, and telling me that if this is how we deal with all major crimes then it's no wonder we've got a rapist on the loose. Jumped-up little shit."

"What's he on about?"

"A bloke called Andy Huxton has reported that his father, John Huxton, a wealthy businessman, is missing. The coppers have told him there's nothing to suggest foul play so there's bugger all they can do. They had a look at his flat and have spoken with a couple of the people who work at the apartment block, but there was nothing untoward. He was last seen driving out of the underground car park. Our guys tried to reassure him that his dad would rock up sooner or later. That didn't cut any ice and Huxton Junior has taken to Twitter to give us a kicking. And guess who is Andy Huxton's best mate?"

"Jed Forrest," Lee groaned.

"Yes indeed. I know you've got shit hitting the fan, but I need to show willing here. I need you to go and see Andy Huxton. Have a chat, see what you think. I'm sure there's nothing in it, but at least having a DI come and talk to him should get him to stop tweeting and get Winston fucking Churchill off my back."

Lee felt the blood rise and knew his neck and face had gone red. "Come on, boss, give me a break. A mis-per? I'm up to my eyes in the worst series of rapes this city has seen, topped off with the murder of a young student, and you want me to take time out to keep some preppie MP happy? You have got to be bloody joking. We are in serious shit here, sir, and it's every man to the pump before this nutter does it again."

Lee edged back in his seat as his Boss shoved his chair away from the desk and pushed himself upright, pointing an accusatory finger. "Hey," he shouted, "that's enough. We're all under pressure and if you want me to continue to shove every resource this force has at your disposal, then I don't think it's too much to ask, for you to spend an hour on a legitimate investigation into the disappearance of a prominent Leeds citizen. Or is that below you now? Anyway, I'm not having a fucking debate. You've got more coppers on this than they had extras in Ben Hur, so get them to find this killer and you go and see Huxton. Today." Authority reasserted, Jones sat back down and gave a dismissive nod. "Thanks, that will be all."

"Sir," said Lee. The door closed behind him and he leaned on the wall as uniforms raced past. Lee checked his phone. No messages, no missed calls. Chad, where the fuck are you?

CHAPTER 13

Chad opened his eyes. Where the fuck was he? The ceiling offered the first clue. Kitchen. The bottle of Highland Park on the floor next to him confirmed this. He had to get up, shit, what had he done? The silver foil next to the bottle presented an uneasy explanation. He counted the empty sockets in the foil. Seven. Christ. He felt for his phone in his trouser pocket. "Don't be fucking broken." The screen lit up. Six messages. One theme.

"*Where the fuck are you?*" Five from Lee.

"*Where the fuck are you?*" One from Angie.

He typed. "On my way."

* * *

Chad pushed the door of room 106 open with his shoulder and shuffled to the desk by the window. "Sorry I'm late guys, wasn't thinking I'd be in today so didn't have my phone with me." Brazen it out, he'd decided. A text from Lee had brought him up to speed on the murder, so he expected a sombre mood in the room. Jas smiled at him but everyone else was looking at the floor or out of the window. Chad hoped no-one would pay too much attention to him today. If he looked anything like he felt they'd be calling a fucking ambulance. He looked down, read his notes and tried to concentrate.

Lee walked to the front of the room. "Okay, well you're here now so let's crack on. I know that this murder scuppered the plan to get to Leeds Laundry and the other one, Eco something, first thing but let's do that as soon as we finish here. Joe, bring us up to speed with what we know about the victim."

"Not much more to tell, Boss, the victim is Katie Archer, she was covering a shift for someone off sick, finished work and started walking across Roundhay park, to her parents' house. Multiple stab wounds but no sexual assault. Found at 23:45 last night by a man walking his dog. She was only a couple of hundred yards from home. Forensics have done a prelim but are yet to make a full report."

"This has got to be our rapist, hasn't it? What the fuck's happened to make him kill I don't know, but I can't see past him for this. Does anyone disagree?" asked Lee.

Silence. Chad scanned the team from his vantage point at the back, and saw the tension evident on their faces. They'll be in the weeds again. He knew blue-sky thinking was required. Why had the perp killed her? What was the catalyst? Chad had an idea but needed to see if the team could get to the same place.

"I'm with you, boss,' Jas found her voice, "too much of a coincidence. Why kill her?"

"That's the million-dollar question. I don't think it alters the fact that our suspects are working at these laundry firms. It's the delivery guys from both these places that would have met or, at least, seen our victims, so I want them interviewed pronto. Let's see where they were last night. Jas, you go and view the CCTV from the Roundhay Fox, call me when you've reviewed it. Joe, Luke, get yourselves to Leeds Laundry, Debbie, Sally go to the Eco place. Anything else?"

The time had come to interrupt, Chad thought, or they'd miss the main point. "Lee?" he said.

"Yes, Chad, what?"

"Look, I know that this murder changes things, but I think it's his first mistake, and therefore our first big opportunity. Nothing was going to stop him once a couple of things happened."

"Okay, Chad, what things?" asked Lee.

"I'd guess that the perp can't understand why his intended victim, the regular barmaid, isn't there. He's planned it, watched her. He knows when she works and her night off. So, when he saw she wasn't there, things started to unravel for him. But by this time his urge to rape is overwhelming. Remember the intervals between his attacks have been reducing. The gap between his first and second was ten days but now it's been less than forty-eight hours since he attacked Emily Barrett. He's been building himself up for this, and the anticipation will be fuelled by adrenalin, he wouldn't have been able to call it off and go home. This is where the desire to rape is greater than his ability to be calm and stick to his planning. And that is his mistake."

Schmidt rocked back on to two legs of his chair. "The keywords in that monologue were the first two. "*I Guess.*" Why did he kill her and not rape her?" he asked.

Chad ran his hand through his hair; he could give this fucking copper John the Baptist's head on a plate and he'd still want an ID parade. Chad moved so that his body language was non-defensive and moderated his tone of voice as he said, "Because, Joe, my friend, he's not in control of events now, he's winging it. He is now the opportunist you guys all believed him to be from the start, and as I told you yesterday, opportunists make mistakes. Also, remember the words he's whispered to each of his victims."

The team looked at one to the other.

Chad stared at them. "Come on, it's not a trick question, someone fucking answer."

"He says 'scream and I'll kill you,'" said Jas.

"So, what?" said Joe.

Chad stood from where he'd perched, rubbed his knee then scanned their faces. "Why kill her and not rape her like the others?

First, because he's unstable and behaving erratically and second," he paused and thought Joe would have a fit when he said the next bit. "Because I think Katie Archer screamed. That would explain the escalation, and why he killed her."

To be fair, they handled it quite well, he thought, no bitching him off just the odd shrug. He understood their point, no-one will ever know. Lee was opening the door.

"Right, guys, us turning up at the laundry should set the cat amongst the fucking pigeons so let's get on with it. Jas, I want that CCTV asap okay?"

"Yes Boss, on it."

"Mind if I tag along?" asked Chad.

Lee answered for her. "No, Chad, I want you to come with me. Everyone back here at 13:00 please, and in the meantime, I've got to run an errand for the Chief fucking Super."

CHAPTER 14

Chad huddled into the car seat and tried but failed to find a comfortable spot for his leg. He looked out of the window. He'd taken seven yesterday, what the hell had he been thinking? The weather matched his mood, rain swept in horizontal lines across the puddle-strewn road and water gushed out of the metal drain covers. Pedestrians avoided the curb-edge, no-one needed a soaking. The windscreen wipers swayed hypnotically. Lee had been on the phone for the duration of the ride, one call firing impatient instructions to staff, the next talking to his Boss and the one he was on now, his wife to check how, Hannah, the youngest, was. She's got the flu, Lee explained. Chad had been glad of the calls, but he guessed what was coming.

"So, what the hell happened to you then? I was texting you from midnight right through to 09:00?"

"The clue is in the time. From midnight to 9:00 a.m most normal people are asleep. I was one of those. I'd left my phone on the kitchen table, I agree that was stupid, but nothing more sinister than that."

"Well, you looked like shit when you came in this morning. The rest of them may not have noticed, but I did. I look fresher than you and I've been up all night with Hannah. So much for beauty sleep. If you're going to work with us, you're going to have to play by our rules. Phones on twenty-four seven."

"Okay, Boss." Chad watched Leeds speed by in a haze of water. No hiding place from Lee he thought.

Chad, hunched against the rain, still devoid of a fucking umbrella. He limped half a yard behind Lee, as they walked down Park Row to the offices of Andy Huxton. Why had Lee made him tag along to this interview? He looked up and a thought arrived from nowhere. So he could get bollocked for last night of course. The rain found its way inside his coat. Fucking hell.

* * *

"Hi, I'm Andy, come through, I've booked the boardroom so we can talk in there. Tea? Coffee?" Andy Huxton looked from Lee to Chad.

"I'm fine, thanks, but some water would be nice," replied Lee.

"I'll get a black coffee please," said Chad, thinking: God, do I need a caffeine fix.

The sea of heads obscured Chad's view of the boardroom. The main office was open plan, maybe fifty people. They seemed to be in team groupings, two desks facing another two. Most of the staff were staring at screens or their mobiles, some were talking on the phone. No chance any of this lot would get served in a bar without producing their ID. The office had a glass perimeter giving a 360-degree view of Leeds, and at the far end was a series of partitioned private rooms, the centrepiece of which was a large boardroom. Huxton held the door open and invited them in, then poured water from a dispenser into two opaque blue plastic glasses, keeping one for himself and giving the other to Lee. He put a capsule into a fancy looking machine which dispensed coffee into a mug which he put in front of Chad. Chad let the aroma envelope him. No-one had been in such dire need of caffeine as he was now. He eased the second tablet of the day out of the foil wrapper and into his hand. And in need of one of these. He'd become a bloody expert at palming the tablets like a croupier or a magician like Dynamo.

"Sorry, what did you say your name was?" Huxton asked.

"Chad, Chad Hilton"

"He's working with us on some cases we're running and I thought it might be helpful to bring him along today," said Lee.

"No, that's fine, I just seem to remember hearing the name Hilton somewhere but can't think from where so never mind." Huxton moved an impressive leather chair away from the table and sat down. "So, I get no assistance from you guys till a few words in the right ear and, hey presto, I get a DI rocking up. Better late than never, I suppose."

"Why don't you start from the beginning and tell us when you last saw your father, and why you think something may have happened to him?" said Lee.

Chad glanced at Lee. Impressive, he thought. It must be his training. He'd kept calm and measured in the face of Huxton's provocative tone. Lee needed a medal and Huxton needed a fucking slap. He sipped his coffee and looked out of the window. Glistening glass and metal structures stood on the opposite side of Park Row. That's Angie's office, Angie. Shit. He needed to ring her as soon as he got out of here.

Huxton interrupted his thoughts. "I spoke to Dad on the phone at around 2:30 p.m on the day he went missing, which was last Friday. He was fine. He said he was off to play tennis a bit later and we chatted through a transaction we're involved with."

"So, do you and your father have business interests in common?" asked Lee.

"Yes, Dad and I are shareholders in this business, Excelsior Recruitment." Huxton indicated his universe with an expansive sweeping gesture of his arm. "He's got the majority, seventy per cent, and I own twenty per cent. The other ten is distributed between key staff. And that's the reason I know he wouldn't just disappear. We've had an offer for the business and we're coming to the end of Due Diligence. We're expecting to complete the deal within the next couple of weeks and Dad's shares would give him fourteen million quid. I'd get four million.'

Chad had expected to be bored, but he shuffled in his chair and stared at Andy Huxton. Jesus, fourteen million quid. That was a hell of a reason for Huxton not to disappear. And perhaps a reason someone else might want him to.

"We're at the stage," Huxton continued, "where we will have thousands of papers to sign, warranties to undertake and if Dad's signature isn't on those papers then the deal can't happen. And he's a complete control freak, there's just no way he would bugger off now. Something has happened to him and it's now five days later and you guys are still pissing about."

First impressions counted, thought Chad. Huxton had been a prick from the get go and was doing nothing to improve that opinion.

"As I understand it," Lee replied, "your father was seen driving away from his apartment at Bridgewater Place. The garage attendant confirms this and I believe there's also CCTV that further corroborates that. Constables have been into his apartment and you confirmed that there had been no break-in and nothing seemed to be missing. So, from a procedural point of view, there's nothing for us to go on. No crime appears to have been committed. As an adult, your father is entitled to go where he wants, when he wants, and he's under no obligation to tell anyone."

"Lee may I ask Andy something?" said Chad.

Huxton looked at Chad like he'd forgotten he was there. Lee nodded.

Chad sought eye contact with Andy Huxton. "I understand that it is very strange for your Dad to go missing at this point in the deal. So, if he hasn't gone off his own volition, are there people who might wish harm to your father? Is that what you're suggesting to us Andy?"

Chad watched as Huxton swivelled in his leather chair and

looked out of the window. Obviously hadn't liked the eye contact, Chad thought. A couple of seconds later Huxton swivelled back. "Not that I know of. Don't get me wrong, he's been an absolute bastard over the years, not least to me. Tells me regularly that I'm "as thick as pig shit" and I'm sure there are people out there who have been shafted by him, but not in the recent past. He's mellowed and this was to be his last deal."

"How did he make his money?" asked Chad. He made a mental note to congratulate John Huxton on his choice of description.

"He's always been in the recruitment industry. He built his first business from scratch back in the early nineties and sold it for shedloads. Since then, he's backed young recruitment entrepreneurs that want to go it alone. He'd put cash into the business and taken a shareholding then Dad's lawyer would draw up the contract and some naive kid would sign without checking the small print. As the businesses needed cash to grow, Dad would put more in, taking a greater slug of the equity in return until it got to the point that Dad could sell the business at any time irrespective of whether the guy who set the business up wants to do that. I know a number of those guys made peanuts when Dad made millions. I'm sure some of those would be pissed off with him but as I say he hasn't done much investing for years. I suppose it must be five or six years since he did a deal like that. He knew he'd make millions from this business so was content to play a bit of tennis and take it a bit easier."

"Okay, we'll need a list of all those businesses going back over the years, do you have that information?" said Lee.

"God, no. He has a lawyer called Tom Nichols and an accountant called Steven Holding, they've been with him since the start. I'll email their numbers to you."

"Great, thanks. Anything else you can tell us, anything at all?"

"No, I don't think so," said Huxton. "What happens now?"

"Okay," said Lee, closing his notebook. "We'll go back and revisit the CCTV and interview the garage attendant. I'll also check out his tennis club. Which is that?"

"It's the Rawdon Tennis Club."

"Fine, I'll get back to you in the next day or so. If you hear anything in the meantime, call me," Lee said as he handed Huxton a business card.

"Andy," said Chad, "have you had a ransom demand or message from anyone since your father disappeared?"

Andy Huxton straightened in his chair then looked from Chad to Lee. "No, not at all." He said.

Chad stood and rummaged in his inside pocket. He pulled out a business card amongst other detritus and as he passed it to Huxton a strip of Fentanyl fell to the floor. Andy Huxton bent down and retrieved the pills and gave them back to Chad. "You don't want to lose those do you?" he smiled.

* * *

"What a tosser," said Chad as they left the building into the rain. "I couldn't do your job, having to be nice to jumped-up wankers like him. Leaving that aside though, there's just no logic to his dad going AWOL at this point. Not when there's fourteen million quid on the table. Doesn't make any sense. But he's not told us the whole truth, that's for sure. Did you notice that Huxton looked like he'd been expecting the question about ransom demands and how he coloured up a bit?

"Yeah, I did, and I agree he's a wanker, but he's well connected," said Lee. "Anyway, that visit should buy us a little time and get him off Twitter. And, with a bit of luck, it should get that MP off the Chief's back, which will mean he gets off mine. My problem is that all our manpower is focused on catching this rapist turned murderer and I can't allocate anyone to Huxton till we've nailed the bastard. Come on, let's get back and see what the guys have got for us."

CHAPTER 15

Voicemail. "Hey Ange, I'm sorry, but I need to take a rain check on that coffee today. This case with Lee has taken a turn for the worse and I'm needed. It's murder now, so, hey, I can't say no. Been thinking about what you said, and I agree, we should sit down with someone who can help us work through the issues together. So, let's find a therapist or counsellor, whatever. But I also think you need to be transparent with me about who this guy is, how it started, and why. Not knowing everything is killing me. I've been reading loads online. I know, I know, typical me. But everything says that reconciliation is based on truthfulness and clarity. No secrets. So, maybe you could think about that before we meet. Sorry again about today. Call me when you get this and we'll rearrange. Bye, babe." Chad ended the call. Had he gone far enough by agreeing to counselling? perhaps. The ball was in her court, he thought, he'd have to wait and see if she'd now meet him half way and tell him the name of the wanker she'd been seeing.

He checked his watch,12:30 p.m. He'd had two so far but he needed another. "Aaargh," he yelped and hopped. "Fucking cramp." He swallowed the third of the day. Seven yesterday. Christ, he'd end up killing himself if he went on like this. What the hell had happened? More to the point why had it happened? He wasn't some kid that hadn't a clue that drugs and alcohol weren't a good mix but he'd done it anyway. Woken up on the kitchen floor, for Christ's sake, what was that about? No control, that's what that was about. In fact, it was the other way around, the pills were controlling him, and there was only one way that ended. He'd have a chat with Freddie, see if he knew anyone who could help. Maybe another Consultant who might be able to do something on his leg where everyone else had failed. Maybe. Maybe not. Right, what the coppers have discovered, he thought.

* * *

"So much for that theory then," said Joe Schmidt to the team assembled again in Room 106.

"Jesus Christ," Lee shouted at the ceiling. "How the hell can we be so wrong?"

Chad looked around. Silence. Eyes to the floor. Not even Jas able to look at him. Sally Plunkett had discounted Eco Laundry, as they subcontracted their deliveries to Leeds Laundry, it had to be them. "Joe, tell me again. Run the whole thing from the start, from the minute you got there. Everything."

"What else can he tell us, Chad? He's been through it thread to needle for fuck's sake." Lee had lost patience and his leg twitched up and down, beating an incessant rhythm.

"Once more won't hurt," Jas said.

Joe sighed and began. "So, we drive to the Laundry. Just off Armley Road. A set of ramshackle old buildings. We parked in the yard at the front, outside the office. There's the main laundry works to the right, and the loading bays extending from it. Looks to have had some money spent, at least on the machinery if not the buildings. A lot of new kit. The office has got a couple of desks and that's where the manager a guy called Jamie Lawlor was."

"What's his job?" asked Chad.

"He's responsible for scheduling collections and deliveries, staff rotas and dealing with any customer queries or complaints.

There's also an accounts clerk called Jane Welsh who works in the office. Apart from those two, there's a factory manager who is responsible for the cleaning, drying and pressing. He has three girls working in the laundry with him. We can count him out, though. He's fifty-three and has more time off sick than he's there, according to Lawlor." Joe paused and looked at Lee, then Chad. "So, there's only one delivery team and that is Bainbridge and Shopland. They were out on their rounds and wouldn't be back until 18:00 tonight. Lawlor gave me the number for Bainbridge and I rang and spoke to them both. If your profile is correct, neither of these two can be our perp. Tom Bainbridge is Irish with a full-on Dublin accent which he uses to charm the girls, and Shopland is from Cornwall. And he only has one hand, the other is prosthetic."

Chad shuffled in his seat. That fucking prick Schmidt was loving this, he thought. But what had he got wrong?

"What happens when those guys take holidays or are sick?" asked Jas.

"The husband of one of the girls in the laundry steps in. He takes time off his job and does it cash in hand. He's in his fifties as well."

"Tell me about Lawlor," said Chad

"What's to tell? He's a Leeds lad, maybe twenty-five to thirty years old. Worked there for the last two years. Doesn't get out of the laundry so has no face-to-face contact with the clients or the victims. Married. Lives in Burley."

"And the smell," asked Chad, "was the smell of the place as Emily said?"

"Well, yeah. Chemicals, plastics. Yeah, the place and everyone in it reeked of it."

"What do you want us to do now, boss? Go back to the beginning and look at other possible lines of enquiry?" Deakin asked.

"No, not yet. What about the CCTV from the Roundhay Fox,

Jas? Anything on that?"

"Yeah, CCTV at the pub shows a figure wearing a motorbike helmet approach. He looks through the window and stays there for around a minute. He then disappears. The guys at the pub also saw him but didn't think anything of it particularly as he left the place fairly quickly," said Jas.

"What time was that?"

"23:05"

"And what's the regular barmaid called?"

"Her name is Claire Bullough and, on a normal shift, she'd leave at 23:15 give or take five minutes. Katie Archer can be seen leaving at 23:12, and this guy then leaves the pub car park on foot one minute later. That's it. Oh, and we've checked the bike licence plate. Stolen three months ago."

Chad interrupted. "Lee, let me go and see these drivers. Jas could take me. Let me have another shot. We are not wrong. He's a laundry worker. We're just missing something, that's all."

The struggle was written all over Lee's face. "Okay, go and find these drivers. Meet back here at 18:00 sharp. Joe, Luke come to my office there's something else I want you to have a look at."

Lee walked across and put his hand on Chad's shoulder pulling him in close so the team couldn't hear. "You'd better be fucking right, Chad."

CHAPTER 16

Chad moved a Snicker wrapper from where it had got trapped under his leg. He looked out of the window in Jas' Beemer. He wasn't wrong. He couldn't be. Or was this part of his life going to shit like all the rest of it? He looked at his hands and focussed. What would be happening to the perp's behaviour now? The guy would be beginning to panic, for sure, and the way he acted would be out of kilter, so someone would notice or he'd make another mistake. Emily's reaction to the smell had been positive and accurate. A laundry. Leeds laundry was the only firm that delivered to all the victims' workplaces. So, what then? What had he missed? He needed to clear his head. Clear his head and breathe. Relax and breathe.

Jas was on the phone. The sound boomed through the car's audio system, "Mr Lawlor, I'm not going to argue with you. You need to tell me where your delivery van is right now and where it is going to be over the next hour or so. This is a murder enquiry and I will have you arrested for obstruction if you fail to answer my question."

"Okay, okay, I just don't get how you are connecting my guys with this murder. It doesn't make sense. After those coppers spoke to them this morning, the detective said the drivers could be ruled out, so I'm just wondering why you want to see them? A small business like ours can't afford something like this getting into the press and anyway, what the hell makes you think it's someone from a laundry in the first place?"

Jas remained silent.

"Let me check," Lawlor resumed. "they'll be at the Doubletree at Granary Wharf now, after that they'll be going around the corner to the Hilton, to be there at 1:30 p.m." The tip-tap of punched computer keys filled the car. "Then they collect from the Metropole before going on to the Dakota for 2:15 p.m. Those are all city-centre drops and collections, then they head out of town. I'll call them and tell them to wait at the Hilton if you like?"

"No, just text them and tell them to wait there till you tell them they can go. We'll be there in ten minutes." Jas clicked the call off. "Why did you push the Boss to let you meet these guys? If one's from Dublin the other from Cornwall with only one arm, neither can be our perp?"

"Maybe, but maybe not. I want to see them for myself. It's not that I don't trust Joe, but whatever else he is, he ain't a psychologist. We are missing something so let's just see what they say. Trust me, I'm not wrong on this, our perp works in a laundry and has a local accent. If it's not these guys then it's someone else that works there."

"How's your leg? asked Jas. "It must be pretty bad. I've noticed you seem to take pain killers a fair bit and your limp gets worse the longer the day goes on. Can't they do anything for it, like operate or something?"

Chad looked at Jas and thought where the hell had that come from? One minute we were on laundries the next we're on his leg. "I don't know why I'm laughing and I wish they could. I've had eight operations on my leg over the years. I've got pins in the top half and the bottom half which makes it impossible to replace my knee and that's what needs to happen. It's a right laugh going through the security scanners at airports. I'm not moaning, well not much anyway, but yeah, the pain can be debilitating at times.

Not that anyone would feel sorry for me, I'm sure. Loads of people think a bit of pain is a small price to pay for a career in football and all that money. We're overpaid prima donnas the lot of us, seems to be the consensus."

"Well, if I had all your money I'd be going to the States or somewhere and getting a second opinion. There's always something they can do. Painkillers won't help. My Nan was on those for ages and they did her no good at all. She had arthritis. When she stopped taking the tablets, she was better off 'cos she didn't have the side effects any more. You should think about that."

"What the hell? No offence to your nan and her arthritis but I'm only forty-nine not seventy-nine. I'm still clinging onto the hope that a treatment will come along to help me but until then painkillers are the only thing between me and jumping off Malham Cove."

"Alright, I was only trying to help."

Chad grimaced. Dickhead, he thought, he'd now pissed off the only copper that was on his side. He looked at Jas and said, "Yeah, I know. I'm sorry."

The city centre whizzed by. Bridgewater Place Apartments appeared on his left. Chad had read articles about the building. It was the tallest in Leeds and had gained an unwanted notoriety for its resemblance to a Dalek. Shit, yeah, it did look like one, So, this is where John Huxton had lived

"Left here, what do you reckon, round the back for deliveries?" asked Jas.

"Yeah, I'd have thought so."

They turned down a side street in front of the Hilton Hotel and, fifty yards later, made a right which brought them to the back of the hotel. Sure enough, Chad saw a 7.5-tonne lorry with the Leeds Laundry Services motif on the side was parked at a loading bay. Once parked Chad pulled the door handle and, holding onto the top of the door he pulled himself upright, then stood and let the blood circulate so he didn't fall over when he let go. Once stable he started to follow Jas to the truck.

"Well, what da fuck, pardon me French," said the driver as he saw Jas' warrant card. "There's me t'inking I'd answered all the questions from yir man this morning. What have I done now? Do ye mind if I climb down?"

"Please, yes that would be helpful. You must be Tom Bainbridge?" said Jas.

"The very same."

Chad thought the guy had to be putting on the comedy Irish for their benefit, but maybe not, maybe it was his accent that pulled the girls. Anyway, how funny would a Yorkshireman sound in Dublin? But whichever way he looked at it, Bainbridge wasn't the perp. Not with that voice. Fuck.

Bainbridge and a surly Shopland climbed down from the truck. Shopland walked around to the front of the lorry his left arm hung by his side. Chad watched him and thought, this guy couldn't be the perp either. No way. The victims would have noticed if they'd been attacked by a guy with one arm. Fuck. Apart from having only one arm he was thin, pale and unhealthy not 'muscly.' Chad scratched his chin and thought how had he got this wrong? He looked across at Bainbridge who was attempting to flirt with Jas and clearly thought the whole thing was one big joke. Fuck, fuck, fuck.

"Okay, thanks for your help." Jas had run out of questions. "Chad, anything you want to ask the guys?"

Chad looked at the truck and something glinting in the windscreen. "Yeah, what's that?"

"It's our dashcam, so it is. There's one at the back as well. They're on all the time for insurance purposes, so Jamie tells me."

"Show me how they work," said Chad.

Bainbridge opened the cab door and said, "I have a display here that'll show ya whatever the camera is filming, and it also feeds back to base onto Jamie's computer, so if I'm ever in an accident or something goes missing, we've got a record. Clever, eh?"

The monitor displayed live pictures of an empty storage area inside the loading bay. Maybe, just maybe. Chad said, "Can you just pull the truck forward a bit, and, Jas, could you jump into the storage area for me?"

Bainbridge started the engine and moved the vehicle a couple of feet forward. Enough for Jas to climb up onto the loading bay and stand in the entrance, giving him a look that said *why the fuck am I doing this?*

"Great, clear as day, the pictures are quality, high resolution. I'm surprised." Chad shouted. Of course, he thought, it was so easy when you thought about it. And clever as hell. "And can this dashcam take still shots as well?"

"Oh aye, if needed it can. If you had a smash, you'd get the live feed data which is stored in something called the cloud, according to Jamie, but if I were to press this little button here it would take a lovely photo of your lady friend. I didn't know they made coppers as pretty as her now and I can tell ye, she's a vast improvement on the ones I normally run into."

Chad smiled, thanked God for the Irish, and said "Jas, come on we've got to go. Thanks, guys, you've been very helpful."

Jas caught him up. "What was all that about, why did I have to let those two weirdos ogle me?" she pushed her hair behind her ears and glared.

"Jas, think about what we know and what we've just been told. We know from Emily that the smell is from a laundry. We know that only Leeds Laundry Services do the deliveries and collections. I'm now with the rest of you, the perp can't be Bainbridge or Shopland for all the reasons that everyone's been through. But we now know that there is an opportunity for someone else to see the victims using the live feed or stills from the dashcam like I just did with you in the loading bay. I reckon we need to get to the Laundry in Armley and check out this guy Lawlor pronto. What do you think?"

"I think we'd better run it past the gaffer before we do anything.

It's his neck on the line if you're wrong." Said Jas.

Chad manoeuvred into the passenger seat, "Go on then, ring him."

Chad heard Lee's voice before any ringtone. Lee's been waiting for this call, he thought. "Hi Jas, how'd you get on, any joy?"

Chad mouthed *tell him*.

"Maybe, Boss, maybe. We think there may be a new angle we should look at. We can defo rule out these two delivery guys but there may be a chance the Laundry manager, Lawlor, has access to the victims."

"How so?" Asked Lee, a tension in his voice clear to Chad.

Chad saw Jas signpost for him to take over. "Lee, Chad here. Listen, mate, it's possible that he's identified the victims from dashcams that are installed in the truck, the live feed is on constantly and projects direct to Lawlor's desk top. He can see anyone the drivers can see. We did an experiment with Jas standing in a loading bay and the pictures were clear and vivid. As I said, the dashcams play straight back to his computer so he'll have just seen the pictures of Jas as well. If he is the perp, that might alert him that we're onto something so I think we should head over there. Can you get there?"

"Chad are you sure about this? The guy told Joe and Luke he'd never been anywhere near the places the victims worked, and the woman who works with him said he never leaves the office."

"He doesn't need to, Lee, that's what I'm telling you. He can pick the victim from the dashcam footage and then stake them out in his own time. Look, we'll head to Armley now. We'll see you there."

* * *

"Doesn't this thing go any quicker? It's not like in the movies, is it? Hurtling through traffic, sirens wailing, and Will Smith shooting out the window. Not us, no we're stuck behind a bloody bus on

Wellington Street. Fast and Furious my arse. More like slow fucking motion." Said Chad. He looked out of the window at the stationary traffic. He'd done it again, he thought, mouthed off at the only copper who didn't think he was a total dickhead.

"Fuck off, Chad, I'll get us there as fast as I can. And tapping your fingers on the dashboard won't make us go any quicker so stop it. What made you think about the cameras?"

"I don't know. I was trying to work out how we'd got it wrong. Listening to those guys answer your questions it was clear it couldn't be either of them, which left Lawlor or if not him, then someone who works at the main Laundry and has access to the dash cam footage. Then I saw the camera and thought, maybe, that's how he does it."

"Remember," said Jas, "no-one likes a clever dick."

"It's not clever. If it couldn't be either of them it had to be Lawlor or someone else back at the Laundry. But hey, let's not count our chickens, the way our luck is on this case we'll find the footage has never replayed back."

Traffic ebbed away and Jas floored the Beemer. Leeds sped by. "I've always wanted to know how they came up with the name Armley Gyratory for a roundabout. Why Gyratory? What does that even mean?" he asked

"I dunno. Sounds vaguely rude, doesn't it. City planners for you."

The sign for Leeds Laundry Services was ahead on the right. Jas indicated and pulled in. Schmidt was wrong about most things but he wasn't wrong about this place, ramshackle was the best word to describe the buildings. Jas parked. The familiar clawing in his stomach began, the right leg started to itch, the knee required massaging as the ache grew to more acute levels. Warning signs he needed another. 2:15 p.m. Not even two hours since the last one. Wow, he thought, those intervals were getting shorter, but he couldn't take one now. Not now. He needed to stay focussed and the pain might help with that. Door first. Upright second. Hold third. Release fourth. Walk fifth. The five-step plan to functioning.

Jas was already at the office and he saw her give him the thumbs-up with a look of concern on her face. She'd waited for him at the door. "You okay?"

"Yeah, fine. Just takes me a bit longer to get from A to B. Let's do this." Before Jas could open the office door, a loud screech of tyres and blue flashing lights announced Lee's arrival. He abandoned his car just inside the entrance gates, making it impossible for anyone to enter or exit without moving it first, then jogged down to them. "Okay, in we go, and I hope you're fucking right."

The office was rectangular, with two desks facing each other at either end of the room. Separating the desks from each other were four tall filing cabinets standing like sentries against the wall. A Health and Safety notice filled the space behind them, alongside a Public Liability Indemnity insurance certificate. An A4 sheet showed a twenty-four-hour on-call number, only to be used in an emergency, and was signed by Jamie Lawlor, Manager. At the desk on the left sat the man himself. The other desk was empty.

"Mr Lawlor, I'm Detective Inspector Lee Wallace and this is my colleague Detective Sergeant Jasmin Carter. This is Chad Hilton, a consultant working with West Yorkshire Police."

"Hi, apologies as you can see, I can't offer you all a seat," said Lawlor, waving his arm around the room to highlight the lack of chairs. "How can I help you guys? I thought you were at the Hilton having another chat with Tom? How did that go? A dead-end is my guess, I told you they're good guys. Anyway, what can I do for you, I thought I'd answered all your questions with the other detectives this morning?"

Chad listened to him answer Lee's questions. No, he didn't know any of the victims, no he'd never been to their work, he didn't know where he was on those dates, but he didn't go out much and he'd check but thought he'd been at home. Last night? Home all evening, went to bed around 11:45 p.m. Yes, his wife would confirm that. Check with your other detectives I've already told them all this. The body language said cool, relaxed, in charge. The face asked are they buying it?

"Fuck me, how many times do I have to say this? I have never been to any of our customers' premises or met any of their staff. If there are queries or issues, I resolve them over the phone. It's a straightforward business. We collect dirty laundry, wash it, clean it, press it and deliver it back. To be honest, there's not much that can go wrong." Lawlor said.

Chad raised an eyebrow at Lee who nodded. "Mr Lawlor," Chad began, "we've just been to have a chat with your drivers as you know and one thing they did say was of particular significance. They showed us the dash cams in the truck and explained they operate on a live feed straight back to your desktop. Is that correct?"

"Yes, that's right. What of it?"

Jas joined in, "Well that would mean that the live feeds would give you sight of anyone your drivers could see. In this case perhaps, the victims?"

Before Lawlor could answer, Lee said, "And that enables you to visit your clients' premises and see their staff without ever leaving the office."

Chad watched as Lawlor's eyes roved from one face to the other. The quick-fire questions from the three of them were beginning to shift his calm demeanour he thought.

Lawlor had begun to fidget and Chad sensed an anxiety in his quick response. "Don't you think I've got better things to do all day than watch a dash cam video. For fuck's sake, you're clutching at straws there. The feed is downloaded every day and is only ever needed if there's an insurance claim or a complaint about non-delivery or collection."

Chad saw Lawlor's mobile was on the desk. iPhone 13, the latest. What if? A thought emerged. How could he test it? Chad took his older iPhone from his inside pocket and while Lawlor waxed lyrical about how his day was far too busy to watch fucking videos, Chad dialled the emergency number on the wall. The phone on the desk vibrated. Lawlor looked at it then answered it. Chad clicked the call off.

"You like all the latest gizmos, don't you?" said Chad. "Mind if I look at your phone? I'm due an upgrade soon." Lawlor looked at him and then handed across his phone. It was unlocked.

"Nice weight, and slim, but a bit on the large side for me. I prefer them smaller." Lawlor held out his hand for the phone but Chad ignored it. Instead, he scrolled across the phone looking at the apps. "There we go. 'Find my iPhone'."

Chad smiled, "This is very helpful, DI Wallace, Jamie here has his "Find my iPhone" app switched on, which means that Apple has been tracking his movements. As you know whenever you move past a mast your whereabouts are triangulated with other masts, which is how the app works. Simple, and dead easy to corroborate Mr Lawlor's account of his whereabouts. I'm sure he won't mind you checking all that out."

"You can't take that, you fucking twat, give me that phone back right now," Lawlor shouted. Chad replaced the phone on the desk in front of Lawlor. As he'd hoped, Lee picked up the reins

"I suggest we nip across to our HQ, Mr Lawlor, we're only ten minutes away and we can get our tech guys to check out the phone then you can have it back and we can eliminate you from our enquiries," said Lee, with a smile.

Lawlor wriggled. Chad knew what was going through his mind. To refuse would look bad, to comply maybe worse. "Oh, and could we take your computer, please, and any back up of the files you store in the cloud that hold the data from the dash cams." Said Lee

"No, you fucking can't. Not without a warrant. This is fucking harassment."

Chad said, "Deleting them won't help you know. Nothing is ever permanently deleted so you might as well show us, we'll find it anyway. Same goes for the phone, you don't want us to check because it's going to show that you've been at all the wrong places at all the wrong times. And the files, are going to have pictures and videos of the victims, except, there won't be a photo of the poor girl you murdered last night, because she wasn't planned. Isn't that right, Mr Lawlor?"

Lawlor jumped to his feet and pushed the desk in front of him. "Fuck off, get out, the lot of you and no, you're not fucking right," he walked around his desk, brushing past Chad. "I'll show you everything when you come back with a warrant. Now fuck off." Lawlor moved towards the filing cabinets and then, in one quick movement, turned swinging his arm. Chad heard a loud crunching sound in his ears and then a flash of bright light before the four filing cabinets seemed to rearrange themselves. He tried to steady himself but that was doomed. Shit, he thought. The floor rushed up to meet him and he rolled over, winded, onto his back. Schoolboy error, what a dick. A rush of arms and legs flew past him. Jas and Lee. He didn't know where Lawlor thought he was going 'cos they were going to nail his arse. Something human and heavy hit metal. Chad crawled to the door in time to see Jas push Lawlor's face into the roof of her BMW while Lee pinned his arms behind him mouthing something into his ear.

"Freddie's right,' Chad muttered, "whatever they're paying me isn't enough for this shit."

CHAPTER 17

The noise of laughter filtered down the corridor to where Chad stood at the top of the escalator. Well, they sounded a hell of a sight jollier than they had earlier. He felt the foil in his pocket and counted the spaces. Four. Not bad. If he could manage with six today and no whisky then that would be a start, a step in the right direction. He felt his phone vibrate, a voicemail from Angie. He'd deal with that later. He walked in as Lee banged his hand on the desk, the team quietened and Chad managed to find a perch on the desk nearest the door.

"Thanks, guys, it's been a successful day. We're not home and dry yet but I think we are on the way. We can hold Lawlor for twenty-four hours, but I've just been told that Lawlor's phone places him at the site of each at least three victims and we are still checking the rest. Initial screening of the files on his computer also shows hundreds of images of our victims. Sally Plunkett is with his wife right now and says she's confirmed that he often went out at night and came home in the early hours. And wait for this," Lee paused, "she says he rides a motorbike. Ha. He told her he'd bought it three months ago and keeps it in a lock-up near Burley Park train station. I've got a couple of uniforms going over there as we speak. Lawlor is now lawyered up and 'no commenting' but if the bike is the one in the CCTV from the pub, I think we'll have enough to charge him. Well done, everybody. Chad, how's the jaw?"

"Yeah, okay thanks. I've had worse elbows from centre-halves back in the day, but I was paid a lot more then." The hubbub of conversation, the laughing and banter reminded him of the locker room after a good win. The only thing missing was Freddie strutting around with a towel around his waist leading the party.

"You pulled that out of the hat for us, Chad. Thanks buddy," said Lee. "Even the Chief Super is happy. He's now claiming credit for hiring you. All his idea. I'm afraid there'll be no mention of you in the Press, as we agreed, hope you don't mind?"

"I don't mind at all. I'd rather not be in their spotlight, thanks very much. It's a bit like having Sauron's eye on you, it never bodes well. What happens now?"

"We dot Is and cross Ts and make sure we have all the evidence we need for a conviction. Having Lawlor off the streets is the main thing. The process will take its course and could be months before we get to trial, but we've done the first part, nicking him. Now we need to get on and prove it to the satisfaction of twelve jurors. You've done your bit though, mate, and thanks again. By the way, after we met with Andy Huxton this morning, I sent Schmidt and Deakin across to Bridgewater Place to interview the garage attendant and security. Told them to have a look round Huxton's flat. Do you have to shoot off or do you have a minute to get their feedback?"

"Yeah, interested to hear what they have to say."

Chad's phone vibrated. A direct message to his Twitter account.

@therealchadhilton If you had two weeks to live what would you do? Travel? Bucket list? Holiday with the wife? Oh sorry, forgot, she's left you. Two weeks isn't long Ha, Ha #napoleoncalling.

Chad re-read it. Where the hell had that come from? And how did anyone know about him and Ange?

CHAPTER 18

"Right guys, bring us up to speed," said Lee. "Is this a mountain out of a molehill or has something happened to John Huxton. What's the story?"

Chad kneaded the muscles in his thigh and looked across at Schmidt, who opened his notebook.

"Let me run through this boss, and see what you think," said Schmidt. "We spoke to George Hampsthwaite, the garage attendant at Bridgewater Place. He said that on Friday, he'd seen Huxton standing by the side entrance to the car park. He was waving and signalling to explain he'd left his entry fob. Hampsthwaite can open the door from a control panel in his hut, so that's what he did at 2:57 p.m. His hut is about forty metres from the car park door. Then at 3:02 p.m. Mr Huxton had driven his Porsche Cayenne, it's the big SUV not the sporty job, out of the garage and turned left onto Water Lane."

"Each resident has a fob to give them access to the car park from the outside, and from inside the building they access the car park via the lifts," said Deakin.

"Okay, so at 2:57 p.m. Huxton gains entry to the car park and 3:02 he drives out. Correct?"

"Correct, boss. We then had a look at the CCTV and the digital display records the Porsche leaving at 3.02."

"Can you see that it's Huxton driving?" asked Chad

"Clear as day. It was him."

"So, what then?" asked Lee.

"We went inside the building and spoke to the security guard on duty in the foyer. Bridgewater Place is a mix of office space and residential apartments. From the ground floor to level ten are the offices, then from ten to thirty-two are the private apartments. Huxton's is a penthouse on the twenty-ninth floor. The car park is underground spread over two floors. The security guard gave us access to Huxton's apartment," said Schmidt.

"Fuck me, Boss, how the other one per cent lives," said Deakin "This place was huge. Floor-to-ceiling windows, massive rooms. You could fit my whole flat into his en-suite bathroom. Nothing out of place. He seems to be a bit of an obsessive. No sign of a break-in or forced entry, which would have been nigh-on impossible anyway as the locks on the door are straight out of Fort Knox. Nothing at all to suggest any type of foul play."

"Was his fob for the garage there?" asked Chad

"No, we didn't see it. Why?"

"Just wondering. If I go out and leave my keys, I find them on the kitchen table, interested where he left his."

"Andy Huxton told us that he'd spoken to his father at 2:30 p.m. and that his Dad said he was going to play tennis later. Which fits with where he was going when he drove out at 3:02," said Lee. "We need to check if Andy knows where his father was when they had their call."

"We've done that," said Schmidt. "I called him half an hour ago. He knows his dad was in the flat when they spoke because they needed to check some documents and his father was using his MacBook, which we found on his desk in his study."

"And this is where it gets a bit odd, Boss."

"Go on," said Lee, "what's odd?"

"If he's in his flat until sometime after 2:30 p.m. and we know he's outside Bridgewater place without his fob at 2:57 p.m, then he must have left the building at some point, but he doesn't appear on the CCTV in the foyer, which is the only way out except the car park," said Deakin. "So, if he left through the door in the car park, he's somehow let the door shut behind him and then needed to get Hampsthwaite to let him back in. Whichever way you look at it, it's a bit weird."

Deakin's right, Chad thought, that was a bit weird.

"How about CCTV in the car park what does that show?" asked Lee.

"Out of action, Boss. Waiting for it to be repaired."

"Oh, that's brilliant. Okay, I'm going to have a chat with the Chief Super, round up stuff on Lawlor and then I think we need the full team together to go over this Huxton stuff before it starts to get messy. I'll text you the time later."

Chad opened the door to find a young, pretty WPC standing outside.

"Come in, come in, are you after me?" said Lee.

"Yes sir, I am. The desk Sarge told me to come and find you. We've been told you are the Chief Investigating Officer on the Huxton missing person case?"

"Bloody hell, am I?" said Lee. "When did that happen? When the Chief Super said, I suppose. What is it?"

"Well, sir, it's just that we've got another one."

"Another what?"

"Mis-per, sir. He's a priest, sir, gone missing from a nursing home."

"Are you sure he's missing and not just wandered off? How long's he been gone?"

"Well, only a few hours, but the nursing home know that something's wrong 'cos he went out with one of the carers to meet a chap that the priest had taught when he was younger. They never arrived at the pub for lunch, and the carer's phone isn't switched on. The priest doesn't have a mobile."

"What's this got to do with Huxton?"

“Not sure, sir, just told to bring it to you.”

“Okay, thank you, I’ll get someone to look into it.” Lee looked at Chad. “This is what happens here, the Chief Super nails Huxton to my tail and then I get landed with every other frigging problem that no-one else wants.”

Chad closed the door behind her and smiled at Lee. “Looks like you’re now the mis-per guru.”

* * *

Leaning on the wall for support, he checked his phone. Angie had left him a voicemail.

“Chad, it’s me. Got your message, shame we couldn’t meet. Glad you’ve come around to the idea of counselling, and I hear what you said about transparency. It’s just difficult, I don’t want to hurt you any more than I already have so maybe it’d be better if we can deal with that when we are with the counsellor if that’s okay? By the way, I may be getting a bit paranoid, but I thought I was being followed yesterday. There was a black guy, I’d never seen him before, and he followed me to Park Row. I drove home and when I got back into Harrogate, I went to Waitrose to get some bits and saw him again in there. Maybe nothing. Just unnerved me. How are you? Are you keeping a check on those pills you’re taking? Right, babe, I’ve got to go. Call me when you get a chance and we’ll re-arrange meeting up. Bye.”

Followed by a black guy, what’s that about? His phone vibrated. Twitter.

@therealchadhilton I forgot to tell you to make sure you have enough of your little pills for the next fortnight. You won’t need them after that. Ha-ha. #napoleoncalling

What the actual fuck? He clicked on Angie’s name and waited. Straight to voicemail. “Hi, babe, got your message. Go ahead and book the first appointment with the counsellor, send me a diary invite and I’ll make sure I’m there. I don’t like the sound of this guy following you. Drop me a text if you see him again and I'll get across to you. The knee is okay."

He scrolled further down and dialled Freddie's number. Voicemail again. Fuck it, I'll text him.

Freddie, you okay *? Look, I'm getting trolled by some nutter calling himself Napoleon but whoever it is he knows about my painkillers. No idea how. Wondered if he has a contact in the drug world, I thought you might be able to keep an ear to the ground. See if anyone is mouthing off. Take it easy, bro. Let's grab a beer soon. Also, can you get me some more F for next week? Cheers buddy.*

CHAPTER 19

"I wonder how Chad fucking Hilton feels about Napoleon being on his arse? Wanker, I hope I've put the shits up him." I keep a watchful eye in my mirrors for any sign of police but there were none. "Don't need to get pulled for anything daft, so indicate here, and turn." I swing into a small industrial estate, where my unit is at the far end, solitary, isolated, which is why I'd chosen it. Planning, that's what sets me apart. That's why I've opted for the hashtag Napoleon, no better strategist than him. I drive into the parking space in front of the two-storey breeze-block building and pull up. Caution has become my watchword over the years, so I check my mirrors again before opening the car door and climbing out. The warehouse has a corrugated shutter door which is padlocked to two steel ground anchor hoops I'd bolted into the concrete. I scan the estate. A couple of units are busy but no-one is paying me any attention. Why would they? I unlock the padlocks and push the shutter halfway up, then duck underneath, and have a look inside. All good. Right, let's get this Porsche in here and out of sight, it's bloody enormous and sticks out like a sore thumb. I push the shutter to the top, jump into the Porsche and drive it into the warehouse. My footsteps echo on the harsh concrete of the floor as I walk to the wall and switch on the lights before rolling the shutters back into place. "That's better, I can see what I'm doing."

Now the low hum of the Porsche's engine cooling is all that breaks the silence. Still and calm just the way I like it.

"Okay, let's see how things are in here,"

In the centre of the warehouse is a red shipping container. The guy at the Container Base at Stourton had told me that it was the regulation size. It complied to the International Organisation for Standardisation measurements: Eight feet wide, eight feet six inches high and twenty feet in length, cash, no receipt. Self-collection. Perfect. It had been a bit of a pain getting it inside the warehouse, but a couple of bottle jacks, some rollers and a high-tensile chain attached to my truck had done the job.

The wrought-iron handle lies flat against the container door, attached to a long vertical pole descending from the top, which creaks and calls out a metallic groan as I wrench the arm away from the metal to an angle of ninety degrees. The door to the right of the two opens a fraction.

"Let's get this show on the road. Fuck, it'll stink in there so I'd better get masked up." Armed with a pair of latex gloves, a tub of Vic's VapoRub and a face mask from the car, I head back to the container, then stop. "Come on, mate, follow your own rules. Safety first." I walk back to the car open the glove compartment and pull a pistol from within, then slip it into the side pocket of my hoody. Tugging the heavy doors open I poke my head in. All just as I'd left it.

"Thank fuck I brought the Vicks." I flinch as the overpowering stench of excrement and urine permeate the ointment. In the middle of the container is the table I'd bought from a factory clearance. It's square and metal and does the job. No unnecessary frills. Like the container, cash, no receipt. I'd arranged metal chairs in the middle of three sides of the table. Positioning was mission-critical. Measure twice, cut once, my dad had told me. Good advice. I'd welded the legs onto brackets which were bolted to the floor. The seat in the middle of the three is occupied by a man, chin resting on his chest.

I say, "Fuck, John, it stinks in here." But the guy in the seat makes no response. Guess there's not much he can say. As I look at the long side of the container though, my disgust evaporates and I smile. On a shelf welded to the wall are three Tasers each facing the mid-point on the chairs at the table. "Loving my work, buddy. Loving my work. Okay, time for visitor number two."

Every sound in the warehouse seems amplified and the ping of the boot opening bounces around the walls. The boot swings upwards and I take a pace back. These are the rules, better safe than sorry. I'll be amazed if this one is any trouble but you never know. I look inside. "I was right, in your condition you weren't going to try an escape, were you? Come on, up you get. Got a friend for you to meet."

I lean inside and grab the figure by his collar, hauling him over the rim and letting him fall to the concrete. A shallow groan tells me the priest is still alive. "Come on, paedo, there's someone I want you to meet. Jesus, you're a weight, fat bastard."

I drag the old man across the floor, his heels leaving tracks in the concrete dust. Once in the container, I dump him in the chair on the left of the three, nearest the doors. The chairs have metal restraints on the arms and legs, and I clamp them into place.

"Snug as a bug in a rug and welcome to your home for the next couple of days. There's only one house rule." I look at the two figures, both slumped in their seats. Neither of them has their eyes open. "Pay attention," I yell. "A little slap should wake you up." The men lift their heads. Good, I don't need them croaking on me yet.

"That's better, now listen up. The Tasers you can see on the opposite wall are wired to a sensor that is triggered by sound. You two can chat along, but only at a decibel of 45. That is the level of a whisper. Anything over that will trigger the sensor and… Hey presto! Not sure either of you will survive that, but hey, that's your problem." I nudge Huxton. "Hey, John, Father Murphy may be able to hear your confession, I bet that would be interesting." I shake Murphy's shoulder. The priest raises his head. A picture of misery. Excellent. "I doubt that Father Murphy will ask you to hear his though, John. Just too many kids to remember, isn't that right, Declan? Okay, that's it. I'll be back at some point, and when I'm back there'll be some food and drink, and a little bit of work for you to do, John, okay?"

Not anticipating an answer, I turn, walk over to the Tasers, switch on the sensor and take a quick glance around. All good. Nothing to see here. I leave the container, sliding the long arm into place. Locked. I check around the warehouse, then turn the light off. Once outside I pull the roller shutter down and re-fit the padlocks. No-one around, no-one watching. It's a ten-minute walk to where I've left my car but that's good, some fresh air after the stink in there. It'll be worse next time with two of them. Still, it's a small price to pay. I just love it when a plan comes together. And it's been easy. Very easy. A memory comes flooding into my head. I'm at Elland Road back in the nineties. Manchester United playing Leeds, with that tosser Hilton in their side. I'm a red. We thrash them and take the piss out of their stupid fans. What did we sing? Oh yes, I remember. "So fucking easy, that was so fucking easy."

How apt.

CHAPTER 20

Chad was early for the 8:15 a.m. meeting. He typed a message to Angie. *Hey Ange, sorry to bother you, but just checking you haven't told anyone about the Fentanyl?*

Three little dots blinked.

No, babe. No-one, why?

Just wondered. The news appears to have leaked that's all. Not to worry.

* * *

Lee began, "Let me bring you all up to speed then we can crack on. First, we'll be tying up all the evidence over the next few days, and awaiting forensics which I believe will allow us to charge Lawlor with all five rapes. Sally Plunkett will be leading on that. We have found the bike in his lock-up, the same one as in the CCTV. Even better, in the luggage holder on the back was a knife. It's with forensics now, but no reason to think it's anything other than the murder weapon. Great result, but Sally, make sure you double-check everything. I don't want Lawlor sprung on a technicality."

"Will do, Boss."

"Okay, moving on. As some of you may know, we have a businessman missing. He's got friends in high places and there's a fair bit of political noise around this, which I don't need getting out of hand. His name is John Huxton and he disappeared without a trace last Friday. Today is what? Wednesday morning?" He received a nod of confirmation. "So, we are on day five. Apart from the political sensitivity around this, there's a couple of issues that make us think that this may not be a straightforward misper case. Huxton was due to complete on a business deal with his son, Andy, in the next couple of weeks which would have put fourteen million quid in his back pocket. Very odd time to bugger off. Before driving out of Bridgewater Place at around 3:00 p.m. he had managed to lock himself out of the car park and the attendant had to let him in."

"What's strange about that, Boss?" said Jas. "I'm always forgetting my keys."

"Yeah, but this guy is slightly more organised than you, Jas," he laughed. "There are only two ways for Huxton to have been outside. One he goes down in the lift, for some reason decides to exit the car park by the side door and lets it close behind him. He's forgotten his fob so needs to be let back in, then drives out. That scenario doesn't add up to me. The most obvious was for him to have exited the apartment block through the Bridgewater Place foyer, in which case he'd appear on CCTV leaving the building. But he doesn't."

Better get my thoughts out in the open, thought Chad. "Just a couple of things. Or maybe it's me thinking they're strange."

"Go on," said Lee.

"The attendant lets Huxton into the car park at 2:57 p.m. He then drives out at 3:02 p.m. Confirmed on CCTV. What is he doing in the car park for five minutes?"

Lee scribbled, *five mins in the car park, why?* on the board. "Yeah, okay, weird. What's the other thing, you said there were a couple?"

"No sign of a ransom demand as far as we are aware."

"You're right. I'll keep close to Andy Huxton on that. Joe and

Luke, will you follow up with the Rawdon Tennis Club and find out if Huxton turned up to play on Friday and if so, what time and when did he leave. Also, check out what's on his Mac. The tech guys should be finished with it later this morning. Let's circle back around after lunch on that. Now, it must be the mis-per season in Leeds because we have another, and courtesy of the Chief, it's landed at our door. A Father Murphy has gone AWOL from a care home in Alwoodley. Again, some sensitivity on this. The Super grabbed me first thing and said he's already had a call from the Archbishop asking that we devote some resource to this. Jas, can you get yourself up to the care home, it's called the Ashfield Grange, and check out what they know. Chad, don't know if we'll need you any further but you're booked for today anyway, so if you're at a loose end why don't you go with Jas. Let's see what the score is on that. Right, if there's nothing else, get cracking and meet back here at 1:30 p.m."

* * *

Chad popped a pill from the strip and swallowed it. Third so far. Jas pinged the car open. "Christ, Jas, how do you get your car so full of crap so fast?"

"It's a particular talent I have, but if you want a lift, I'd keep your comments to yourself and just move the shit off the seat and shove it in the back. Or do you have a problem with that?"

"Fine with me, just don't shout when you can't find the shit you need." Chad stretched his leg into the footwell and checked his phone. Nothing. Who the fuck was this troll, he thought, and how did he know about me and Ange? And the Fentanyl? Who knew about both? Freddie knew about the drugs but not about me and Ange. Or did he? Angie knew about both. His best friend or his wife? Freddie's whole business was based on being able to keep things quiet, no loose talk. Certainly, wouldn't be good for business to let it be known who his clients were. That left Angie.

Jesus, Ange, what the fuck have you said and to whom? His phone vibrated. Freddie.

Hey, buddy, all cool with me. Put out some feelers will let you know what I hear. Nutters, man, should be locked up. F ok for Friday, but we need a serious conversation. Okay?

Chad smiled. Freddie was quick to identify whole swathes of people he believed should be locked up. Except himself. Freddie didn't do irony.

CHAPTER 21

Stop staring at her, Chad thought, she'll clock it soon and then what? She'll box you off as a perv. Chad followed Jas across a pebbled car park and onto the driveway of Ashfield Grange.

"That old boy looking out the window there, watching me hobble, is thinking I'm one of the residents and you're my carer."

"Ha, that's funny. I mean yes, you're old, but not ready to be in here yet. Soon, but not yet." She raised an eyebrow, checking he was taking it as a joke. She didn't know him that well yet. "And I pity any poor sod that ends up with me as their carer. By the way, why don't you get a walking stick or a wheelchair?"

"Fuck off, Jas."

"No, I'm being serious. Until you get that leg sorted, a stick would help you walk. It would make you look distinguished. You could pretend to be some sort of war hero."

A cane? he thought. Might not be a bad shout.

* * *

"We're here to see Mrs Grogan," said Jas. "I'm DS Jasmin Carter and this is my colleague Chad Hilton."

The young Asian carer looked from one to the other. "Would you mind signing in for me, please? The visitors' book is just on the desk there."

"Of course."

"Do you get visitors every day or is it mainly at weekends?" asked Chad.

"To be honest, we don't get many visitors at all. Our residents used to be priests, you see, so they don't have much family."

"Are all the residents former priests?"

A strident voice interrupted. "Yes, they are. Thanks, Sudipta, I'll look after our visitors now. I'm Mrs Grogan, my husband and I own the Nursing Home. This is a terrible and very worrying time for us all, I do hope you'll be able to find Father Murphy. And, of course, Mr Bannister. Do come this way, we can talk in my office."

Mrs Grogan gestured for Jas and Chad to follow her. Chad trailed behind the two women, along a short hallway and into a small office behind the main staircase. "It's so awful about Father Murphy, I'm just praying he's okay. I can't begin to tell you how shaken up we all are about it. Do take a seat."

Chad rubbed his knee. "I'll stand if you don't mind."

"So, shall we start at the beginning," said Jas. "Tell me what happened yesterday."

Mrs Grogan took a deep breath. "It was a little after 10 a.m when the call came into my office. The caller was a very polite man who gave his name as John Nicholson. He explained he'd been given my number by a gentleman to whom he'd spoken at the Diocese administration offices, and that he was hoping to come and see Father Declan, as he called him. He told me he had been taught many years ago by Father Murphy." She smiled at Chad, "I'll stick to calling him Father Murphy so we don't get confused."

Chad nodded.

"He said that it would be nice to repay him in a small way, and asked whether it would be okay to take him out for a spot of lunch to The Deer Park on Street Lane. I thought how wonderful it was that someone would remember an old teacher like that and said as much to Father Murphy when I told him about it. It never occurred to me that anything was strange, given that the Diocese had told him where to find Father Murphy. I thought it must all be okay. I mean why wouldn't I? We've had requests like this before. Not often though, I grant you."

"So, what happened then?" said Jas.

"I told Mr Nicholson to call back in half an hour and that I would have a chat with Father Murphy to check he was happy to go. Father Murphy was in the lounge and I went to tell him. He did start to get a little anxious. He's a very quiet, introverted man, and keeps himself to himself. But that was when Ronnie overheard us talking and said he'd be happy to take Father Murphy to the pub, get him settled and wait there to bring him back. If Father Murphy wanted to leave at any stage then Ronnie would bring him home straight away."

"Did Father Murphy remember teaching John Nicholson?" asked Jas.

"He couldn't place him, no. But as he said, he'd taught a lot of children over many years so it wasn't surprising he couldn't remember the name."

"Didn't you think the whole thing a bit odd? A former pupil who Father Murphy can't remember rings out of the blue and wants to take him to lunch that day. All a bit hurried and urgent wouldn't you say?" said Chad.

"That's what Ronnie said, which is why he offered to take him. I thought that was a lovely gesture."

"Please, go on," said Jas.

"Mr Nicholson telephoned again at around 10:45 a.m. I told him that Father Murphy would be taken to The Deer Park by one of our staff and I asked what time they should meet. Mr Nicholson was very charming, thanked me and said he understood why Father Murphy would want to be accompanied. He said to meet at 1:00 p.m. I gave him Ronnie's mobile number in case plans changed or he was going to be late. Father Murphy doesn't have a phone. Mr Nicholson then gave me his mobile number to give to

Ronnie or in case I needed to call him. About five minutes after the call had finished, I found Ronnie and told him I'd given his mobile number to Mr Nicholson. He was fine about it."

"What then?"

"That was pretty much it. Ronnie helped Father Murphy into his car, that was at 12:45 p.m. and off they went."

"When did you start to get alarmed?"

"I suppose it was around 4:00 p.m. when I asked Sid, the girl you met earlier, if she'd seen them. She said they weren't back. By five I was alarmed and rang The Deer Park. The chap said there was no one resembling Father Murphy or Ronnie in the pub, and there hadn't been all afternoon. That's when I rang the police."

Chad looked at Mrs Grogan clasping and unclasping her hands. "Tell us about Ronnie, Mrs Grogan."

"Ronnie, Ronnie Bannister, he's a volunteer. Comes and helps every so often. A half-day here or a full day when he can. All the residents love him. He'll take them shopping or sometimes just for a walk. Places like this couldn't exist without people like Ronnie."

"How long has he been with you?"

"Oh, he's only very recent. Started about a month ago. I can check the exact dates."

Jas said, "Did you ring the mobile number Mr Nicholson gave you, or Ronnie's?"

"Yes, of course. Both were switched off."

"Do you know of anyone that might want to harm Father Murphy or Mr Bannister? Or any reason that they both might have chosen to disappear."

"No, of course not. That's a preposterous idea. Father Murphy is a sick old man and Ronnie has a heart of gold."

"Does Father Murphy have any relatives?"

"None, I'm afraid. As with most of our residents, God was his only family." Mrs Grogan crossed herself.

"Can you let us have a recent photograph of both of them please, we'll need those to get posters and TV appeals done."

"Of course, I've got one for Father Murphy but I don't think I do for Ronnie. As I said he's a volunteer so hasn't got a personnel file. I've got an address for him if that helps."

"Yes, thank you. Can you describe him for us?"

"He's a tall man in his forties. A man of colour, as we now have to say."

Jas shimmied across the car park rummaging in her handbag.

"If it's the keys you're after, they're probably on the back seat," he said.

She flicked him a finger. "What do you make of all that?"

"I don't like it at all, what about you?"

"Likewise. Let's get back and update the Boss."

CHAPTER 22

Chad checked his watch, it was 1:30 p.m. He perched on the desk near the window again in Room 106. And shit, the pain in his leg was excruciating. It felt like someone was inserting a large blunt chisel into his knee and then twisting it. He rubbed it to ease the muscles loose. Fuck. He counted back, he'd had three, one before bed would make four. Two left for the rest of the day felt nowhere near enough. He needed to make it till 2:30 p.m. He could last another hour.

The door pushed open, Lee came in followed by Schmidt and Deakin in conversation. "Okay, Jas, kick-off. What news of our missing priest?"

Chad checked his phone as Jas gave the team an abbreviated account of their visit to Ashfield Grange.

"That's about it, Boss. No sightings of either of them and no clue as to where they went when they left the Nursing Home. Zilch. Nada."

"Every day," said Chad, "there's something on the news about abuse at care homes and how stringent the vetting of employees must be, and here we've got a home full of ex-priests and the owner hasn't got a clue who one of her volunteers is. This Bannister guy could be anybody off the street. No checks, not even a bloody photo. We know he's black with a heart of gold. So much for the

Care Quality Commission."

"Getting Bannister's home address checked out by uniform as we speak, Boss," Jas added.

Chad watched Lee make some notes on his iPad, then Lee looked up and said "Okay, thanks, Jas. What was the name of the guy who Murphy was meeting? Oh yeah, Nicholson. Anything on him?"

"Nothing. We are checking with the Diocese to find out who spoke to him, but right now, we can't confirm anything about him, so can't list him as missing. We'll get an appeal out for Murphy and Bannister onto Look North, the Yorkshire Evening Post and all the local radio programmes. Unless we get some sightings or Bannister's family give us anything, that's about all we can do. I mean how far can Murphy go without his medication? My guess is he'll be struggling very soon so I'll alert the Leeds General and St James' as well."

"Fine." Lee looked at Chad. "I think we need a session on strategic handling of the press on both these cases, but for different reasons. A priest going missing from a care home in circumstances that are, at best, out of the ordinary, will attract national as well as local interest. A businessman going missing at the same time and in the same city might lead some of our more innovative journos to start thinking there's a bigger story. We need to control that. I'll talk to the Chief Super about it. MPs on one side, Bishops on another, we just need a General to go missing to add a military flavour and we'll have a job lot. I shouldn't tempt fate, should I?"

"A bit like the buses, Boss, none come for ages then two come at once," said Deakin.

"Yeah, okay, Luke, very funny. Now, what have we got from the tennis club and Huxton's Mac?"

"The MacBook," said Joe, "confirmed that the deal he'd been doing was very much alive and kicking. Lots of correspondence back and forth with lawyers and accountants. Appears there was to be a whole heap more paperwork this week and they'd got a target deal completion date in the diary for next Monday. Nothing in his emails that looks sinister. If anything, Boss, this guy was all over the deal like a rash. He's the one pressuring the other parties to get the Due Diligence completed. He's the driving force."

Luke Deakin joined in. "His calendar showed this week's scheduled meetings. Pretty hectic for him. This is not the diary of a guy who is planning on doing a runner. His calendar also showed that at 4:00 p.m. last Friday he was booked to play tennis at Rawdon. I contacted the tennis club and spoke to the Secretary there, a guy called Neil Cawthorne. He says that Huxton plays most weeks. Outdoor in the summer indoor in the winter. He doesn't have a regular playing partner but puts his name down and either makes up a doubles game or someone matches up with him for singles. Huxton had his name on the list for a game on Friday at 4:00 p.m. which ties in with his diary. Cawthorne then tells me that Huxton called the club on Friday morning, said he's going away for a few days and can't make the game. Apologises and rings off."

"But hang on," said Lee, "Andy Huxton, told us that when he was talking to his Dad at 2:30 p.m. John Huxton tells him he's going to play tennis later. So, why did he say that if he'd already cancelled? And for a guy as meticulous as he appears to be, why didn't he cancel the game in his diary? This whole thing just makes no sense."

Chad's phone vibrated. Freddie.

One of my boys tells me that he overheard a punter, big coke head, been saying how the press would pay good cash for a story about a footballer he knows who's a junkie. Trying to find out more. Will let you know bro. Do you want me to take care of it?

No, let's catch up Friday let me know if you hear anything else. Cheers bro.

Lee stood up. "Let's get the hard yards done, guys, it's the only way we'll get a break. Joe, Luke, follow up with Huxton's lawyer, Tom Nichols. And his accountant, Steven Holding. Let's see what they have to say. They've worked with him since he started. Also, try to find any of these businesses that Huxton ripped off in the past. See if that gives us anything. Anything we've missed?" Silence. "Okay let's meet at 6:00 p.m. and see if we've found the buggers."

Chad shuffled off the desk and waited as the coppers filed by. "Lee, I've got a few ideas buzzing around my head. Do you mind if I go and visit Bridgewater Place and talk again to the security guys and this car park attendant? I don't want to tread on any toes, just want to sanity check what they told Joe and Deakin."

"Go for it, buddy. These guys all think you're the dog's proverbials after nailing Lawlor, so they won't mind what you do. I'll get a Constable to take you there so he can make notes. Let me know if you get anything."

CHAPTER 23

"Never noticed that before. What is it?" Chad asked.

George Hampsthwaite, the car park attendant looked past Chad at a metal structure that hovered above the road at the entrance to Water Lane. He was maybe late sixties, early seventies, Chad thought, with a full head of white hair and a white moustache and goatee. He wore black trousers beneath a beige padded anorak jacket that zipped at the front with additional buttons. George just needed a trilby and he could have been David Jason as Inspector Frost.

"It's a windbreak. When they built Bridgewater Place, they didn't realise they were creating a wind tunnel. It's been a bloody nightmare. Lorries toppling over, pedestrians were blown away, and a couple of years ago one poor chap died when a lorry was blown onto him. So, they built that to disperse the wind."

"Really? Some poor sod had a lorry blown onto him? I bet that was one hell of an insurance claim." Chad looked up. Bridgewater Place towered over him. He'd heard the place was visible from twenty-five miles away which, now he stood beneath it didn't surprise him

"Does it work?" he asked

"I think it must help, but we never get to find out because now when it gets windy the Council close the roads around here.

Typical isn't it? Bolting the stable door but only after they've built the bloody thing."

"Yep," said Chad, "you'd think, wouldn't you, that these things wouldn't get past the planning committee stage without finding all that stuff out. Money talks I suppose." Chad pulled his temporary Police ID card out and showed it to the old boy, while the Constable that had accompanied Chad stood to the rear.

"There can't be two Chad Hiltons so, you must be the one I used to pay to watch?" said George.

"I am, and I hope you got your money's worth."

"Yes, I don't go as often now, but my grandson tells me Bielsa's got them playing well. I loved watching you and Freddie Jackson taking on the likes of Man Utd and Liverpool. Good memories. So, you're with the Police now?"

"I'd say helping rather than with full time, but yes, I'm having to work for a living now."

"Aye, you and me both. Now, what can I do for you, don't think there's much I can say as I haven't already told the detectives?"

Chad smiled and said, "Can you remember, George, you don't mind me calling you George, do you?" George waved him on, "whether Mr Huxton was carrying anything when you let him into the car park?"

"No, I don't think so, in fact, I'm sure he wasn't, 'cos he was gesticulating with both arms tapping his pockets." George mimed the actions for extra effect.

"Right, I see. Just so I'm clear, you let Mr Huxton into the car park by that door down there," said Chad, looking past Hampsthwaite to a steel door on the side of the building. George nodded. "And, did you see him come out of that door as well?"

"No, I never saw him come out, I happened to glance across and there he was waving like crazy."

"How long would it have taken Mr Huxton to get up to his apartment and back down again once you'd let him in."

"Well, that depends on the lifts which can be temperamental.

You can wait for ages sometimes. But assuming it came straight away then he could have been up and back down in three or four minutes I'd have said. But he didn't do that."

"What do you mean, how do you know he didn't do that?" asked Chad.

"Well, because the fob to get into the garage is the same as the one to activate the lift. To go up to his apartment he'd have needed his fob. He could only get as far as the ground floor without it. Security reasons."

"I see, so he'd have had to get out at the ground floor and then get the security guard to override the lift so he could get to his apartment?"

"Yep, that's it, you've got it."

The constable was making notes in a black notebook.

"But what if another resident had been in the lift at the same time, couldn't they have used their fob to get Mr Huxton up to his floor?"

"No, not in this building. Each fob is floor specific. So, if I live on floor twelve, for example, I can go to all floors up to twelve but no further. Mr Huxton would have had to have been in the lift with the residents of floors thirty or thirty-one to enable him to get to his floor. You'll have to check with them but I know that they didn't drive in or out of the car park that day."

"Isn't that a bit of a pain for residents?"

"No, not much. They just go to security, confirm who they are, and he gives them a temporary fob."

"I see," said Chad, "that's very helpful. Can you remember what Mr Huxton was wearing when you saw him?"

"Yes, he had on a pair of jeans with a hoody top, blue I think, but you'll be able to tell from the CCTV."

"Thanks, George, do you mind if I take a wander down there and round the back of the building. Just want to get my bearings."

"You crack on, young fella."

Chad limped down to the car park with the copper for company.

To the side of the steel door was a fob activated electronic pad. A good forty yards to George's cabin from here, he thought, then walked along the side of the building. Well, bugger me, it takes me to the back of the apartment block and out onto the main road. It does a loop.

"George, one more thing. Mr Huxton could have come from the back of the apartment block around the side there, and you'd have only seen him when he got to the door. Is that right?"

"Yes, I suppose he could have. But to get out of the building he'd go through the foyer and be on CCTV or he'd come out of the car park and I'd have seen him. That's a bloody awful limp you've got there, lad. Is that from your playing days?"

"It is, George. Still, better to have played and ended up like this than never to have played at all. Or so my doctor tells me. See you later, George, thanks for your help."

* * *

The security guard in the foyer of Bridgewater Place stared at Chad and the constable. "Yes, I'm aware you spoke to the detectives earlier, but there's just a couple of additional questions I need to run by you, if you don't mind?" Said Chad.

"Okay, but I ain't got long. I'm busy here, man."

"Fine. Can you confirm that Mr Huxton did not exit the lifts on the ground floor at 3:00 p.m. and ask you to give him access to his apartment on the twenty-ninth?"

"No, he never did that."

"Thanks, and are there security cameras around the back of the block facing the main road into town?"

"No, just inside the building."

"You've been very helpful. I guess you must have been off work the day they did that?'

"Did what?"

"The customer engagement course."

Chad typed into his Notes app. *Where's his tennis kit? What did he do in the car park for the 5 mins before driving out at 3:02 p.m.? Why isn't his fob in his apartment? How did he get to the garage door without being spotted on CCTV?* "Can you write up your notes please," he said to the policeman that had been with him, "and let DI Wallace have them."

"Of course, sir, will do."

CHAPTER 24

I'm sitting on one of the two plastic chairs I've brought with me. The Bulgarian Makarov pistol lies on my lap, good for focusing the mind I find. John Huxton is sitting opposite me. Have I gone too far? The man looks near the end. I've fed him each day and given him half an hour to exercise and clean himself, which is gross, but he still doesn't look well. I need some cooperation tonight so I hope the extra tuna sandwich I gave him with the bottle of orange juice will have done the trick. Doesn't look that way though. He looks a picture of misery. Well, he's had the carrot, now for the stick.

"Time for choices, John," I say, "you've got two. Choice one, you comply with everything I tell you to do and you will be released from here tomorrow. No harm done. Choice two is that you do not comply. In which case, you'll die tonight. As I said, choices." I follow Huxton's eyes as he watches me slide my hand over the Makarov. I think he's getting the hang of it.

"What do you want me to do?" Huxton's voice croaked.

"John, I need you to concentrate on what I'm going to tell you. You need to get it right because if you don't, you haven't complied and you know what that means?"

"I'm okay. For fuck's sake get on with it."

Grumpy bastard. "Good. In a few minutes, you'll make a call

to your son's mobile, you'll say that you are okay but being held captive and that failure to follow the instructions you give him will result in your death. Then, tell him to get hold of both your lawyer and your accountant. No excuses. You'll call him back in exactly fifteen minutes. If all three are not on the call, you die. Clear?"

"Yes, I'm clear." murmured Huxton.

"Good, so on your second call, you'll tell them they are to go to the Kirkstall Lane entrance to Headingley cricket ground. They should meet there tonight at 6:45 p.m. Outside turnstile B is a waste bin in which is a bag with three mobile phones. They take one each. Taped to the base of the phone is the number of the other two phones. That's how they'll communicate. You will then tell them that a sum of five million pounds is to be available at 7:55 a.m. tomorrow. You will give them the account details for transfer tomorrow at that time. I have written the instructions on cards so you don't have to worry about forgetting any of what I've just told you. Understood?" I watched him shuffle in his plastic seat. He's trying to think of ways to worm out of this, but I've got all my bases covered. He runs a veiny hand through his unwashed hair, and the smell of him seeps into my nose.

"A movement of that amount of cash will need my sign off, without that it can't happen." He says.

Disappointed really. I'm disappointed that he went for the most obvious delay tactic. He doesn't understand how far ahead of him I am. "Really John, is that right?" I look shocked and pretend to be at a loss, then say, "Your accountant can move money from any or all of your accounts up to the tune of ten million with any two signatures from yourself, himself and your lawyer. So, don't give me shit. Is that understood?" Huxton raises his head. I know he's wondering how I know this and who from his inner circle has betrayed him.

"How do I know that you'll let me go when the cash has been transferred, you could just leave me here to rot."

"And there you have it, well done," I start a slow handclap. "Now you're getting the hang of things. Because, you don't know anything, you have no guarantees, no cards to play. For the first time in your miserable life, you do not hold the upper hand. How does that feel, fuckwit? But as you've asked, I'll tell you. Letting you go poses no risk to me at all. You don't know who I am or where you are. Therefore, as soon as the money is confirmed in my account, I'll give you back to your devoted family."

There was a moment's silence.

"Okay, I'll do it."

* * *

I savour the deep crimson colour of the Malbec, then take a large drink and put the glass on the table. There are four mobile phones also on the table. I pick one. Showtime, the sequel. My call is answered after two rings. "Yes, I'd like to speak to Bishop Benedict please."

"I'm afraid that's not possible, he's giving a lecture."

"Yes, yes, he's giving a lecture to a group of fresh-faced young clergy. He needs to call me back on the number you can see within ten minutes. If he doesn't then he'll forever have to answer why he considered a lecture to young priests was more important than saving the life of Father Murphy. Ten minutes. The clock is ticking."

The phone lies alone, away from the other three. I see it light up displaying a number. I have it on silent but answer after two or three seconds. "Well done, I love punctuality."

"This is Bishop Benedict, to whom am I talking?"

"No, no, no, let's start as we mean to go on. The rules are mine, not yours. So, you only have two things to do. Listen, and comply. Simple stuff. Do you understand?" Silence. Just breathing. "Do you understand?"

"Yes, I understand."

"Good. I have Father Murphy, and he's not a healthy man. He needs his medication, or I think he may well die soon. We'd better get a move on. You have until tomorrow morning to get the sum of five million pounds available to be transferred to me. At 8:00 a.m. I will give you the account details into which you transfer the money. As soon as I see the money, I will release Father Murphy into safekeeping. Clear?"

"You know I cannot possibly raise that amount of money."

"Oh, I think you can. Your brother, the UK's version of Bill Gates, has got a huge stash of cash. I'm sure he can help his little brother out in his time of need. Call it Christian charity. Oh, and I forgot to mention that if you don't do this, the full and gory details of Murphy's paedophilia will be released on social media and to the press. That'll include the names of hundreds of children he abused over the years, the schools that you placed him in allowing him to continue his abuse, and all the silences you've bought. And all the Diocesan officials that worked so hard on his behalf, including your good self. I'll give all of it to the press. What a cover-up. All to protect one of your own. One amongst many. I reckon Ashfield Grange must be home to more paedophiles than anywhere else on earth. A clever strategy, I grant you, most of your bad apples in one place, but I'm not sure the good citizens of Leeds will see it that way." Silence. "Good, I think you're getting with the program. 8:00 a.m. Or he dies and I'll release it all."

"How do I know you won't do that anyway?"

"To be fair, you don't. However, I'll accept the cash in exchange for my laptop which I'll leave with Murphy. Everything is on there. No copies. 8:00 a.m. Don't be late."

I end the call and reach for the Malbec, then swirl the wine around the glass. "I fucking love this job."

CHAPTER 25

Andy Huxton fidgeted, his head flicking from side to side. At 6:45 p.m Yorkshire County Cricket ground in Headingley was shrouded in darkness. The spectator stands loomed out of the gloom and there was a faint hum of distant traffic as rush hour faded with the last stragglers heading to the suburbs. Only two cars in any otherwise deserted car park. His own and one other. Phones in a fucking waste bin, he thought. What the fuck, was someone taking the piss? Can't be. It had defo been his dad on the phone, he hadn't sounded good but he was alive. He glowered at the waste bin outside turnstile B then turned towards the other car parked a few yards away. "See if there's a fucking bag in that bin," he yelled to the lawyer and accountant standing beside a Range Rover. His voice sounded inordinately loud and his fidgeting was getting worse. Each nerve ending pulsing of its own accord, independent of the rest of his body. He couldn't control it. Keep your fucking voice down or someone will hear, he thought. Jesus, what the fuck is going on?

Nichols looked around him then walked to the large recycling bin put his hand inside and pulled out a Sainsbury's carrier bag.

"Are they in there?" said Huxton.

"Yes, they're here," replied Nichols.

"Right," said Huxton, "we do as he said, we use these, till we get

Dad back." He looked at his father's oldest allies. "How the fuck can we get that amount of cash by tomorrow?"

"Calm down, Andrew, it'll be okay," said Nichols, looking around again, "and keep your voice down we don't want to be attracting unwanted attention. We may be able to arrange it."

"Don't you tell me to keep my fucking voice down. How the hell can you arrange that?"

"Many years ago, your father gave me access to all his accounts because of the need to be able to transfer cash, at short notice, into escrow accounts for acquisition purposes. Any movements require two of the three of us, Mr Huxton, Mr Holding here and myself to give the necessary authorisation. So, there's two of us and we will be able to make the transfer."

"Jesus, wow, fuck, I didn't know that. Okay," muttered Andy, "I suppose we should tell the police, what do you think?"

"I think that would be unwise. We don't know that whoever is holding your father isn't watching us, or may have hacked our mobiles to see if and to whom calls are made. Sudden police activity may well put your Dad's life at risk. And we can't rely on the police not to make a dreadful mistake," said Nichols.

"I agree," said Holding. "Let's get the money ready to transfer and then look for some assurances when the call comes tomorrow."

Andy Huxton stared at them both in turn, "Right, call me and let me know when you've sorted it."

CHAPTER 26

Chad checked his phone.

Lee. "*Guys, need to move mtg from 18:00 to 19:00 p.m. Sorry.*"

He tapped on the phone icon then scrolled to Angie.

She answered. "Hi, babe, how are you?"

"Yep, fine, thanks. Just thought I'd call while I've got a minute. How're things with you?"

"I'm okay, hectic at work but other than that, fine. I've booked our first meeting with the counsellor for next Wednesday, so a week today. I'll send you a diary invite because otherwise, you'll forget."

"Okay, that's great, I'll be there I promise," he paused, then said, "Ange, are you sure you didn't mention our situation to anyone? That's what we agreed, isn't it? We'd keep it between us until we got some help or sorted it out? I ask, because you and I are the only people who know we're not together and that I take painkillers."

She paused. "Jesus, Chad, you've sent me a text about that and I told you I hadn't but I suppose it's possible, in conversation, you know. I can't remember everything I say to everybody."

Jesus, he thought, she wouldn't be so blasé if it were her getting trolled. Don't get irritated, keep calm. "Who might you have told, Ange?"

"Chad, I've just said I don't think I have, but people are always asking after you and what you're up to. I can't remember. Why is it important?"

"Because I have some weirdo trolling me every day."

"So, it must have been me. That's what you're saying? Typical, always my fault. Can you remember everything you say to people? No. It's just as likely to have been one of the coppers you're working with or any of your mates. Freddie? What about him? You two are as thick as thieves. But no, it had to have been me."

"I didn't mean it like that. I want to find out who it is so I can put a stop to it. Has that guy you thought was following you showed up again?"

"No. Not so far. I've got to go. Make sure you accept the diary invite."

The phone went dead. How long has it been like this, he thought? One of us jumping down the other's throat at the smallest thing. He pulled the strip from his pocket. Four down.

* * *

Lee kicked the meeting into life. "Dead ends everywhere on all of these then? No sign of Father Murphy, Huxton senior or Bannister? Jas, what did you get from Bannister's address?"

"Nothing boss. He rented a bedsit in a house in Harehills two months ago but hasn't been seen much. The room told us nothing, obviously been in use but nothing for us to go on. He paid cash for the two months and the rental runs out next week."

"Shit. Joe, did you get anything on Huxton's previous businesses?" asked Lee.

"We've made a start, Boss," said Joe, "but it's going to be a long job. We've set up meetings tomorrow with Nichols and Holding, the lawyer and accountant. They should be able to give us more info."

Lee frowned, then said, "I phoned Andy Huxton and the Catholic Diocese during the afternoon and both said they hadn't received any ransom demands. Nothing, radio silence. Chad, any thoughts? Oh, how did you get on at Bridgewater Place?"

"Yes, okay. Raised more questions than answers."

"What are the questions?"

Chad checked on the notes app. "Where's the fob, and where is his tennis kit? How did he get out of the apartment block without being seen? Oh, and what was he doing in the car park for five minutes from going in, to driving out? That's just a few of them, let me put them all down in some sort of order and I'll get them across to you. In the meantime, there's not much I can do in terms of perp profiling, because we don't know how many perps we've got. I'm taking it there's nothing to link Huxton's disappearance with that of Bannister and Murphy?"

Joe jumped in. "No, nothing we've seen to suggest that."

Chad nodded, then looked at Lee. "Except that it's a weird coincidence that in the space of a couple of days we've got three mis-per cases. There's a section on your website which is interesting. It details how you grade each mis-per case, high, medium or low risk, based on various factors, age, sex et cetera, and some stats show most mis-pers rock up within twenty-four hours of going missing. The fact that ours haven't, and that there are question marks at best around their disappearance, puts our boys in the high-risk category. What're the chances of that? Three high-risk mis-pers in the space of a couple of days. Strange, if you ask me."

"Yeah," said Jas, "you're right, that does seem like a coincidence, but I'm not sure what it tells us."

"All I'm saying is that it's out of the ordinary, something for you guys to think about. Anyhow, I can't build you a profile until you find evidence one way or the other that they're linked or not linked. Whether we're dealing with one perp or two. There's also something bothering me about Bannister and Nicholson."

"What about them?"

"We know fuck all about either of them. They stick out because we know so little, whereas we know plenty about Huxton's life. We know how he made money, we know he's well connected and we know he has a family. Likewise, Murphy, we know he was a priest, that he lived in a care home and that he'd been a teacher. They both have past lives, people know them, we can dig into those lives. But Bannister? Who is he? What do we know about him? How does he fit? I don't see it. Same for Nicholson, he's a name that's all, no address, no description just that he says Murphy taught him which we haven't been able to check."

"Fair enough, but we can move faster with Huxton and Murphy because we know more about them. I agree, let's not lose sight of Bannister and Nicholson but let's concentrate our efforts on where we can get the best chance of a result. Joe, Luke, you stick on Huxton. Keep searching into those businesses, and until we have evidence to the contrary, we'll treat Huxton's disappearance as a separate case from Murphy and Bannister. That's about it for today. See you all in the morning."

CHAPTER 27

He was like a pea on a fucking drum, thought Chad. A massive four-seater settee with him perched in the middle. This house had been too big when there'd been two of us but now he was flying solo, it was ridiculous. Anyway, he had to concentrate. There was nothing that linked Huxton to Murphy, no connection, so why was he feeling that there was? Why? He began to type.

Huxton and Murphy??? If kidnapped, why no ransom?

Bannister and Nicholson are spectral, we know nothing about them. Are they linked? do they know each other? Victims, or perps?

Why now?

What's the catalyst?

He folded the iPad, took another sip of whisky and wondered how Emily Barrett was doing? Maybe he should check, not just walk away. He'd ask Jas how coppers managed to box each case off and not worry about the victims afterwards? Fucked if he could. He looked at the iPad screen. What connected Huxton and Murphy? The perp, of course. Just like the rape cases, the victims didn't know each other but the perp linked them. But how in this case? He took his metallic strip from his pocket and held the foil in his hand. Bedtime, he needed to give the old grey matter a rest. And the body for that matter. He put a pill on his tongue and looked at the whisky bottle and the empty glass next to it. Maybe one small one, he thought. A large measure splashed into the glass and the heady aroma brought a smile to his lips. He added a couple of drops from the water bottle then downed the whisky in one gulp. God, that was good. He fingered the Fentanyl foil and counted. Six today, that was an improvement, so he should try and stick to that tomorrow.

Pushing the foil back in his pocket, it grated on something flexible and metallic. "What the hell's that?" He emptied his pocket and a second Fentanyl foil emerged. He stared at it and his heart sank. One space. Fuck, when had he taken it? That morning, shit, that made seven. Oh, no, not again.

CHAPTER 28

The phone on the table vibrates, juddering on the glass top. Interesting. I let it buzz twice more, then answer. "Good evening, Bishop, this is a surprise. What can I do for you?" The tracking mechanisms on the phones are disabled so I'm not worried that they can be traced, even if any of them had been dumb enough to go the police. But I know my quarry and I know they haven't.

"I can't get you five million. There's not enough time and I need to be able to explain it to my brother. Yes, he's a friend and benefactor to the Catholic Church, but he wants to know what I need the money for. I can't tell him the details. Not yet. It's going to take a few days. I can get you some of it by tomorrow, but not all." The Bishop's voice trailed away.

Not a surprise, it would have been a bonus if old Brother Benny had managed to wheedle five million from his brother. I let him stew for a few seconds.

"How much can you get by tomorrow morning?"

"I think I can get one million."

"Call me back in five minutes," I replace the phone and select a second mobile from the ones laid out on the table. There is one number programmed, I dial it.

"Nichols, here." The voice is breathless. Anxious.

"Slight change of plan. It's nine million, not five. No debates.

Just do it, or bye, bye to your meal ticket. Good night."

The phone vibrates again. I let it buzz, same as before. Then say, "This is what we are going to do Bishop. You will transfer one million as planned. But for that, you only get Murphy. The laptop and all the evidence you get when you pay me the remaining four. That will be no later than 6:00 p.m next Wednesday. One week today. If it doesn't reach me by that time, I will publish and be damned, to quote someone whose name I forget. Anyway, while I mull that over, make sure you get that million in place by the time I call you in the morning. We'll make further arrangements when you've confirmed you've got the other four. Good night"

CHAPTER 29

"Father Murphy, Father Murphy!" The boys were calling to him and he could smell the cut grass and the linseed oil. Summertime and boys were playing cricket. Lots of boys. Somewhere in the distance, he could see them. He answered, and shouted. "Over here, Andrew, over here, Stuart." The blue sky was awash with cherubic white clouds and oh, was that the shed over there? The sun was shining through the cracks in the wood. There would be hay bales warm from the sun. Soft and warm. "Come quickly, come quickly, boys," he called. Somewhere he could hear a voice, he didn't recognise it but it was close, in his ear.

"Shh," it said. "Shh."

"Come on, boys, in here," he called.

"Shhh." The voice was low and deep and insistent. He didn't need to be quiet, no-one would hear him, not in the barn.

"There, yes, just there. That's right. Good boy. Keep doing that Andrew. Stuart, lovely boy, come here. Lie down next to me. Is that nice? Do you like that? You do, I know you do, stop pretending. Don't cry, Stuart. Oh, Andrew, that's so nice, show Stuart how to do it."

"Shh." And again, "Shh."

Stop saying that, go away whoever you are, I'm with my beautiful boys.

"Oh, yes, yes. Oh, boys, don't stop. Oh yes. Oh."

CHAPTER 30

It's funny how some things stick with you. For me it's the three Ps. Piss Poor Planning gives Piss Poor Performance. I'd learned that on the first day of the management course and had adopted the mantra to every facet of my life. I check my watch. 6:00 a.m. Matchday. It's all about the preparation, and you can never be too careful. The industrial estate looks quiet but, all the same, I check for any activity. Give people a busy place and they'll see and remember nothing. Give them one man at an industrial unit at 6:00 a.m. and they'll remember every detail. All quiet, no-one around. Lazy bastards, no wonder the country's up the Suwannee. I follow my routine, place the padlocks on the ground and roll up the shutters, duck underneath then close them. Once inside I smell the fetid air.

"Jesus, that smell is horrendous. Glad today's the last day."

I reach up and place a leather briefcase on the roof of the Porsche. "Don't be a dickhead and forget it's there when you drive off," I laugh. No chance of that. There are advantages to O.C.D. The obvious one being that you don't overlook the small details that would fuck the plan up. I'd packed a bag the previous evening and had already checked the contents several times before leaving home. P.P.P. I check them again now.

"Hoody, joggers, trainers. No brand names. Labels removed.

Excellent. These charity shops are great. Where's the cleaning stuff?" I reach into the bag, "There we are. Okay, let's get Huxton cleaned and fit to be reunited with the family." I apply the VapoRub, under my nose, then put on the latex gloves and release the locking bar, before pulling the doors of the container wide. It's Murphy I see first. His head is slumped forward, his mouth is gaping open and two wires stretch from his chest to the Taser on the shelf. I look at Huxton. The same.

"What the fuck? Stupid twats, what have you done? Fuck, fuck, fuck." Jumping into the container I feel for a pulse in Murphy's neck. Nothing. His face is cold to my touch.

"Shit, stupid old fucker, you weren't meant to die yet. You had to die when I said so, not before, and not fucking now." I feel my stomach turn to water and my legs are weak. I stare at Huxton. "Don't tell me you've gone as well?" I touch Huxton's neck. Warm. "Thank fuck for that," I shake Huxton's shoulders. "Wake up." I pull out the two sharp barbs dropping them onto the table.

Huxton lifts his head from his chest. "Will I live?"

Pathetic old git. Relief floods through me. "Of course you'll fucking live, if it doesn't cause a heart attack straight away, you're fine."

"You've killed him," Huxton shouts, saliva frothing around his mouth. "Fucking moron, you think you're so fucking clever, don't you? Well, look where that's got you. You'll be going down for murder."

"I didn't fucking kill him, and call me a moron again, you old twat, and I'll blow your fucking head off right now." Calm down and breathe, don't lose it now. "I told you to speak in whispers. One of you must have made some noise. What happened?" I inhale several deep breaths and feel my composure returning. I've got this, I'm in control.

Huxton looks up. "The fucking perv you locked me up with must have been dreaming. It was disgusting. He was talking in his sleep, I kept telling him to shut the fuck up but he was out of it. Shouting, groaning, it was fucking horrendous. Then there's a bang and I felt this god-awful pain in my chest. I must have blacked out. When I came to, I couldn't hear him breathing. What are you going to do?"

"I'll sort that out, you should be worrying about whether they've got the money ready. It's a couple of hours 'till we make the call, so sit still and shut the fuck up, I need to think."

Huxton is staring at me with a quizzical look on his face. He says, "Who are you, I feel like I know you?"

"You do, you just don't recognise me. That's the plan. What?" I stare at him, "all black guys look the same, do we? I suppose you've shafted so many people in your time that they must all begin to blend into one. Just a bunch of losers in your mind. Well, not today, buddy. We'll see who the loser is today."

"Your plan's going up in smoke fella, so why not just let me go and I won't say anything about our dead priest. How about that?"

He's got some balls I'll give him that, but he's way out of his depth. He just doesn't know it. I stand behind Murphy. What to do? I look at the matted hair on the back of Murphy's head and make my decision.

"My plan's right on track, and the old paedo dying won't change a thing, so you need to calm down before you have a heart attack. I'm going out for an hour. When I'm back we'll clean you up and make the calls. Just think, a couple of hours from now you'll be back home and this will all be a distant memory."

* * *

The tarpaulin makes a loud *thwack* as I drop it onto the floor of the warehouse. This should do it. I check my protective CSI style gear. Careful is the watchword. Unlocking the container, I release the doors and, stepping in, take a small key from my pocket and unlock the arm restraints holding Murphy. Grabbing the dead priest by the shoulders, I bend him forward to rest on the table, then I kneel to unlock Murphy's legs. "Oh, fuck that's gross. Dirty bastard."

"He wouldn't be like that if you hadn't brought him here, then fucking killed him," yelled Huxton.

"Shut the fuck up, Huxton, and worry about yourself."

"Fuck you, wanker," screamed Huxton.

Leaving the container, I unfold the tarpaulin and pick up the strapping I'd put inside it, then walk back into the stinking prison. Standing behind Murphy, I wrap the strapping around the dead man's chest, bringing it together underneath each arm. Unpleasant, but the ends will justify the means. "Right, let's get you out of here." Holding each end of the strapping, I haul him upright, taking the weight of priest's body.

"Fuck me, fat bastard." I drag him out of the container and drop the body onto the open tarpaulin. "Come on, I'll wrap you up nice and tight."

"He looks like a maggot," I chuckle as I survey Murphy trussed in the tarpaulin and secured with the strapping. I open the boot of the Cayenne then bend and lift the body before lugging it along the concrete floor to the car. Sweat is trickling inside my hoody. Pausing to get my breath, I manhandle the corpse in its black plastic shroud, onto the rim before tipping it over the edge and into the boot. "Back where you started," I close the lid with a slam.

Reaching onto the roof of the SUV, I pick up the leather briefcase. The hinges click as I open it. Inside lies a Makarov pistol, and a long black cylinder. I screw the silencer onto the thread at the end of the barrel and push it into my waistband, then count the single-stack magazines inside the case. Five. Don't think I'll need all those, but, hey, better safe than sorry. "Here's the plan," I lean on the container door and say, "I'm going to unlock you and we'll get you out. I've brought all sorts for you to clean yourself up with and some clean clothes to change into. Any funny business and I'll introduce you to my mate." I pull the weapon from my waistband and wave the gun in front of Huxton's face.

* * *

"That's better, isn't it. You look a bit more human. Not long to go. Now, hold your hands out in front of you." I tie his wrists together with a plastic tie, then leave Huxton standing by the car, and walk behind the container, returning with one of the plastic chairs. "Now, sit down, relax and remember. You do exactly what I say, right?"

"Right," muttered Huxton.

CHAPTER 31

Chad forced his eyes to open. That he was in bed and not the kitchen floor was progress of sorts, he thought. Weak sunlight filtered into the bedroom and he looked through the windows opposite the bed and saw the top of the large silver birch swaying in the wind. He couldn't remember going to bed and it was obvious that he hadn't closed the curtains.

"I can't keep doing this, one day I won't wake up. So why am I?" The bedroom remained stoic in its silence as he let that question drift across his mind. Maybe, he thought, there was some dark part of him, somewhere in his subconscious that urged him to keep taking them until he fell into oblivion? No more shit, no more pain. He let his hand fall onto Angie's side of the bed. What was the point anyway? Look how fucked up life was. The pain in his fucking leg was incessant, his marriage was broken, and he'd got a drug habit to boot. And to round it all off he had a nutcase that trolled him. There was no light at the end of the tunnel. No fucking tunnel for that matter.

* * *

He looked at himself in the mirror. "You got away with one there," he said, "you don't look as bad as you should, considering." His watch said 7:30 a.m. and he stared into the blue eyes looking out from the mirror. What if today turned out to be a long day, how many would he take? Seven? What about eight? Twice he'd blacked out after seven so would eight kill him? Or would eight become nine? What was the alternative, hit the booze instead? He was doing both now wasn't he? He was caught between a rock and fucking hard place. If he took more than he should then whoa, blackout. What happened if he was driving and he blacked out? Fuck, anything could happen.

"You can't stop taking them, can you Chad?" he said to the mirror. "Admit it, you're addicted to them. You've heard all about the alkies that need a drink as soon as they get up. What about you eh? You need a pill, now, don't you? You're getting anxious already 'cos you haven't had one. Admit it, Chad, you are fucking hooked." He looked away from the mirror and picked up his toothbrush. Where could he get help? Did he even want help? The answer crept into his mind. Freddie. If anyone could help Freddie could. He would know someone, a surgeon maybe. But was Freddie part of the problem, he supplied the Fentanyl after all? Who else was there? No-one. Freddie, it had to be Freddie.

He looked at his phone. It was too early to call so he left a message. "Hey, Freddie call me back. I'm listening to you about these painkillers. Trust me, I am. I just don't have many options. Give it some thought for me buddy, maybe you know some surgeons I haven't already seen? By the way, have your guys found out anything more on the coke head?" As he dialled off, his phone pinged. That was quick, then he saw it was a message from Lee, not Freddie.

"*Can we meet for coffee, compare thinking on what happened to Huxton? Not at HQ, I've got to be in Leeds. Starbucks? Headrow? Nine ish*?"

"*No probs, see you there.*"

He popped the blue-and-white capsule from the foil. "Hello darkness, my old friend."

* * *

"So, where's your head about Huxton? You said you needed to clear your thinking, have you managed to do that? I hope so, cos we've got fuck all to go on and I've got the gaffer belly aching at me again."

Chad looked at Lee over his coffee cup. "I don't know about clear my head, the whole thing seems a bit of a mind fuck, but I have managed to isolate the bits that just don't add up."

"Fire away, let's see if between us we can make some sense of them."

"Remember, Lee, I'm coming at this from a psychologist perspective which means I'm looking at the way people act and think. That makes for some ambiguity, but here goes. Start with what we know about Huxton. He's ruthless and well organised. A control freak, his son says. The apartment's spotless, nothing out of place. His diary's a masterpiece of Teutonic efficiency, and he does it himself, no P.A. Every paper required for selling this recruitment business is ordered and filed but he still has time to chase up the lawyers and advisors to make sure they are completing their Due Diligence on schedule. A classic case of obsessive behaviour. Right?"

"Yeah, that's right, but so what?"

"Do you believe that a man like that would forget his fob?"

Chad looked around the café as he waited for Lee to answer. Coffee shops, same the world over, he thought. Businessmen in a rush, acting calm but letting their eyes bore holes in the backs of the Baristas urging speed. Young mums with the day ahead of them, and students on their way to college. Chad watched Lee push his coffee cup away from him then pull it back towards him then slide it around the table in some sort of hypnotic circular pattern.

"You keep going on about this fob, everyone forgets things sometimes." Said Lee

"Lee, I'm telling you, mate, this man wouldn't. It's just not in his nature."

"Chad, you can say what you like, but you can't dispute the fact that Hampsthwaite had to let him into the car park, because he'd forgotten his fob. End of."

"Okay, Lee, answer me this. Hampsthwaite lets Huxton into the car park. What would Mr Organised do next?"

Lee sipped his coffee while he thought. "Okay, I see where you're going. He'd go back to his apartment and get his fob. Granted I'll give you that, fair enough"

"Correct. And we know that he didn't do that because the security guy would have had to override the lift for him, which he said he didn't and CCTV confirms it. So, where is the fob now? It should be in his apartment but it's not? Which brings me to the next issue. He didn't go to his apartment, so what did he do for the five minutes between entering the car park and driving out?" Chad bit into his granola bar then lifted his cup of Black Americano to his lips and savoured the taste as the bitterness of the coffee mingled with the sweet gooiness of the snack.

"What do you think he did?"

"I don't know," Chad said, swallowing. "I'm just highlighting this illogical set of circumstances against the known character traits of Huxton. This behaviour is out of kilter. And then, of course, there's the tennis."

"What about tennis?"

"According to the club secretary, Huxton calls on Friday morning to cancel the game and tells him that he's going away for a few days. But, John Huxton, the man who is pathological about organisation, does not remove the game from his diary and nor is there anything in his calendar about him going away for a few days. He then tells his son on his call at 2:30 p.m. that's he's playing tennis later. And, finally, where's his tennis kit? If he had cancelled the game his kit should be in his apartment, but it's not. All very weird."

"Where do you think he was going?"

"Lee, I don't fucking know, I'm just making the point that the facts as we see them do not match the behaviour patterns of Huxton. So, either the facts are wrong, or our man began to act out of character."

"What the fuck?" said Lee.

"Then, there's motive. If he has been kidnapped, why kidnap him before this deal goes through? After it, he'd be fourteen million quid richer so a bigger payday. Not only does it happen before the deal, but there's also no ransom demand."

"Maybe, the kidnapper doesn't know about the deal. Or what if Huxton has just had enough of everything? Maybe there are some mental health issues we don't know about? Maybe he's in his Porsche at the bottom of Fewston Reservoir? That would certainly explain his erratic behaviour."

Chad leaned back in his seat, and took another bite of granola. Could be, he thought, but really? He sipped his coffee. No, not a fucking cat in hell's chance but don't say it like that to Lee. "You're right Lee," said Chad "it might explain his behaviour. But Andy Huxton says his old man was fine just half an hour before he drove out of the car park. Fine one minute, suicidal the next?" he looked across the table at Lee.

"It's improbable, I know but it is possible, I'll get the guys to check his medical history and see if he's been prescribed anti-depressants or has any other treatment for depression." Lee said resuming his tour of the table with his coffee cup.

"I bet you a tenner there'll be no record of mental health issues and there'll be no other significant medical issues either. He seems the sort of guy who would take going to the doctor as a sign of weakness. I'm telling you, Lee, there's something not right about all that palaver with his fob and the car park. I don't know what. Just something not right."

"Okay, well, keep mulling it over. We need a break, something to happen. I've got to go, let me know if you come up with anything.

See you later."

Chad's phone pinged. A direct message to his Twitter account.

@therealChadH. Not long now till I tell the world about your drug habit. You and @FreddieJ may be sharing a cell soon. #napoleoncalling

"Shit."

CHAPTER 32

"When I've dialled, I'm going to give you the phone and you'll read out everything on the pieces of card I'll hold in front of you. I'm going to put it on loudspeaker so deviate in any way from those words and I'll kill you. Do you understand?"

Huxton looks up. "Yes, let's just get on with it."

Taking one of the mobiles from my pocket, I dial the number, then give it to Huxton.

"Nichols here."

"Tom, It's me, John Huxton. Put this information into your phone. Do not write it down. Understand?"

"Yes." said Nichols, "hold on while I put this on speaker. I can't type into it and listen at the same time."

I can hear the lawyer's anxious breathing as he fiddles with the phone. Huxton's hands are shaking.

"Okay, I'm ready." Said Nichols

"Account number 56482319. Sort code 458134. Reference Asset Acquisition. Account Name, People Enterprises. Did you get that?"

"Hold on, hold on, say it slower I can't type that fast."

These two are like the fucking Keystone Cops, I think. Bungling idiots.

Huxton repeats the information. "Okay?"

"Yes, I've got it." Nichols reads back the information he's been given.

Huxton says, “Okay, that’s right, call back on this number to confirm you have transferred the money. If you don’t call back within five minutes from now, I will be executed.” His voice wavers. “Confirm you understand this.”

“Confirmed.”

“When you call back, I’ll give you further instructions regarding my release.” Huxton looks up and holds the phone towards me.

I take it and click it off. “So far so good. Now for the next one. As you and Murphy managed to set the taser off, we are going to have to improvise a bit. You’ll do what you did with Nichols except this time you will be playing the part of Murphy. My guess is our Bishop friend wouldn’t recognise Murphy’s voice from Adam, but we’ll see what he says.”

Huxton nods.

I take a second phone from my pocket and dial then hand it to Huxton.

“Bishop Benedict here.”

“Bishop, it’s me, Declan Murphy. Put this information into your phone. Do not write it down. Understand?”

“Yes.”

More nonsense as the idiot cleric can’t find the speaker icon. How this lot have got to be captains of industry and in the upper echelons of society I have no fucking idea. Holding the sheet in front of Huxton’s face, I smile encouragement as Huxton reads the same details that he’s just given to Nichols. I nod as Huxton finishes by asking for confirmation from the Bishop that the information is received and understood.

“Confirm you understand this.”

“Confirmed. Father Murphy, I need to speak to the man who is holding you. Is he there?”

“Yes,” Huxton passes me the phone.

I can almost smell the fear and stress coming down the line.

He wants to push back but he's scared of what I might do. I'll play along. For now. "Good morning Bishop, I trust you have the money?"

"Yes, yes, but I need confirmation that the er, person I've just spoken to is Father Murphy."

I'm right, his voice is warbling a couple of octaves higher than when I'd last spoken to him and I can hear the rustle as he shifts in his seat. "Trust seems to be in short supply Bishop, but very well. How shall we do that?" I pause, "I know, let's ask him a couple of personal questions. Mm, what about though? He's old, so his memory will be shot. Asking him the names of children he's molested over the years may prove fruitless. Simply too many, isn't that right Bishop?" Ha, a nice reminder of the stakes he's playing for. "I know," I resume, "what about questions regarding the care home which only a resident would know."

"That seems reasonable, okay." The Bishop stutters "What about the name of the owner and his bedroom number, that would work."

"Let me just put the phone on speaker," I say, but press mute instead. I quickly write two words and a number on one of the pieces of paper and in the blink of an eye I'm shouting into the phone. "Your line went dead on me Bishop, can you hear me, are you there?"

"Yes, I'm here."

"I've put the phone on speaker so fire away. Father Murphy can hear you,"

"Father Murphy, what is the name of the person who is in charge of the home where you live?" he asks.

I hold a sheet of paper in front of Huxton. *Mrs Grogan,* it reads.

"Mrs Grogan," says Huxton.

"Thank you, and what is your bedroom number?"

On the same sheet is written the number fifty-six.

"It's room fifty-six."

"Thank you," says the Bishop, "and don't worry we'll have you back safe and sound today. Could you pass the phone?" Huxton gives it to me.

"Satisfied?"

"Yes, but how do I know you'll keep your side of the deal? How do I know you'll release him?"

"Look, Bishop, I don't want to spend a minute longer with this smelly old git than I have to. I'm interested in the money. It's the price for all the abuse. That'll do me. Just get the four million lined up for next week. Now, Bishop, you need to get on and transfer the money. You've got five minutes. Call back on this number when you've done it." I click the call off.

All going to plan. God I'm good at this shit. The mobile in my pocket rings. I accept the call and put it on speaker.

"This is Nichols here. The money has been transferred as instructed. What now?"

I hold another piece of paper in front of Huxton.

"When I receive confirmation that the money has hit the account, I'll call and give you collection instructions," says Huxton.

The second phone rings. Speaker.

"This is Bishop Benedict; the money has been transferred. What happens now?"

Huxton repeats the words and ends the call. He stares at me as the noise from the calls filters away and the silence returns.

"See, that wasn't hard. Now sit back and relax everything is going to plan."

Two new email notifications pop up. I read them and laugh. This is just so fucking easy. What do the Americans say? It's like taking candy from a baby. These fuckers are so stupid they deserve to have it taken from them. Or maybe it's less that they're dumb and more that I'm smart? Plenty of time to consider that soon, but in the meantime the final pieces need to be put in place. "Okay, well, the money's in so let's call them back. Same as before, just read."

"Nichols here."

Huxton blinks rapidly but focuses on the words. "These are the instructions. You will call Holding and tell him to be at your house at 10:30 a.m. He must bring the phone he was given. You must both call your respective workplaces and tell them that you won't be in this morning. A family emergency. Tell them nothing more. Your wife and children will be out. Can you confirm that?"

"Yes, my wife is at work and my daughter is at school."

Huxton shifts in his seat. I stand behind him and double check he's reading it correctly. PPP. I can tell I'm making him nervous as his head turns slightly and his eye catches mine. I walk away a pace or two. "Next call my son, and tell him to go to work as normal. He's to stay there until you communicate further with him. No other message. If he deviates, I die. You and Holding will walk to the Whitehall Industrial Estate on Whitehall Road, take nothing with you except the phones. My Porsche Cayenne will be parked in the first bay on the right as you turn in at the entrance there and the keys will be on the driver's side wheel arch. Touch nothing, merely get in and drive out of Leeds, picking up the A1 northbound. Stay on it till you pick up the A19, towards Middlesbrough. Make sure that the phones you were given are switched on. Drive for nine miles and turn left at the sign for Potto. One mile down this road there's a small track on the left. Take it and you'll see there's a clearing on the right. Reverse into it and wait there. The journey is fifty-five miles and should take a little over an hour. You need to arrive at midday. Not before and not after. I will be there waiting, and my captor will be watching. If the police come, or anyone else, then I will be killed. Understand?"

"Yes, I understand. But..."

I draw my hand across my throat so Huxton clicks the call off. He's brighter, perceptibly perkier, having read his release instructions. I aim to please.

"Right, just Bishop Benny and we are done," I dial the number. "Bishop, no need to make notes this is very simple. Father Murphy will be waiting outside the Leeds General Infirmary main entrance at midday. I would imagine he'll need his medication so I thought hospital might be the best place. I'll be watching. If anyone other than a clergyman arrives, he'll be killed. Do you understand?"

"Yes, I understand."

I end the call.

"You are an absolute bastard," says Huxton.

"Trust me, I'm just getting started." I reply. The dust motes are fluttering in the sunlight coming in the window upstairs and the silence is oppressive. I stand a few feet in front of him and turn to face him. "Now, I'm sorry, John, but there's been a last-minute change of plan. You know how it is sometimes, circumstances change and the plan needs to change with them?" Reaching behind my jacket, I pull the Makarov from my waistband, the dull, black silencer sticking out from the barrel.

Huxton stares from the gun to me and back again. I read disbelief in his eyes. Disbelief tinged with fear and, to my surprise, defiance. "What the fuck are you going to do with that?"

"I'd have thought that was pretty obvious to a man of your intelligence, John, but hey maybe I was wrong about you."

Huxton's eyes open wide.

Not much more to say, I think. Actions are louder than words and all that. I squeeze the trigger. Twice. Two shots to the chest. I fire again as he begins to topple, a headshot, all over. The silencer does its job. So little noise, more 'phut' than bang. Smoke trickles from the end, and I lay it on the ground to cool. But no rest for the wicked, work to be done. I walk to the SUV and open the boot. Leaning inside there's a tarpaulin that is wedged against the side. I drag it out and turning, lay it out on the floor. Huxton is taller than Murphy but not as heavy, so dragging him to the tarpaulin and trussing him is somewhat less of an effort. When I finish, Huxton lies on the warehouse floor, wrapped tightly in his plastic pall. I haul him to the 4x4 and heave him over the rim to fall inside next to Murphy.

"Yes sir, please see for yourself, the boot has ample space. Ideal for camping trips with the family or to put it another way enough for at least two corpses. Ha!"

CHAPTER 33

Chad stood in the doorway. The bar looked different with no-one in it. Then again, most bars did. Sky Sports still dominated the TV screens, but no throbbing music and no heavies in suits. The chefs stood chatting behind the counter. No orders yet, no punters yet. Lunchtime, so most of the regular clientele would be heading off to bed around now. He saw Freddie alone at the bar. His footsteps rang out on the stone-flagged floor.

"Hey, buddy, how are you?"

"Cool, bro, cool." Freddie bear-hugged him as usual. "Where you at, everything okay? What can I get you?"

A different barman, but a replica of the guy who'd been serving the last time. "Just a Diet Coke, please." The barman nodded and shuffled away. "How's business, Freddie, is the bar doing well?'

"Yeah, we're flying. Better than I could have hoped for, and mainly legit. Ha. Now, Chad, man, you are worrying the shit out of me." Freddie slipped six more rectangular silver foil sheets under Chad's hand. "It's only a few days since you were last here and you need more of this shit. What are we going to do?"

"I know, Freddie, I know." He rolled a beer mat between his fingers. "As I said on my message it's worrying the hell out of me but I feel like I'm caught between a rock and a hard place. Without the drugs, the pain is too much and I can't function, I can't even leave the house. The drugs let me get through the day. But," he paused. Tell Freddie about the blackouts or not, he thought? He inhaled. "Look, Freddie, it's worse than just needing the drug to function, I'm taking more and more each day to keep going. I think I'm getting hooked on them. The intervals between me taking one and needing another are getting shorter. Buddy, it's fucking me up. Twice in the last three days, I've blacked out."

Freddie's eyebrows twitched in surprise.

"I've been lucky that I've been at home each time and it's been late at night. Once I woke up in bed but the first time, I woke up on the kitchen floor. There's no fucking warning. I take one too many, then pretty much that's it, I struggle to get my breath, then bang, I'm out. What happens if I'm in the car? Shit."

Freddie pressed himself further into his bar stool and shot a glance at Chad. "Fucking hell, bro, that's even worse than I thought. And these Fentanyl things are strong, man, those bitches take no prisoners. We've got to find a way to get you off 'em, somehow. I need to think about how we do that. What's Angie have to say? She can't be happy finding her man sparko on the kitchen floor, she must be worried sick as well?"

Chad saw Freddie sneak another sidelong look. What did that look mean, he thought, did Freddie know already that something was wrong between them? Should he tell him anyway? "We're not together at the moment, Freddie." There, he'd said it. It was out, it couldn't be unsaid.

The barman put Chad's drink down on a mat and moved away. Chad held his friend's gaze.

Then Freddie said, "I know bro, I know. I have been so worried about you and these fucking drugs that I spoke to Angie. She said there was some shit going down between you but she didn't say what. I didn't push it. What's gone on man?"

"You won't believe me when I tell you."

"Try me, bro."

"I found out Angie had been seeing another guy."

"What the fuck? I mean, what the actual fuck? That can't be right man?" He paused. "No, sorry buddy, I'm not doubting what you're telling me, it's just a shock."

"I know, it was a fucking shock to me."

"Is it over? Where are you guys at now?"

"She's told me that she's finished it with this guy, but I don't know who he is or how long it had been going on. Not knowing is killing me, but when she tells me the details, that'll kill me too. We've arranged to see a counsellor, starting next week. Freddie, your old mate's life is one big crock of shit. And then there's this." He called up his Twitter account and passed the phone to Freddie.

Freddie read the Twitter trail, his body tensed and his frown deepened, then he passed the phone back. "Shit, this guy is a weirdo," he said "and he's getting worse each time he messages you." Chad and Freddie both stared straight ahead lost in thought, each looking at the array of optics behind the bar. "Any idea who this is, or why he's doing it?"

"No idea at all." Said Chad. "He came out of the blue. Never had anything like this before and then last Friday this shit started happening. Whoever it is knows me and you, Freddie. By the way, Ange mentioned that she thought she was being stalked by some black guy. Not sure if she was but it seems a fucking massive coincidence."

Freddie sipped his drink then carefully replaced the glass on the mat. He turned to face Chad. "You should tell Lee. The feds need to be involved to get this guy."

"I can't tell Lee yet, buddy. I'd have to tell him about me and Ange, and probably the Fentanyl as well. He'd stop me working, and that's about the only thing that keeps me going. I'll tell him, but just not yet. Anyway, I think our best lead is this punter who's been mouthing off. Any more on him?"

"No, but I'll push a bit harder. He's a coke head, so I might just hold the supplies back for a day or two and see who comes out of the woodwork. Buys a lot of it, so if he can't get what he needs, I'd guess he'll start squealing. Leave that with me. Now, buddy, call me tomorrow, I'm going to talk to some people I know and find out how we get you off these painkillers and keep you functioning at the same time." Another hug.

Chad limped away from the bar.

Freddie called out. "Chad?"

"Yes, mate?"

"We've got this bro. You might stumble, but I won't let you fall."

"Cheers, buddy."

"Yeah, well fuck off now and catch some crooks. Ha."

CHAPTER 34

I don't mind waiting. I have patience, it's a skill I've taught myself and it's why the strategy is mapping out exactly as planned. Good things come to those who wait, someone once said. Well good things are coming my way. In a Porsche. I sit in the car I've borrowed for the day, I'm facing South, the opposite way from where the Porsche will arrive. The borrowed car is nice to drive but the owner has a shit taste in music so just Talk Sport to keep me company. Not long now. A quick final run-through, check the details, piss poor planning and all that. 11:57 a.m. "Okay, come on, where are you?" A glint of sunshine on metal catches my eye. I can see the shape but at this distance can't make out if it's the Porsche arriving. "Go on, indicate." The car slows and indicates then turns left off the main road and onto the small side road. "That's them." Good to go. I reverse out of sight of the approaching Porsche. Leaning across to the passenger seat, I open the glove compartment and lift the Makarov. I check the magazine. Three gone, plenty left. Should be fine.

* * *

I pull the hood of my sweatshirt over my face and bow my head a fraction as I walk the few paces from the roadside to the clearing.

The Porsche is parked as instructed and from underneath my hoody I can see Nichols and Holding in the front seats, confusion on their faces. They'll have recognised the wheels I'm driving. Walking to the driver's door, I indicate for Nichols to roll down the window. Adrenalin is flowing like a tsunami around my veins. I'm alert to everything, to any slight move this fucker might try and make. An electric hiss releases the glass and I look inside checking their hands are not holding anything that could be a weapon. Careful is my watchword. There's nothing, just their fear which I can see sweeping across their faces. It is palpable, I can almost touch it. It has a presence. My right arm is behind my back and I swing it slowly round in an arc bringing the pistol to the open window. Their eyes, in unison, slide from the gun to my face then back again. Their mouths hang open. Synchronised dying. The rush of power makes every nerve end tingle. This is better than sex. I register the look of shock from inside the car. Then. *Phut, phut.* The pistol spits. Nichols slumps against his seatbelt. *Phut, phut.* Holding's body arches into the backrest of his seat. I pull Nichols' hair so his head falls back against the headrest and fire again. Headshot, all over. Then pointing the gun at Holding's head which has flopped onto his right shoulder I fire. Job done. Between the seats is a tray holder for drinks, keys and other bits and pieces, where two phones are propped upright. I open the car door, lean in and lift them out, checking the numbers on the back. All good. I type a text into Nichols phone and press send. *We've got your dad but he's in the boot and we can't release him till we get back to Leeds. You've got to leave the office now and go to Starbucks at The Light. Wait there and we'll contact you with further instructions. We are being followed so comply.*

Putting the phones in my pocket, I close the door of John Huxton's Porsche Cayenne and walk back to my borrowed wheels. I take care to cover my footprints with leaves as I go. Excellent. I look back at the Porsche partly hidden. From where I stand it looks like a couple of blokes having a nap. I whistle. So fucking easy.

CHAPTER 35

Chad stretched his leg out in front of him and massaged his knee. 1:00 p.m. and he was three down. Not too bad, he thought, he'd finish the day on six at this rate. He looked up from his perch at the back of the room. He needed to concentrate despite the pain.

Joe was updating the team. "Neither Nichols nor Holding is at work today. Both rang into colleagues claiming some sort of family emergency. Meetings with them both rearranged for tomorrow."

"What, they both have a family emergency on the same day which coincides with both having meetings with you? Don't like the sound of that. Push them on it tomorrow," said Lee. "Jas, did you get any further with Bannister or Nicholson?"

"No, boss. I've been through Social Services, births and marriages, and there are seven Ronald Bannisters that fit age and location, so I'll be tracing those during the rest of the day. A big fat zero on Nicholson. I rang the Diocese and they say that no-one rang to enquire about Murphy and had they done so, that information would not have been given out. It would breach all sorts of confidentiality, and it appears even the Catholic Church is wised up to GDPR. I've asked them to provide a list of schools that Murphy taught at but they're not keen to give that information out. Mind you, Boss, he taught for nearly fifty years so we'll have a mammoth task tracking thousands of pupils. Even then, we may not find Nicholson or Bannister. It happens."

Lee caught Chad's eye. "Chad, any thoughts?"

Chad eased off the desk and steadied himself. "We were talking yesterday about whether these disappearances might be linked. Well, they are, by the fact that there's a load of weird shit surrounding them that you don't find in your average mis-per case. Are we saying that it's just bad luck that in the space of a couple of days we've had three high-profile disappearances under mysterious circumstances? Is that what we're saying?"

"We're not saying anything Chad, we just haven't got any evidence to suggest for one second that anything links them. Why would anyone kidnap Huxton and Murphy? Let alone Bannister? Remember, we've had no ransom demands either."

"True," said Chad, "but strange. I suppose you could be right and Huxton has topped himself. Must be worth putting an alert out again to see if anyone's seen the car?"

"We've done that, haven't we?" said Lee looking around his team for confirmation.

"Yes, boss, did it this morning," replied Joe. "Nothing so far."

Lee looked past Chad out of the window. "We've got nothing. We need a break. Go back to the beginning, guys, check everything, review the statements of everyone we've interviewed already and see if we've missed anything. Jas, can you take Chad back to Ashfield Grange and have another chat with Mrs Grogan? Maybe have a word with some of the other staff and residents. Joe, Luke, get up to the tennis club, dig around, find out who took the call from Huxton the day he cancelled. Okay, that's it, let's re-group at 18:00"

* * *

Chad fidgeted in the passenger seat, unable to get comfortable.

"So, what do you reckon to this Bannister, Nicholson double act, it doesn't seem to make sense to me?" asked Jas.

"I'm not sure yet. Interested to see what we can find out today. I had an idea back at HQ but it was random, so I'll keep it to myself for a bit. Don't want to be looking a dick."

"Hey, you're the star of the show after that whole Lawlor exposé, come on, you can share with me, you know I won't tell," she laughed.

He shook his head, "Not yet. Anyway, the Boss needs to know first, he's paying me not you."

"Okay, spoilsport. But tell me if you work it out. Come on then, Hopalong, let's see what Mrs Grogan has to say this time."

* * *

Jas opened her notepad. "Mrs Grogan, we understand that it is a mandatory requirement of the Care Quality Commission that all staff working with vulnerable adults have certain checks undertaken. Criminal record check, references, that sort of thing. When we were last here you said you had no information on Mr Bannister. Given that it's a legal requirement, why didn't you undertake any checks into his background?"

Mrs Grogan crossed her legs and shifted in her chair. It was clear, Chad thought, that she realised she'd been far too open in her discussions with them previously and intended to make amends. She's hard-faced, he wouldn't want to get on the wrong side of her.

"Ronnie started doing some odd jobs around the place, maintenance, that sort of thing, you can't imagine how much that helps a place like this. He wasn't in contact with the residents so no checks were required. But, yes, I grant you, when he started having more to do with them, we should have undertaken the necessary checks. You know how it is, though, they all loved him and we needed the help. It was an oversight that's all, and it wasn't as though he was doing personal care tasks. That is what the regulations are for." The smile didn't reach her eyes.

"So, have you undertaken the necessary checks on all the other staff you employ?"

"Oh, yes. You are more than welcome to check our files. The last CQC inspection rated us as "Good" overall. I wanted "Excellent" but still, they had no complaints or recommendations."

Mrs Grogan's shoulders relaxed and she smiled, sitting forward in the chair. Chad thought that this was safer territory for her.

"What can you tell us about Ronnie Bannister? What made the residents like him so much?" asked Chad.

"He was always cheerful, making them laugh with little jokes. He'd talk football with the residents that were interested in the sport, and he seemed to be very well informed. Nothing was too much trouble for him. Some of the staff, often the younger ones, can be a little surly sometimes, but not Ronnie. The more able-bodied residents enjoyed taking a little stroll around the grounds with him and, as I told you last time, he'd take some shopping or to the café at the garden centre from time to time."

"Is he from Leeds, does he have a Yorkshire accent?"

"Oh, yes, I'd say Leeds through and through."

Jas said, "And do you keep a record of his attendance, Mrs Grogan? How often did he volunteer?"

"Yes, we do, I can get the dates for you before you go, dear."

"Mrs Grogan, do you know what Mr Bannister did for a living outside his volunteering work?" asked Chad.

"The girls may know more than me, but I did ask him once and he laughed and said he had a boring office job which is why he liked to come here in his spare time. I don't think he told me what sort of an office job though."

Christ, thought Chad, and you couldn't be bothered to ask him.

"What else can you tell us about him? Can you describe him for us?" said Jas.

As Mrs Grogan opened her mouth to answer Chad said, "Or, better still, can you give us a list of the shops and garden centres where he took residents? Some may have CCTV."

Jas gave him a look and he got the message. *Butt out, Chad, that was my next question.*

"Well, yes. I'm sure we'll be able to get you a list of those. Ronnie is a tall black man. Am I allowed to say that? Anyway, yes, tall. Six feet at least. Well built, I'd say mid-forties. No real distinguishing features. A little odd to look at. I don't know how to describe it. Like he hadn't quite grown into his skin, or like he's lost weight and the skin sagged a bit. Not unpleasant looking and not something you'd remark on. I think I'm just more observant than most."

"Of course, I'm sure you are," said Jas.

"What about Father Murphy, Mrs Grogan. What can you tell us about him?"

"He's an odd fish, but I suppose if I'd been fifty years a priest and a teacher, I might be like that too. He kept himself to himself, didn't get any visitors. He liked to read and to walk around the garden, but for the most part, kept his own company. He didn't join in with any of the activities we organise, he preferred to stay in his room."

"So, Mr Nicholson ringing must have been a real shock to him?"

"Yes, it was. That was why he didn't want to go. But as I always say, we must all compromise. I think it was very kind of the gentleman to want to take his old teacher for lunch. Although, that never quite happened did it? Oh dear, I do hope they're alright."

"Yes, so do we."

"Mrs Grogan, have you always only had former priests as residents?"

"No, when we first set the home up, oh, when would that be? Must have been ninety-nine. Or was it two thousand? Anyway, never mind, the first few years we took all sorts of residents. But over time we took a couple of priests, then the Diocese got in touch and asked if we could take more. They'd pay more than private residents, so that was commercially very good for us, and it's grown from there to where we are now. I think the Church sees us as an extension of their pastoral care."

"And do you have a waiting list?"

"Not a waiting list as such. We have eighty beds, and we work closely with the Diocese to make sure we are always full."

Chad smiled, "Thanks, Mrs Grogan, you've been very helpful," he said. "Cast your mind back to the first time Mr Nicholson telephoned. Can you go over that again for us?"

"Really?" She shuffled in her seat and looked hard at Chad. His smile held. "There's not much to tell. I took a call at around 10:00 a.m from a well-spoken chap."

Chad interrupted her. "When you say well-spoken, what do you mean?"

"He was very polite, friendly and sounded, I don't know. Polished, professional."

"Accent?"

"Posh Yorkshire, probably Harrogate but I didn't ask."

"So, as I explained last time, he told me that the diocese had told him that Father Murphy lived with us and that he was a former pupil and would very much like to see Father Murphy and take him to lunch."

"Okay," said Chad, "when the call came in can you remember where Mr Bannister was?"

"Ronnie? No, I don't remember."

"But, if you took the call here in your office, then you'd have been able to see if Ronnie was in the lounge area with the residents? Try and remember."

"I'm sorry. I can't." She looked beyond Chad and Jas into the lounge across the hallway. "No, I don't think he was in there but I can't honestly remember. Is it important?"

Chad didn't answer, instead he posed another question. "And when Mr Nicholson called the second time, was Ronnie around then?"

"No. Now that I can remember because after I'd finished the call, I went out of my office to look for him and he was coming in from outside."

"Right, okay. Thank you, Mrs Grogan, that's helpful."

"Would it be okay for us to have a chat with some of the residents and staff, Mrs Grogan?" asked Jas.

"Yes, of course. But don't be getting them agitated."

Chad needed number four but would have to wait. The lounge was excessively warm and the cloying smells of urine and yesterday's dinner clung to the place and its occupants. Large upright seats with wooden armrests were arranged around the perimeter of the room. All had plastic covers of different colours. More functional than made for comfort, he thought. Easier to wipe down when they've made a mess. There were four old men in the room but little by way of camaraderie. Each sat some distance from the others. Jas sat down on a seat next to a small man, Father John, that a nurse had pointed out to them. He had a face like a ferret and seemed to have shrunk with age. His hair was thin and there was a couple of days grey stubble on his chin, but his eyes were bright and alert. He wore a thick blue cardigan just beginning to lose its elbows, over a white shirt, and the obligatory black cleric trousers. Jas held his hand. Chad smiled at the old boy as Jas asked him about Father Murphy.

"What was he like?"

"Same as the rest of us. Dying. Some quicker than others."

"Had you known him before you both came in here?"

"I'd known of him. By reputation, but hadn't met him."

"Oh, and what was Father Murphy's reputation? Good was it?"

The priest turned towards Chad and raised an eyebrow.

"Good? You're kidding? He was a pervert, a molester, a paedophile. I wouldn't call that good, would you?"

He thinks we're idiots, thought Chad.

"Really?" Said Jas. She let go of the priest's hand and leaned in towards him. "And that was common knowledge was it?"

"Loads of 'em in here. It's where they put them out to pasture. All the wrong 'uns."

Chad looked around the room but no-one was paying them any attention. He spoke in an undertone, "And are you a wrong 'un?"

"Not that sort. I may have had my hand in the collection boxes and up a blouse or two from time to time, which I know is a sin, but I don't think I'll be going to the same place as Murphy when I die. There's a special corner in hell for him and his ilk. The powers that be want us all in one place so when we get dementia and start shouting and carrying on, we won't have anyone hearing us. No secrets getting out. That's what I think, anyway."

Jas didn't let it drop. "But apart from hearsay, do you know for certain that Father Murphy abused children? Was he ever prosecuted?"

"I don't know," said the old boy shifting in his chair "I doubt it though. The church tries to keep its dirty linen hidden so they would have moved Murphy at the first sign of trouble. One thing is for sure, the powers that be would have been very aware."

Jas circled the word *paedophile* in her pad then changed tack. "What did you think of Ronnie Bannister, Father?'

"Seemed a nice enough fella. Can't say I thought much about him one way or the other. Spent a fair bit of time with Murphy though."

"Would you say Ronnie spent more time with Father Murphy than he did with other residents? Were they particularly close?"

"Maybe. Murphy didn't talk to any of us very much so I noticed that he did seem to chat on with Ronnie. Probably got more sense out of him than most of the nutters in here." He said looking around the room.

You've been very helpful, Father. Have a lovely afternoon." Jas closed her notepad and dropped it in her bag. She stood and walked past the priest out of the lounge, Chad followed. The priest was mumbling something he couldn't catch.

"I'll get the list of places where Bannister took the residents and his attendance record. I'll see you outside," said Jas.

Chad limped to the front door, opened it then turned and looked back at the lounge. What a rats' nest, he thought.

CHAPTER 36

Andy Huxton leaned forward and placed the two phones side by side. His personal iPhone 11x, sleek, black and silent. The other, from the cricket ground, the phone he'd come to see as a harbinger of doom, blinked at him announcing a new message.

We've got your dad but he's drugged in the boot of the car and we can't release him till we get back to Leeds. You've got to leave the office now and go to Starbucks at The Light. Wait there and we'll contact you with further instructions. We are being followed so comply.

"Shit," he said. "Shit, shit, shit." 12:03 p.m. Standing, he pulled his jacket from the back of his chair and walked across to the door. It was lunchtime, so the staff in the office were thinning out, some were in the kitchen, others had gone into town. He looked across the heads and saw his PA. Waving, he signalled he was going out.

Starbucks at The Light was busy. Finding a stool, he perched on it looking out the window at the throngs of office workers on The Headrow. Sipping his latte, he tried to regulate his breathing. His heart rate was through the fucking roof. He looked at the phone again. Nothing. He tapped a cigarette packet on the table in a staccato rhythm, and noticed that the noise was annoying the girl on the stool next to him. Fuck her. He ran his hand through his hair and then checked his watch. 1:10 p.m. *Ping.* The phone screen lit up. Swallowing hard, he took a deep breath and opened the message.

Okay, go back to the office and wait for me to call you on your phone. All okay. Won't be long. Drop this phone in the bin on the wall outside your office. Don't use it again. Dad's okay.

"Thank Christ for that." He wiped away a tear and let the relief seep through him. The sun was warm on his face as he left the coffee shop and, for the first time in days, he smiled. Jesus, he could use a few beers now, he thought. He walked fast and let the blood course around his limbs. He felt alive and alert. The waste bin was bolted to the wall outside the entrance to the office on Park Row. It had a plastic bag inside to catch the garbage. He pulled the phone from his inside pocket, had a quick check to make sure no-one was watching, then dropped it into the bin. "Good fucking riddance." He said, breathing in the fresh air. The phone had been like a Sword of Damocles but now it was gone. The reception area was busy but he managed to sidestep into the crowded lift. As the lift doors opened, a colleague was waiting to get in.

"Hey, boss, mind where you're going. You look happy, just closed a deal?"

"No, better than that, Stu, better than that."

CHAPTER 37

Chad took the chance to slip the fourth into his mouth as Jas made the introductions to the manager of the High Trees Garden Centre. She explained what they wanted.

"Thanks very much Mr Brown, as I mentioned when I rang, we are investigating a missing person case and believe that the individual may have been here last Wednesday the fourteenth between 2:30 p.m. and 3:30 p.m. We're hoping you'll have the CCTV footage and we'd like to see it please?"

"Yes, we'll have it. If you'll take a seat here, I'll get the head of security to come in and you can have a look at whichever days you need. I won't be a moment."

Chad massaged his knee and lower thigh. He steadied himself against a desk as he waited for the rush to hit him. The yellow lights to come.

Jas said "And don't think I didn't see you have another of those tablets, 'cos I did. I looked them up on the internet the other day. They are the strongest pain killer you can get. How many are you taking?"

Chad took a breath as the surge arrived, then said, "Jesus, don't you start. You're at the back of a long queue of friends and family all telling me I should take less, and find some other way to control the pain. Trust me, Jas, if there was something I could do, I would.

Thanks for your concern, though."

"I still think you should take my advice and get a walking stick. It'd help."

"No way, I'd look like my fucking grandad."

"Don't be ridiculous, anyhow you can get some funky ones these days. After we're done here, we'll go to Jeffrey West in the Victoria Quarter. My brother was getting some shoes there at Christmas and I went in with him, they've got all sorts of cool designs. Okay, they're canes, but they look great and will defo help you. I think it would suit you, it'd go with your image. Changing the subject, how weird what that priest said, that the home is full of wrong 'uns. I've sent a photo of my notes to the Boss and Schmidt as well. I've asked for background checks to be made on all residents. If it is full of paedos we might be opening a whole different can of worms and it generates a motive for Murphy's disappearance. What if Nicholson, the ex-pupil, was a victim of abuse?"

"Yeah, the old boy seemed compos mentis so no reason not to believe him. I can see Mrs Grogan cutting a nice deal with the church to look after these characters if the price is right. But we still don't know how the kidnapper found out Murphy was at Ashfield Grange."

"Why were you quizzing Grogan about where Ronnie Bannister was when Nicholson was calling. What does that matter?"

"I was just trying to check my theory out," he looked at Jas. "Yeah, the one that makes me look a dick if it's wrong."

"And is it wrong?"

"Put it this way, nothing Grogan said put the kybosh on it."

"Interesting. Remember, you promised to tell me first when you've sorted it out in that head of yours."

"I didn't promise anything."

The door opened and a uniformed security guard entered edging his way to the desk-top. "What date and time are you after?" he asked, pushing his khaki-clad arse into a seat too small by half to accommodate it.

"Wednesday the fourteenth between 2:30 p.m. and 3:30 p.m."

The manager's office gave a view into the open-plan shopping area of the garden centre, which heaved with punters. Chad stared out. Since when had bedding plants become a national pastime, he thought? He'd rather be shot than end up where a trip to a garden centre was the social highlight of his week. For that matter he'd rather finish it all at Dignitas in Switzerland than wind up in a place like the Ashfield Nursing Home.

The security guard scrolled through the tapes. "Here you go. 2:30 p.m. you said. Just scroll from there and it'll show through to the end of the day. I'll leave you to it." The chair groaned in relief.

"You sit, I'll stand," Jas said.

'No, it's okay, I need to keep it moving or the knee seizes up. Let's start."

* * *

"Here you go, that has to be them," Jas said, pausing the tape and pointing at the screen.

A tall black guy in hoody and jeans looked down at a hunched old man with grey hair, wearing a pair of glasses from the seventies and a thick anorak over dark trousers. "Yep, that's them." Jas wound the tape forward and the incongruous pair made their way through the store to the café. "Why's Ronnie wearing gloves, do you think?"

"Don't know, maybe cold?"

The old priest made his way through the aisles. Ronnie a pace or so behind. Every so often, the priest would look over his shoulder and say something. They reached an aisle with small potted plants in trays. Murphy pointed to a plant on the top row of a set of shelving. Ronnie reached up and claimed the chosen pot before giving it to Murphy.

The camera in the café picked up the pair, and Ronnie brought two mugs and what looked like biscuits back to a table where Murphy sat. "They're a bloody odd couple. I wonder what they're talking about?" said Chad.

"Yeah, they're chatting on, aren't they? Murphy seems quite comfortable with him."

"And if Ronnie is a bad guy, he doesn't look like CCTV is bothering him, or worried at all about who sees him."

"Maybe, we should play it again and instead of keeping our eye on Murphy and Bannister, look out for anyone that may be watching them?"

"Good idea," said Chad.

Jas rewound the tape and they watched again as the pair entered the store and began to weave their way through the assorted bulbs, trees, and plants.

"Stop it there," said Chad.

Jas paused the tape. "What is it?"

"Well, bugger me," Chad said.

Front and centre, Bannister and Murphy were looking at an array of bedding plants laid out on a large rectangular table. There were other shoppers also inspecting the plants, but Chad pointed to a man standing away to the left of the screen looking directly at Murphy.

"Who is that?" said Jas.

"That's the cat amongst the pigeons, right there."

CHAPTER 38

Chad checked his emails as Joe updated the team. "The lady that took the call from Huxton is the daughter of the club secretary. She was helping for the day, so doesn't know Huxton at all. Couldn't say if it was Huxton or not. Just a voice."

"Great,' said Lee. "Jas, did you get anywhere at Ashfield Grange? And Chad, what the bloody hell is that?"

Jas laughed and said, "That, boss, is a very fashionable walking stick to help my mate, Hoppy, keep up when we are out and about."

"Jesus, I thought I'd seen everything. Did you have to buy one with a silver skull as a handle?"

"Don't listen to them Chad, I think it's great."

Chad said, "I'm sensing you disagree with Jas' assessment, guys?"

Deakin grinned and said, "It's more an offensive weapon than a walking stick."

"Anyway, enough on that, what happened at the nursing home?" said Lee. "I got the notes you sent through. Could be explosive if what the priest said has some truth in it. We're getting the background checks done now, but I think because of their ages unless a prosecution succeeded, we'll be unlikely to get much."

"We had a profitable afternoon, boss. Mrs Grogan wasn't much help, just became defensive about not making any checks on

Bannister. She told us he worked full time in an office but didn't know what sort of office or where."

"Is that it?" asked Lee. "Apart from the old boy's comments, which could be just malicious, doesn't sound profitable to me."

"Wait, boss, I'm coming to the good bit."

"We got the details of the places where Bannister had taken Murphy. Shops etcetera. There's a garden centre out near Adel that they'd gone to, and it's got CCTV. We went up there and we got our first look at Bannister. This is a still photograph from the CCTV," said Jas. She walked to the front of the room and pinned the enlarged photograph onto the board. She stood by the board and played to the gallery. "But it gets better. We thought Bannister and Murphy looked very comfortable together so went back through the tape to see if we'd missed anything. And, hey presto, we found this guy." Jas pinned another still onto the board.

"But, that's…" Lee's voice trailed off. "I don't get it."

"Don't leave us in the bleeding dark," said Joe. "Who is that?"

"That," said Jas, "is Andy Huxton." She paused to let the information sink in.

"Wow," said, Deakin.

Lee said, "It could, of course, be a coincidence, but at the very least we need to know what he was doing there and why he's staring at Murphy."

Chad coughed. "Lee, we have Andy Huxton, son of our first missing person, in a garden centre staring at the other two mis-pers. That's got to be too much of a coincidence, hasn't it?"

"Still no proof they're linked, Chad, but we need to give it serious consideration from here on in. What of Nicholson, Jas, did you find out any more on him?"

"Chad's got a theory boss."

"Course he has," muttered Joe.

"Come on, then, let's hear it," said Lee.

"It is only a theory, I have no evidence, so don't bite my head off. But," he took a breath, "I don't think Nicholson exists. I think it was Ronnie Bannister that made those calls."

"So, why do you think that?" asked Lee

"One, the diocese says that they did not receive a call asking for Murphy's whereabouts. They have no reason to lie about that. If that call didn't happen, then we can assume that someone already knew where Murphy was. Bannister knew. Two, we know that Bannister exists, but apart from a voice on the end of a phone, we have not a jot of evidence to suggest Nicholson does. We also know that Bannister was outside when Mrs Grogan received the second call from Nicholson. Bannister could have made that call. That's it. I did say it was just a theory, but if I'm right it takes Nicholson out of the equation and makes Bannister a suspect as well as a potential victim." The team were silent. It was only a few days since they'd have argued the bloody toss with him, he thought, but that Lawlor case had changed everything. He had a gravitas now. His ideas were worth hearing. That felt good.

"Well, yes, it's a theory," said Lee. "Not sure if it creates more questions than it answers but let's see if there's any evidence to support it. Jas, do we have anything more on Bannister?"

"No, Boss, I haven't had a chance to follow up on the list I made earlier but I'll make a start now."

"Okay, thanks, everyone. Let's keep digging. Joe, push hard on Nichols and Holding when you see them. Family emergency, my arse."

CHAPTER 39

Andy Huxton checked his watch. 2:45 p.m. Why hadn't he had a call? What the fuck was going on? Pacing his office, he looked out across the shiny, rain-soaked rooftops of Leeds. "Something must have gone wrong. Shit." The screen on his phone shone black. Silent. Nearly two hours and they'd said everything was okay. Had he got it wrong, misunderstood the instructions? No, they'd told him to dump the other phone and they'd call on this. So, why hadn't they? Fuck, they should have gone to the police, he'd told those fucking idiots they should have done that. Fucking morons. Now what? He'd better call the copper that came to see him, but what could he say? "Oh, yeah, sorry but we paid a ransom of nine million quid and I still haven't got my dad back." He couldn't do that. He'd give it another hour, see if they called.

* * *

4:15 p.m. "What the fuck am I going to do?" he stuttered. "Let's go and get that phone out of the bin, maybe they rang on that." The lift arrived and he pressed G. Then pressed it again. "Come on, come on, so fucking slow." He lurched as the lift stopped on the ground floor and the doors pinged open. Hurrying outside, he felt inside the bin on the wall. It was empty. Shit. What time had he put the phone in there? One ish? So, no more than a couple of hours ago. They couldn't have emptied the bins in that time?

A large recycling bin stood on the corner of Park Row and he began walking towards it. Still, some distance away it was obvious that it hadn't been emptied. "What the fuck is going on?" he yelled.

CHAPTER 40

No tweets today. Maybe he's given up? Maybe not. Chad typed. "*Hey babe, just checking in. Any sign of your stalker today? Btw, would you recognise him if you saw him*?" He poured another whisky into his tumbler. The bad guys in the old cowboy films asked the barman for two fingers of red-eye. Good name for it. The whisky warmed and soothed. "It's a pretty lethal combination. Strong painkillers and strong whisky. Feels good right now, though." His phone pinged. Ange.

"*I'm okay. No sign of the stalker today. Don't know if I could pick him out, but maybe. Why?*"

"*No reason, just wondering. This guy you were seeing, was he a black guy?*"

"*No, Chad, he wasn't. Goodnight.*"

It was just a thought. There was a catalyst somewhere. Why would he start getting trolled at the same time as Angie starts being stalked? That's if she was being stalked, she might have been mistaken, and he hadn't resurfaced. Stalkers are meant to stalk, the clue was in the title. His phone pinged. Freddie.

"*Yo, bro, how're things? Been talking to Emma Williams, remember the physio when we were at Leeds? Told her about you. She's saying that you should consider acupuncture. I'm going to check that out 'cos I know you won't be arsed. There's a Chinese fella on Street Lane does it. I'll call him in the morning. Night bro. Oh, no word from our coke head today. I'll keep you posted."*

Acupuncture. Why not? he'd tried everything else. The doctors told him to exercise, he did. They said control your weight. He did. They said take these pills. Hell, yes. So, why not acupuncture? Chad picked up his whisky. Bedtime. Six down. The boy had done good today, only six. '*The boy's done good today*,' He sounded like Harry bloody Redknapp. One before bed? Only if you're in bed, no sparko on the kitchen floor antics. Where were they? Chad stared at the table top but there was no silver foil. Where the fuck were they? He moved the coaster and glass. Nothing. A coldness spread through his body. What had he done with them? He slapped his hands against his jeans pocket then stood, delving deep into them. Nothing. "Fuck," he yelled. "Jacket. They must be in my jacket." He hobbled as fast as he could through the lounge into the kitchen feeling the panic subside as he saw his jacket hanging on the back of a chair at the dining table. He felt inside the pockets. Empty. He spun round, threw the post pile onto the floor and dived on it. He tore at the paper. Nothing. He felt bile sting his mouth and his legs turned to dust. His head snapped back. "I can't have fucking lost them." He opened the kitchen cupboard nearest to him and looked inside, then hurled the contents onto the floor and fell to his knees sifting through the broken jars and contents.

"No, no. They're fucking here, in the kitchen. I know they are." He leaned forward until his forehead almost touched the floor. He could smell the scattered herbs around him. Crawling forward through the broken cups, he grabbed the edge of the breakfast bar, then hauled himself up and turned to face the carnage.

Smashed crockery, two cabinets with the doors off their hinges. Only the overwhelming fatigue had stopped him. "This is where you die, you fucking prick. Surrounded by shit having wrecked your house. Fuck it, who cares. I don't." He turned his head away in disgust, then his mouth dropped open.

Glinting at him from the fruit bowl, like a whore beckoning an excited punter, was the silver strip of Fentanyl.

CHAPTER 41

He looked at his reflection in the mirror. Shame oozed from every pore. He didn't know which was more worrying. The fact that he'd trashed the house to find them or that he'd taken a seventh and hadn't passed out. God, maybe now he'd need an eighth to make that happen. He moved the razor over his chin. No, never do eight, he thought, he didn't want to find out. His phone lit up, perched on the marble washbasin. Lee. He didn't pick up. Let me at least shave for fuck's sake, he thought. The screen flashed, Lee again.

"I'm just shaving can I call you back?" Chad could tell from the background noise that Lee was driving.

"No. We've found Huxton's Porsche."

"Oh, well that's good news."

"Not good news if you're one of the two corpses inside it."

"Shit."

"Yes, shit. I'm heading there now. We had Nichols and Holding reported missing by their wives last night, so fuck knows what's going on. Andy Huxton rang the office a couple of times as well but didn't leave a message. Jas is on her way to pick you up from your house. Harrogate is en-route to the crime scene. The Porsche is in a clearing off a track near the A19. She'll be with you in ten minutes."

Chad picked up his razor and looked in the mirror. Two bodies, what a mess. But which two?

* * *

"Good morning, nice place you've got here," Jas called through the open window of her BMW. "My Beemer's making the place look downmarket, the neighbours will be complaining. Is it compulsory to have a Bentley to live around here?"

Chad gave her the finger and walked to the passenger side. He hated to admit it, but the cane did help, it eased the stress on the knee. "Usual crap on the seat I see. Is your bedroom like this, shit everywhere, or do you reserve the mess for the car?"

"Just get in. And wouldn't you like to know what my bedroom's like?" Jas chuckled.

Yes, he would but better just ignore her, answering that question could get him in a lot of trouble. "You're very jolly given that there's a car with dead bodies in it waiting for us."

"Yeah, sorry. But now we've got something concrete, we're not chasing shadows. The Boss is stressed though. The Chief Super's been kicking off at him as if it's our fault. Tosser."

Chad stretched his leg into the footwell and leant his cane between the door and his good leg. "He'll be rolling shit downhill that's all." He said. "The Super will have been getting his arse kicked by that MP Jed Forrest. Not sure about something concrete though. We've still got three mis-pers cases and Lee reckons Nichols and Holding have disappeared as well. So, five mis-pers and two corpses." Chad looked out of the window as Jas drove past the vast public open grassland in Harrogate called The Stray. Early spring sunshine flickered on the dew. Not long till the cherry blossoms would give the place a fairy-tale feel. They ground to a halt on Wetherby Road. "Do you know who the victims are?" Chad asked.

"No, not yet. Forensics will be there. Everyone and their brother will be there. Not quite sure why you have to come to this though?"

The Beemer crawled forward. "From a profiling perspective, there is no better start point than seeing the crime scene first hand. It will help me. It's like you guys need the crime scene for evidence, I need it to get inside the perp's head. That's if Lee's going to hire me to help on this one. I'd better check that."

"Okay, well we need this traffic to move or everything will be over by the time we arrive."

CHAPTER 42

Jas signed him in as Chad showed his ID to the uniforms blocking the junction where the track left the main road to Potto. "Don't know why, but I always thought Potto was somewhere in Scotland. You must have seen those massive wagons with Preston's of Potto on the side?"

"I've never even heard of it," Jas replied. "I don't think we'll be able to drive too far down here, there are loads of cars, vans and ambulances already down there. Will you be okay to walk if we turn it around and park here?"

"No probs, a good idea of mine to get a cane wasn't it?"

Jas punched him on the arm. "You'd still be hobbling and having to stop every couple of yards if I hadn't made you get that. So shut it, Hopalong, and make sure you keep up at the back."

He looked down the track. Must be about four hundred meters. Two ambulances were parked with lights flashing and various white-suited forensic guys moved in and out of the trees. He could make out Lee, leaning against a car, talking to two other men. Looked like Schmidt and Deakin. Let her go on ahead, no point trying to keep up. Why here? How did the perp know this place? The horizon seemed miles away and middle of nowhere didn't do the place justice. Our boy was a planner, he thought.

Chad reached Lee and the team. "Hi, Lee," he nodded at Joe

and Luke. "Guys."

"Hi, Chad," said Lee. "What a fucking job we've got on our hands here."

"Who are the victims?"

"Nichols, the lawyer, and Holding, the accountant. Professional job by the look of it. Both shot twice in the chest and once in the head. Forensics reckon they've been here for up to twenty-four hours, but they'll know more when they do the full examination."

"Lee, do you mind if I go and look? It'll help me. Assuming you want me on the case?"

"Yes, we do, I've cleared it with the gaffer. Jas, take Chad up there. Get him kitted out."

Lee's outstretched arm was pointing to a forensics guy pulling various items of protective clothing out of a box in the boot of one of the cars. Walking over, he sat on the rim and pulled on a pair of shoe covers, then gloves.

"That'll do," said Jas. "You'll be kept away from the car so you won't need the full suit."

He looked past Jas into the clearing and could see the front bumper of the car. It's visible from the track, he thought, why not hide it?

The perimeter tape stretched from tree to tree. He picked his way through the leaves. Forensic technicians had set up lighting equipment to shine into the car and were hustling between the vehicle and evidence boxes laid out on a table. Two guys were unloading a tent from a large plastic box. Jas showed her ID and Chad stepped through the tape to stand just a couple of metres from the imposing bulk of the Porsche Cayenne. Christ, he'd never been this close to death, he thought. The horror of it made his mouth fill with acid reflux. Nothing glorious about this, no Hollywood treatment here. Cold, brutal. A man in the passenger seat stared past him. There was a hole just above the man's nose, out of which blood had trickled like a small tributary. In the driver's seat, another man was slumped with a small circular bullet hole in his forehead and his shirt was dyed crimson. Stepping away, Chad, gulped some air and looked around. Why was the Porsche facing towards the track? Weird. The obvious thing would have been to drive it off the track straight up into the clearing as far as it would go, then hide it. Leaving it visible just attracted attention.

"Anything?" Jas asked.

"No, I was wondering why the car was reversed in and not just driven in from the track."

"Yeah, why would you do that?"

"I don't know, but seems to me like whoever did this told them to park like that. The obvious thing to do would be to drive in off the track. Not reverse. Whatever, one thing's for sure, it was done for a reason. Whoever shot these guys went to a lot of trouble to pick the spot, so I don't think anything here is haphazard." Chad had seen enough. This guy's organised, clinical and ruthless, he thought. For the two victims to be dead in their seats, no attempt to escape, our boy executed them before they had a chance to think. An area on the track verge had been cordoned off. Tyre marks were visible, and a tech guy with a camera was taking photographs.

Further down the road, Lee was waving to them.

"The Boss wants us," said Chad, and leaned on his cane as he hobbled to join Lee with the other detectives.

"Okay, guys, we've got a complete shit show here," said Lee. "Too many questions, not least what are they doing in Huxton's Porsche? First off, Joe and Luke, go to see the families and get family liaison involved as well."

"DI Wallace?" A uniformed officer came running towards them from out of the clearing.

"Yes, what is it?" said Lee, as the copper got to them.

"Sir, you'd better come. They've opened the boot and there are other bodies in it."

"Fucking hell," said Lee.

Chad limped a few paces behind the detectives as they strode back towards the Porsche.

"What have you got?" asked Lee.

"There are two more victims, sir, both wrapped in tarpaulins in the boot of the vehicle."

The pathologist and a forensic scientist worked partially hidden underneath the lid of the boot. "Lee, come and take a look," said the pathologist.

Lee moved to the rear of the vehicle. Chad stayed put, he could hear a muted conversation but couldn't make out the words. Lee emerged from behind the car and walked back to the track. Chad reached them in time as Lee stood in front of his team.

"It's Huxton and Murphy," said Lee. "Let's get back to Leeds. And find out where Andy Huxton is before he gets wind of this from the press. We need to be the ones breaking the bad news."

Chad's phone pinged. Twitter. *@therealchadhilton. Having a good day dickhead? Ha. I'm going to make sure that you get what you deserve #napoleoncalling*

CHAPTER 43

This would be the sixth, but fuck he needed it. He slipped the tablet from the foil and into his mouth. 5:55 p.m. The team was assembled, seated on desks and chairs. Jas stood. The collective body language oozed tension. Yeah, this wasn't good, Chad thought, four dead, one still missing and the press all over them like a rash. The door swung open and Lee walked in, hair tousled and his suit lacked its usual sharpness.

"Okay," Lee said, "the guys at the mortuary are still carrying out tests, but we've got the prelims. Nichols, Holding and Huxton have been formally identified by next of kin. We're awaiting identification of the fourth body, but I expect that to be confirmed as Father Murphy. What we know at this stage is that John Huxton, Nichols and Holding were each shot three times at close range by nine-millimetre parabellum bullets."

Joe asked, "What about Murphy? Was he shot?"

"No, it appears he died of a massive heart attack. The pathologist found marks on his chest consistent with having been hit by a Taser."

"Jesus, that's horrendous," said Jas.

Lee nodded. "Murphy died around twelve hours before Huxton was shot. Looks like Murphy spent longer in the boot than Huxton. So, in chronological order, the perp kills Murphy with a Taser at some point in the last thirty-six hours. Then a few hours later Huxton is shot, tied up and put in the boot of the Porsche with Murphy. Nichols and Holding were shot sometime between 11:00 a.m. and 2:00 p.m. yesterday. First, Joe and Luke, you take the lawyer and accountant. Find out as much as you can, personal and professional. Talk to their wives And Joe, try and be sensitive."

"Yes, boss, will do."

"Interview their work colleagues. What they were working on most recently and who have they met with? Get as much as you can." He paused then looked at Jas. "Jas, I want you to interview Andy Huxton. Dig into his business dealings. Who were they selling the business to? Find out and then talk to them. What was he doing at the garden centre at the same time as Murphy? And get as much as we can on John Huxton, his links to Nichols and Holding and what ties all this together. Once you've seen Andy Huxton, let's see what more we can find out about Murphy." Lee had barked out the instructions like an army sergeant, he took a breath then shouted "And where the fuck is Bannister?" he paused "yes that was rhetorical but we need to find that fucker. Chad, stay close to these guys, and I want a profile on our perp as soon as you can. We are going to be in the weeds so you try and step away, see the bigger picture, see if we're missing anything. Okay?"

Chad nodded.

"I've asked the Chief Super to pull rank and get the various pathology, forensic and ballistic teams to work on this overnight, so we should have full and comprehensive reports first thing tomorrow. I'll forward anything I get by email. Let's meet at 08:00 tomorrow."

Chad looked at his friend of twenty years. Poor sod he thought, he'll have the Chief Super giving him shit and of course, it'll be Lee's fault if this goes pear-shaped. Come on, Hilton, let's go home.

CHAPTER 44

Chad stared at the Highland Park and Fentanyl standing side by side on the kitchen table. What a combo, he thought. No danger of losing either tonight. Seven down and still standing. His tolerance levels must be increasing. That was a fucking worry. He needed to think. No more whisky. He began typing.

What sort of guy are we dealing with?
Detailed, ruthless, good planner, smooth talker. Could apply to A. Huxton?

Must have a motive, what is it?
Love? Lust? Loathing? Greed? Revenge? Priest, abuse? Huxton business? Why were Nichols and Holding there?
Money? (No ransom?)

Bannister
Where is Bannister? If dead why not left with the others? If perp not bothered about bodies being found so why not Bannister?
Could Bannister be the perp?

He reached for the whisky and poured then added a drop of water and watched as the amber liquid quivered, like the ripples on a pond. "Will power's another of your strong suits." He said. His phone pinged. Twitter.

@therealchadhilton *Had a good day did ya? You might as well start crossing them off, you've not got many more. And when you're gone, I'm going to have some fun with that ex-wife of yours. Night, night, dickhead #napoleoncalling*

"What the fuck?"

CHAPTER 45

08:00. Lee stood at the front of room 106. "You've all had the reports I sent through, but in case some of you haven't read them yet…"

Chad avoided eye contact. He looked a mess and knew it. The tweet last night had sobered him and worried sick, he'd tried to reach Angie. She hadn't answered so he'd had more whisky. Then more, until there was no more.

"I'll summarise. Huxton, Nichols and Holding were killed with 9mm parabellum bullets. Both Murphy and Huxton have restraint marks on their wrists and ankles and it looks like some form of manacle was used to detain them. Both have bruising and puncture marks on their chests consistent with being hit by the barbs from a Taser."

"So, Huxton was tasered as well?" said Jas.

"Yep, but in Murphy's case, the Taser triggered a massive heart attack which killed him. Both were also found to have contusions to the base of the skull behind the right ear. Some form of recent blunt trauma. So, where were they detained? Someone must have seen or heard something, and where was the Porsche kept for the last week? Let's check city centre and highways CCTV for sightings in the last two days."

Lee sipped his coffee then continued. "There are two sets of tyre tracks at the Potto crime scene, these have been confirmed as belonging to the Porsche and a large SUV, possibly a Range Rover judging by the track distance between the back wheels and the width of the tyres. We need to identify that car."

Chad looked up. "Lee, you've mentioned the bullet type and the other injuries to Murphy and Huxton, what about Nichols and Holding, were they tasered? Any restraint marks or head injuries to either of them?"

"No, just gunshot wounds. Right, that's it, let's get on it. Update by email during the day, and we'll meet back here at 5:00 p.m. I'll fend off the press. Off you go."

* * *

"Hey Jas, I've got a few things I need to do, so I'll meet you in town later, okay?" Chad was limping behind Jas as she neared the car. What a body, he thought, not for the first time.

"Okay, but I want you in on the interview with Andy Huxton so what time will you be free?"

"How about I meet you outside Harvey Nicks at 3:00 p.m.? I should be done by then."

"Okay, I suppose." Her tone said the opposite.

"What's up?" said Chad

"Oh, nothing, looks like I'll be working Saturday and Sunday. After clearing the Lawlor case I was hoping for a weekend off, but no chance of that now. The life of a copper, eh?"

"Coffee's on me at 3:00 p.m. That'll cheer you up."

"Last of the big spenders!"

CHAPTER 46

Chad looked up at windows of police headquarters behind him. The whisky hangover was somewhat diminished and the sweats had stopped. He looked west away from the football ground, and saw a gleaming black and silver car was making sedate progress towards him. Freddie hadn't come in the roller, had he? It came closer. Jesus, he had. Typical bloody Freddie, Chad thought, keep it low key he'd said, don't draw attention. No chance of that. The car came to a halt and the driver peeled himself out, moved to the rear passenger door, and held it wide for Chad to get in. He looked like one of the bouncer types Chad had seen in Freddie's club. Leaning on the cane he edged towards the door and bent to look inside.

"Yo, Chad, bro get in, get in man. It makes me nervous being within two miles of this place, let alone right outside the door. You okay?"

Chad eased himself into the cavernous depths of the car. "For fuck's sake, Freddie, you couldn't be more obvious if you tried. Black and Silver roller, a driver who looks like Odd Job and you sitting in the back like Lord of the fucking Manor sipping Champagne. What happened to low key? I just hope Lee didn't see me. Let's get out of here."

"Okay, okay. Remember I'm doing you a favour here bro, so no need to shout. Champagne?"

"No, I'd better not. So, is this acupuncture guy any good?"

"Man, would I take you to someone who wasn't? Yeah, I have it on good authority he's the best. I've booked a table at Whitelocks afterwards, we'll get a bit more privacy there than some of the flashier places."

"Why not your bar?"

"We'll just get disturbed, staff and punters all wanting a bit of Freddie so I fancy somewhere quieter."

Chad leaned back into the soft leather upholstery. Fingers crossed for acupuncture.

* * *

Chad gave his name to the girl behind a glass counter and looked around. The waiting room was full. "I didn't know acupuncture was this popular," he said to the receptionist who was typing his details into her desktop.

She smiled back at him. Whatever was on her computer seemed to jolt her into action. "Mr Hilton, please come this way, Doctor Woo will see you now."

Freddie, he thought. Freddie's had a word and I'm getting priority treatment. What was he like? The corridor was white and antiseptic featuring a series of closed doors. She led him to the door at the end and knocked. "Mister Hilton to see you, Doctor."

"Do come in Mister Hilton, please go behind the screen and remove your clothes and put on the gown, I shall be with you in just a moment."

Jeez, he thought, Doctor Woo doesn't look old enough to be out of school, let alone running an acupuncture practice.

* * *

Chad lay on the bed and let the acupuncturist examine his legs. His hands roamed, squeezing here and probing there, before starting at the foot and working his way up to the hip on his injured leg. The young doctor's hands glided over Chad's skin, pausing at the swelling around the knee which was inflamed and angry. His leg looked awful, Chad thought, the skin was grotesque, almost opaque. It looked like it'd had some vicious demon come to live inside it. A bit like the kid in The Exorcist, only it was his leg that had been inhabited not his head. It was killing its host.

The doctor's hands were soft and supple but still managed to cause Chad to cry out as he applied slight pressure to the knee, before sliding down to apply similar pressure to the ankle joint. Less agony just short, sharp, stabbing pain. Even though he'd had a couple of pills the pain was still horrendous. Imagine if he hadn't had any. Jesus. The doctor stepped away from the bed and removed the latex gloves, then looked at Chad.

"You don't need me to tell you, Mister Hilton, that you have arthritis in your joints, and that in your knee it is profound. My experience tells me that the extent and acuity of it would make getting out of a car and walking into my surgery as you did a few minutes ago very difficult. I would expect someone presenting with your condition to be wheelchair-bound. So, Mister Hilton, if I am going to be able to help, you must be completely honest with me. Do you understand?"

Chad paused. He didn't like the way this conversation was going. He nodded at the doctor.

"Mister Hilton, I know that you must be taking a high level of strong pain killer as well as the usual anti-inflammatory drugs like Ibuprofen. Which painkillers are you taking?"

The doctor held his eye. Now or never. Chad blanched and remembered the fear when he couldn't find the pills. He knew it was getting out of hand. He made up his mind. "Fentanyl," he said.

"I see, I assume that the prescribed dose is four tablets a day?"

"Yes."

"And how many more than the prescribed dose are you having

to take each day?"

How the fuck did he know that? Freddie. Twat. "Sometimes two more, sometimes three."

"So, six or seven each day? And, for how long have you been taking that amount?"

"I don't know, maybe three or four months."

Pulling a chair from against the wall the doctor moved it closer to the bed and sat down. "Thank you for your honesty."

Chad held his gaze.

"And, I will be honest with you. Whether you admit it to yourself, I don't know, but I believe you'll be aware that you are addicted to the drug?"

Chad looked away; silence took hold. He was aware of the sunshine through the window, the white walls reflecting it, and the stillness in the room. He nodded, his shame compounded.

"The quantities you are taking now will become insufficient very soon, and you will increase the dosage. It will not be long until you will be taking more than double the recommended daily dose. You will suffer blackouts, heart problems and a range of other physical complications. If you continue in this way, then you will be dead within six months. However, I think the likelihood is it that you'll have less time than that."

Anxiety spread like ice-cold water through Chad's body. Cheery fucker, he thought.

"You must be acquiring the drug through illegal sources as no doctor anywhere would prescribe such amounts. That presents a further danger. We must address this."

Chad found his voice, "Am I a lost cause, doctor? Or do you think there's hope for me yet?"

"If you are prepared to pursue the courses of action that I will describe, then there may be a way in which I can help you. But it will not be easy and, in the short term, you will have to make some dramatic changes to your life. I am recommending four courses of action that must happen in parallel. Counselling for the addiction, Methadone or similar, to reduce the craving, Electro-Acupuncture for your arthritis and a change of diet to also assist."

Chad nodded.

"As you know I am a homoeopathic doctor, but I will write to your GP, with whom you must be candid. There are medications like Methadone and Buprenorphine that your GP can prescribe which reduce the craving for the opioid. This must happen. I am going to use Electro-Acupuncture to ease your arthritic pain. It's an electrical nerve stimulation known as P.E.N.S. and has proven to be very successful in the treatment of this type of arthritis. I would also recommend that you remove gluten entirely from your diet. Gluten in the bloodstream makes the body generate Fibrin, which builds up around your joints and causes the pain. You should also reduce your Omega 6 intake and increase your Omega 3. There's a leaflet on diet by the door, please make sure you take it and read it. You are not an old man and apart from your right leg you have a high level of muscular stability, so I am confident Mr Hilton, that if you adopt the changes I have described, then we can restore your health and help you live as close to pain-free as possible."

Chad jolted. "Wow, you are the first person to offer me any hope at all, so, whatever happens, thank you for that. When can we start the acupuncture?"

"My receptionist will book a course of treatments for you on your way out. Could you leave the name and address of your GP with her, and I will write today? You must book an appointment with them as soon as possible. Mister Hilton, your willpower will be the key determinant of success or failure. Now, I suggest you take a Fentanyl to ease your current pain."

CHAPTER 47

The cane click-clacked on the old cobbles as he made his way up the narrow path to Whitelock's tavern where Freddie held the door for him. Chad edged past him into the bar. The ceiling was low, amplifying the noise of the diners and the bar area was full of office workers out for a Friday lunchtime pint. Dan, the manager, smiled and nodded to a table at the far end of the pub tucked in a corner. Great, now to get through this lot, Chad thought. Some of the punters were staring trying to remember how they knew him, but recognition was instant as soon as they saw Freddie. C'est la vie, toujours comme ça. Freddie was fist-pumping a guy at a table and then stopped to have a selfie taken with a couple at the bar. He fancied somewhere quieter. Yeah, right.

Dan had been as good as his word, the table was in a corner away from the main dining room, so their conversation wouldn't be overheard.

"Come on, man, you haven't said a word since you got in the car, don't keep me hanging. What did the doc say?" said Freddie

"The good news is that he thinks he can help me as long as I turn my life around. The bad news is, if I don't, I'll be dead within six months. He didn't pull any punches I'll give him that. Had you already told him about these?" Chad tapped his jacket pocket.

"Well, I had to tell him you were taking some shit, but I didn't tell him the whole story."

"Well, he's got it now."

"So, you're going to do what he says, right?"

"Yeah, I'll make an appointment to see the GP, that'll get the ball rolling. I'm also going for my first acupuncture session next week. Then it's three sessions a week. He gave it to me straight, no bullshit, but he did something none of the other fuckers has done."

"What's that?"

"He gave me hope. He said he thought he might be able to get me pain-free. Fuck, I can't remember what that feels like. So, thanks buddy, thanks for making me go and see him. Oh, and whatever you said or paid them, I got preferential treatment."

Freddie grinned.

Chad reviewed the menu. Freddie was so predictable, he thought, he just had to know that his influence had paid off. Ego the size of Argentina. "The doc reckons that my GP will be able to prescribe something to stop me needing the Fentanyl. It'll be weird not taking them. I just hope I don't get hooked on whatever the replacement is."

"I'm going to make sure you don't, bro."

Chad stretched his leg out underneath the table. "Oh, and I've got to change my diet. No bread, pasta, nothing with gluten. Apart from that, life will go on as normal. Ha."

He waited till Freddie had finished eating and the plates had been cleared, then he passed his phone to across the table. "Twitter. Have a read of those."

Freddie, squinting, began to read. Chad listened to the low buzz of conversations in the bar as Freddie scrolled.

He'd always liked Whitelocks, he thought, it was a proper pub with its dark wood panelling and hidden booths, not the artificial "cocktail" bars Ange loved and that proliferated in Leeds. How the pair of them had lasted twenty-one years was a mystery.

Freddie looked up. "Fuck, this guy is getting out of control. Am

I reading that right? He's threatening to kill you?"

"Looks that way to me, buddy."

"I've told you once, bro, and I'm telling you again, you need to let Lee see these, he might be able to do something we can't. Trace where they're coming from."

"I told you, I can't, not yet. Lee's got enough on his plate. Let me show you something, look at this one." He picked up the phone and scrolled back through the messages till he found the one he wanted. "Here."

Having a good day dickhead? Ha. I'm going to make sure that you get what you deserve.

"What? I don't get what you mean. Why does this particular one bother you?"

He leaned towards Freddie, "So, you've heard about these murders, bodies found in a Porsche in Potto?"

'Yeah, I heard about that on the news. What of it?"

"I was there, at the scene, with the coppers and forensics, ambulances everywhere, they've just found these guys in the car, shot dead, when this message came through. I thought at the time, does this guy know what I'm doing? Does he know where I am? How could he know that?"

"I think that's a bit of a leap, bro. I think, "*Having a good day dickhead"* is just an opening shot like he's saying hello."

"Yeah, you may be right. This shit gets in your head, it's making me paranoid. Have you heard any more from your guys looking out for the mouthy coke head?"

"He hasn't popped up yet, but when he does, I'll be the first to know."

"It can't be a coincidence. A coke user telling your dealers that he's going to make some money by telling the press about an ex-footballer with a drug problem, and then at the same time, this guy starts trolling me. It's got to be the same person. I reckon the quickest way of finding him is your network, mate. Still don't get what he's got against Ange though."

"Talking of Ange buddy, what happened? I still can't believe what you told me."

"Well, it's true. I couldn't believe it either."

Freddie leaned closer across the table and lowered his voice. "You two were, like, so close. I'm gutted for you both. You want to tell me what happened?"

Chad shook his head and shuffled in his seat. "Not right now buddy. I'm not holding out on you, but you know what, while there's still a chance Ange and I can work things out, patch things up and move on I don't want to wash the dirty linen. Even with my best mate. I'm hoping we can get things sorted out. If we can do that, then I want to put this behind us and move on. Forget it ever happened. If I've gone through the whole thing with you then it'll be hard for you not to take sides, and I don't want that. If we can't resolve it and split up for good, then for sure I'll tell you about it. Do you understand?"

"I think so, bro. I've always looked at you and Ange and thought, that's what a relationship should be like, that's how it should work. I've never had that. Buddy, do what you must do and I hope you guys can work it out. Tell me only what you want, when you want. If you never tell me that's okay too. What can I say? I love you guys. Now, ring that GP and get yourself booked in."

Chad's phone pinged. He looked at Freddie, then opened the message.

@therealchadhilton Enjoying your lunch, dickhead, or are you too doped up? Wifey's looking hot today. Can't wait till you're gone and I'm shagging her. Not long now #napoleoncalling

Freddie read the message and stared. "We need to find this fucker and deal with him."

CHAPTER 48

Chad emerged from Turk's Head Yard onto Briggate, bustling with shoppers. The tweet had rattled him, but seeing Freddie anxious made him even more worried. He'd tried again to get Ange but his call went straight to voicemail. "Ange, babe, look call me when you get this. The nutcase that's trolling me seems to know your whereabouts and movements and his threats are ratcheting up. Call me babe." He ended the call. Fuck who was this guy? He checked the time, 3:05 p.m. Shit, he was late. Jas had been grumpy earlier so being late wouldn't help. Hobbling as fast as he could he saw Jas standing outside Harvey Nichols. "Hey, sorry I'm late, you okay?"

"Yes, I'm fine. You'll be pleased to know I've cheered up since I last saw you. Found out that there's a whole posse of cousins, aunts and uncles coming for the weekend so I'm better off working than having to entertain that lot. They never strike a bat, and I'm expected to wait on them hand and foot. Anyway, don't let me go in there," she tilted her head at the entrance to the store, "I'll end up loading the credit card."

"Right, well let's walk on by, do we have time to grab a coffee?"

"Yep, we're interviewing Huxton at 4:00 p.m. Follow me."

Chad trundled after her as she walked into the Victoria Quarter.

"Have you eaten? I'm starving," said Jas.

"Yeah, I've had lunch but why don't we go to the Harvey Nicks café, I can have a coffee and they do great soup and sandwiches, so you can eat."

"Cool," said Jas, leading the way through the dome-shaped stained-glass roof of the shopping arcade.

Chad scanned the shoppers while Jas read the menu.

"I'll get the soup please, and a brie and grape sandwich. No chips." She said when the waiter arrived. "And a black Americano for my friend here."

The waiter took the order and scuttled off. The Victoria Centre was busy, small independents cheek by jowl with the big upmarket chains attracting the wealthy. Normal people doing normal things. Nothing normal about his fucking life.

"Are you okay, you seem a bit preoccupied?" said Jas.

"Yeah, sorry, I'm fine. Are you going to ask Andy Huxton what he was doing at the garden centre watching Bannister and Murphy?"

"Hell, yes," said Jas. Her tongue shot out, trying and failing to stop a grape falling from her lip onto her plate.

Christ, how sexy was that he thought. He squeezed his leg hard underneath the table and pain seared upwards. He'd just left a message for his wife who was being threatened by some psycho and now here he was just two minutes later getting hot for a colleague. For fuck's sake stop it.

She was looking at him over the sandwich. He hoped she hadn't clocked that. "Okay, how are you going to play it with him?"

"I'm going to be sensitive to the fact his dad has been killed, but also quite firm given that he's also a suspect."

"I'm interested to see his reaction."

"Oh, and I rang the Catholic Diocese and arranged to see the Bishop at 5:30 p.m. I've told the Boss, so he's put the debrief back till 7:00 p.m. Have you had any more thoughts?"

Chad sipped his coffee. "I feel like I'm in a game where one player knows how it ends and knows what move you're going to make before you make it. It feels like this guy is watching us, knowing what comes next and knowing how we'll react. Like we are following a pre-set plan. Or, I don't know, like we are actors in a play, we just don't know it. It seems a bit obvious that killing Murphy could be an act of revenge for abuse in his childhood. At a stretch, someone might kill Huxton, in revenge for some business deal gone bad. Nichols and Holding make no sense yet. They're part of our perp's plan, though. I just don't know how or what the fucking plan is. While you guys do the legwork, I want to go back to the beginning, go over everything we know about the disappearance of Huxton and Murphy. Check again and make sure we haven't missed anything. There are still loads of things that I think are weird. Are you okay with that?"

"Good idea, cos that's where it all started."

"Eat up then and let's get going."

CHAPTER 49

Through the glass partitioning, a plethora of heads busied themselves like ants in a nest. "Decent size business this, I never knew there was so much money in recruitment," said Chad.

Jas followed his gaze. "Yeah, it is. Must be fifty or more in there. You've got to do a lot of recruitment to pay for that lot. How does it work?"

"What? How do they make money?"

"Yeah, don't they just find people temp jobs?"

"No there's more to it than that. A company might be needing to hire, and rather than go through the hassle of placing an advert, dealing with the response and all that, they put the job with an agency like this. These guys then do all the work and present the client with a shortlist for interview. If the client hires, then the agency charge a fee."

"Mm, never knew that. Maybe they could help me."

"Nah, you're a copper to the core."

A young woman with blue-tinted hair pushed open a door in the partition and said: "Please follow me, Andy can see you now."

The woman led them through the cluster of desks. The noise was a constant low hum like an engine as the occupants talked into headsets or mobiles. She knocked on the door marked Boardroom and held it for Jas and Chad to walk through. "Andy, the Police," she said.

Andy Huxton turned.

Jas held out her hand. "Hello, I'm DS Jas Carter and I'm very sorry for your loss, Mr Huxton. We'll try not to take up too much of your time."

Huxton shook Jas' hand then turned to Chad. "We've met, right?"

"That's right," said Chad, propping his cane against the table and taking in Huxton's appearance. He looked like shit, thought Chad, his hair was unwashed and he had at least three days' stubble. He was wearing the same suit he'd had on last time, but he looked like he'd slept in it. He wondered if he had. The guy's world had gone up in smoke in less than a week. A bit like Chad's own. Kindred spirits. "Mr Huxton, we have no wish to intrude on your grief any more than is necessary, but I need to ask you some questions. Are you okay to answer these today?"

"Yes, I'm okay, better to get on with it."

"Thank you." Jas smiled at Huxton. "I'm aware that you made two phone calls to our switchboard the evening before last, can you tell me the reason for those calls?"

Huxton looked out of the windows, then turned to Jas. "I wanted to know where you had got to in trying to find my Dad. I was worried."

"I see, but you'd met DI Wallace and Mr Hilton that morning, did something happen to make you call?"

"No, nothing, I just wanted an update that's all. No other reason."

Chad spotted the tell-tale body language that said Huxton was lying. The eyes looking up and to the right, the arms folding, the fidgeting. But why was he lying, he thought?

"Have you had any contact with Mr Nichols and Mr Holding during the time your father was missing?"

"Yeah, once or twice, a couple of phone calls to see if they'd heard anything. Nothing other than that."

"So, they didn't mention anything to you about contact from any third party, asking for a ransom maybe, or anything else that might shed some light on how these events unfolded?"

"No, nothing."

"Can you think of any reason that Mr Nichols and Mr Holding may have withheld information from you regarding your father's whereabouts?"

"No, none. I mean, why would they?"

Huxton's demeanour continued to contradict the words he was saying, thought Chad.

"I don't know but, strangely, they are found dead in your father's Porsche, and we need to understand how that happened, do you know of any enemies they may have had?"

"No, sorry, I've no idea. They worked a lot with my father but I only had dealings with them in the last couple of months during the sale of the business."

"Ah, yes," said Jas. "How is that going? Will it still go ahead?"

"I have no idea, but it's the reason I'm in here today, I've got to try and keep it warm."

Jas reached into her bag. She placed a photograph in front of Huxton.

"Do you recognise these two people, Mr Huxton."

Huxton looked at the photo of Murphy and Bannister in the garden centre, then back to Jas. "Both seem familiar somehow, but no, I'm not sure."

"Could you look again, please, Mr Huxton."

He pulled the photo closer and Chad saw him squint at it.

"As I said, they both look familiar but no, I can't place them."

This time, thought Chad, his body was in synch with his words. He was telling the truth.

"Did you notice them when you were at the garden centre?" Jas continued.

He didn't seem phased by Jas' question.

"No, I don't think so, no not at all."

"What were you doing at the High Trees garden centre mid-afternoon on a weekday?"

"Is it important?" said Huxton. His anger was evident. His nostrils flared and spittle sprang from his mouth with the words.

Jas didn't answer.

Huxton stared at her then said "I don't know why I was there. I think I went to get some spring bulbs to put in the window-box at my flat, that's right, I did. I'd been to see a client in Adel and called in on my way back."

Jas pulled the photo across the desk and put it back in her bag. Chad looked across the desk. Poor sod had just lost his father, he thought, he must be struggling to hold it together.

"Mr Huxton, where were you between 8:00 a.m. and 3:00 p.m. yesterday?"

"What? I mean, what the fuck, am I a suspect now?" He shouted. Huxton pushed the chair away from the desk and slammed his fist onto down on the table. "You lot do fuck all to find my father till you get an MP up your arse, and when it's too late and my Dad's dead you try to pin it on me."

Jas let things settle for a few seconds, "We have to check the whereabouts of everyone with any links to the deceased, Mr Huxton, so if you wouldn't mind, where were you between 8:00 a.m. and 3:00 p.m.?"

"I was here pretty much all that time.' He paused, breathing hard. "Yeah, I went into town for a while to get some lunch but that was it."

"And what time was that?"

"I'm not sure, I think I went out about 11:00 a.m. and came back about one-ish. Something like that."

"And did you meet anyone?"

"No, I wanted to get some headspace, it's been a very difficult time. I wandered up to the Starbucks at The Light and had some coffee."

"Did anyone see you there?"

"I've no idea, maybe the guy who served me?"

Jas changed tack. "Okay, just a couple more questions Mr Huxton. What make of car do you drive?"

"What? I drive a Range Rover Sport, blue. Why?"

"Where do you garage it?"

"It's in the basement. I keep it here. Why?"

"When did you last use the car?"

Chad pressed himself backwards into his seat. Huxton's going to lose it big time any second, he thought.

"I don't know, a few days ago, look what's this about? What's my car got to do with this?"

"I'm just crossing off details so that we can eliminate individuals from the enquiry," said Jas. "So, we won't take up any more of your time, one final question if I may. Mr Huxton, which Primary School did you attend?"

Huxton went up like an exploding bottle of pop. He jumped up and yelled "Jesus, what is this? Primary school? Are you fucking mad? My Dad's been murdered and you want to know where I went to school as a kid. You're fucking nuts."

Jas remained silent and tapped her pen on her pad.

Huxton stared across the table. "I went to St Patrick's. Why?"

"Can you recall if there was a teacher there by the name of Murphy, a priest, Father Declan Murphy?"

"Murphy." Huxton's facial muscles tensed. "Yeah, there was a priest called Murphy. A right pervy bastard. What's he got to do with this?" He paused, then leant forward towards Jas. "That was him in the photo wasn't it? I thought I recognised him."

Jas pushed her chair back and stood, so Chad grabbed his cane and hoisted himself upright. "Thank you, Mr Huxton, you've been very helpful. We may have more questions so we'll be in touch. We can see ourselves out."

Chad smiled at Huxton then turned and followed Jas out of the door. "Not as green as you're cabbage looking, D.S. Carter," he said.

Chapter 49

Chad stood next to Jas in the lift, facing the doors. He watched as her finger hovered over the numbers on the panel. She pressed B. "Thought so," he said.

"Well, seeing as we're here it would be rude not to. No alibi for at least two of the deaths makes our Andy a nice suspect."

The lift juddered to a halt and the doors opened. They were in a short corridor with bare walls and a concrete floor, to the right was a large metal door. His cane tapped on the pre-cast. He said, "I'll hold this open in case it locks when we shut it."

"Cool, I'll go have a look. Are there no frigging lights in here?"

The light from the corridor shone through the doorway into the otherwise black underground space. There was a lone vehicle in the car park. Jas moved towards the car, walked around it then squatted to look at the front tyre. She pulled something from her bag.

"What are you doing?"

"Police work," she said.

"Very funny. What can you see? Anything?"

Jas stood and walked towards him holding a clear plastic bag with something dark and solid inside. "I don't know where he's been recently, but somewhere muddy, that's for sure. We'll get this analysed, could be interesting. Right, we'd better get a shift on and go and see God's representative on earth."

"Oh, ye of little faith," said Chad.

CHAPTER 50

The lady that answered the door introduced herself as Miss Eastley, the housekeeper at The Bishop's House. She was around four feet ten tall, Chad thought, and about four feet ten wide. She had white hair in a bob. Chad smiled and Jas showed her police badge.

"Please come through and take a seat. The Bishop is over at Hinsley Hall, but I telephoned him when you rang earlier, so he should be back any minute. Can I get you anything? Tea, coffee?"

"No thanks, I think we're okay," said Jas, looking at Chad for confirmation.

"We're fine thanks," said Chad. The ageing housekeeper shuffled out and closed the door behind her. "Imaginative bunch, eh?"

"Who?"

"Whoever was on the house naming committee," he adopted a nerdy voice. "What shall we call a house where the Bishop lives? I know, let's call it The Bishop's House."

"Ha, ha. Very funny. You should do stand up."

"Nice place, anyway. A bit like your Police Headquarters, no expense spared."

The room was adorned with the sort of Catholic paraphernalia that would have had Oliver Cromwell turning in his grave. Crucifixes and paintings of Jesus Christ, in life and death, covered most of the wall space, but one wall was entirely given over to books. Hundreds of them. Chad loped across and looked at the titles. Worthy tomes from assorted saints, theologians and philosophers. Not his cup of tea, but hey, each to their own. The opposite wall was dominated by large windows overlooking the lawns and flowerbeds, which even at this time of year looked well maintained. A loud slam in the hallway followed by energetic pacing outside announced an arrival. A vision in black filled the doorway. Baggy black suit, black shoes and a shirt. The only relief a white dog collar which accentuated the saggy jowls that it appeared to support. Bishop Benedict, Chad presumed.

"Hello there, many apologies for my tardiness, I was over at the Hall, it's the hub for the administration of the Diocese."

The man waddled across to his desk as Jas made the introductions. Every part of him wobbled as he moved, like a seal heading up the beach, wheezing, sniffing and, in the Bishop's case, sweating. His shirt buttons were in the middle of a tug of war being pulled from both sides as the cloth strained across a waistline that had never met a Weightwatchers diet plan. His face had an unhealthy pallor highlighted further by a huge, bulbous red-veined nose indicating a lifelong endorsement of good wine. Not a primate that's adopted the Jesuitical vow of poverty. More a twenty-first-century Friar Tuck.

"Terrible, terrible business. Such a dreadful thing to have happened to Father Declan. I've instructed all our Parish priests to remember him in their prayers and I am saying mass for him tomorrow. Do you have any theories yet or some potential suspects? The Archbishop has asked me to keep him informed as to your progress, and I believe he is an acquaintance of your Chief Superintendent, so he will no doubt, be keeping himself abreast of developments. Anyway, how may I be of assistance?"

"We are trying to understand the motive for the attack on Father Murphy and wondered if you could shed any light on his past?"

"I'm afraid not. I understand that Father Murphy taught in many of the schools in Leeds and the surrounding parishes, but our paths only crossed at the end of his career when I was appointed Bishop. I was, until then, working as a priest in Stockport. I never met him in person, we exchanged some correspondence when it became necessary for him to be cared for in a residential setting. I engaged with the Diocese to take care of those arrangements."

"I see," said Jas, "and who chose Ashfield Grange for his care?"

"I believe we've had an arrangement with Ashfield Grange over many years. I understand that it's an environment conducive to elderly priests living alongside each other. Shared pasts if you will. As priests reach that time of their life, we check availability with Ashfield Grange first. They've always been able to accommodate us. Why do you ask, is there a problem with the home?"

Jas was deadpan. "Well, not as long as you don't count employing a volunteer with no background checks, who subsequently disappeared with Father Murphy, a problem. Then no. No problem."

"Oh, I presume that is this Bannister chap. Was he another of the victims?"

"No, he wasn't. He's still missing. Do you know him, or whether Father Murphy had any connection to John Huxton and his son Andrew Huxton?"

"Again, I'm sorry I have no idea about Bannister and no knowledge of any connection between Father Murphy and the Huxtons. I'm afraid I can't help you."

Let's prod this fat fucker, thought Chad. "Bishop Benedict," he said "when we were at the Ashfield Grange, we had a chat with another resident. He told us that it was common knowledge that Father Murphy was a paedophile and that the home serves as a dumping ground for problem priests. As he put it, all the church's bad apples under one roof. What can you tell us about that?"

"Well, I'm shocked anyone would say anything to impugn the reputation of a fellow priest. Moreover, I can assure you without equivocation, that the Church does not have a policy of *dumping*. That is untrue and you should be very careful about sharing those remarks outside of this room." The fatty wrinkles on his forehead bunched in what passed for a frown. "As to the specific allegation against Father Murphy, I am aware that there were suggestions of impropriety in the past but nothing was ever proven and no claims were ever made against him."

He's a lying bastard, Chad thought. Smug, self-righteous, assured, but a shifty fucker. "Has the Church ever paid a ransom?"

The Bishop narrowed his eyes and increased colour spread from the jowls upwards, as the cleric considered his response. "Why on earth would you ask that? Of course not."

If he had lost some composure, he'd got it back damn fast. "No reason, I wondered whether anything like this has happened in the past, that's all. As a matter of interest, what would happen if demands for money were made? Blackmail, that sort of thing?"

"As it has never happened, I can't say for sure, but I imagine we would report it to the police and engage our lawyers. Now, if there's nothing else I can help you with I need to prepare my sermon for tomorrow's remembrance mass for Father Murphy."

Jas stood and turned to go. Shifting his weight from his bad leg, Chad leant on his cane and pushed himself upright then shook the clammy, chubby hand proffered by the Bishop.

"That leg looks extremely painful. You should consider joining our pilgrimage to Lourdes. There are many examples of healing from the waters at the shrine to Our Lady, I'll send you the details," said the Bishop.

* * *

Jas started the car. "We got bugger all out of him. He gave me the creeps though, all that flesh and sausages for fingers." She shivered. "Do you think he was holding back?"

"Did you notice how his eyes slanted a bit when I asked about paying a ransom? I thought his colour heightened as well. Though any more colour in that nose and you could use it as a lighthouse. I think there's something he's not telling us but no idea what. Come on, let's call it a day."

"So, I take it you'll be booking a trip to Lourdes then?"

Chad grinned. "Fuck off."

CHAPTER 51

This is what sets me apart. Planning, picking the time and place with precision and care. Easy enough getting into the car park with plenty of time to put on the protective gear required, now I've just got to wait. Bless him, Andy won't see fuck all once he closes the door, too dark, poor sod, I almost feel sorry for him. I've checked the car park enough times, it's always deserted. Except for Andy. Only Andy ever parks in it. More money than sense. Why have the hassle of driving into town and paying over the top to park, when the office was so close to the train station and buses? Typical Andy, money no object. The place smelled of diesel and rubber. Butterflies, I smile, always good to have some nerves, keeps the mind alive. I'm ready. I was born ready. 6:30 p.m. He won't be long.

I hear the lift make a loud *ding* as it arrives and a *whoosh* as the lift doors open. Three steps to the door. One, two, three. Turns the door handle. Pulls. The hinges creak and the metal door groans. Two steps inside. One, two. Let the door swing shut. Clang. Go, go, go.

He's in front of me and to my left, perfect for the swing of my right arm. I slam the ball-pein hammer down onto the crown of his skull. He drops like a stone, I pause, not a sound.

Bending down over the crumpled heap, I smile, he's out cold

but not dead. Perfect. It's all in the detail. I feel in Huxton's pocket and pull out the keys to the Range Rover. "Okay, fella, this is what all those weights in the gym have been for, let's do it." Squatting, I stoop over the unconscious body and grabbing the right arm, I pull it around my neck and push through my legs to straighten. Andy Huxton's body lifts from the ground. Reaching behind, I swing the right leg over my shoulders then stand. A classic fireman's lift. The sound of my steps seems deafening in the emptiness of the car park. "Let's get you in and lie you down." I ease Huxton's limp body onto the back seat then reach for my backpack. "I'll put these on." I fish out two plastic ties. "Not tight, just enough, in case you wake up. I don't think you will, but better safe than sorry. And let's get this towel under your head in case there's some blood." The stillness and silence return as the echo of the car door closing fades. All good. "Right, let's get the hell out of here."

* * *

"No-one for fucking miles." The wind whistles up from the water below, billowing my jumpsuit and parting my hair. I knew I'd be alone here. No-one came during the day let alone at 7:30 p.m on a cold evening. Come on, let's get this finished. Huxton lies prone on the back seat. Hooking my arms underneath the body and heaving him out of the car, I let Huxton's weight fall onto my shoulder, then manoeuvre him into the driver's seat. On a panel on the driver's door is an automatic seat positioner. I press 1. The seat moves forward to the memorised driving position Huxton had programmed. Seat belt or no seat belt? Nah, no seat belt. Let's get the ties off. The magazine in the Makarov still holds enough rounds, but I eject it then wrap Huxton's fingers around it and drop it onto the passenger seat. I make sure that my victim's fingerprints are on the new stack before clicking it back into place. Huxton's head droops and the wind howling from the water below ruffles his hair. "Hold your nerve, mate. You've been building towards this for a long time don't lose it now." My voice gets lost on the wind. The pistol feels cold, and the smell of the oil I've used to clean it wafts past me, carried on the breeze. I need to get the angle right so the bruise from the hammer gets obliterated. Holding the pistol tight I jam the suppressor hard under Huxton's chin, pushing his head back. I fold Huxton's hand around the gun and position his finger on the trigger. I pause hearing the waves on the water far below, then pull the trigger. Blood and bone spatter the roof lining. "Right, let's get the fuck out of here."

CHAPTER 52

@therealchadhilton Tick, tock, another day has gone. Not too long now, dickhead. Can you handle the suspense? I can't wait to give your missus what she's been waiting for. Tick, tock. #napoleoncalling

Staring at the screen, Chad released a capsule from the foil and put it on his tongue. He began to type.

Hey babe, haven't heard from you, all okay? I left you a voicemail earlier, so call me when you get a chance. Night babe.

Rolling over he reached for his iPad and hunched himself up the bed to lean against the headrest, propping the tablet on his knees. He opened the Notes app, then rested his fingers on the keypad and gazed, unseeing, at the settee against the far wall. Scrolling back, he re-read the tweets from the day they had begun. When was that? Just started on the Lawlor case when the first one came through, and they've gone from vague trolling about drugs through to full-on death threats, in what? One week? Chad felt sweat, prickling cold against his body and there were goosebumps on his arms. He couldn't tell whether the turmoil in his stomach was last night's excesses or fear. He was certain there was no-one, apart from Ange and Freddie, that knew anything about the Fentanyl. So, it had to have been one of them that had spoken out of turn. Chad pushed his hair behind his ear and spoke to the empty room. "Even if Freddie had been loose-lipped why would someone he'd told decide they wanted to kill me? They'd have wanted money, wouldn't they? Blackmail me into giving them cash so they didn't go to the press, that's what they'd have done." But Freddie wouldn't have been loose-lipped, he'd bet the house on that. So, who does that leave? Shit, Ange. He kept coming back to her. She couldn't remember if she'd told anyone, so that meant she probably had. So, who had she spoken to, and why had they hated him enough to send death threats? The rain tapped out a rhythm on the window. Chad gripped the iPad. "Oh, fuck," he muttered. "Of course."

CHAPTER 53

Chad parked the car and checked his phone. Still nothing from Ange. She hadn't replied to his voicemail yesterday afternoon or his text of last night. What the fuck? He typed another message.

Ange, give me a buzz back when you get this. I'm still being trolled, and the nutter is getting more threatening by the tweet. I need to know you're okay. Had an idea about who's sending them. Anyway, just call me when you can.

Come on Ange, he thought, call me.

* * *

"Morning."

"Morning, Chad, happy Saturday, welcome to the mortuary." Jas beamed.

No-one needed that jolly shit when you're at work on a Saturday, Chad thought. "Yeah, well, some of us have been up and at 'em for a while. Were you out on the vino last night, or playing happy families with the cousins?" he said.

"Neither. But since you ask, I went out for a meal with a friend, over your way, in Harrogate, we went to The Bengali Lancer for an Indian. It was fabulous."

"You should have said, I know the owner well. He'd have given you a discount."

"Great, now you tell me. Right, let's crack on. The pathologist is a mate of mine, Martin, and he's doing me a favour by seeing us today. So, play nice."

Chad laboured up the steps of the hospital using his cane as leverage and trailed in Jas' wake. The place had the smell of disinfectant and cabbage that someone at the NHS seemed to have bought the rights to. Why, he thought, was he bothered that Jas went to dinner with someone? Jesus, as if his life wasn't complicated enough, now he was getting jealous. There were signs for the Mortuary, above each set of double doors. He'd have got a taxi if he'd known it was going to be this far.

Jas pressed the buzzer outside the door and used the hand cleanser on the wall. Chad followed suit. The doors opened, and a tall, athletic, man in his thirties came through them and smiled at Jas. He had thick blonde hair and patrician features. Despite wearing green scrubs and white Adidas trainers, he was far too handsome for his own good, Chad thought.

"You owe me, young lady," he said, "how are you? Come on through. Oh, sorry, I'm Martin, you must be Chad?" His accent was two parts public school one-part expert. Confident and assured.

Chad felt his hackles rise. Why was he annoyed? What the fuck was wrong with him? First, she had a meal with a friend, and that annoyed him, now he was pissed that she smiled at this bloke. Get a grip and check the mirror, he thought, the last thing Jas needed was a cripple with a cane and a drug habit. And he needed to get his wife back.

"Hi," said Chad.

"In here," said Martin, holding open a further set of double doors.

The room gleamed, everything spotless, anaemic, antiseptic. So, Chad thought, this is where we end up, is it? To the left were a bank of four metal doors, each with nameplates at vertical intervals. A further bank of six occupied the other side of the room, and an extendable, hydraulic gurney was in the middle of the room. Everything was white. The ceiling panels generated a harsh bright beam. The place smelled of ammonia.

Martin turned to face them, "So, Jas, how can I help you? Your text said you'd got a couple of questions from the post-mortem report?"

She looked at the pathologist. "Yes, we'd like to know what more you can tell us, about the blows that Huxton and Murphy received to the head? And, what else can you tell us about the marks on their wrists and ankles?"

"The head wounds are interesting. Each was hit just behind the left ear, wait, I'll show you." Martin pulled open the second door on his left. Inside were three trolleys, each holding a body in a white body bag. He pulled the middle occupant out and unzipped the shroud. John Huxton. He moved the dead man's head to the side, pointed to a spot behind his left ear.

"So, as I said, it's interesting, because the blow extends from here on the Parietal," he pointed to an area on the upper rear of the head, "down to the Temporal." His finger traced a path to the side of the skull near the ear. "That means that the weapon used, was approximately fifteen centimetres in length, and perhaps, no more than three centimetres wide. I'd say, cylindrical."

"So, what, a piece of piping?" asked Jas.

"I can't be certain, but a piece of metal piping in all probability would have caused greater damage, fractured the skull and caused the skin to break. I'd be more inclined, to think it was something like a cosh."

Chad had been half-listening, but was transfixed by the sight of the body. This is how death looked he thought, just a slab of flesh on a trolley. This guy, this John Huxton, once walked, talked, laughed, but whatever it was that had given him life was well and truly gone. And if he kept on with the Fentanyl this would be where he ended, a specimen being rolled in and out of a fridge unit being inspected by a bunch of Med students. He felt a weird and morbid need to touch the body. He wondered what that would be like. Chad looked up and away from the body. What had Martin said? something about a cosh?

"What, the sort you see the gangsters using, in the movies?" he asked.

"I'd say so, yes, or something very similar." He unzipped the bag and moved Huxton's left arm out. There was a purple discolouration around the wrist, stark against the pale flesh.

"The restraint used on the wrists and ankles was a metal bracelet. Five centimetres in width, the clasp came over the top of the wrist and fastened at the side. The bruising is extensive and consistent on the arms and legs of each of the victims. I'd say that the bracelet was in a fixed position, probably welded to something, meaning that the victims remained static. The gluteal muscles in both show significant damage, so they'd been seated for some time. Sitting for long periods also increases blood pressure which, in Father Murphy's case, weakened his resistance to the Taser."

"That's very helpful, thanks, Martin," said Chad. "So, the chairs they were on must have been in a fixed position, otherwise they could have tipped over?"

"Yes, I'd say so. There are no other injuries consistent with either man falling over, which would have happened when the Taser hit."

Jas looked at Chad and said, "So, what? What does it matter about whether the chair was fixed, or not?"

"I'm not sure, but if the chairs are fixed it tells a little more than we knew about where he held them. I don't know. Just something else to think about."

Jas raised an eyebrow. "I'm not sure if any of that matters, but hey. Martin, did either of them have any personal effects?"

Martin walked to a small desk at the far end of the mortuary. "Yep, over here. Not much I'm afraid."

"Is this it?" said Jas.

There were two metal trays. On one was an old Omega watch with a worn leather strap, on the other, a Rolex and a gold ring. "I take it the Rolex and ring belong to Huxton?" Chad asked.

"That's correct."

"Okay, well thanks again," said Jas. "We'll get out of your hair, and let you get back to Jacqui and the kids."

"Great, yes, we're going to the Yorkshire Sculpture Park this afternoon, so I need to be getting off. I'll get Jacqui to drop you a text, and we'll meet up for a beer. Haven't done that for ages."

"Yes, lets, I'll look forward to that. It will be good to see you without dead bodies for company."

Chad leaned on the wall outside the LGI. "A cosh, now that is interesting."

"Why is it interesting?" said Jas.

"Because it's unusual. He could have used anything, but a cosh is very specific. You can check the database for any other crimes where a cosh has been used. It may throw something up."

"I suppose so, but it's not much to go on, is it?"

"No, not by itself, but it's a start. Also, we know they were seated, and for the restraint bracelet to have been fixed, it must have been welded to a chair of some sort. Metal. So, where would you keep a couple of people, seated and locked down, without anyone knowing?"

Jas looked up at the rain clouds overhead. "I don't know, maybe a disused building, there are loads at the back of the station. Or a warehouse maybe? Christ there's thousands of places I suppose."

"True, but it's another small piece of the jigsaw. Have you sent that sample from the Range Rover to forensics?"

"Of course. Are you telling me how to do my job, Hopalong?" She smiled. "Come on, I'll give you a lift."

His phone pinged. Ange. *I'm away for the weekend with the girls, so whatever it is, you'll have to wait till Monday.*

Relief flooded through him. At least she'd replied. Chad looked at the message then at the morning shoppers headed into town.

She was on the piss with her mates, he thought. Not a care in the world, meanwhile some nutter wanted to kill him. "Brilliant" he said "fucking brilliant."

"You're very quiet," said Jas, turning to look at him.

Chad stared out of the car window. "Just trying to get my head around our meeting with the Bishop yesterday. I think he was lying, but I just can't work out what he was lying about. Andy Huxton was also lying but again, what about and why? I don't know, we seem to be wading in treacle. By the way, it's worth checking if Bannister went to St Patrick's with Huxton."

"Okay, remind me when we get to the office, and I'll get someone on it."

CHAPTER 54

The radio in Jas' car crackled into life. "*All units, we have a Blue Range Rover, registration Tango, seven, Hotel, Uncle, X-ray, found at Swinsty Reservoir. The driver is inside. Suspected fatality. We have a car on the scene and an ambulance has been called, please advise.*"

"Jas, I'm in the car on my way. You attend, I'll meet you there." Chad could hear the strain in Lee's voice.

"That's got to be Andy Huxton's car." said Jas.

Chad looked across. "Yep, it does, and that doesn't bode well."

* * *

The flashing lights of an ambulance lit up the grey sky. The narrow country lane had been closed off, and Jas parked as close to the tape as she could before running across to where Lee stood with a couple of forensic guys.

Chad swallowed a tablet, the smooth surface negating the need for water to wash it down. Third today, and not even lunchtime.

"He's with me, I'll sign him in." Jas shouted over her shoulder to the copper asking Chad for ID.

"Shit, that hurts," he grumbled, ducking under the tape and leaning hard on the cane. The ground was soft and puddle strewn and the wind threw drops of rain at him. Lee was standing near the blue Range Rover Sport. He yelled at them to get protective gear on before coming closer. Pulling on the shoe covers, Chad looked over at the Range Rover. Yeah, that was the car they'd seen in the garage. Huxton's. No doubt about that.

Jas had reached the open driver's door. He squelched towards her. Christ, he thought, was he ready for this? He hadn't done too well in the mortuary where everything was clean, and he knew this would be worse. "Don't be sick." He whispered. He edged closer, and looked over her shoulder, into the SUV. Andy Huxton's chin rested on his chest, at a slight angle, and the top of his head was a mass of congealed blood and bone. The ceiling of the car was stained red and pink. He saw lumps of brain tissue sticking to it, some of which formed gruesome grey stalactites dangling down. Fucking hell, he thought, He couldn't look at that. Bile tasting of battery acid filled his mouth, he gulped air into his lungs and swallowed hard, then fought back the contents of his stomach. A pistol with a long barrel was lying in Huxton's lap, his right hand clutching it and on the passenger seat was a dull metallic magazine. Chad stepped away shivering and leaned on the wall overlooking the waves splashing a couple of hundred feet below. Poor fucker, he thought, Christ, was it only yesterday he'd been interviewing this guy?

Lee joined him at the wall. "Are you okay, you look a bit green?" He didn't wait for an answer. "God knows how we piece all this together, it's a complete shit show. Not much doubt that Andy Huxton's shot himself. The press will have a feeding frenzy, not to mention his buddy, the MP. Bound to be our fault. Anyway, subject to what we get back from forensics, doesn't look like I'll need that perp profile you're working on, mate. Still, stick around till we know for certain what we're dealing with." Lee walked away.

Chad's phone pinged. Dread clawed his stomach. Twitter.

@therealchadhilton Another day, another....? Ha. I'm going to make sure that you get what you deserve #napoleoncalling.

Chad glared at his phone. '*Another day, another...?*' Another body, he thought. Chad looked up at the thunderous clouds and fought back his anger. This fucker knew where he was and what he was doing. But how? He must be here, now, he thought. Chad's brain felt too big for his skull and panic reminiscent of the previous night flashed through him. Where was this ghost? Chad stared around him at the hustle and bustle of coppers and paramedics. It must be one of these, but it couldn't be, it wasn't possible. "Where are you, Napoleon fucking Bonaparte?" he muttered. Logic cleared the debris out of his head and some clarity returned. He knew Napoleon couldn't be there at the reservoir now but how did he know Chad would be there? '*Another day, another....? Ha.*' A thought flashed into his head. If he's not here, how does he know there's a body? Unless...No. That's not a runner. Huxton's shot himself, not been shot.

Chad put the phone in his pocket and looked around for Jas. She was in deep conversation with Lee and one of the forensic guys, so he walked back to the BMW and leaned on the roof. The Range Rover stood twenty metres to the right. Blue was such a bright optimistic colour, in contrast to the sullen grey water in the reservoir. What a place to die. Cold, windswept, miserable. He didn't suppose it mattered where though, once someone had made their mind up. The clouds scudded past overhead, and the bleak sky merged, with the water below. He shuddered as a gust of wind blew up from the choppy waves so pulled his jacket tight around him. The feeling of being watched wouldn't leave him.

A hand touched his elbow. "I've been shouting at you for five minutes,' said Jas. "You're miles away, what are you thinking about? You look like you've lost a bob and found sixpence."

"My dad used to say shit like that. You're far too young to know what a bob was, or a sixpence."

"I know, but my nan used to say it, and I always thought it was a good way of describing that look."

"How am I meant to look, when I've seen more dead bodies in

forty-eight hours than I've ever seen in my life?"

"Yeah, it's shit, isn't it? Anyway, get in, the Boss wants a full team meeting in two hours."

CHAPTER 55

Chad shifted on the desk at the back of room 106. Food was the last thing on his mind but loud rumblings from his stomach told a different story. The muddy footprints on the carpet reminded him of the wet grass, the biting wind, and the back of Andy Huxton's head. Jesus, how awful was that? He had to concentrate on something else to take his mind off the scene at Swinsty. And that fucking tweet.

"Okay," said Lee, "everyone listen up. Ballistics will be able to check the bullets from Swinsty and Potto and will confirm tomorrow whether they were all fired from the same gun found in Huxton's hand. I think it's a safe bet that it is. An empty magazine on the seat, and a Makarov in his hand would be too much of a coincidence. Luke, you check the gun with Special Branch, but I'm not hopeful. These Makarovs are ten a penny in Europe, but where the hell did Andy Huxton get it? I think we'll also find the mud sample Jas took from his Range Rover matches the specimens we took at Potto." Lee paused. "Good work by the way, Jas."

She smiled. "Thanks, boss."

"If they are, then we know Andy Huxton was at Potto. So, we'll know the who, and the how, but not the why. Andy Huxton was taught by Murphy, so if Murphy abused him as a kid there's a motive. Albeit we don't know why he decided to do something about it now. I can't see how we'll prove that abuse but, Jas, trackback see if any complaint was made at the time."

"Will do."

"We don't know why Andy Huxton killed the other four if that's what ballistics and the mud prove, but I want us to find that motive. Joe, did you make a start with Nichols and Holding?"

"Yes, boss, we got hold of their desktops, laptops, and tablets and got the tech boys onto it. I'll chase them later."

"Good, with luck, they'll provide our answers. Chad, I know you were building a profile of our perp, did Andy Huxton match it?"

Chad looked up. "He did apart from a couple of anomalies."

"Like what?" asked Lee.

"Do you remember when we interviewed him after he'd reported his Dad missing?"

"Yeah, seems like a lifetime ago. What of it?"

"He told us that his Dad used to say he was as 'thick as pigshit', his words not mine. Whoever has done this isn't thick."

"Fair enough, but maybe his Dad was saying that without meaning it. Anything else?"

"No, I don't think so."

"Boss," said Jas, "Chad suggested that while we put all the evidence together, he reviews all the CCTV from Bridgewater Place and the Garden Centre to see if we missed anything and if he can find out what happened to Bannister. I think it would be a good idea."

"Chad, buddy, I pay you to profile and I don't think we are going to need one. If you want to look over things and make sure we've not missed anything, then okay, but I can't pay you for that."

"Taxpayers' money, I understand. Still, if you're okay, then I'll keep going on it. The Bannister thing is a puzzle, and I want to get to the bottom of it even if it turns out he's sitting at home watching daytime TV."

"Fine," said Lee, "but as soon as the guys are finished pulling all the evidence together, that's it, case closed, okay?"

"Yep, that's fine," said Chad.

"Right, let's meet back here in twenty-four hours, and wrap this up."

* * *

'Got a minute?" Chad yelled.

Jas was thirty yards ahead, walking to her car. She waved and smiled. "What's up?"

"Don't forget to get someone to check the database for assaults where a cosh was used."

"Okay, I won't. Well, I had, but I'll get onto it."

"Just one more thing for you to think about. It might not mean much, but you never know."

She put her hands on her hips as he caught up with her. "What's that, then?"

"Why would Andy Huxton be so careless as to take his car to Potto, leave tyre tracks, and not clean the mud off?"

"They all make mistakes, that's how we catch 'em."

"But, sometimes, if it looks too good to be true, then it probably is."

"Touché. See you tomorrow. Are you doing anything tonight?"

"Nah, off home. You?"

"Likewise."

She smiled and held his eye. Chad smiled back and hoped it didn't look like he was leering. She stood for a couple of seconds. Was she waiting for him to say something, he thought? Should he ask her for a drink?

Jas turned. "Night, then."

"Goodnight," said Chad. The lights on the Beemer flashed. "That troll is right," he muttered, "you are a dickhead."

CHAPTER 56

Chad felt his phone vibrate. Freddie.

Chad, bro, think we've had contact. He's wanting to meet his man, tonight, 9:00 p.m. outside the Brown Hare, on Harehills Lane. You around? Pay this guy a visit?

Chad replied. *Too right. Meet you in the pub, 8:30 p.m?*

8:05 p.m. Plenty of time to get from Beeston to Harehills. "Right, you bastard, let's find out who you are." His phone pinged. Freddie, replying with a thumbs-up emoji.

* * *

The car park of the Brown Hare was deserted. He'd stick out like a sore thumb if he parked in there, he thought. Chad took the next left and parked in the Office of the Traffic Commissioner. He smiled, they hadn't had Freddie's sort of trafficking in mind when they built this. Rows of red brick terraced houses stretched east and west along Harehills Lane. Three youths loitered at the bus stop outside the pub and began to take an interest in him. Easy pickings. White guy with a limp and a cane. He met their stare, as he walked past the opening to an alley, at the side of the pub. "Evening boys," he called and waved. One of the youths sloped out of the shelter towards him so he limped faster to avoid further contact. Inside the lack of any patrons emphasised the vastness of the pub. A large circular bar occupied the centre of the room, behind which a lone barmaid was using her phone. A corridor stretched away with signs for a games room somewhere in the far distance. Like seeing a sign for Land's End when you're at John O' Groats.

"I'll get a Diet Coke please," he said.

In the contest for the least interested employee, maybe the security guard at Bridgewater Place would have given her a run for her money. But maybe not.

"One pound seventy-five." She said, putting the drink in front of him.

"Is ice extra?" he asked.

"You should have said," she replied, making no effort to remedy the situation.

Chad gave up, picked up his drink and made his way to a table, which gave him a view of Harehills Lane. The youths were still at the bus stop and turned their heads as one when a silver-and-black Rolls Royce approached. "Freddie, for fuck's sake, man, what happened to unobtrusive?" He heard Freddie before he saw him. There must be an entrance to the pub near the games room because Freddie boomed greetings to whoever was in there. He emerged from the other side of the bar.

"Hey, Glenda, darling, how're you keeping? Looking fabulous, as ever, you, sexy little minx." Freddie leaned across the bar and pecked her on the cheek. "My usual please, darling, and could you bring it over?"

Glenda gave Freddie her best attempt at a sensuous smile before she turned to the optics to pour a vodka.

"Local of yours is it, Freddie?" said Chad.

"I own it, bro."

"Of course, you do, how did I not guess that?"

Glenda swayed across the floor and put Freddie's drink in front of him, taking the opportunity to run her other hand over his back. Chad smiled. Glenda ignored him.

"So, what do you know?"

Freddie sipped his drink. "I got a call about an hour ago from Errol, he runs some errands for me, and he told me that our coke head had called him to arrange a collection. Errol usually delivers. Like Deliveroo. But our dude doesn't want that, he wants a meet, somewhere he can collect, and disappear. Doesn't want Errol knowing where he lives. He's careful, I'll give him that. So, Errol, tells him to meet here at 9:00 p.m"

"Where exactly? In the car park? Outside? Where?"

"Outside the pub, there's an alley. Only one way in, which is from Harehills Lane. There's an eight-foot fence at the other end, so he's got to come out the same way he goes in."

"Yeah, I saw it coming in. Okay, so we wait for him to rock up."

* * *

Chad checked his watch. 9:15 p.m. "Doesn't look like he's going to show," he said.

Freddie's phone lit up.

"Is it Errol?"

"Yeah, he's been waiting twenty-five minutes and doesn't want to hang around any longer. Says he'll text when he knows what's gone down."

"Fuck," said Chad. "Never mind, we'll get him soon, he wants his fix. Right, buddy, I'm going to get off. Scintillating though this bar is I'm going to go and get a takeaway."

Freddie rose, embracing him as always in a massive bear hug. "Take it, easy bro, I'll be in touch. Did you make an appointment with your GP?"

"Yeah, I did. Tuesday next week. Doctor on Tuesday, acupuncture and counselling Wednesday, could life get any better? Night buddy, stay safe."

"You too, bro."

CHAPTER 57

Fucking little dickhead thinks I'm going to turn up without checking things first. Wanker. Disrespectful wanker. Inside the entrance to Harehills Park, the shadows from the trees cast a dark blanket around me. As always, I've done my homework, even if Errol hasn't done his. Any minute now, the little shit will be here and won't be expecting to see me. I touch the butt of the Makarov I've tucked in my waistband. I'm statue still and silent. Patience, my virtue. Footsteps. 11:00 p.m. Errol's nothing if not punctual. I remain in the shadows. Let the little fucker get past me then I'll give him the shock of his fucking life.

"Errol" I whisper. Errol turns and fear spreads like a stain across his face when I press the Makarov against his chest. I love this bit. The power I hold over him. "Move a fucking muscle, you little shit, and I'll blow your fucking brains out. One more dead drug dealer in Harehills, who'll give a fuck about that? No-one."

'What do you want?" stammers Errol.

"You tried to set me up. Don't think I didn't see your Boss turn up in his limo, and don't think I didn't see his crippled mate, trying to be clever and parking next door. I saw them both. Now, why were they there I wonder? Because Errol fucking told them, that's why. And, why did he do that?" Sweat is bubbling on Errol's top lip, but the kid stays silent, not quite as dumb as he looks.

"So, Errol if you want to live this is how it's going to work," I stare into the kid's eyes. "I want the coke you had for me, now. I want the same amount again on Monday, but I also want two strips of Fentanyl, and one of Rohypnol."

"But, man, that stuff's difficult I don't know if I can get it," Errol began, blabbering.

"You can, and you will. If you don't, you'll wind up in the canal. I'll pay you over the odds, and I'll text you the meeting place and time. Now give me my fucking coke."

Errol took the small silver backpack off his shoulder, pulled out a transparent plastic bag, half full with a white powder.

"Right, there's the cash, less a fifty per cent discount for inconveniencing me. If you ever try and pull a stunt with me again, my little druggie friend, you'll be dead. Understand?"

Errol nods.

"Right, fuck off," I push Errol in the chest with the barrel of the gun, turn, and walk out of the park. Job done. And a couple of free lines to snort. An evening well spent.

CHAPTER 58

The roller shutters of the car park at Bridgewater Place juddered as they rose, and the Porsche emerged. Rubbing his eyes, Chad leant back in the chair and watched the tape for the seventh time. "There's got to be something." The digital clock on the wall said 11:17 a.m. How long had he been here? Must have arrived around 9:30 a.m., so nearly two hours of looking at this tape and nothing.

The Porsche idled up the ramp and came alongside George Hampsthwaite's cabin. Chad waited until it was right outside, so he got the best view of John Huxton.

Is it him? he thought. Looked like him, but to be fair he'd only ever seen Huxton dead on a trolley. "Right," he said to the empty room, "let's change the movie and watch Murphy and Bannister at the Garden Centre, see if I can spot anything on that one."

The tall black guy loomed across the screen, reaching up and plucking a plant from the top shelf of a metal rack. The ill-matched pair browsed the aisles, and Andy Huxton came into the shot, standing at the same table as Murphy. What was wrong with that frame? There was something, but what? He watched the tape through to the end, rewound, and watched it again. Bannister reaching up. He paused the tape at that moment. There was something not right with that shot either. He cursed under his breath; he was watching but not seeing.

He eased himself out of the chair and stood gazing out of the window for a moment, where the stadium stood bathed in the early spring sunshine. He hobbled back to the desk, sat and stretched his leg. One more run-through, then he'd call it a day. Start with Bridgwater Place, again, he thought, what was he missing? John Huxton looking straight ahead, both hands on the wheel, about to drive past the cabin. Chad stared at the image. Huxton's face looked strange, but why?

"Jesus, this is frustrating." He shouted and slammed his hand on the desk making the keyboard jump. He pressed pause. "What the..." He rewound a couple of frames, pressed play, and stopped the tape at the same spot as before. Smiling, he put his hands behind his head. "Well, Hilton, maybe you haven't lost your touch after all."

He typed a text. *Hey Jas, happy Sundays, you ok? Just been going through the CCTV. I think I've spotted something on the Huxton tape.*

Come on then, smart arse, what have you found?

He grinned as he typed. *Ha. If you're not doing much, pop down I'm at HQ.*

On my way.

* * *

"I'll play it from the beginning and see if you spot anything. I was on my eighth re-running before I saw it. Damn nearly died of boredom. It's hardly Spielberg. So, you can have one run through then I'll show you."

"Patience is not a virtue for Mr Hilton then," Jas laughed.

"Okay, here we go." He pressed play.

The clip lasted fifteen seconds. Jas was riveted to the screen. "Okay, I give up."

"Budge up then, and I'll show you."

Jas moved her chair and Chad pulled into the vacated space.

He paused the tape with Huxton outside Hampsthwaite's cabin. "Right, do you see anything there?"

"No, just Huxton. What am I missing?"

Chad leaned forward and pointed at Huxton's hands gripping the steering wheel.

"Oh, my God," said Jas. "You clever bastard."

"We aim to please."

CHAPTER 59

Chad had said he'd buy Jas lunch to celebrate their find so they ended up at the Old Peacock. Never darkened the doors in all the time he'd been in Yorkshire but now he'd come twice in a week.

"Now then, Mr Hilton, nice to see you again, how are you, can we tempt you with some food this time?"

"Yeah, I'm good, thanks, Eric. How're things with you?" Eric puffed out his chest. Everyone liked to be remembered.

"I'm keeping well, thank you. You still helping with the police?" he asked, nodding towards Jas.

"Yes, bits and bobs, nothing much. By the way, thanks for pointing me at Leeds Laundry, that was an enormous help."

"Ah, well, I'm glad they caught that blighter. Now, what can I get you?"

"A couple of Diet Cokes, please."

"Fine, you sit yourselves down and I'll bring the menus across."

Jas chose the table, sat and weaved a beer mat through her fingers. "So, Huxton's not wearing his watch or his ring, what does that tell us? I mean, there may be a perfectly reasonable explanation. Maybe he takes them off when he goes to play tennis. Maybe they're in the car somewhere."

"I don't know what it tells us, and you could be right, he'd just taken them off. But they turned up on his body and it's another annoying loose end that creates a glimmer of doubt. I think things will become clearer when we get ballistics back, and when Joe Schmidt has followed up on Nichols and Holding. If there's a money trail leading back to Andy Huxton then, that's pretty much it."

Jas was peering at him over the rim of her drink.

"What?" he said.

"Your wife must be understanding, doesn't she mind you working on a Sunday?"

Chad shuffled in his seat and looked across the table. Another dramatic change of subject, he thought, off on another tangent. And an uncomfortable one at that.

"Sorry, I didn't mean to pry," said Jas.

Fuck it, he thought. "She would, but we're not together. I'm hoping that it's a temporary situation, but we'll see. I've been on my own for a few weeks, and I'm no bloody use, that's for sure. Working with you guys has kept me occupied and taken my mind off things but it's like toothache, it doesn't go away and you can't forget about it. Sorry, I don't want to burden you with my shit." He smiled. "What about you, do you have a man in tow?"

"Hey, look I understand it must be tough, and no, no other half for me, when would I get time to meet someone? I'm always bloody working."

"There's always Tinder?"

"I really can't be arsed with that. It's just a bunch of weirdos looking for a shag."

"Sorry, I don't understand. What's wrong with that?" He laughed. "Only joking."

"Yeah, that's probably why I don't have much luck in the relationship department. I tell it like it is. Men don't seem to like that, or can't handle it. One or the other, I need to learn to button it."

"Nah, that wouldn't be you. You'll find someone who likes you, warts and all. If you get what I mean?"

"Oh, that's charming. Warts and all? There's nothing like getting a compliment to keep a girl interested. And that was nothing like a compliment."

Chad's phone vibrated. Twitter. Fuck.

@therealchadhilton Working on a Sunday, dickhead? Make the most of it and enjoy, it's the last one for you. #napoleoncalling.

He clicked it off. Jas was staring at him.

"What was that? It can't have been good, judging by the look on your face."

In for a penny, he thought, she may as well know the rest of the shit going on in his shambles of a life. He passed the phone to Jas. "Scroll to the top and have a read. I'm interested to hear your thoughts." Her expression became more serious as she went on.

"Have you shown these to the Boss?"

"No, just a mate of mine, and now you. What do you think?"

"I think he's right, you're a dickhead. You should have mentioned them. This guy is a serious nut job."

"A mate of mine is trying to track him, he has good networks. We were close to getting to him last night and, anyway, I don't want Lee to divert resources away from the Huxton case, onto what may turn out to be a random nutter."

"I don't think he's random at all. Would this mate of yours be the infamous Freddie Jackson?" She stared at Chad, then raised an eyebrow. "I bet he has more resources than us. So, tell me, Mister Profiler, what do you make of this troll?"

"He knows a lot about me and what I'm up to, which suggests that he's watching my movements. I'm trying to think of who else knows about the drugs, and who might have a reason to want to harm me. Disgruntled opposition fans are way in the past and wouldn't know about the drugs anyway. There's only one person I can think of."

"Go on," said Jas. "Who's that?"

"Ange and I split up a few weeks ago because I found out she was seeing another guy. I confronted her. Cutting a long story short, she ended it with whoever it was and we decided to give each other some space to come to terms with things and decide what we both want to do. I think the guy trolling me is the guy my wife had an affair with. Why he wants to kill me I have no idea."

"Why do you think it's him?"

"By a process of elimination. There's no-one else. Suppose he blames me out for not being able to see Ange again? I don't know, Jas, but he's the only one I can think of, and the timing works. He started direct messaging me on Twitter, just as I started on the Lawlor case, which coincides with when Ange told me she had stopped seeing him."

Jas was deep in thought. "Who is he, this guy she was having an affair with, do you know him?"

"No, I don't. She won't tell me, says it's more important to understand what went wrong in our relationship than who the person was. She says it's over between them, so to her, it's not important. We're going for counselling next Wednesday and she says she wants to talk about things in a safe environment. She'll tell me then."

"Does she know that he's threatening to kill you?" Jas' tone oozed exasperation.

Chad watched her body language go from open and supportive to urgent and angry. "Well, no, she doesn't. She's also said she thought that she's been followed once or twice by a black guy."

"For fuck's sake, Chad, come on, this is serious shit. Do you want me to make an official call to your wife and question her under caution?"

"Don't be ridiculous."

"I'm not. You are by not demanding she tells you who this guy is. Do it now, go on, call her. She needs to be aware that there's an explicit threat of sexual assault against her, have you thought about that? What the fuck is wrong with you?"

"Alright, alright, no need to get shitty, I'll call her now."

"You haven't seen me shitty yet, trust me you'll know it when you do. Now ring her."

Angie answered, "Chad, I told you, whatever it is, will have to wait until tomorrow."

"Don't hang up, Ange, this is important. I've shown the messages from whoever is trolling me to the police, and they're concerned. They think he's serious. Ange, the only person that I can think of that might be doing this, is the guy you were seeing. He's the only person who might be pissed off enough, to be sending these. You've got to tell me his name, it can't wait. If nothing else, the police can have a chat with him and check it out, that might be all it needs for him to stop. The cops are talking about questioning you under caution. Ange, this is serious."

"Jesus, Chad." He heard suspicion in her voice. "Is this another little ploy of yours to find out his name and give me grief before we go for counselling, because if it is you can bugger off it won't work?"

"Seriously Ange I'm with one of Lee's colleagues right now, I can put you onto her if you like?"

The line went quiet. Chad could hear her breathing into the phone and somewhere in the background glasses clinked and female voices were raised in laughter.

Angie whispered a name; he could barely catch it.

"Just repeat that," he said.

Angie repeated the name, then as silence descended, she said, "Chad, say something, you're scaring me."

"Okay, don't worry, that's fine, I'll call you later."

He clicked the call off and looked at Jas. "You're not going to believe this."

"Try me."

He paused, and looked out of the window. What the fuck, he thought? He looked back to Jas and said "She said his name is Andy Huxton."

"Fucking hell."

"So, where do we go from here?" Chad said.

"The Boss is going to have to know. This is looking a whole lot bigger than some vendetta against you. Jesus Christ, has this got something to do with the murders?" Jas looked at him, "I'll leave you to tell the Boss, much better if it comes that way and, also, preferable that he doesn't know that I'm aware. Make that call Chad. I'll leave you to it, see you tomorrow."

She looked back and smiled at him as the door closed behind her. He shivered, stood and walked to the bar to pay the bill.

CHAPTER 60

Chad tried to get comfortable on a stool at the breakfast bar. Lee's kitchen was spacious and modern with a host of top-of-the-range appliances, granite work surfaces and kitchen units in slate grey which Chad had always thought were tasteful and chic. The walls were decorated in matching grey paint, with the sills and ceiling in a slightly off white. A huge double oven stood next to an American style, double-door fridge freezer, adorned with school timetables, shopping lists, and Lee's work rota, all held in place by a variety of fridge magnets.

"So, tell me, what's so urgent. It's not like you to come around on a Sunday. What happened to Super Sunday on Sky?" said Lee.

The kitchen door burst open and Hannah, Lee's seven-year-old, hurtled in. "Dad, dad, can uncle Chad stay for dinner, please dad, we never get to see him. Mum says he can. Go on dad, don't be mean."

Thank God she grabbed the good leg, Chad thought. Wouldn't have been the best start to a tricky conversation if he'd been sprawling on the floor in agony.

"I'm sure Chad, has better things to do than listen to you and your sister."

"He doesn't. Do you Chad? You want to stay, don't you?" She beamed at him.

Lee answered for him. "If Chad wants to stay for dinner, he can with pleasure, though who would want to eat their meal with you lot, I don't know. Anyway, it's on one condition."

The Tasmanian she-devil stared at her father. "What's that then?"

"That you give Chad and I an hour of peace to do some work. Okay? Is that a deal?"

"Deal," said Hannah, and evacuated the room with the same devastating burst of energy as she'd entered.

"Bloody hell, I'd forgotten what a livewire she is. Gorgeous though," said Chad.

"You won't be saying that when she and Carrie bombard you with questions at dinner. Then they'll bicker, fall out and demand that you play some game or another with them. You'll be searching for the indigestion tablets before you go. Glass of wine? Beer?"

"I'm driving, so I'd better not."

"Hey, I just remembered you said Ange was away, so why don't you have a few drinks and stay the night? Go on, have a beer."

Chad could not think of anything he'd rather do, but gave Lee an escape route. "You might not be saying that when I've told you the full story."

Lee opened two bottles of Peroni and gave one to Chad. "Let's hear it then," he said.

Chad sighed, "Okay, buddy, here goes."

* * *

An hour later, there were three empty lager bottles in front of him, and Lee was opening a fourth. At one stage, after Chad had told him about Angie, Lee had stood up and walked around the breakfast bar, then clasped Chad to him. The tears fell, and Chad held on.

"I'm so sorry, buddy, so sorry. I wish we'd known. We might have been able to help."

Thereafter, Chad left nothing out, no point, even on the occasions where the narrative involved Freddie. He'd given Lee his phone, as he'd done earlier with Jas, and Lee had read the tweets with increasing consternation.

"Fuck, Chad, this is no keyboard warrior. This guy is serious."

"Yeah, and it gets worse," Chad brought Lee into the present, "I decided to tell Ange that she has to let me know who this guy is, otherwise I'd get you to question her under caution."

"I bet that went down well," said Lee.

"As you can imagine she wasn't pleased, but it did the trick, she told me his name."

"And, who is it?"

Chad paused, took a breath and said, "She said his name's Andy Huxton."

Lee's head shot up and an involuntary shout exploded from him. "Get the fuck out of here!"

A voice came from the hallway. "Stop swearing, daddy, we heard you, and we'll tell Mum."

"Sorry," he yelled.

"How weird is that?" Lee muttered then took a pull on his Peroni. "I need a bit of time to think all that through. Fuck I don't know where that takes us. One thing at a time, do you mind if I go and tell Helen about you and Ange? She'll be upset and I'd rather the kids didn't see that. Then we can think about Andy Huxton and the tweets."

"No, mate I don't mind, she should know. I'm sorry I haven't told you both earlier."

"Don't worry about that, why don't you grab another beer, or wine, whatever you want and go and entertain the two monsters while I have a think and a chat with Helen."

* * *

Helen moved around the kitchen in a blur of activity. Chad had always been in awe of her culinary skills but now marvelled at her ability to control two exuberant kids, serve up the food, load the dishwasher, and keep the flow of conversation going. Multi-tasking as an Olympic sport. He waited for Lee to grab the third bottle of wine from the rack, before slipping another Fentanyl onto his tongue. He'd now had seven and needed to be careful, he was in company. No blackouts pal, he thought. Lee had been right, the two girls had kept him occupied throughout dinner, and were now demanding that he play football with them in the hallway. "I'd love to girls, but I don't think your mum would be too happy, and I've got this dodgy leg, so I'd be useless."

"You can go in goal," said Carrie.

Goalie, he thought. So that's what he'd become. The adult version of the fat kid in the playground. How the mighty fall.

"Girls, it's school tomorrow, go and get your bags ready," said Helen.

"Ah, no mum, not now, we'll do it later."

"Now," said Helen. "Then you can come and watch some TV with Chad, before bed.

The girls sprinted for the staircase, yelling hysterically at each other.

"Blimey, they're full-on, aren't they? Just as well I never had kids, I'm not sure I would have coped, I love yours to bits, though."

"And for some reason, they love you to bits. And Angie," said Helen. "Chad, Lee told me what's happened. I'm not going to give you platitudes, just know that we are here for you, and we hope that you two can sort it out. We've known each other for a long time, and we love you both." Helen wiped away a tear and walked around to where he was sitting. He felt the warmth of her body as she hugged him tight and kissed him on his head.

"Why don't you two go and discuss your work stuff in the study, and by the time you've finished, the girls will be back downstairs."

* * *

He was seven down, had a glass of wine in his hand and no idea where the girls had put his cane so Chad made his way with careful steps down the hallway. Now was not the time to go arse over tit, he thought. The study was small and functional, with a large desk occupying most of the available space, and the rest of the room filled by a leather armchair. Bookshelves climbed vertically on one wall, opposite which a window looked out onto the driveway. Lee turned the chair by the desk. "You'll be better on that," he said, "I'll have the leather."

"Something occurred to me during dinner, which makes this even crazier," said Chad, stretching his leg.

Lee looked up from twirling his wine around the glass. "Shit it's crazy enough as it is. What is it?"

"I've had two tweets in the last twenty-four hours. One when we were at Swinsty Reservoir, the other earlier today. So, unless we have some supernatural shit going on here, whoever sent those can't have been Andy Huxton 'cos he was dead, it must have been someone else." He felt for his phone. "I've got an idea. I'm going to check something. I'm sure somewhere in the case notes, there's a photo of Andy Huxton. I store all this stuff in the cloud, let's see. Yep, there it is." He gave the phone to Lee.

"I don't get it, what good is that?"

"Let's see if Angie recognises him. I'll forward it to her now." He downloaded the photo and sent it on a text to Ange.

They sat in silence, both staring at Chad's phone. It pinged, making them jump.

"Chad, I don't know who that is, but it's not Andy Huxton."

Chad passed the phone. "I don't get this," said Lee.

"Ange, do you have a photo of the guy you were seeing, if so please send."

"No, idiot, of course, I don't."

"Okay, thanks, call you tomorrow."

"Where do we start with this? It's just so bloody strange. If you are not Andy Huxton, why say you are? Anyway, first thing tomorrow I'll get our tech team to go through the tweets and see if they can trace this guy. Has Freddie got any further since last night?"

"No, not that I'm aware of. He'll text if he does. I've had a go at tracing the troll but he doesn't follow anyone apart from me, and no-one follows him."

"What do you make of all this, Chad, it must have been tearing you up?"

"Yep, it has and trying to step away and take an objective view of the facts is difficult, but on the couple of occasions I've been able to, I keep coming back to one word. Revenge. The reason that Andy Huxton shot his father, and killed Murphy, can be explained only if he was exacting revenge for something done to him in the past. And, the only sensible explanation for the tweets is that the guy wants to exact revenge on me, for ending his relationship with Angie. Lee, this is fucking bonkers."

"Agreed. Let's sleep on it," said Lee. "Come on, I can hear those two piling down the stairs."

Hannah and Carrie were tucked under each arm. Both had snuggled in, heads on his chest, chuckling at Toy Story Four. There were familiar photographs in frames, on every shelf and table. A family history in pictures. To the left of the vast TV screen was one that hadn't been there the last time he'd been for dinner. He could remember it being taken as if it was yesterday. Pissed, outside the Original Oak, must have been 1998. Lee was to the left, with his arm around Helen, laughing, and saying something to the camera. Helen was smiling and looking at Ange, who stood next to her, eyes sparkling, hair blowing back, and arms aloft, in celebration. Chad, to the right, was also looking at Ange. It had been Freddie behind the camera. Twenty-one years, Jesus, where's that time gone? Helen was watching him and smiling. He smiled back. Should he go for the counselling, or was he just kidding himself? What about Jas? Did he feel something for her, or was lust taking over? Whatever, it wasn't a good basis for starting a reconciliation process, by fancying the pants off someone else was it? God knows. Friends, time, love. Who knew what was in store? He gave the giggling girls a tender cuddle.

CHAPTER 61

"Why is my life so fucking difficult?" Errol raged at the swings in the empty kids' playground. He kicked at an imaginary stone and considered his predicament.

"This fucking nutcase punter is defo going to shoot you if you tell Freddie, right? Right."

The grey sky failed to inspire. He tried to rationalise "But, if you don't tell Freddie, you can't get the Fentanyl and Rohypnol, 'cos he controls the supply. What the fuck?"

"If you do get it from Freddie, he will want to know who it's for. Lie to Freddie, and bad things gonna happen. Very bad things. But he won't shoot you, right?" He thought about that and concluded. "Nah, he won't shoot you, but you'll never work in Leeds again, you'll have to leave."

Fuck. What to do? Errol lit a spliff and took a deep draw. Life always got a little easier with a spliff. He grinned as he formulated his plan. "I know, I got it. I'll tell Freddie everything, but when the punter connects with the time and place, I'll tell Freddie a different time. That way the punter goes off happy and I say to Freddie, he turned up early. Simples.

"Errol, mum always said you were one smart cookie. One day it'll be you in the black-and-silver Roller."

CHAPTER 62

Monday 8:00 a.m.

The staircase was steep and long. Chad looked down. Fuck, he remembered watching the Hahnenkamm Downhill on Ski Sunday. This was worse. The only way to navigate this without falling headlong was to place the good leg on each step, then move the dodgy one to join it. Could be lunchtime by the time he got down. He heard the kids in the kitchen, shouting and running about like Duracell bunnies on a full charge.

"Uncle Chad, Uncle Chad, will you take us to school? Please," yelled Hannah.

"Yes, that would be such fun, please," implored Carrie.

The smell of coffee and toast kick-started his metabolism.

Helen shouted to make herself heard over the racket. "Not a chance, Chad's very busy. I'm taking you, and you've got five minutes to make sure you're ready. Coffee's in the pot, Chad, help yourself."

He hoped a conspiratorial raise of the eyebrows and outstretching of the palms would help the girls understand that he would have loved to have taken them, but their mum wasn't having it.

The coffee was home-brewed, strong and black. Perfect.

Lee walked into the room, holding a pair of trainers. "So, which of you two would have been doing PE today with no trainers?"

Hannah let out a shriek and bolted towards Lee. As she grabbed for the trainers, Lee raised his arm, holding the shoes over his head. "Your mum told you to get ready, but you, young lady, are too busy making a racket to listen."

As Hannah jumped up, her blouse extricated itself from the waistband of her skirt, revealing her tummy. Lee tickled it which made her squeal even louder.

Chad's coffee remained halfway between the table and his mouth. What had he just seen and what did it remind him of? It couldn't be, could it?

Lee caught the query and the look. "What?" he said.

"I've got to get off, thanks for letting me stay."

Helen pulled Chad close and whispered, "You take care of yourself, and I hope the counselling goes well for you both. If you need to come and stay, don't ask, just turn up."

"Thanks, Helen." Chad leaned down and gave first Hannah, and then Carrie, a hug and a kiss. "Now, you two be good. I don't know how your mum and dad cope, you'd exhaust me."

"Ha!" they yelped in unison.

"I'll see you out, have you got everything? Where's your cane?" said Lee, prompting more shrieking before Carrie found it behind the bin.

At the front door, Chad turned. "Sorry, mate, didn't want to talk shop in front of the kids, but I need to have another look at that CCTV. Something just struck me. I'll call you, okay?"

"Fine. I'm going to get those tweets looked at. When I know more, I'll buzz you. Don't forget the team meeting this afternoon."

"I won't. Oh, by the way, how about getting an artist to meet Ange and draw a portrait of the bloke she was seeing? At least we'll have a clue what he looks like, even if we don't know who the hell he is."

"Yeah, that's a good idea. Call her and let me know if she's okay with that and I'll get it set up. See you later."

* * *

He dug his phone from his jacket pocket and dialled Ange's number. No answer. Christ, come on Ange. "Hey Ange, it's me. Lee's tracing the tweets today and suggested that a police artist comes to meet you, to sketch the guy you were seeing, so we have an idea who we are looking for. Are you okay with that? If so, I'll get Lee to call you and arrange times, et cetera. Okay, babe, let me know."

He walked to his car on legs made more unsteady by the beer and wine from the previous evening. It's normally whisky and pills, he thought. A change was as good as a rest, apparently. He opened the car door, threw his jacket onto the passenger seat and undertook the ritual of getting himself in. He put his phone in its holder on the dash. It pinged.

Angie. WhatsApp message. *"If I must, I suppose I'm okay with that. Get Lee to call."*

He stared out of the windscreen. Why didn't she just answer the bloody phone, he thought? Jesus. *If I must* for fuck's sake, very sorry to have interrupted your hectic fucking schedule, but it's not a frigging game. He replaced the phone in its holder and fired up the engine.

CHAPTER 63

Monday 9:30 a.m.

Tight blue distressed jeans and a white top. Her neck was the colour of milk chocolate, and tapered to where the top few buttons of the blouse were unfastened. Chad, sitting at ninety degrees to her, caught a tantalising glimpse of the swell of her breasts under the shirt. Was he becoming a perv, he thought? Just stop it.

Jas paused the tape from the Garden Centre. "Show me again, and if I can't see anything, then you'll have to point it out."

"Okay."

On the screen, Bannister was standing at the end of a table full of plants, Murphy was next to him and, at the other end of the table, was Andy Huxton. They moved around the table like sequence dancers until Murphy and Bannister moved out of sight.

"What?" she said. "I don't get it, what am I meant to see, or what can you see that I can't?"

"Forget Murphy for the moment," said Chad. "Focus on Huxton. What's he doing?"

"He's not doing anything."

"What's he looking at?"

"The plants, he's looking at the bloody plants."

"Exactly," said Chad.

"You've lost me. What's your point?"

"Remember when we interviewed him, and he said he'd been to the Garden Centre to buy plants for his balcony? Maybe he was telling the truth. It's clear that he doesn't recognise Murphy, and that Murphy doesn't recognise him. He's simply shopping."

"What does that prove?"

"It shows that someone else wanted them to be on CCTV together, to make sure we linked Huxton to Murphy. That could only be Bannister."

Jas held her hand up. "Hold on, how could Bannister have known when Andy Huxton was going to the Garden Centre? That's ludicrous." She paused. "Unless they know each other I suppose."

"Yep, unless they know each other. But if they do, how come Andy Huxton doesn't acknowledge Bannister, they're only a couple of feet apart, and he looks straight through him?" Chad pointed at the screen, showing Huxton looking at Bannister.

"None of this makes sense," said Jas, "and the more I watch the less I understand."

"Which brings me on to the next bit," said Chad. "This has been bugging me. I've thought there was something wrong with it, but couldn't work out what, until this morning. Have a look." Bannister stretching, grasping at the top shelf, his hoody and tee-shirt had ridden up exposing his stomach.

Jas' eyes opened wide and she turned to Chad. "What the juice?" she said. "That's barmy."

Chad swivelled in his seat. "I know, how do you explain that?"

"That's white skin, right?" she asked.

"Looks like it to me. He's a person of colour, with what appears to be a white stomach. I've no idea how that happens."

CHAPTER 64

Monday noon.

Chad sat in his usual perch at the back of the room. He slipped another Fentanyl, fourth already, and not even lunchtime. He was popping them like there was no tomorrow. Maybe, he thought, because there was no tomorrow as far as those babies were concerned. The foil crinkled in his pocket. The idea of never taking another scared the shit out of him. What if the acupuncture didn't work and he was left with the pain and some second-rate Fentanyl substitute that didn't work? But what if it did work and he got rid of the pain and the blackouts, how good would that be? Anyway, dead within six months if he didn't stop was a sobering thought, and one that brooked no argument. The Doctor's tomorrow, what the fuck would he have to say?

"You've got that foggy look in your eyes like you're somewhere else," said Jas.

"Sorry, I was miles away."

"I got the information through, on cosh assaults," she said.

"Oh, right, anything interesting?"

"Maybe. There's been one victim, ten days ago. A guy called Nick O'Connor gets off the last bus and is walking to his apartment in Meanwood when he's whacked from behind. The wounds, and bruising, an exact match for our guys. No witnesses and nothing more to go on. The guy's in a coma, and they're not hopeful of a recovery."

"Mm, doesn't give us much does it? But the timing is interesting, ten days ago would have been the day after Huxton was kidnapped."

Lee interrupted the buzz of conversations around the room. "Thanks everyone, let's crack on. From what I've been hearing it looks like we'll be able to close this off, but Joe, take us through what came in over the weekend."

Okay," said Joe, "we've had the ballistics report. The Makarov used by Andy Huxton to shoot himself was also used to shoot Nichols, Holding, and John Huxton. The bullet recovered from the Range Rover was a 9mm parabellum same as the rest, and, Andy Huxton, as you know was found dead holding the Makarov. Powder burns are evident on Huxton's hand and the trajectory of the bullet that killed Huxton supports our suicide theory. That's it, Boss."

"Thanks, Joe, that's about as conclusive a ballistics report as we could get. Luke, bring us up to speed on the financial stuff Nichols and Holding were working on before their deaths."

Luke Deakin marched to the front, chest out, looking very pleased with himself.

'Thanks, Boss. We've spent the weekend at Holding's offices, he's the accountant, and we had Iqbal with us," he nodded to a young guy in a smart blue suit, standing next to Joe. "For those of you that don't know him, Iqbal is also a Forensic Accountant, specialising in the detailed examination of accounts, accounting practises, and a whole range of other numbers related stuff, that I don't understand."

He laughed, a signal to the rest of the team to expect good news. "According to Iqbal, the whole thing was straightforward. Maybe you want to talk us through it?" Luke held out his arm, gesturing for the young man to take the floor.

Iqbal walked with the awkward manner of a man out of his comfort zone. Give him an Excel spreadsheet, he would be fine. People, maybe not.

"Okay," Iqbal began, "to be fair, Holding had made no effort to conceal the transaction. He'd been meticulous in filing and cross-referencing the movements of cash, from one account to another, which made things plain sailing for me. The day before the shooting, Holding had transferred nine million pounds from four of John Huxton's business accounts and placed the cash into an escrow account. That is an account specifically set up to hold monies before a transaction takes place. Last Thursday morning, at 8:00 a.m, the nine million was transferred to an account belonging to a shell company. One signatory on the account of the shell company was Andrew Huxton, but that's not to say there aren't other hidden signatories we can't trace. Now, without going into too much detail because it gets complicated from here, there are thousands of subsidiary companies attached to the shell, but they're in different countries and different tax jurisdictions so tracing the money through those will take months, maybe years. But before the cash was distributed into the subsids, four separate payments of two hundred and fifty thousand pounds were made to four charities, who work with the victims of child abuse. I contacted them and none were expecting any such donation." Iqbal paused for breath. "It may never be possible to trace where the remaining eight million has gone, but it no longer sits in the holding company to which it was transferred, that's empty."

Iqbal gave a nod to Luke and returned to his position by the door.

"Looks like a ransom payment to me," said Joe.

"Yes, I can't see how it could be anything else. So, let's check what we know for certain," said Lee. He picked up a marker pen and began to write on the wipe board on the wall at the front of the office. "Ballistics have confirmed the same gun killed everyone except Murphy. Andy Huxton was found holding that gun and his prints are on the empty magazine found in the car. The tyre tracks at Potto match the mud from his Range Rover. Andy Huxton was taught by Murphy and cash has been paid to child abuse charities, sanctioned by a company of which Huxton is an authorised signatory. Did I miss anything?"

There were general murmurings from the team, but no one spoke.

"Well, guys, I think this is rock solid, we haven't got motive but the evidence is conclusive, no doubt about that. Maybe we'll get a better idea of motive as we gather evidence of Huxton's business dealings and Murphy's abuse of kids. But as of now, well done everyone."

Neat and fucking tidy, Chad thought. There's too much that doesn't add up, but you can't argue with a ballistics report and five dead bodies he supposed. If he was Lee, he'd be closing it off as well.

Lee held up a hand. "However, before I see the Chief Super to put the official stamp on this, I want to check we haven't missed anything. There have been loads of anomalies which we should try and explain so nothing comes back to haunt us down the track. The last thing any of us needs is this to be the subject of some frigging documentary in a couple of years." A murmuring went around the group. "I want Chad to play devil's advocate for us and lead us through the inconsistencies. Let's see if there's anything that warrants further investigation. Chad, what do you think, can you walk us through the bits and pieces that don't quite add up?"

Fair play, mate, Chad thought, Lee had been thorough and at least hadn't ignored the inconsistencies. His phone vibrated. Twitter, it would have to wait, even death threats had to join the queue. "No getting away from it, the evidence points to Andy Huxton. But, as Lee said, several things are odd, and as they say, if it looks too good to be true, it probably is." He caught Jas' eye and she smiled. "Let's review these anomalies in chronological order, and see if they tell us anything."

A voice was in his head, a half-forgotten tutor. Be concise, succinct and clear. Don't waffle. He walked to the only clean wipe board and listed numbers one to four in a line down the board. "Before we deal with the murders, let's look at the kidnappings. Start with John Huxton. Four things for you to consider. Our Mr Organised forgets his fob but somehow manages to get himself outside the car park, without being seen on CCTV exiting the building. How does he manage that?" *How does he exit the building?* He wrote against the number one.

Joe shrugged.

Chad continued. "After George Hampsthwaite lets him into the car park, he spends five minutes inside before driving out. What is he doing in there, when he can't get back to his apartment without going to security?" *Five minutes in the car park unaccounted?* Inked against number two.

Third, he spoke as he wrote, "*Where are his fob and tennis gear now?* Not in his apartment, we know that. But it gets weirder. Jas would you mind rolling the CCTV please?"

"Sure." She connected her laptop to the screen and paused the CCTV with John Huxton in front of Hampsthwaite's cabin. "There you go."

"Thanks. Okay, you're all familiar with this, yeah?"

"Yes, I think we are," replied Lee.

Chad opened the laptop holding the photos of John Huxton's body laid out on the tarpaulin at Potto. In one, Huxton's left arm was visible and he clicked on it, then split the screen, so that on the left, the team had Huxton at Hampsthwaite's cabin, and on the right, the photograph from the crime scene. "So, spot the difference," said Chad. He scanned the team as all eyes flicked from one shot to the other.

"Come on, Chad, put us out of our misery, what are we looking for?" said Lee.

"You can see in the photograph at Potto, that Huxton is wearing his watch, and has a ring on his little finger." He pointed to them on the screen. "Now, look at him driving. Where are they?"

The team leaned towards the screen to get a better view.

"Well, bugger me, that's weird," said Luke.

"Agreed," said Chad. "Weird." *Why wasn't he wearing his watch and ring?* He wrote. So that's the four anomalies you guys need to get your heads around and, if possible, get answers for." His mouth was dry, the pills always had that effect. He poured himself some water. "Right, there's also a couple of other things for you to consider. He turned back to the board and wrote the word Potto which he underlined. He continued to talk as he wrote. "*Why did Andy Huxton drive his car to Potto and leave tyre tracks for us to find?*" He faced the team. "Maybe in the heat of things he just made a mistake, but that's not in keeping with everything else." Chad watched the reactions closely. How they dealt with all this, he thought, would be very revealing. "Think about it." He said. The second issue is this. He wrote *Porsche* on the board. "Under what circumstances do Holding and Nichols come to be in the Porsche with the two kidnap victims, dead in the boot? How did they get there? Where did they get the car? All rhetorical questions guys, but their families will want answers." As a hubbub of conversations arose Chad finalised the notes on the board.

Like a cricket ball getting old, a little bit of shine had come off their certainties. "Okay, moving on to the kidnapping of Murphy. Lots of weird shit here, too. First, who is Nicholson? Why is he necessary to the kidnapping?" Silence. "Secondly, who is Bannister? What's happened to him? Why can you find no trace of him? Is he an accomplice? If so, how is he known to Andy Huxton? Just think about that while I fire up the CCTV." Andy Huxton, Murphy, and Bannister were in the shot, looking at the plants. "Right, have a look at this. It's not so much what you do see that's important, as what you don't see." He played the tape. "Anybody?" he asked. The silence held a tension, everyone staring at the screen.

"Nope," said Joe, "I didn't see anything."

"I'm going to show it frame by frame, and tell me if Andy Huxton, or Murphy, show that they recognise each other." The tape inched forward in slow motion. "I'll take that as a no. Now look at Bannister, what's he doing?"

"He's staring at Andy Huxton," said Lee.

"And what about Huxton?" The tape moved forward a couple of frames to show Huxton looking straight at Bannister. "Any recognition there?" Silence, they could see there wasn't. "I'd argue that our common denominator is Bannister. The tape shows he recognises Huxton and he obviously knows Murphy, but neither Murphy nor Huxton knows the other, that's clear from the tape. Your case is that Huxton killed Murphy in revenge for abuse, right? So, if he's going to kill him a few days later how come he doesn't recognise him here? Andy Huxton told us he's been to the Garden Centre to buy plants, remember?" asked Chad. Joe nodded. "Well, you guys need to consider, whether that is just what he was doing and that Bannister staged the meeting for our benefit. If so, how did Bannister know that Huxton was going to be at the Garden Centre, at that time?" The team stayed silent. More shine off. "Okay, and the last, and the weirdest piece of the whole thing." Bannister, stretching for the plant. Chad ran the tape at normal speed a couple of times. "Anybody see anything?"

"Nope," said Luke.

Chad paused the tape. "Now?" he asked

"That's still a big no from me," said, Luke.

Chad picked up a pen and pointed at the still. "So, you tell me, guys, how does a black guy have a white stomach?"

He stood back from the board. Watching the detectives. Great song. And better than the debate going on Chad thought. They'd convinced themselves black was white. Or in this case, white was black. Bannister's stomach colour was a technical fault on the CCTV which they'd get the IT boys to look at. The tyre tracks were simple. Huxton fucked up. So much for keeping an open mind. Joe's voice rose above the hubbub.

"Look, it's clear that Chad has highlighted lots of issues. The question is, what can we do in practice to resolve any of them? Not much, unless we can find Bannister. He could be dead if he was in cahoots with Huxton. We can't explain Huxton's tyres, or Nichols and Holding driving the Porsche. Yes, it's weird, but even if we put the whole team on it, I don't think we'd get answers."

Chad couldn't disagree.

"There's one thing we can do," said Jas. "A guy called Nick O'Connor was assaulted in Meanwood a week or so ago. The weapon used was a cosh, and the head wounds were an identical match for the wounds suffered by Huxton and Murphy. We can dig into O'Connor and see if he ties in anywhere."

"Okay," said Lee, "let's wrap things up. Joe, I want you to go back to the Bishop and shake his tree. We now know a ransom was paid for Huxton, so was one paid for Murphy? Also, dig again and find out everything you can about Nicholson and Bannister. Jas, follow the O'Connor lead and let us know where that takes you. One final thing, a bit sensitive but, Chad, are you okay if I run through the basics of this?"

Chad nodded. They'd have to know at some point, so it may as well be now.

"Chad has been receiving tweets from an unknown troll. In the space of a fortnight, he's escalated from some low-key slagging off to death threats. Some content links this troll to the murders so I'm taking them seriously. On several occasions, he seems to know Chad's whereabouts. Keep this front and centre and watch each other's backs. If Bannister or Nicholson is out there, then they might be responsible."

The talk of Twitter reminded Chad he hadn't read the latest.

@therealchadhilton Nearly time to put you out of your misery, loser. Hope you've said your goodbyes. #napoleoncalling

It pinged again. A text, Freddie.

Looks like we're on tonight bro. Our guy is meeting Errol at 9:00 p.m. tonight at Unit 12 on the Whitehall Road Industrial Estate.

Tell Lee, let me know how he's going to play it. I'm going to be there whatever. This guy is pissing me off.

No-one needed Freddie going solo, Chad thought, that spelled trouble. He'd better show this to Lee.

Lee read the tweet first and then the message from Freddie. "Joe, Luke, here please." Lee showed them the message. "The troll is the guy mentioned meeting at 9:00 p.m., so, get a couple of uniforms down there and we'll meet on Whitehall Road outside the estate at 8:45 p.m. Let's nail this guy."

CHAPTER 65

Monday 7:00 p.m.

Errol read the message from his punter for the tenth time. It had come in as he was eating his KFC at lunchtime but the sense of unease had stayed with him all day.

So, fuckwit…

"Fuckwit, like, who's he calling fuckwit?"

"*…you'd better have the goods. Meet me tonight at 8:00 p.m., back of unit 12, Whitehall Industrial Estate. I see anyone with you, you die.*"

"Whitehall Industrial Estate?" Errol shouted, "I mean, where the fuck is that?" He checked Google Maps again, but the location got no closer, no matter how many times he checked. Fucking hell, it wasn't anywhere near Harehills. He only did shit in Harehills. Taxi, he'd get a taxi. But how did he get out of there, if anything went down? That's why he only did Harehills, and why he had a fucking bike. The air filled with the clawing smoke of the spliff. What the fuck? He'd told Freddie the meet was at 9:00 p.m. So, maybe he could stick around and wait for him to come, explain the shit to him, and then get a lift back to Harehills, he'd be bound to have brought some of the boys, and they'd have wheels, right? Might even get a ride in the Roller. He was getting top dollar for the gear, the dude didn't quibble about the price, so Freddie wouldn't be too pissed with him. Yeah, fuck it, he'd do this shit, any trouble, he'd cut the fucker and run.

CHAPTER 66

Monday 8:00 p.m.

Always choose the terrain you want to fight on. I'd learned that years ago at school. Julius Caesar said it and Napoleon followed it. If it was good enough for them it was good enough for me. It's a calculated risk, bringing Errol to the Industrial Estate, but worth it. My home patch, better than playing away in Harehills. The little shit will be like a fish out of water. I look out of the window of the mezzanine floor of the warehouse which gives a clear view of the main road and Unit 12. There's one entrance and exit from the main road, so covering it is easy. It's what had attracted me in the first place. That fucker Freddie will come, Errol will have told him. His life wouldn't be worth living otherwise. So, execute the plan, no hanging around. Time to up your game, fella, which is good, gets you in the right frame of mind for the next two. Headlights turn into the estate and a taxi pulls up on the curb at the entrance to the estate. Errol gets out, looks around, and then starts walking. Unit 12 lies at the furthest end of the second cul-de-sac on the left. The road is quiet, no sign of anyone else, yet. The walk from the main road to Unit 12 is one hundred and fifty yards and takes two minutes to walk if you know where you're going. I know I've paced it. But for those who don't, like Errol, it'll take three minutes. I time my route in my head. Thirty seconds to unit 12 from here, thirty seconds back means that if Jackson hasn't arrived by the time Errol gets to unit 12, I have four minutes to get there get the job done and get back. No problem. Let's go. Showtime.

* * *

Errol is jigging from one foot to the other. A funny sort of bouncing-on-the-spot motion. He's nervous. Good. The road is still quiet, nothing, no-one. Maybe Errol's more of an idiot than I thought and hasn't told Freddie. Maybe. "Errol," I keep my voice just above a whisper. It still makes Errol, jump.

"Hey, bro, where are you? I can't see you."

"I'm here. Walk across, and don't do anything stupid."

Errol walks out of the gloom towards me, peering into the shadows. "Where, man? Oh, I see you, what are you standing there for? There ain't no-one here, 'cept us."

"Are you sure you haven't told your boss?"

"No, man, I swear."

"Right, let me see what you've got for me."

Errol's hand is shaking as he shows me the products. Anxious, stressed. Good. I inspect the foil strips. Good stuff.

"Like I told you, bro, I can get whatever you want. You want more of that, just let me know."

"What about the coke?"

"Oh, yeah, man, I nearly forgot." Errol recovers a clear plastic pouch from his jeans, the white powder is translucent in the gloom. "You get through some of this shit man, that's for sure."

"Who the fuck asked you?"

"Sorry, bro, just saying."

Thirty seconds left. "Okay, how much did we agree on? Seven hundred was it?"

"Yeah, man, seven hundred."

I undo the ties on my backpack, drop in the strips and the coke and pull out a wad of cash. Fifteen seconds.

"You'd better count it," I say.

Errol begins counting, eyes only on the cash. No thought to the pistol sliding out of the backpack. I'd banked on that, and as usual I'm right. Ten seconds. "Errol,"

Errol looks up and stares. "What the fuck?"

Time up. Phut, phut. Errol's legs buckle and he collapses backwards onto the tarmac, still grasping the cash.

"I'll have that, thank you," I take the cash and push it into the backpack. One more for luck. Headshot. All over.

* * *

I could get used to the view from here. I'm standing by the windows of my temporary home, which has a great view of the Industrial Estate. How the other one percent live eh? Yeah, well I'm one of them now. Anyway, no time for admiring the scenery, what the fuck is happening down there?

I check the time, 8:44 p.m. A black BMW, four by four, pulls up outside the entrance to the industrial estate and a tall guy in a suit emerges from the driver's side. Who the fuck is this? Doesn't look over the top enough for Jackson. Police maybe? He looks like a plod. Shit, what are they doing here? The passenger door opens and a smaller man supporting himself on what looks like a cane climbs out. "Chad, fucking, Hilton," Why the hell has he brought the law? I thought it would be just him and Jackson? The pair make their way to the estate directory sign and then peer in the direction of Unit 12. A flash of light from the main road draws my attention.

"I was right, here comes Freddie Jackson. Flash git, he's come in that poncey roller he drives"

I watch the Rolls Royce pull up then see two other cars rolling in behind. Three enormous black guys get out of each. "They've come mob-handed, that's for sure. Just a teeny bit late."

Freddie Jackson walks over to the guy with Chad Hilton, who points towards Unit 12, then looks at his watch, and back down Whitehall Road.

"What the fuck? Jackson is working with the cops? How does that happen?"

The group start walking towards the cul-de-sac, I can see the light from the street lamps gleaming off Jackson's head and his hired muscle following a couple of paces behind. They're checking around them as they walk. "Too late I'm afraid guys." More headlights turn into the estate. Two squad cars. "Jesus, the cavalry as well."

Hilton and co stand in front of the unit, looking around, seeing nothing, then they move around to the rear of the building. Shame, I was enjoying the hide and seek. Down below all hell breaks loose. Phones are coming out, blue lights and sirens coming on, and the muscle is running backwards and forwards before the tall guy has a word with Freddie Jackson, and he rounds up his men.

"Ha, how funny's that? Talk about headless chickens." An ambulance arrives. Hilton, Jackson and the tall cop stand in a huddle.

"Wonder what they're saying? Are they onto me? Why are they here together? I don't get it." There's a nagging worry that's creeping around my brain. But, whatever. Adapt, innovate and push on. Let's finish this, bring the plans forward a day or two."

Chad Hilton turns and looks up, it seems like he's staring straight at me.

"Tomorrow, mate," I raise the glass of wine in my hand "Your turn tomorrow."

CHAPTER 67

Monday 11:45 p.m.

He'd overdone it this time, Chad thought. The need to sleep was overwhelming, fighting it impossible. His heart rate had slowed. "Any slower it'll fucking stop," Chad muttered. He'd had the eighth pill just after they'd found Errol, and knew as soon as the tablet started to take effect that he'd made a huge mistake. When taking seven every day had become the norm, he understood that he was delivering on a self-fulfilling prophecy, and here he was, checking out. Somehow, Freddie had bundled him into the roller but he hadn't been able to speak in the car, although Freddie slapped his cheeks. From somewhere faint and indistinct he listened to a soundtrack of Freddie delivering a verbal rant interspersed with screams of abuse at whoever had shot Errol. The out-of-body feelings remained after Freddie and someone else had stripped him and put him to bed. They'd tried to make him sit up but gave up and let him fall onto the pillows. His fingernails were pale blue as he clasped the sheet and he knew it was different this time. He'd passed out before after seven, but now after eight he was still conscious, which was somehow more serious. As if both mind and body had crossed an invisible line, and were wandering away, leaving him.

His body seemed to be saying, "Your problem, pal, not ours, we're off." He tried to re-connect but couldn't. He was slipping, he sensed the darkness. Faces were floating past. Ephemeral, spectral. They were wearing masks. Why masks?

CHAPTER 68

Tuesday 8:05 a.m.

Chad opened his eyes. The ceiling looked familiar. He allowed the thought to linger. Unless the afterlife furnished its rooms with crystal chandeliers, then he was alive. His mind adjusted to the fact, then he found his voice.

"You are a fucking idiot! You can't be trusted with those fucking things. You'll tell the doctor the truth today, you fucking tool." Anger gave way to a feeling he didn't recognise, or at least, one he hadn't been in touch with for some time. Elation. He was alive. "Why do you have to jump eh? Lots of people stand on the edge, then walk back, but not you, no, you fucking jump. Fucking idiot. No more. Ever." He turned and looked at his phone. 8:07 a.m. Two messages.

Lee. "*Call me when you get this.*"

Freddie. "*I need to know you're alive. Call, bro.*"

He sent a text to both. "*All okay will call soon.*"

The events of the previous evening began to resurface. Errol on his back staring at the sky, a wistful smile on his lips. Melancholy, rather than fear. Like the outcome was not desired but expected. Freddie had blamed himself, he shouldn't have let Errol go off the patch. He was only a kid and he shouldn't have let it happen.

Freddie had checked the last message he'd received from Errol, confirming that the meet was at 9:00 p.m. The first pathologist on the scene had said he thought death had occurred nearer to 8:00 p.m. Why had Errol said 9:00 p.m. when he meant 8:00 p.m.?

It was clear to him that the guy who shot Errol was the same nut job sending the tweets. Keep your wits about you, he thought, till they've caught him; he's done it once so don't become number two. There was something else bugging him, and he tried to release the idea that was nagging away, somewhere in his brain. He eased his legs out of the bed and sat on the edge. What was it? Something he'd thought of last night? Masks, that was it. Picking up his iPad he opened Google and keyed 'Masks used in crimes' into the search engine.

"Well, fuck me," he muttered.

CHAPTER 69

Tuesday 9:00 a.m.

Lee answered the call. "Hi, mate, are you okay, did Freddie get you home safe?"

"Yeah, I'm fine, thanks. Look, I've got some ideas that I think hang together."

"Well, just hold on," said Lee, "I'm keeping the Huxton case open. Ballistics have confirmed that the ammo used on the kid last night was the same as the others. No spent cartridge cases, the shooter must have picked them up. Not conclusive without a weapon, but add it to the shot pattern, two to the chest, and one to the head and the MO's the same. If you've got ideas on how these are all linked, drop it on an email to me, cos I've got to jump into a meeting now. Oh, by the way, we need to keep you and Angie safe 'till we nail this psycho, so I'm talking to the Chief Super in an hour to get you both some protection."

"Okay, thanks, and yes I'll pop my ideas on an email. Can I ask a favour?" said Chad

"Yeah, mate, fire away."

"I've got a doctor's appointment at midday, wondered if Jas could pick me up afterwards, and get me across to the team meeting this afternoon. I don't like to ask, but I'm going to be coming off the Fentanyl today, so just a little anxious about driving."

"Hey, buddy, delighted to hear that. Yeah, Jas is over Harrogate way this morning, so, I'll get her to pick you up."

"That's great, tell her I'll meet her at 12:30 p.m at the train station, it's easier for her to park there."

"Will do. See you later. Oh, shit, I nearly forgot, our artist has arranged to meet Ange on Wednesday so we should be able to make some headway after that. I'll get the photofit onto Look North."

"Thank fuck for that, I thought she might stall, but that's good news. Someone must recognise him."

"Let's hope so, see you later."

* * *

Chad's phone vibrated. Jas. "Hey, how are you? Did Lee get hold of you?"

"He did. I understand that as well as a highly trained police officer, I'm now your fucking chauffeur? Only joking. I'm in Bramhope this morning, so Harrogate's not a million miles out of my way. Going to the doctor's, I hear?"

"Yeah, I'm starting my treatment this week, and the acupuncture doctor says that I need to get weaned off this shit. There are other drugs they can give me that lessen the withdrawal symptoms, but I'm not expecting life's going to be a lot of fun for a few weeks."

"For the best though, in the long run. Remember what I told you about my Nan. How are you feeling about what went down last night? A shocker, wasn't it?"

"Yeah, the poor kid. I mean, I know selling drugs is a risky occupation, but to get mown down like that. Shit, just awful."

"How's your mate Freddie taking it?"

"Not well. I spoke to him a few minutes ago. He's outraged. Not sure if the bloke who's done this knows what it's like to get on the wrong side of Freddie, but trust me, it's a place you don't want to be."

"Mmm, I can imagine. You'll need to have a word with him and calm him down. Taking the law into his own hands and exacting some sort of retribution is going to land him behind bars for a long stretch, and I know loads of coppers who would just love that" She paused. "Right, I'm picking you up at 12:30 p.m. at Harrogate train station, yeah?"

"Yeah, thanks, I've got lots to do before then. I think I'm beginning to understand how everything links together, and I've told Lee I'll pop it in an email for him."

"Cool, sounds interesting. By the way, I found out a bit more about Nick O'Connor, the guy that got coshed. Don't know if it helps much but, anyway, he lives alone in a flat in Meanwood. Thirty-five years old, he worked at the Yorkshire Playhouse."

Chad felt his heart skip a beat. "Yorkshire Playhouse? What did he do there? No, don't tell me, let me guess. He worked in makeup?"

"How the fuck did you know that?" said Jas.

"It just fits with the other stuff. I'll fill you in when I see you."

"Okay, sounds very mysterious though. Good luck with the doctor. See you later. Bye."

"Now, let's try and write all this down so it makes sense," he murmured and began to type.

CHAPTER 70

Tuesday 10:30 a.m.

Odd Job held the door of the Rolls Royce open and Freddie, climbing out, looked up and down Harehills Avenue. There were fifteen back-to-back red-brick terraced houses on the street. He cast an appraising eye over his properties. Some better kept than others, he noted. He charged peppercorn rents to the occupants because they were all friends or relatives of his. Having eyes and ears on the street also helped. Odd Job had parked in front of number seventeen. Fuck, this was terrible. Eighteen years old for fuck's sake and taken out like he's been executed. Freddie walked through the gateway and up the three stone steps to the door. It opened before he could knock.

"Oh, Freddie, Freddie Jackson, God bless you for coming."

The distraught figure standing in the doorway opened her arms wide. Freddie wrapped Errol's mum in a long embrace and whispered to her. "I'm so sorry, Veronica, so sorry. I should have taken more care of your boy and for that, may God forgive me. But I will find who did this to him, and I will make sure that he pays. God will also make him pay, in the next life."

He felt Veronica squeeze tighter, holding him in, before he released her arms, and guided her inside.

* * *

He closed the door behind him, the misery of Veronica's wailing following him outside and growing louder as her sisters and cousins joined in. Shit, that was awful. Loyalty was top of his value set and it was good for the community, he thought, to let them see him here, to let them see he cared. Odd Job held the rear door open.

"Get everyone to the club, today 1:00 p.m., no absentees, no excuses."

Odd Job nodded. "Wait. I need to make a call." The anger he'd felt last night hadn't abated, and he began to pace. The shimmer of curtains up and down Harehills Avenue told of watching eyes. Loyalty was a two-way street. "Shit, I need to do this," he scrolled through his contacts, found the name he wanted, took a deep breath and dialled.

"Freddie?"

"Hi Lee, is now a good time, can you talk?"

"Yes," said Lee, "just let me find a room."

Footsteps, a door opening and closing, then Lee came back on.

"Hi, yes I can talk freely now. Are you okay, has something happened?"

"No, bro, but there's something that's come my way, that I think you need to know."

"Okay, what's that?"

Freddie paused. A friend of Chad or not, Lee was still a cop. "So, the word from the street is that the goods Errol's punter bought last night were way out of the ordinary. Apart from nearly five grams of cocaine, which I'm told costs around four large ones, this dude bought two strips of Fentanyl. Each strip has ten tablets. He also bought one strip of eight Rohypnol tablets. Some serious drugs there, bro, and some serious cash. Now, am I right to take it you know about Chad and Fentanyl?"

"Yeah, he didn't think I knew but it was pretty obvious. He's going to the doctor's today to start coming off them."

"Yep, that's right, but in the last few weeks, he's been taking way more than he should. Now, I'm telling you this because we go way back and you, like me, are his friend. Our paths in life may have taken different directions…" He paused. He was beginning to sound evangelical, he thought, cut that *life direction* shit out.

"But I'm also telling you this because you're a cop. We know this dude has been threatening Chad, and Angie, so those specific drugs may be important. I just felt you need to know."

"Thanks, Freddie. I'm organising some protection for them both, but I'm not sure what good that will do. I mean, shit, he's going to have to be close to them if he's going to give them drugs."

"I'm organising some protection too, Lee and, with all due respect, I may be a bit closer to how this goes down than you." Freddie listened to Lee breathing down the line.

"You know about Chad and Ange splitting up?"

"Yeah, bro, I know. Gutted doesn't cut it. What're your thoughts?"

"Like you, gutted. I mean Ange has always been a bit out there, a party girl, life and soul, but I always thought she was just having a laugh. Flirting at worst. She's always been like that. I never thought she'd do anything."

"Me neither, bro. Anyhow, we can't let anything happen to either of them and we now know what this mother is capable of."

"Freddie, don't do anything stupid and don't do anything that means we end up on different sides. Make sure you call me if you or your guys hear anything." Freddie caught the threat in Lee's words. They'd been here several times over the years but never had they stood at such clearly marked demarcation lines.

"Let's be clear, Lee, this dude killed one of my boys, and there will be a price to pay for that, one way or another, but he's not going to take Chad as well, or Ange. Talk soon, bro, yeah?" Freddie waited in silence. He'd crossed the Rubicon and knew it.

"Freddie, we've known each other for years, and crossed swords a few times. But don't let that happen now, or the consequences will be different. And believe me, I won't hesitate. Understand?" Silence. "And yeah, Freddie, talk soon."

Odd Job was still holding the door. "Take me to the club."

CHAPTER 71

Tuesday 11:30 a.m.

"It makes sense to me," said Chad, re-reading his email to Lee. Fuck me, but this bastard is clever, he thought. We need to get him and get him sharpish. He stood up, holding the desk for support. He'd better call a cab to the docs, and he'd take the iPad with him, give himself some headspace while he was out, then have another read through in the car. Check he wasn't making a complete tit of myself before he sent it. The automated voice of the taxi firm asked him to press one if he wanted a cab, for as soon as possible, from his home address, or press two for pick up from the Fat Badger, his local boozer. He chuckled and pressed one. So, even the taxi firm knew he went from home to the Badger, and back again.

* * *

The lift doors opened and Chad stepped out into the ground floor reception of the doctor's surgery. There were four GP practices in the building so the place was heaving. The looks he got from other patients said *lazy bastard, young guy like that, take the bloody stairs.* Then they would turn their heads away as they saw him limp towards the exit, his cane clicking on the tiled floor.

The air outside held a hint of spring. Well, at least he'd been honest with the doc, so the guy knew what he was dealing with, Chad thought. He couldn't hide his shock at the development of the addiction and had hastily checked his notes to make sure he hadn't overprescribed. Where there's blame there's a claim. He'd been only too pleased to prescribe a substitute. Methadone. Four each day, no more. The doctor also wanted Chad to go to addiction counselling, which he agreed to do. Just the thought of giving up the Fentanyl had caused the odd panic attack, so maybe it would help. He was being counselled for everything else so why leave this out? He was pleased the doctor had been positive about the acupuncture, he'd told him that he knew of several similar cases, where that treatment had worked. In his jacket pocket was his last strip. The doctor had agreed for him to finish these today, and then start the Methadone tomorrow. Maybe the Doc had agreed that 'cos he'd told a little porky, and said there were only four left. There were seven, but hey, he could cope with that. He slipped one out of the strip and put it on his tongue. 12:15 p.m. three down, but there'd be some in his system from last night, so he might not need seven today. Anyway, last day, he thought, No more after today.

CHAPTER 72

Tuesday 12:15 p.m.

Jas looked at her phone. The Boss. "Hey, hi Boss, everything okay?"

"Are you on your way to Harrogate?" asked Lee.

He sounded stressed. "Yep, I'm just coming to Pannal, should be at the station for 12:30 p.m"

"Okay, good, don't be late."

"What's up Boss, you sound worried?"

"I spoke with Freddie Jackson an hour or so ago. He told me that the guy who shot Errol Gray was buying Fentanyl and Rohypnol so make sure you get our limping friend in your car at 12:30 p.m. and deliver him here. I've been trying to get hold of his wife, but her phone's off."

"Roger that, boss. Will do."

CHAPTER 73

Tuesday 12:27 p.m.

Chad turned onto Station Parade. Bloody hell it was quiet, he thought. Midweek he supposed, but still. More 'To Let' signs than open shops. The retail industry was up the chute but the same people buying online from Amazon would be the first to write to the Harrogate Advertiser and complain about the lack of shops in Harrogate. Crazy. He smelled cigarette smoke drifting from the small bus station where a driver leaned on a double-decker number 76 finishing a fag. Chad's knee complained by sending stabbing pains into the rest of his leg. Shouldn't have walked, still the train station was only another fifty yards or so. Out of the corner of his eye, in his peripheral vision, something moved. A sign telling him to get a meal deal at Subway was the last thing he saw on his way down. Then day became night.

* * *

The sky came into focus. Next came the pain, a deep throbbing, at the back of his head. Then, the noise. People shouting.

"Give him some air, he's coming around."

"What happened?"

"He fainted."

Another voice. "Here, give him some water."

A hand holding a bottle of water put it to his lips, saying, "Here, drink this, fella, it'll help, you've had a funny turn that's all."

Someone raised his head, the pain intensified. He opened his mouth and drank the water.

"Good, that's good. Have some more. We've called an ambulance, it's on the way, so don't worry. Lie still."

The water tasted bitter and as the last drop touched the back of his throat, he knew. His breathing slowed, everything slowed, he could feel his heart begin to shut down. And he understood. The sky receded, along with the voices. Silence now, except for his heartbeat, becoming softer, like a muffled drum, fading. He acknowledged the darkness, approaching without a sound and he recognised the end as if he'd known it all along.

CHAPTER 74

Tuesday 12:30 p.m.

Tapping her fingers on the steering wheel, Jas waited for the lights to change. Six sets in under a mile and all had been red.

"Typical, the one time I can't be late, I'm going to be. Whoever's in charge of traffic planning here needs their head looking at."

She accelerated as the lights changed and swung right onto Station Parade, but braked immediately when she saw an ambulance to her left, just past the bus station, lights flashing. Something caught her eye, on the pavement. "Oh, fuck." She pulled up behind the ambulance. Two paramedics were attending to someone on the ground. She couldn't see him but she knew it was Chad. His cane was what she'd seen, lying half on the pavement and half on the road.

"Hey, move please, police," she barked, flashing her badge, and began pushing her way through the small group of bystanders. Chad was lying on his back with an oxygen mask clamped over his nose and mouth. A tidal wave of panic overwhelmed her. She opened her mouth but couldn't speak, her eyes were fixed on Chad's face and her body was frozen in motion. A jolt of electricity through her veins brought her back. "What's happened?" she asked the paramedic leaning over him.

"Not sure, a guy here said he fainted, but he's got a wound to the back of his head, maybe happened when he fell. He's been unconscious since we got here, and I can hardly feel a pulse, so we need to get him to A and E pronto."

The paramedics placed Chad onto a stretcher, and she moved aside to give them space to lift him. "I'm coming with you, he's a colleague." She said and flashed her warrant card in front of their faces.

"Come on, then, let's get a shift on," said the paramedic.

Picking up Chad's cane and shoulder bag, she ran a couple of paces to her car leaned in and placed her police sign in the windscreen, slammed the door and locked it.

Chad's face was white and his hands were folded on his chest, but there was little sign of him breathing. One of the paramedics, who's name badge identified him as Brian, looked at Jas.

"Do you know if he was on any medication? His pulse is very slow, his breathing is shallow and those blue nails are a worry. His blood pressure is in a dangerous place, low too."

She remembered her conversation with Lee, only fifteen minutes earlier. Fuck. "Yes, he took Fentanyl to control the pain in his leg. He'd just come from seeing the doctor, he was going to stop taking them." That sounded pathetic, she thought.

Brian looked at her, then over to his colleague. "Radio that in," he said. "Fentanyl. Shit. That might explain it. But with these symptoms, I'd say he's overdosed. Right, let's get him sitting upright and awake, the worst thing we can do is leave him like this."

The second paramedic was rummaging in a waste bag. "I picked this up at the scene," he said and gave Jas an empty bottle of Harrogate Spa water. "One of the people who attended to him gave him some water."

Jas looked at the bottle. The Boss had been worried that the attacker may try and get Chad to overdose. Maybe this was it. The copper's instinct in her came to the fore. "Keep it and get it tested," said Jas. "And work on the assumption he's overdosed. By the way, the wound to the back of his head, can I see it?"

Brian moved Chad's head to the side. A long, inflamed welt ran up the side of his head past the left ear and upwards. About fifteen centimetres long and three centimetres wide. Fuck. Fuck. She found her phone out and dialled.

"Have you got him?" said Lee.

"Boss, listen, I'm in an ambulance on the way to the hospital. Chad's been hurt. It looks like he's been coshed, and they think he's overdosed. I'll stay with him and keep you posted."

"Overdosed?" Lee's voice wobbled and shook. Then anger flew down the line. "How the fuck has he done that? He's just been to the doctor." Worry, concern and a hint of desperation were evident to Jas as she held the phone to her ear. She'd never heard her Boss like that.

"We don't know. Someone gave him some water when he regained consciousness, people thought he'd fainted, but it may have been spiked. We've got the bottle to test."

"Shit, fuck, so how's this fucker got to him? Fuck. Is he okay, I mean he'll be okay, right?" Lee's panic hit her full on.

Brian had overheard. "I couldn't say, love, not yet."

"I don't know Boss, I don't know."

"Stay with him Jas, I'm on my way. I'll try and get Angie. Where are they taking him? Harrogate or the LGI?"

"Harrogate, I think."

Brian nodded. "Yeah, Harrogate."

She clicked the call off. Brian was trying to wake Chad. "Did you say his name was Chad?"

"Yes, that's right."

Brian and the other paramedic began lifting Chad into a sitting position. Brian had one hand on Chad's back and with the other he massaged Chad's face and said "Come on Chad, let's wake up now, come on, you're okay, let's sit you up."

The ambulance seemed stifling and Jas felt the cold crawl of sweat down her back. Chad's fingertips and nails were the colour of a soft summer sky. Please don't die, she thought.

CHAPTER 75

Tuesday 12:50 p.m.

"Angie, answer the goddamn phone," Lee shouted, ending the ninth call to her voicemail. The blues and twos he'd triggered moved the congestion in Leeds out of his way, give or take the odd moron who took it as a licence to drive faster. At the bottom of Scott Hall road, he dialled Freddie.

"Hey Lee, what's happening?"

"Freddie, Chad's in trouble. He's in an ambulance on his way to Harrogate District. The paramedics think he might have overdosed on Fentanyl and Jas has said he's also been coshed. Given our previous conversation it would be too much of a coincidence for it to be an accident. He's not good Freddie, Jas is with him, and I'm on my way across. I've been trying to get hold of Angie but her bloody phone's off." Silence on the other end of the line. "Freddie?"

"Yeah, bro. I heard. I'm on my way right now, I'll meet you at the hospital. I'll get my boys to try and find Angie. Lee, I'm going to find this fucker and kill him."

* * *

The generals Freddie relied on to control his empire on the streets were sitting at various tables in the cavernous underground bar. Three of them were women. They looked up as he ended the call. The urge to smash something, anything, made him clench his hands into fists the size of melons. From his playing days came the muscle memory: Control the rage, harness the anger, lead the line.

"You have one job, find the fucker who killed Errol. We find him and we deal with him. Our rules. Tool up, and get as many boys on the streets as you can. I want this fucker found. I need to go to Harrogate."

The group knew better than to ask why. Odd Job emerged out of the shadows to get the roller.

CHAPTER 76

Tuesday 1:00 p.m.

That's gone even better than I could have hoped. Planning again, it's always in the planning. Half power with the cosh did the trick, but getting the do-gooder to give him the water was inspired. No fingerprints, clean as a whistle. Hanging around for a bit was great fun. Watching it all unfold.

"And the copper that arrived was fit as a butcher's dog. Yeah, I might try and have a dabble there when this is over. I should have some Rohypnol left."

Anyway, fingers crossed, that's the end of Chad Hilton. Payback is so sweet. A car speeds past me near Harewood House heading in the other direction, lights flashing, sirens wailing. I wonder if that's his mate, the copper? Ever so slightly late. Again. I turn on the radio, T Rex, I love to Boogie. Don't I just. Ten minutes later, at the Moortown roundabout, a silver-and-black Rolls Royce with a driver the size of a house is heading towards Harrogate. "Not been a good twenty-four hours for you, Freddie lad, a dealer dead, and now your best friend. Losing your grip, fella. Wonder if someone else will start to muscle in on your turf? Not that it matters, I'll be a long way from Leeds, when I next need to buy, but that won't be a problem, every city in the world sells coke."

I focus on the job ahead. The last part of the plan, the final piece in the jigsaw, and they still haven't got a clue. I've checked her usual arrangements are in place by phoning her office. Afternoon off, they said. That's what I like, consistency, dependability. First Tuesday of every month, Spa treatments at Rudding Park, then into Leeds for a long, cocktail-fuelled lunch with her mate, Karen, at All Bar One, before catching the train back to Harrogate. This is the only part of the entire plan where I need a bit of luck. Would Angie have confided in her friend, that she and Chad had separated? Unknown. Naturally I've got a contingency if she has, but I figure that a friend she sees once a month is unlikely to be the confidante of choice. Plan A depends on Karen being unaware. Angie had also told me, back then, that Chad didn't know about her Tuesday sessions, that it was a girly thing and everyone needed a secret. Well, I, for one, am delighted she keeps her secrets.

* * *

Executing the plan hinges on timing. But I pride myself that timing is another of my strong suits. The one-way system takes me on two full circuits before the parking space I want becomes available. Twenty or so paces from the bar but close enough to get her to the car without carrying her, which might attract unwanted interference from some do-gooding pedestrian or worse. Paying for two hours at the meter on Greek Street, I'm aware that days later when the cops check the city centre CCTV cameras for clues, they'll see me, but I couldn't give a shit, they'll know who I am by then anyway, and I'll be long gone. I've been several steps ahead of them all along. Bumper-to-bumper traffic on East Parade pollutes what little clean air there is, as I make sure the passenger seat is as far back as it will go. Keeping my head down I walk past the bar a couple of times with my phone pressed to my ear. Greek Street is packed with lunchtime punters and the inevitable hen party. Don't they have any work to do? Still, it all helps me remain unnoticed. Nerves are causing a twittering in my stomach. No problem. Sometimes a plan needs a high-risk solution and this is one such, but knowing it doesn't make it easier. I've considered alternative solutions but none has the same risk-to-reward ratio like this one. The windows of the bar look out onto the street and from where I am, afford a good view of the inside. On the third walk past, I spot them. It's as she turns to look towards the bar that I see her. They're sitting at a table, maybe twenty feet from the bar, but adjacent to it. Karen has her back to the wall and can see the whole bar. Angie is facing her so won't be able to see anyone behind her. That has advantages in my plan. Okay, let's do this.

There's a reasonable lunchtime crowd of suits and skirts, milling around the bar and most of the tables are taken. So far so good. A table is free at the opposite end of the bar from Angie and the menu, a large printed affair, provides ample cover. The opportunity presents itself sooner than expected. Karen squeezes herself out of her seat. She'll no doubt describe herself as voluptuous. To me she's just fat. She chats to the barman and then points towards the ladies' toilets. The guy smiles and nods. Shielding my face with the menu in case Angie turns around, I stroll to the spot that Karen has just left. "Can I grab a Diet Coke when you get a minute, please?" I ask the barman.

"Sure, buddy, no worries. Any food with that?"

"Not for the moment thanks, I'm still choosing."

"Okay, I'll just finish these and I'll be right with you."

The tablets make a pinging sound as I pop a couple out of the foil in my trouser pocket. It seems loud to me but no-one seems to hear or notice. The barman has two cocktail glasses on the bar and is using the cocktail shaker in that preposterous 'look at me' way that waiters use. Not attracting the admiring looks he is hoping for, he stops shaking and starts pouring. Fuck, they're both having the same. Angie always drinks Margheritas, and this is not a Margherita. The tap of high heels on stairs reverberate. Karen is approaching the bar.

"Are those the two porn star martinis?" she asks.

"Indeed, they are. Not like Angie to try something different, but a change is as good as a rest, eh?" says the barman.

"We'll see if she likes it, if not, back to the usual."

Karen picks up the two drinks from the bar and makes her way back to Angie, I turn away, so that Angie would only see my back. Fuck.

"Diet Coke, sir," says the barman placing the drink in front of him.

* * *

The minutes tick by but I make my drink last, listening to Karen and Angie shrieking laughing, and having a debate about whose round it is next. The illicit smell of someone else's chips hit me, as a plate is put on the next table. Christ I could just eat those.

Karen stands and walks towards the bar.

"I'll have another porn star please, but Angie wants her usual this time. Cocktails go right through me. I need the loo again." She laughs. The barman laughs with her. Timing. The waiter puts one glass on the bar and begins to pour. I edge towards the bar and arrive as the barman turns his back and reaches towards the alcohol bottles, arranged behind him, then slip two white tablets into the Margherita.

"I'll be with you in a second, sir."

"It's okay, I can see you're still on cocktails and they take forever, I'll come back when you're finished." The crowd around the bar part to let me through. No-one says anything, so no-one has seen anything. Excellent.

Karen pants as she reaches the bar. She should lose some weight and get to the gym, I think. She exchanges more banter with the barman and then carries the drinks back to the table. Thirty minutes for the effect to hit. Let's check for any breaking news. Chad Hilton's death must surely be newsworthy. I search Google and BBC News. Nothing yet on the main channels, although the BBC in the North carried a story about an incident in Harrogate earlier. Let's drop a little tweet into the news desks.

Hearing that #therealchadhilton, has been rushed to hospital with a suspected overdose. Critical condition.

That should keep them busy.

Across the bar, Karen is leaning towards Angie with a look of concern on her face. Showtime. The Gents toilets are at the far end of the room, behind Angie. Slowing, as I approach the two women, I walk past them, stop, and look back over my shoulder. I should have been on the stage.

"Hey, Ange, I thought it was you, how're things?" I say.

Angie looks up at me with vacant eyes, the pupils' tiny pinheads, then puts her head in her hands. "Ange, are you okay?" I ask, then turn to Karen. "Is she alright?"

"I don't know, she was fine a couple of minutes ago."

Angie starts to slump sideways in her seat, and I reach down and hold her shoulder. "She doesn't look well, you'd better call Chad. Or, better still, maybe you two should call it a day, drive her home, and call Chad on the way," Her reaction will determine Plan A or Plan B.

"I…" she paused, "don't have his number, and we both came on the train."

I absorb this. If she knows they've split up she would be saying so. Good news, Luck's in. Plan A it is. "Okay, I'll ring him," I go through the pretence of scrolling and clicking, then lift the phone to my ear.

"Voicemail," I mouth at Karen. "Oh, hi Chad, it's Neil, neighbour Neil. Listen I'm in All Bar One in Leeds and have run into Ange, she's with a friend of hers," I question her with my eyes.

"Karen."

"Karen. Anyway, Ange is feeling a bit poorly, and I'm heading back to Harrogate, so will pop her home. No worries if you're not in, Jane will look after her at ours. Buzz me when you get this," I mime finishing the call. "Right, come on Ange, you'll be laughing about this tomorrow." Lifting her from the seat I drape her arm around my shoulder. She stumbles on her way towards the doors so I smile at the inquisitive faces, and give them the 'she's had a little too much' look.

Karen holds the door and Ange slumps further into me as the fresh air hits her.

"Are you certain about this? I mean I'm sure she'll feel better shortly, maybe I should just wait here with her? Karen looks at me then glances anxiously up and down the street.

"Well, of course you could do that but I'm not sure Chad will thank you if the police come along and she's slumped like this. Up to you though?"

I see the doubts and potential scenarios flit through her mind, then she says, "You're probably right, better to get her home. Do you have her address?" She's checking I am a neighbour. Fair Play.

"I should think so, I'm a neighbour remember. Ange lives at 47 Kent Road and I live at 51 Kent Road."

Karen smiles, she's relieved to hand the responsibility on, I think. Guiding Angie across the road was easier than I thought it might be. Karen opens the passenger door, and I hold onto Ange and lower her down into the seat. Her head flops to one side. "Are those her things?" I ask.

"Yes, they are." She puts the bag in the footwell. "Do you think she'll be okay?"

"I think so, was she mixing her drinks?"

"Well, yes, a little, but we haven't had much just three or four cocktails." Karen is on the defensive.

"Sometimes, drinking at lunchtime can have that effect if it's on an empty stomach." Karen's eyes speak of guilt and regret. "Okay, Karen, what's your number, and I'll send you a text when I drop her off. I'll also tell Chad to make sure to call you, and let you know she's okay." Karen reels off her number, and I type it into my phone. Angie smells of perfume and tequila as I stretch across her and fasten the seat belt.

"Right, I'll be off. Don't worry, she'll be fine." I wave out of the window as I indicate, and pull away from the kerb. Karen is standing, looking lost, in the middle of the road.

CHAPTER 77

Tuesday 3:00 p.m.

Impotent, Lee thought. That's how it feels waiting for someone else to feed me information. Waiting for someone else to determine how the next part of my life is going to play out. Impotent. The waiting room was gloomy. Ten years of austerity's knackered any hope of a refurb in here. Christ, we are a tiny bloody country but the NHS is the fourth largest employer in the world, and someone's decided to put photos of most of them on the wall of the waiting room in Harrogate District Hospital. Large jolly people in uniforms and smug-looking executives.

Jas scrolled through her phone while Freddie paced the floor, barking instructions at those foolish enough to call him. Snarling menace then gives way to charm personified with the nursing staff. Lee had to hand it to him, Freddie had charisma. Still nothing from Angie. Fuck. He checked his emails and scrolled through to see if any demanded immediate attention. None did. Hang on, Chad said he was going to send me an email. Reckoned he's sussed the whole thing. Where's that? He keyed Chad Hilton into the search box, but the most recent email from Chad had been from two days previously. He nudged Jas. "Chad was meant to be sending me an email, do you know if he did?"

Jas looked up. "I don't know if he sent it, but I know he was doing it. He told me earlier that he reckoned he'd figured the whole thing out and was going to type it up and send it to you. Maybe there's something in here?" She picked up Chad's shoulder bag which lay next to his cane.

"Armani, I mean come on, who has an Armani shoulder bag and works for the cops? Only Chad," said Lee. Inside were an iPad, a pen and a pair of glasses. The iPad was password protected. Fuck. "Do you know the password?" he asked. Jas shook her head. Fuck.

"Try zero, nine, zero, seven," said Freddie.

The screen illuminated, then he was in. "How the hell, did you know his password?" asked Lee.

"Cos years ago, he told me that he never remembered birthdays or anniversaries, but the numbers he did remember were our shirt numbers at Leeds. I wore nine, he wore seven."

Lee smiled for the first time that day. Nothing in the Sent Items. He checked Drafts. One email with the title *'Reckon I've sussed it. Napoleon's Waterloo!'* Let's hope so, Lee thought, Let's bloody hope so. Shifting position to find some comfort on the unyielding plastic chair he began to read.

Lee. After Errol's killing, the MO used in his murder, the tweets etcetera it's crystal clear that it's improbable if not impossible for Andy Huxton to have carried out the executions and his suicide. What you've got in this document is my attempt to show how the kidnappings and murders can be explained, if the killer is someone else.

Start, at Bridgewater Place, and consider all the anomalies we had about timing, about fobs, and CCTV. We've tried to piece these together and make round pegs fit square holes until we were blue in the face. And we did all that because there's been one basic premise we've never questioned:

That it's John Huxton driving the car.

What if it wasn't him driving, but instead it was our perp disguised to look like Huxton? I know it sounds crazy but think about that, Lee. If it wasn't Huxton everything changes. An unsuspecting John Huxton would have been in his apartment so, of course, would not have appeared on the CCTV in the foyer. He would have had his fob and his tennis gear with him, ready to go to Rawdon because he hadn't cancelled the tennis match, the kidnapper had. John Huxton would leave his flat as usual, at 3:00 p.m. to drive to Rawdon, to be there for 4:00 p.m. For the attacker to know all this, he must be an acquaintance of either Andy or John Huxton. I'll come on to that in a moment. I think he approached the car park from the rear. There's a path leading from the main road and round the side of the car park I've walked it. He gets to the side door of the car park unseen, then starts waving his arms around until Hampsthwaite, lets him in. And then there's a five-minute gap between him going in and the car driving out. What happens during that time? He waits until John Huxton comes down in the lift, all his gear with him. As he reaches the car, he's coshed from behind, then maybe gagged and dumped in the boot. Boyo drives the Porsche, out of the car park and away.

Lee, looked up for a moment. Not John Huxton.

But everyone including me says it's John Huxton driving the car and, to be fair, it does look like him. I couldn't figure it out at first. Everything else fitted, but how did the perp pull that off? The idea of John Huxton being coshed in the car park added to the fact that the same happened to Murphy, led me to ask Jas to find out if there'd been any similar assaults in Leeds in the last few months. Just one, and he worked at The Yorkshire Playhouse. He was a professional stage make-up artist. His name is Nick O'Connor, and he's currently in a coma in the LGI. And guess what? He was attacked the day after John Huxton disappeared. Our guy, I believe, paid Nick O'Connor to use stage make-up and a wig to make him look like John Huxton which means he must be of similar height and stature. Tall and well put together. If you check O'Connor's bank account, my guess is you'll find a large amount of cash paid in. If it's not in his account, it'll be at his flat. Almost perfect, and had it not been for the missing watch and Pinkie ring he may have pulled that off. Classic Sherlock Holmes. Remember? 'When you have eliminated the impossible, whatever remains, however improbable, must be the truth.' With me so far? Good, right, onto the Murphy kidnapping, and Messrs Bannister and Nicholson. More smokescreen. Before I go on, come out of this email and go into Google. It's easier for you to read it than for me to explain. Key in "masks used in crimes" and read what comes up.

Lee came out of the email and went into Google as instructed. He keyed in the phrase and waited. As the page hit the screen, Lee began reading.

Silicone masks have been used in bank robberies and by people taking international flights in disguise, with suspects switching gender, ethnicity and looking decades younger or older within just a few seconds. Lee scanned further down the page and read that when shown a photograph, only one person out of one hundred questioned, thought the face they'd been shown, was a man in a mask.

"Jesus Christ," said Lee. He brought Chad's email back up.

Right, freaky isn't it? The idea that Bannister was not a black guy at all, but a white guy came to me when I was watching the CCTV from the garden centre, and we see him stretch and reveal a white stomach. How could that be? There was no logical explanation until I looked at Google, and saw the case in the States, in which a white guy uses a silicone mask to make him look like a black guy. Then, when I read that ninety-nine per cent of people were fooled by the mask, that was the clincher for me. It explains why Murphy doesn't recognise him, why Andy Huxton doesn't recognise him at the garden centre, and why we've found no trace of him since. Because he doesn't exist. Nor does Nicholson. Nicholson is the name Bannister used when he made the phone calls to Mrs Grogan. In summary, there's only one perp. One man disguised himself to look like John Huxton and the same guy then disguised himself as a black man called Bannister. One guy, Lee. Just one.

A nurse came in. Jas and Freddie stiffened. Her blue uniform rustled as she walked the length of the waiting room, and out, through a set of double doors at the back. Lee re-opened the email, took a deep breath, and carried on reading.

What he's made us do is to believe the trail he's laid for us, but it's all a smokescreen. Everything that has happened, kidnappings, murders, all of it, was designed to make us think that Andy Huxton carried out the killings, driven by revenge. Because revenge on Murphy was a believable motive, we've believed everything else. We decided that he'd killed the others out of revenge but there was no evidence for that. Why steal nine million quid and top yourself when you're about to sign a deal to sell your company? It doesn't make any sense. We have been made to dance to his tune, to follow where he takes us, and to believe everything he puts in front of us. Lee, it's all rubbish. The killer is not Andy Huxton. He was a victim, like the rest. Errol was a loose end, so were Nichols and Holding. The murderer doesn't leave loose ends. He kills them off. Here's how I think the murders went down. Murphy was Tasered, which was either an accident or not but the shock of it killed him. He was trussed up and put in the boot of the Porsche. Then I believe once he'd received confirmation that the ransom was paid, he shot Huxton and dumped him in with Murphy. He parks the Porsche somewhere and gets Nichols and Holding to drive it to Potto, no doubt telling them he'll release Huxton when they get there. He gets Andy out of the way for a few hours over lunchtime, takes his Range Rover and, after killing Nichols and Holding, parks the car back in the underground car park. Perfect.

He's had his plans in his head, stewing, probably for years, but Angie breaking things off was his call to action. Maybe the only revenge he wants is against me. Maybe he's blaming me for Angie dumping him. That was the spark for all of this. He's a clever, bitter, psychopath, hiding in plain sight. And he's driven by greed. A motive as old as crime. Money is the reason for the whole enterprise. I believe the ransom money, somehow, makes its way to him. How?

Iqbal said there may be "hidden signatories" our boy will be one. Get Iqbal to drop everything and follow that money. It will lead to the murderer. I think that the Bishop also paid a ransom. I did some snooping around on Google. Did you know that the Bishop's brother is the billionaire owner of software giant Monterey? Worth talking to him, to see if he bailed out the Catholic Church. But there's a bigger pot of cash we haven't looked at yet. Excelsior Recruitment. We know that the company was due to be sold, realising around twenty million pounds. What happens to the shares owned by Andy Huxton, and John Huxton, on their death? Whoever benefits from those, would be someone of interest to us, right? And that person must be close to one or both, of the Huxtons. Could be a motive for murder, don't you think?

Good point. What does happen to their shares? Someone must benefit. He nudged Jas. "Get onto Joe, pronto, ask him to find out what happens to the Huxtons' shares in Excelsior. Who gets them? Urgent."

Money has always been his main driver, but to make us believe that Andy Huxton was the guy behind the whole thing, he had to find something tangible, something plausible, that would lead us to that conclusion. That's where Murphy comes in. The pair are linked because Murphy taught Huxton. Murphy was a paedophile, and we have assumed that Andy Huxton was seeking revenge for abuse in his childhood. The abuse may be true, but we have no evidence for that, it's the circumstances of the murders and the supposed suicide that give the theory credibility. Once we'd accepted that revenge was Huxton's motive for killing Murphy, we simply applied the same motive, revenge, to the killing of his father. Case closed. Lee, I'll bet your mortgage that Andy Huxton and our perp were schoolmates, both taught by Murphy, and if I'm right about the shares in the business, you'll find our perp works at Excelsior Recruitment. Find the beneficiary of the shares, find where the ransom money went, and you'll find our killer. I've got to go but I'll fill you in on how I think the murders at Potto happened when I get to the office.

Lee passed the iPad to Jas. "Read that and let me know what you think," he said. "Can you stay here and call me the minute you hear anything. I'm going back to Leeds to get Iqbal finding where that ransom money went."

"No problem, boss."

Freddie was pacing like a caged tiger.

"Freddie, I've got to go but Jas is going to stay till we get news on Chad. Can you keep trying Angie's number till you get her, or put feelers out with her friends? We've got to get her somewhere safe. Give me a buzz when you reach her."

"Okay, bro. Leave it with me, we'll find her. I'm going to stay here till I know Chad's going to be okay."

CHAPTER 78

Tuesday 4:00 p.m.

Fear trampled through Lee's stomach. Christ, Chad had stayed over at his on Sunday and now he might die. Fuck. What if he didn't make it? He should have done more when he'd read those tweets. Should have got protection sorted there and then. What was he going to say to Helen and the kids, if Chad didn't pull through? Water filled his eyes, he brushed it away. And where the fuck was Ange? "Fuck!" he yelled. Desperation, tension, and anger looked back at him from the rear-view mirror. "Come on, don't let inertia take over. Stop being a rabbit in the fucking headlights. Let's do something constructive. Catch the fucker that did this." He shouted at his eyes in the mirror. Lee activated the voice recognition system in his car. "Call Joe Schmidt."

Joe answered after the first ring, "Hi Boss, how's Chad?"

"No news yet, so let's keep fingers crossed. I've asked Jas to stay at the hospital till we get an update. Look, Joe, have you found out what happens to the Huxtons' shares?"

"Give me a chance, boss, Jas only text me half an hour ago."

"Yeah, okay, sorry." Don't let your stress get to them, he thought. "But this needs to be priority one. Get onto the legal firm that Nichols worked for, they'll have set up the shareholder agreements at the outset, so it shouldn't be too difficult to get a copy. And do me a favour, Joe, tell Iqbal to meet me at the office in half an hour. Tell him it's not a request it's a fucking instruction, okay?"

"On it, Boss."

"And one more thing. Get hold of Excelsior Recruitment and find out who's in charge now that the Huxtons, aren't around. Get hold of a list of all employees, names and addresses, oh, and length of service. And don't let them try and fob you off with some GDPR shit. This is a fucking murder investigation and they'll give us any information we need."

"Right, I'll crack on with that. What time are we meeting today?"

"Team meeting at 18:30. Let's hope we've heard how Chad is, by then." Lee killed the call and asked the system to connect him to Jas. She answered before he'd heard it ring.

"Hi Boss, still no news here. I'm not sure Freddie will last much longer; I think he'll strangle someone if they don't tell us something soon."

"Well, I'm in the no news is good news camp. What did you think to Chad's email?"

"It all fits. Silicone masks, bloody hell, I'd have never thought of that. And getting made up to look like Huxton, Jesus. Crafty bastard."

"Yes, clever. By the way, can you get hold of the make-up guy O'Connor's bank account records, and let's get a warrant to get into his flat. He may have kept details of work he undertook outside the Theatre. Can you ask Freddie if he's got hold of Chad's wife yet?" There was a muffled noise, as Jas covered the phone, to talk to Freddie.

"No joy, Boss. He says he's got feelers out with all her friends. Well, with the ones he knows, anyway."

"Okay, keep me posted on Chad. Dial into the team meeting at 18:30 if you're still at the hospital. Talk later, bye."

CHAPTER 79

Tuesday 5:00 p.m.

This time Chad didn't recognise the ceiling. Was he dead then, he thought? He didn't feel dead, though. What did dead even feel like? If he was dead, it was a real pisser that the pain in his knee was still there. You'd think pain would go when you died. So, maybe I'm not dead.

Chad blinked and turned his head sideways. A drip to his right was feeding a tube attached to the back of his hand. Some sort of monitoring device stood next to the drip. This had to be a hospital room. Always been quick on the uptake, eh Chad? There was an oxygen mask over his mouth and breathing felt easy. His memory jolted into life. Lying on his back with faces peering down at him. Big faces with big features like a Caravaggio painting. A euphoric wave, swept up from his toes. He wasn't fucking dead. The door swung open with a swish and a nurse in an apron walked in, bristling with efficiency and reassurance. No better sight in the world to a man who thought he was dead.

"Oh, you're awake, great. You gave us all a fright, but you should be fine now. I'll get the doctor to come and see you in a minute or two, but let's get you sitting up."

She pressed some buttons on a handheld panel that was

attached by a wire to the bed. As the electric motor lifted the mattress, she helped him sit up then shuffled the pillows behind him, accompanied the whole time by a beaming smile, before moving to the foot of the bed and filling in a form on a clipboard. She came back around to stand beside him.

"Let's see how you do without the oxygen." She reached behind his head, removing the elasticated bands holding the mask in place. "All okay?" she asked.

"Yeah, fine thanks." His voice sounded husky. "How am I… What happened?"

"The doctor will explain, but you've had a bang on the head, and an overdose of an opioid drug. Your chart says we've given you Naloxone which counters the effects. All being well, you should be fine. There's a couple of your friends in the waiting room, they've been a bit anxious, shall I bring them in?"

"Yeah, thanks." She disappeared through the door in a rustle of starch. The water. He spiked the fucking water. He'd known something was wrong even as he drank it. The door opened and calm, ordered efficiency disappeared, as Freddie exploded into the room. The whole damn hospital wasn't big enough to contain him, let alone a small side-ward.

"Yo, bro, how are you doing? Man, you've had us worried. Now just lie there, anything you want, I'll get it for you." The words tumbled out, falling over each other in their rush. Even the American accent slipped somewhat. Chad didn't care. Freddie, the second most reassuring thing in the world.

Freddie stood looking around the small room as if awaiting permission to bear hug him. Jas was standing behind Freddie, and he smiled at her. She smiled back and held his eye.

"I'm glad to see you guys. Do you know what happened?"

Jas sat down on the chair at the side of the bed.

"I got there to find an ambulance at the side of the road," said Jas, "and you on a stretcher, looking like it was only a matter of time till you croaked it. You've got a quick-thinking paramedic called Brian to thank for the fact that you're still here. He was the one who said you looked like you might have overdosed, and then I told him about the Fentanyl. You were also coshed."

A thought came to him, and he looked at Freddie. "Where's Angie?"

"We're just trying to contact her, bro, don't worry. Her office said she'd got the afternoon off, finished at lunchtime, so maybe she's doing a bit of R and R. Do you know where she might have gone, or who with?"

Chad let his head ease onto the pillow. She hadn't told him she was going anywhere but, there again, she hadn't told him anything recently. "No, mate, I don't know where she is. Check my phone, it should be here somewhere and see if she's called me." Freddie fished the phone from Chad's jacket. Nothing. No calls, no messages. Shit. He tried to think of friends that Angie may have gone out with. Chad's head was beginning to throb.

"Okay, let's stay logical here," said Jas. "There's no way that our bad guy could bonk you on the head, try and kill you with Fentanyl at 12:30 p.m. then drive across to Leeds in time to get anywhere near Angie before she finished work at lunchtime. So, wherever she is, I don't think we need to be panicking."

"You're right," said Chad. "Makes sense." He felt better. The door opened and a young Asian guy in a white coat with a stethoscope around his neck came in. He looked about twelve, Chad thought.

"Mister Hilton?" The doctor looked at Freddie and Jas. "Would you mind?" Both got the drift, exit time. He held the door open for them to leave. "You can pop back in a minute, I won't be long," he said, then picked up the clipboard from the end of the bed, scanned it, and came to stand by the side of the bed, looking down at Chad.

"So, Mister Hilton, I think it's fair to say you've been very fortunate. We were able to identify the opioid, and therefore the correct antagonist. Naloxone. That helped to regulate your breathing. However, because you had built up a tolerance to Fentanyl, the effect of the overdose was not as great on you as it might have been in someone else. You got lucky. I understand that Fentanyl has been replaced by Methadone, so please take those as prescribed. I'm going to keep you in overnight tonight. You took a heavy blow to the back of your head, and I want to check for a concussion or any other type of delayed response. Better to be on the safe side. If all is well, you can go home tomorrow. Okay?"

"Yes," Chad smiled and nodded. The doctor turned and left the room.

* * *

Chad checked his phone. Still nothing. "Where the hell is, she?" He looked from Jas to Freddie, who had found a chair from somewhere, and now sat on the other side of the bed from Jas.

"Chad, I've got to get back to Leeds. Is that okay?" said Jas.

"Of course, thanks for looking after me. By the way, did you find my shoulder bag? My iPad's in there, and I was going to send Lee an email. I'd forgotten all about that."

"Don't worry, he's seen it. So have I. Freddie sorted the password."

Freddie beamed.

"We think it makes sense, and Lee's got the guys chasing down the ransom money and the shares. We've got a team meeting at 18:30 that's what I've got to get back for."

"Bro, I'd better get off too. I'm going to find Angie. As soon as I do, I'll let you know. Don't worry, she'll be fine."

Chad smiled. "Thanks, Freddie. I owe you. Again."

A waft of Jean-Paul Gautier and three days stubble rough against his cheek as Freddie said goodbye. Then the soft smoothness of her skin as she leaned in to peck his cheek. What was that perfume? The kiss held for a fraction longer than it needed to, he thought. She stayed cheek to cheek and whispered "You take it easy hoppy.

You gave me a proper fright." He lay back on the pillows and stared at the ceiling. Come on Ange, call me.

CHAPTER 80

Tuesday 6:30 p.m.

"Come on, get the fucking door open," yelled Freddie before Odd Job could get out the car. Traffic was calming as rush hour eased off, but he still had to weave his way through the cars to get to All Bar One on the corner of Greek Street. He looked back over his shoulder. Odd Job stood by the car, the hazards blinking. No time for a chat with the traffic cops. Freddie walked up the steps to the bar. A security guard stood outside.

"Nice to see you, Mr Jackson, how are you this evening?" he said, unused to seeing the Boss.

"I'm good, Gerald, I'm good. Tell me, are any of the bar staff from lunchtime, still here?"

"Let me check for you. Please," said Gerald, opening the door and holding it for Freddie.

The after-work set were reliving the day. He'd already tried Angelica's, The Bar and Grill, and Banyans. His guy on the door at Banyans had told him that Angie sometimes popped in on her way to catch the train. She'd head there, after All Bar One, but the guy hadn't seen her today. He walked towards the bar then saw Gerald approaching with a young guy in a lumberjack shirt, jeans that stopped just below his shins, and a pair of black baseball boots. Looks like a fucking cartoon, thought Freddie.

"Mister Jackson, this is Adrian, he's just finishing his shift. He's the cocktail waiter."

Freddie flashed a smile at Adrian, the same smile that opened women's bedroom doors, and the wallets of the punters in his club. "Hey, Adrian, good to see you, bro. Look, man, I need your help," he placed his huge arm around Adrian's scrawny shoulder. "I'm wondering if a friend of mine was in around lunchtime? Angie, Angie Hilton. Maybe five-seven, blonde hair, blue eyes. A stunner."

"Yes, she was, with her friend Karen. She had to leave after a couple as she was feeling ill."

Freddie lost the smile. "What do you mean, ill?"

"I don't know, she'd had a couple then they each had a pornstar martini, but Angie wasn't keen, so she went back on the margheritas. Then she started feeling dizzy."

"So, what happened, and what time was this?"

The change in tone seemed to alert Adrian. "It was around 2:00 p.m maybe just before that. Is she okay?"

Freddie didn't answer.

"Anyway, Karen came back in to settle up and told me that they'd got lucky. A guy had been going to the toilet and seen Angie. Turns out he lives near her, a neighbour, and he helped get Angie out of the bar and into his car, otherwise, she'd have had to try and get the train. She wasn't in any state to do that." Adrian turned and looked out of the glass frontage. "He'd parked across there. A brown hatchback."

Shit, thought Freddie. His heart was racing and his mouth seemed suddenly bone dry. "So, do we have a name for this guy? And what did he look like?"

"I think Karen said his name was Neil. He was tall, over six feet, a black guy in his forties I'd say. Smartly dressed, but not in a suit. I'd never seen him in here before."

A black guy, thought Freddie. Hadn't Chad said something

about Ange being stalked by a black guy? He looked at Adrian. “Thanks, bro, that’s helpful. I don’t suppose you have a number for Karen, do you?”

“I doubt it, but let me go and check.”

Freddie tapped his foot as he waited for Adrian to return. Come on you little fuck, get a move on. Adrian returned clutching a piece of paper.

“Here you go,” he seemed euphoric at being able to help. “She gave us it after she left her coat here last time she was in, just in case we found it. We never did. Let me know she’s okay, will you? We see her every month, and I’ve been worried about her.”

“Thanks,” said Freddie. “Will do.”

* * *

Freddie sat in the back of the roller and dialled the number. Two rings and it was answered.

“Hello this is Karen, is that Neil?”

Neil? Who the fuck was Neil? “No, no it’s not. My name is Freddie Jackson, I’m a friend of Chad and Angie Hilton, and I believe Angie was taken ill at lunchtime today?”

“Oh yes, she was. Angie’s mentioned you used to play football with Chad, didn’t you? I’ve been expecting a call to let me know she’s okay. Her neighbour, Neil, took my number and said he’d call me, but I haven’t heard, I’m frantic. Is she okay?”

“Listen, Karen, we don’t know. We don’t know where she is. Tell me everything that happened today and what this guy Neil said to you.”

Karen began to sob. “We’d been having a few cocktails, but not many. I think we were on our third. We meet once a month and have two or three, then have some lunch with a glass of champagne. Today was no different, except that Ange had nearly finished her Margherita when she started to feel dizzy. She started slurring her words and everything. Then this guy, on his way to the loo, turns around and says hi to Angie. He says he's her neighbour, and then tells me I should drive her home. But we both come on the train, first Tuesday of the month, so we can have a few drinks. He then says he'll take her home, by which time Angie is looking poorly. So, we get her outside and into his car, and that was it." Freddie heard Karen blow her nose.

"When you say poorly, was she sick?"

"No, she seemed spaced out, like she didn't have control of her body and didn't know where she was. I've never seen her like that before."

"And had you noticed this guy, Neil, before he walked past you?"

"I'd seen him sitting near the bar. Good looking guy, but hadn't spoken to him."

"And did Angie recognise him?"

"As I said, Angie was out of it. She wouldn't have recognised Chad, let alone anyone else." Karen was sobbing again in Freddie's ear.

Freddie tried to keep his tone calm and measured. "Look, girl, we don't know where she is. But one of her best friends is a policeman and he's got his guys looking for her, so don't worry, I'm sure she'll be fine. I'll let you know when we find her."

"That's what the other guy said."

"Yeah, well if you hadn't left her, we'd know where she was, wouldn't we?" So much for calm and measured. He clicked the call off but stared at the phone. He'd got a message from one of his boys, Jonah. "*Hey Boss can you call me like, urgent.*" He dialled.

"Hey, boss, me and the boys think, like, it's weird where Errol got hit. I mean, we never deal off-strip, right? There are the dudes who supply Headingley, others that do Armley and Hunslet, and we do Harehills. Errol's one of us in Harehills. No cross over, safe that way. So why was Errol on Whitehall Road? Like, it makes no sense, boss. Well, it makes no sense unless it was home turf for the shooter. Know what I mean?"

Freddie looked out of the window, "Yeah, Jonah, I think I do. Thanks, bro." He scrolled through his calls, found Lee's name and dialled.

CHAPTER 81

Tuesday 6:45 p.m.

Lee felt his phone vibrate. Holding the door to room 106 open with his foot, he saw it was Freddie. "Hi Freddie, I'm just about to start our meeting, Jas updated me on Chad, great news. Any sign of Angie yet?"

"Lee, bro, I tracked her down to the All Bar One on Greek Street, where she met a friend for lunch. That's where the good news ends. She started to feel unwell, dizzy and spaced out, classic Rohypnol symptoms. Then a black dude comes over to their table saying he's a neighbour called Neil. Persuades her friend, Karen, that it's kosher, and says he'll take Ange home. Her friend believes him and, between them, they load Ange into this prick's car, no make just a colour, brown. Should show up on your CCTV down there though. And that's it, off she goes. That was at around 2:00 p.m., bro. Now, do you remember the barbecue last summer at Chad's place? The neighbours were there but I don't think one was called Neil, and I was the only black face in that crowd. Can you remember?"

"Fuck," said Lee, "I know the neighbours, I've had dinner with them. No Neil."

"I thought so. Something for your boys, to check, though.

Check who owns or rents, the units on the Whitehall Industrial Estate. I have it on good authority that our dude maybe one of them. Let me know if you hear anything."

"Yeah, will do, I should know more after this. Oh, and Freddie, if you hear anything more, you call me, right? Don't go doing anything on your own. Understood?"

"Ten-four. Copy that," said Freddie.

CHAPTER 82

Tuesday 6:45 p.m.

I throw my phone down next to me on the settee. I mean, really? According to some bitch of a nurse, that twat Hilton is not only alive but he's sitting up in bed chatting. What the fuck? How does that happen? I've given him six pills in one dose and he's fucking chatting. And now Angie. I get her back to the warehouse and she's totally zonked. This didn't happen the last time I used Rohypnol. That one was able to walk and talk, not enough to stop me having fun but not totally out of it. "I wonder if that fucker Errol sold me some dodgy shit?"

My phone pings. WhatsApp, Sarah, the receptionist from work. *Just fyi thought you might like to know the police have been calling wanting lists of employees, and who's in charge. I told them Graham is. Still on for next week? Xxx.*

I stare at the message. It's been worth my while cultivating Sarah, an early warning system for anyone prying. My stomach is summersaulting again. Shit, how bad can one day get?

So, they'll have my name on those lists. Quicker than I've planned. Why do they want staff lists, and to know who's in charge? They must have something. But what? Hold it together, come on.

I can feel sweat on my forehead and top lip, a certain precursor of panic. Deep breathe in, hold for five seconds slowly let the air out, and then repeat. That's better, just stay calm, compose your thinking and rationalise things. Come on, it'll be okay. So, they'll see your name, that's it, one name among fifty-seven. Unless? Unless they're tracking the shares. Why would they be doing that? Looking for a motive maybe? Only if they don't believe Andy Huxton has done the shootings. Nah, they haven't got that far, you're seeing shadows where there aren't any, they'll be tying up the loose ends. Let's get some air, been in here too long.

* * *

The metal bracket on the container door groans in complaint as I pull it open. Inside I see Angie's face lying flat on the table-top, eyes closed, a strand of blonde hair across her cheek.

Fuck. This is not part of the plan. Yes, sure, there's been times in the last few days when I've wondered what I'll do if Angie, refuses to come with me, refuses to start our new life together. And yeah, okay, that feeling has grown after the call last week after she'd got shitty with me and told me to fuck off and stop bothering her. But she hadn't meant it, her fucking husband would have put her up to that. She couldn't have meant it because it's only been a couple of weeks since we were having fun, drinking champagne, dancing, nights at the Mal Maison. And the sex was fantastic, she never wanted it to finish. But then she's ended it, says it was a fling that her husband has found out about and she wants to move on. Thanks, and fuck off. But now what? Let's check her pulse. I lean across the table and put two fingers on her neck. The faintest of beats. I've already unlocked the restraints, and tried to get her to drink water, but nothing. How the fuck has this happened? "It's a fucking date rape drug, you don't want them in a fucking coma, it defeats the object,"

My voice bounces off the walls of the container and disappears, leaving silence in its wake. What to do? Can't get a doctor. Obviously. Dick. Okay, think. Lie her on the floor and see if that helps get oxygen to the brain? Pointless, what good will that do? My thoughts are unravelling like wool on an old jumper. Come on, think. Cocaine, let's do a couple of lines, that'll stimulate the brain cells.

Angie looks like an unloved rag-doll, her face is turned sideways. White crystals glint at me from the small round mirror on the table. It's as much the ritual as the snorting that is the thrill. Dividing the powder into two lines using the edge of a banknote fuels the anticipation. Then I roll the note into a long cylinder feeling it fill my nostril, smelling the leather of my wallet on the paper, I close the other nostril with my finger and suck a line up through the other. "Ah, fuck, yes," The residual powder in my nostril hits the back of my throat. I sniff loudly. I'm like a fucking Dyson. I snort the other line. A few specks remain on the glass, so I seek them out with my tongue, hunting the remnants in the rim of the mirror. It reminds me of mum letting me lick the icing bowl on baking day.

"That's fucking better, now come on, you've got this. Let's sort this shit out, and get the fuck out of here."

The rush hits me and a tornado whirls through my brain leaving me ice-cold, clear, sharp and focused. Wow. Okay, so think. Angie is unmoving. Check again, this can't be right. What the fuck has that little shit Errol sold me? Shooting was too good for him. I should have held him out of a window and dropped the fucker. Her skin feels warm but I can't feel a pulse. Fuck. I check her neck. Nothing. Grabbing the mirror, I wipe it on my jeans and hold it in front of Angie's mouth. The mirror clouds. She's breathing. I count to five and hold the mirror again. Try her pulse again. Slight, but it is there.

"Right, hang on Ange, the effects will wear off. I've got to go out, I'll be back soon."

CHAPTER 83

Tuesday 6:45 p.m.

"Evening everyone. Okay, listen up," said Lee, calling the room to attention. "Angie Hilton was last seen around 14:00 being carried out of All Bar One on Greek Street by a guy calling himself Neil and claiming to be a neighbour of the Hiltons. There is no such neighbour. He drove away in a brown hatchback. Luke, get the CCTV from Greek Street and let's find that car. Also, Jas, find out the names of everyone that has a unit on the Whitehall Industrial Estate. I think the perp might be one of them." Luke and Jas sprinted out of the room. "Joe, did you get anywhere on the shareholders?" asked Lee.

"Yeah, I did. On the death of either Huxton, their class "A" shares pass to the surviving Huxton. In this case, after both die, the "A" shares are subsumed back into the business, to be distributed in equal part, but at no cost, to the members of the management team that hold Class "B" shares. The idea, boss, is that the Class "A" shares cannot be gifted to someone outside the business. So, Iqbal has been through the share issues over the last few years and found that Class "B" shares have been bought in dribs and drabs. The problem is they're owned by someone called Diane Beak, and that name isn't on the staff list we received a few minutes ago from

Excelsior."

"Shit." Said Lee. "Okay Joe, call Excelsior now and ask for this woman by name and let's see what they say."

"On it, Boss." Said Schmidt.

Lee turned as the door opened and Jas hurried back in. "Fucking typical, the main letting agent's offices are closed for the day." She said, "If we're going to have any joy down the Industrial Estate route, we're going to have to get the home numbers of the owners of all the businesses on the estate and call them, but that could take hours Boss."

"Fuck, fuck, fuck." Said Lee.

The door hadn't closed following Jas' arrival before it flew wide again, and Lee saw Schmidt framed in the entrance with his phone clutched in his hand.

"Well?" asked Lee.

"Boss, the receptionist at Excelsior says she's never heard of Diane Beak but she's going to ask around with the guys who've worked there longer than her and she'll call me back."

"Come on, come on, we've got to have something. Any names look familiar from the staff list you got?"

"Nah, none that leap off the page, but we're running checks on the names right now."

The sound of Schmidt's phone ringing made Lee jolt. "Yeah, Schmidt here," he said. Silence enveloped the team. "Okay, when was that? And where is she now? Right, thanks."

"And?" said Lee

"Seems someone vaguely remembers the name but says Diane Beak hasn't worked there for years and as far as they know she emigrated to Australia ages ago."

Lee ran his hands through his hair, then rubbed his eyes with his knuckles. "Any ideas anyone?"

"I'll check Facebook," said Jas," See if there's anything on there." She paused. "Hang on a minute though, what if Beak is her married name? Maybe she's related to someone on the staff list.

We could cross reference the surnames of the Excelsior staff to her Christian name then check Facebook, Marriage lists and see if anything turns up?"

"Excellent idea," said Lee. "Divide that list up and share it out between us."

* * *

"Boss, I think we've got her." Shouted Jas. Lee stood behind her and looked over her shoulder. "Facebook, and here's a load of photos from the marriage of Diane Atwell to David Beak. This is one of her arm-in-arm with her brother Stuart Atwell, who is on our employee list." She said.

"That's fucking brilliant Jas. Fantastic work. Okay, listen up everyone, do we have a photo of Atwell? Company websites often have a Meet the Team page? If so, let's compare it to this photo on Facebook and whatever the CCTV on Greek Street shows us. Back here everyone in half an hour. I want that CCTV."

"Stuart James Atwell, Flat 3, Brewery Wharf, Bowman Lane. It's out near the Royal Armouries." Said Jas pinning the wedding photo from Facebook and the screen shot of Atwell from Excelsior's website, onto a wipe board.

Lee ran both hands through his hair as Luke Deakin walked to the wipe boards and stuck a photograph from the CCTV the ones of Atwell

"That's Bannister!" yelled Lee, pointing at the CCTV still. "But look at Atwell, same height, same shaped nose as Bannister, this is what Chad was on about. Bannister is Atwell in a silicone mask. Let's get Atwell picked up. Joe, get onto firearms, let us know when they can get a team together and we'll meet them at his apartment. Get uniforms to the Industrial Estate and make sure no-one leaves there till we arrive. We'll check every fucking unit if needs be. No word to Chad 'till we've got Angie safe, okay?"

CHAPTER 84

Tuesday 7:15 p.m.

"Fuck," murmured Freddie. "How am I going to do this without creating a shit storm?" He leaned on the bar and weighed up his dilemma. The cops would fuck this up. They'd rock up, blues and twos flashing and sirens blaring, the dude would hear them coming when they were still five miles away. He couldn't let that happen. The guy had used a shooter several times so he'd have no problem doing that again if he felt threatened. Then there was Errol. He needed to show that he didn't let one of his own go down, without retribution. Leeds would go to hell in a fucking hand cart, if people thought that Freddie Jackson was going soft. He didn't want to cause problems for Chad with Lee, but Lee was a cop, he knew to expect shit when the lines got blurred. Having said that, he didn't want to create so much bad blood, that the Feds charged all over his business. He'd got to get this right. He looked at the barman, caught his eye and nodded. The barman rang a bell on the bar. Everyone was there, the place was packed. More steroids on show than a WWF challenge event, he thought.

"I think that the cops will get a firearms team to lift this guy, so we need to get to him first. They can have him when we've finished with him. Remember, brothers, he whacked Errol, and very nearly did the same to my best mate." Odd Job materialised at his side and pushed a piece of paper into his hand. He read it, then smiled. "The dude is called Stuart Atwell, and we have an address." He passed the paper to an Asian man with a face like a smacked arse. "Tony," said Freddie. "Take the Harehills boys and pick him up. Don't go mob-handed, just a small team with a back-up. He lives out near the Armouries, should be quiet around there. Position some boys to keep watch, if you're quick the cops will be there after us, so in and out sharpish. Have we got some boys heading to the Industrial Estate, just in case?"

"We've got a crew on bikes, heading down there now. If he's there, they'll call," said Tony.

"The rest of you act as spotters. Check which route the cops will take, and keep us up to speed. Okay, let's pick him up. He has a shooter, remember that. Enough force to nail him and no more. Taser him if needed, but don't shoot the fucker, understood? I don't want him dead. When you've got him, bring him to me at the Brown Hare."

As if someone had just shouted *scramble* in an old Battle of Britain movie, the team ran for the doors. Some Sky Sports pundit was left talking to no-one on the TV above the bar. "Turn that shit off," said Freddie.

CHAPTER 85

Tuesday 8:00 p.m.

I listen. Silence. A creak from the flat above, that's all. Risk a light? Yeah. The place is empty as I'd left it. Nowhere for anyone to hide between me and the bedroom, but don't get careless now. The furniture had gone a couple of weeks ago and the lease runs out today. Just the important bits left, the bits I can carry. In and out, pronto, they'll have my name and address soon, it's only a matter of time. A short hallway leads from the living room, into the main bedroom with its built-in wardrobe. It's a large double, most of the space has been used to hold my suits but I cleared those at the weekend, and they're now hanging in my new, if temporary, apartment. Bending to open the top drawer, the flash of passing headlights gleams in the mirror. Turning and crouching low I run back into the living room and turn off the light. Passing headlights are a problem. Residents of the block park underground, and that entrance is at the other side of the building. Anyone parking here now is on double yellows. Not good. Keeping down, I tiptoe into the bedroom, and duck under the window sill, into the recess of the back wall. My heartbeat sounds like a foghorn breaking the silence of the room. I sneak a look out of the window. The black silhouette of a car stands fifty yards away. Two men emerge from the passenger side, and two heads appear above the car from the driver's side. Not pausing, they move out of my eye-line. They're heading for the main door.

Bzzzzz.

"Fuck." I run from the bedroom into the living room. On the wall by the door is a monitor and intercom, with a remote access entry system. An Asian face is staring into the camera. He's an ugly bastard with several deep cratered acne scars that look like bunkers on a golf course. I sprint back into the bedroom and pull out the drawers, emptying the contents into my backpack. Why did I leave the most valuable until last? Anyway, still time. Looking out all is quiet, so I open the window wide, climb up onto the ledge, and holding the bottom corner of the open window, I drop down onto the grass six feet below, pulling the window closed behind me. I slip on landing and feel the rainwater on the grass dampen my knees through the denim of my jeans. So far so good. The adrenalin rush is nearly as good as a line of coke. They'll spot that the window isn't fully closed, so every second counts. The grass is soft underfoot and my breath floats on the night air. Get the fuck past the car and down to the canal towpath. I crouch under the ledge, making myself as small as possible. Bowman Road runs at ninety degrees to my right. Quiet. Okay, go, go. Squatting low, lactic acid causes my calves to burn as I run to the corner of the building. The car stands twenty yards away. Still quiet. Then, like the floodlights coming on in Colditz, the grass outside the window of the flat becomes bathed in light. No more time. I run and cover the ground fast, then crouch by the bonnet of the car, a Bentley. Not the law, then. Worse, Jackson. The ground slopes behind me, falling seven or eight feet to the canal, okay down we go and then sprint. That's when I see him. A kid on a bike, hoody up, is riding free-hand towards the car. Pressing my face into the wet grass, I lie flat and pull my backpack to my side, ten feet between us, maybe less. The kid stops by the car and slouches, feet on the pedals, one arm resting on the car roof, and a two-way radio in his hand. If the kid turns his head forty-five degrees, he'll see me. I keep my eyes fixed on the youth, and manage to ease the Makarov out of the bag. The suppressor makes it difficult, but slow and watchful as a lion hiding in the pampas, I draw my arm past my head. The youth seems to hear a sound, turns and looks at me. *Phut.* The boy slumps against the car, he makes no sound but the bike grates on the Bentley as it gives way underneath him. Grabbing the backpack, I turn and run.

* * *

Ten minutes door to door flat out. I'd timed it just in case. It takes longer by car, on the one-way system. Pausing and breathing hard I look both ways, along the path. No-one. Ever since that rapist started doing his stuff, the towpath is always quiet. I duck, slip through the hole I'd cut in the fence weeks ago, and scramble up the grass through the wire mesh at the top of the bank, straight to the back door of my unit. A distant hum of traffic the only noise to break the silence. Okay, all good. Let's get Ange and get the fuck out of here before the shit hits the fan.

* * *

Chad scrolled through the recent calls. Still nothing. His phone a mute black brick. He'd called both Lee and Angie eight times in the last hour, but neither had picked up. The last call he'd received had been Freddie, to say he was working on a lead, and that he'd passed it on to Lee. What was that about? Whose car were they after, and why? Where is she? He closed his eyes. Fear owned him. It diminished the pain in his knee by consuming the rest of him. The familiar swish and a trolley emerged being pushed by a different nurse. Shift change.

"Medication time, Chad," she said. "You're to have one methadone, and a sleeping tablet tonight. How are you feeling?

Okay?"

"Yes, thanks, I'm fine. I don't want the sleeping tablet, thanks. I'm waiting to hear from my wife, and don't want to be asleep when she calls."

"That's alright, then, I'll pop back in an hour, and you can take it then. You'll have the methadone now, though." She put the tablet in a small paper thimble, and passed it to him, then poured him a cup of water.

"Thanks," he said and swallowed it. One. Christ, a far cry from his normal intake. Jas, I'll text Jas, he thought. *Hey, you okay? Can't get hold of Lee. Any news on Angie? Have you got any further following the money*? The humming of the monitor next to him created ripples in the silence. Come on Ange, call. "Don't let anything happen to her. Please," he whispered.

CHAPTER 86

Tuesday 8:00 p.m.

The pub was closed to the public. Freddie sat in the bar and waited for the images to come through from the body camera Tony was wearing. They'd replaced Sky Sports on the TV over the bar in the Brown Hare. The only patrons were Freddie's men, waiting for the action to begin. The picture flickered onto the screen as Tony turned on the camera and got out of the car. He walked fast, but unhurried, to the front entrance of the block. Freddie couldn't see them, but he knew the other boys were in close attendance. A hand reached into shot and pressed a buzzer on a panel to the right of the door. No answer. Freddie heard another voice, one of his boys.

"Try seventeen, Tony, he'll let us in, he's one of my regulars. I'll do the talking."

Tony pressed another buzzer, there was a noise, then muffled voices, followed by a loud ping. Tony pulled the door open and walked in. The entrance corridor to the lifts was a few feet ahead. The jerking camera movements picked up the opposite wall where arrows indicated the locations of the ground floor apartments. Flats One to Three were to the left. The camera turned left, past the lifts. Flat One was the first of three doors visible. Flat three had to be the last door on the right. A couple of wobbly movements later and the door to the flat was up-front and centre. The lens picked up Joey, emerging out of the darkness to take up a position to the left of the door. Freddie could see Dozy B to Tony's right, which meant that young Tyler, the fourth member of the team, was watching the corridor. It looked like a military operation, no surprise there. Tony was ex-Special Forces. An arm came into view on the screen and knocked on the door. Then again. Silence.

"Am I going in, boss?' Tony whispered, but the sound boomed through the TV screen.

"Yep, but be as quiet as you can. And be quick." The screen went black. He envisaged Tony kneeling to deal with the lock. Freddie's phone pinged.

"*Pigs flying. Fifteen Minutes.*"

"Tony, in and out in less than ten. Company is on its way."

"Roger that."

The brown colour on the screen lightened as Tony stood. Freddie saw his right hand, with three fingers raised, then two, then one. The door opened and the camera followed it. Dozy B's shape ran ahead into the room. The camera lurched as Tony turned and switched the light on. The place was empty. He walked room to room but each was the same. No furniture, no clothes, no occupant. The camera led Freddie into the living room then down a hallway into a bedroom.

"The window's open, check it," said Tony. "What was that?" The camera swung towards the window.

"Didn't hear anything," said Freddie.

"There was a noise outside."

"Okay, out. Fast. And close the door behind you," said Freddie. "Tony?"

"Yes, boss."

"Take the boys and meet me at the Whitehall Road Industrial Estate. I'll see you there in fifteen minutes."

* * *

"What the fuck?" said Tony.

The camera was bouncing up and the ground shot past in a jumble of shapes. The picture stabilised by the driver's door, a body, indistinct and blurry, but human. There was a bike squashed underneath the figure. The camera shook as Tony stopped and bent down. The boy's features, becoming clearer on the screen above the bar. Freddie saw it was Timo. Sixteen years old. A sentry, no more.

"How is he?" said Freddie.

Tony paused, then said. "He's dead, Boss. Taken one through the heart. No chance. What do you want me to do?"

"You'll have to leave him. The cops will find him in the next minute or two. Are you sure he's dead?"

"Yes Boss, quite sure."

"Well, call an ambulance anyway. Do it now."

The boy's young face filled the TV before Tony turned the camera off, and the screen went black. Freddie put his head in his hands. Come on, he thought, no time for that. Anger replaced the tears, as he wiped his eyes and turned to face the group of men hovering behind him.

"Tool up, get the cars. I'm going to kill this fucker."

CHAPTER 87

Tuesday 8:15 p.m.

I stare at Angie. How's this happened? She's cold, icy cold. She's fucking dead. Oh, God. I empty her handbag onto the table next to her. Make up paraphernalia and a rectangular box. Valium. Oh, for f… Rohypnol, Valium and alcohol. Oh, fucking fuck.

Rage begins to bubble, volcanic and destructive. This is Hilton's fault. They can't blame me for this. Fucking little wanker should have accepted that she'd picked me. The better man. He can't walk for fuck's sake, why would she stay with him? His fault, he should have pissed off, and got on with his life. None of this would have happened if the twat had done that. Angie's head bounces as I slam my fist onto the table. Instead, what have I got?

"Money, yes, but that's not the fucking point," I scream. The container holds the sound, rebounding it from wall to wall.

The plan has always been there, just waiting to be activated, all the parts assembled, but it was Ange who gave it life, Ange who made me do it. With her, I'd have used the cash to go to the best places and live in the smartest houses. Now what? Fuck all. Cash, but no-one to spend it with. I check my watch. The pounding in my head begins to dissipate, hands stop trembling and the insatiable desire to kick the fuck out of whoever I see next creeps back into the dark place in my brain.

Shit, I need to get moving. What to do? I can't drive away from here with her, they know my name, so they'll have traced the Maserati. They'll be watching for it. No, too risky, she'll have to stay here with the car. I look at the Nissan Note I'd used to get Angie and Murphy. Non-descript, the sort of car no-one would ever remember. That's why I'd picked it. I had been planning to drive away in it, but maybe not.

I've always had an Armageddon Plan. A plan B, a contingency. PPP and all that. I've just never thought I'd need it. It isn't fully-fledged, stress tested, proven fit for purpose, because the need for it has been far removed from my thinking. Ready or not, I need it now. Stroking her hair for the last time and, standing behind her, I lift her out of the seat and drag her across the warehouse to the car, then lift her into the passenger seat. Come on, time to improvise, you know the drill, make the decision, then make the decision work. To pull this off I need scale. No point doing anything that doesn't buy time and put everyone off the scent. The bigger the better. Out of the conflicting thoughts comes the plan. I knew it would, I have a higher intellect, so the plan always comes to me in the end. In the boot are four red plastic cans of petrol. The Nissan Note is parked at ninety degrees to the Maserati. Two cars going up will be like bonfire night, no-one's putting that out in a hurry, and the heat will be so intense I doubt there'll be any human remains to identify. If I leave my Rolex in the car for them to find they'll think we were both in here. I remove the cap and douse the Maserati inside and out, then with another can, I repeat the soaking on the Nissan. The smell of petrol clings to every fibre and sucks the air out of the warehouse. I'm beginning to feel better. My *piece de resistance.* In the container, standing against the back wall are four, ten-litre gas bottles. I haven't needed them thus far but they'll come in handy now. Fuck me, this will go pop. I form them in a square around the table, they hiss as I turn the valve on each of the bottles to open. I pour the rest of the petrol around the container. Shit, once I light this, they'll hear the explosion in Bradford.

Okay, good to go, so let's get the fuck out of here. I stop mid-stride. I remember that careful is my watchword. Check all is quiet before I go. 8:15 p.m. Should be fine, no-one works past 5:00 p.m. but better safe than sorry. I take the stairs two at a time to the floor above, keeping in the shadows and close to the wall to get a good view out of the window. The units on the estate are in darkness. Same spot I waited for Errol. God was that only yesterday? Errol, unit twelve, one hundred and fifty yards away. I stare. Out of the shadows, I see someone on a bike, peddle away. Then like swarming rats, more of them, I count five. Five guys on bikes. Nah, I don't buy that. The kid at the flat had been on a bike, too much of a coincidence. I look towards the lights of Wellington Street. Two cars are parked either side of the entrance to the estate. Easy to stop anyone trying to get away. Police? These guys on bikes aren't police, that's obvious. Ah, Freddie Jackson. He's smart, he's taking a punt that I'm on this estate, 'cos this is where Errol copped it. Not as dumb as you look, Freddie, I'll give you that. I crane my neck to get a better view of the tarmac in front of my unit, and to see the adjacent warehouses. All quiet. So, they don't know which one I'm in. Advantage Napoleon, as usual. Edging backwards to the staircase I tiptoe down. Better get on with it, before anyone else shows up. Picking up the last full can of petrol, I walk to the door, pouring as I go. I keep pouring till I'm down the bank. I look up at the warehouse, Christ, I need to be away before this goes bang. Two minutes to the flat, I'll have a ringside seat, it should be a great view. I've left the back door ajar so oxygen will get the place burning quicker. I check the towpath. All quiet. Ditching the petrol can into the canal I take out my lighter. One last check, backpack yep, phone, yep.

"That's it. Goodbye, Stuart Atwell, it's been nice knowing you."

I strike the wheel on the lighter. A flame springs up catching the petrol vapour and blazing a trail up the bank.

"Best get the fuck out of here."

CHAPTER 88

Tuesday 8:15 p.m.

Lee slammed his hand on the dashboard. "I mean, for fuck's sake, how long should it take to get the order signed off. Two hours the armed response unit have been waiting. Two hours we've been waiting. Just because it's not a terrorist threat there's no urgency in the decision making. I've had to jump through every fucking hoop to get this authorised. You can bet you're your arse it'd be a quicker response if it was the Chief Super's wife being held that's for sure."

Joe Schmidt, sat bolt upright, hands gripping the steering wheel and staring out of the windscreen as they tore through Leeds in a convoy of three, heading towards the Royal Armouries. Jas smiled, then resumed watching the city go by in a blur. Luke Deakin grinned. The car radio broke the tension.

"*Squad car attending at Bowman Lane. Ambulance at the scene. Shooting incident, one male suspected fatality. Respond.*"

"Jesus," said Lee. "I told you, we're too fucking late."

Joe answered. "Roger that, we are two minutes away." He pulled the car left onto Crown Point Road, and the speedo hit eighty-five a few moments later, then up to ninety as they hurtled over the bridge. "Hold tight," said Joe and hit the brakes hard, then swung the wheel left onto Bowman Lane. Full-beam headlights coming the other way flooded the car, blinding Lee and Joe, as a black object raced past them across the bridge

"What the fuck was that?"

"Boy racer in a Bentley," said Jas.

Lee felt the seat belt bite into his chest as Joe stood on the brakes behind the first car in the convoy. Ahead, looking like some sort of inter-galactic hit squad, the armed response unit was jumping out of the lead car, doors left open and kneeling behind them. To his right, fifty yards ahead, an ambulance was parked, lights flashing. Next to it a squad car. How did he get here quicker than us? Jesus. Lee got out and approached the first of the firearms team.

"I think we're too late. Can't see anyone still being here, but fill your boots, it's flat three." He pointed to the apartment block and the four-man team bobbed and weaved their way to the entrance. "What have we got?" Lee asked the paramedic by the ambulance.

A uniformed officer answered. "Sir, we've got a shooting. The call came into the ambulance service five minutes ago, and we were in the area so also responded. The victim is a male, I'd say in his teens. Unarmed, that's his bike." He pointed to the frame, twisted where it had slipped away from the car. "We've stopped residents from entering or leaving."

"Thanks," said Lee.

The paramedic looked up. "Looks like he received one gunshot, straight through his heart. Death would have been instantaneous."

Lee saw the armed response heading back to their car. "Anything?"

"Nothing," said the unit commander. "As you said, we're too late. Is the shooter the guy we came here for?"

"Don't know, but I'd be amazed if it wasn't," said Lee. He felt his phone. Freddie.

Get yourselves to the Industrial Estate bro, I'm on my way.

Lee looked again at the message. "Everybody ahead of us again. Last to the frigging party, as usual. Joe, Jas, come on, let's go."

CHAPTER 89

Tuesday 8:25 p.m.

"This is going to be one hell of a show." I mutter racing through the apartment door and over to the window. Way down below, the kids on bikes converge on the entrance to the industrial estate, where the two cars I'd seen earlier remain in position. My eye's drawn to Unit Five, where smoke is seeping out from under the shutter doors and flames surge from the open back door. A sleek black limousine pulls up on Wellington Street. The doors open and four guys get out.

"Let's get this party started."

The four huddle in a group and appear to be recounting the events of the last half an hour with animated gestures. "I bet that's going down well." Another car slows at the entrance. The two blockers move aside to give the new arrival access to the Industrial Estate. "Ah, Freddie Jackson himself. Oh, how cool would that be? Blow the shit out of Hilton's best mate. Justice, I'd call it."

I can see Jackson speaking to the group of eight men, dispersing them East and West on the estate. The kids on bikes assemble around him, and he points to the far reaches of the estate and gestures for them to check each of the individual units. "There are over eighty units, Freddie, you haven't time." On Wellington

Street, the flashing lights of an unmarked police car are being followed by a squad car, sirens blaring. "Great, the cavalry's arriving. Better late than never. Ringside seats, guys."

CHAPTER 90

Tuesday 8:25 p.m.

'Fuck's sake, last to arrive," said Lee.

Joe manoeuvred the car into the industrial estate, and Lee was out before Joe could bring it to a halt next to Freddie's roller.

Freddie was sitting on the bonnet of his car. "Don't start, bro, now is not a good time to be throwing your weight around. Okay? A little sensitivity is required, a close friend of mine was shot and killed tonight. He was only a child. And, bro, we need to find Angie, so, many hands make light work."

Jesus, Lee thought. What the hell is it coming to, when I need this guy, to help me? "I've got uniforms on their way, but I came when I got your text. How do you know Atwell is here?"

"I don't bro, I'm just using my imagination. If Atwell hasn't taken Angie to his apartment, he may have brought her here. The problem is, there are eighty-odd units, and we don't know which, if any, is the right one. Do you?"

"No, we couldn't get the intel yet. And how do you know his name?" said Lee.

Freddie didn't answer.

"For fuck's sake I don't know why we bother trying to keep things confidential, we may as well post it on Twitter." Over

Freddie's shoulder, a rising fog blocked the night sky. "What's that? Shit, it looks like smoke?" He started to run towards where grey ringlets rose from a unit at the furthest point away from them, at the back of the estate. He shouted as he ran. "Joe, get the Fire Brigade." To his left, Freddie's long easy stride ate the ground in great gulps. Kids on bikes overtook him. At a T-Junction Lee stopped, grabbing Freddie's jacket and pulling him back. In front of them was a cube-shaped warehouse unit, with shutter doors some nine feet high and one solitary window on the first floor. Smoke coursed from underneath the shutters.

A kid on a bike came screeching to a halt. "Freddie, like, the whole of the back of the fucking warehouse is on fire, man. No chance anyone can get in there."

"Come on," said Lee, "we'd better move back and wait for the fire guys." Their sirens were distant but unmistakable. But there was another sound. Lee looked to Freddie, then at the warehouse, as a low rumble became a thunderous roar and, without warning, the night sky turned into a vivid orange ball. Searing heat singed his hair and eyes, Lee felt himself being lifted and thrown, hurtling through the air and then falling. Breathing was impossible as the fire gorged on the air and all around him was yellow and orange, bathed in a white heat. He hit the floor, and lifting his eyes he saw a huge, glowing, molten shape, loom out of the maelstrom towards him.

"Oh, shit."

CHAPTER 91

Tuesday 8:45 p.m.

I pour another glass of Malbec, then walk back to the window and inspect my work. "Well, though I say it myself, that couldn't have gone any better. I said I wanted scale and scale I got. And you have a nice view from here, Mr Huxton. Sorry, *had* a very nice view. All you can see now is the inside of a body bag. Or a mortuary. Whatever."

I survey the carnage away to my left. Fire engines haven't got near it yet, the gas canisters have seen to that. Four ambulances are at the entrance and countless squad cars now block Wellington Street. There are at least two helicopters roaming overhead. The Armageddon Plan has been true to its name. Smoke billows into the sky, and flames have reached the units either side. Fire engines are lining their hoses on those first, to attempt to stop the situation getting worse.

"Good luck with that,"

I walk away from the window and sit down on a white leather armchair. Placing my glass on a coaster so as not to mark the glass top of the table, I grab my backpack and empty its contents onto the floor. First out comes the Makarov, I'll pop that with the other one and the ammo. Next, comes the MacBook and iPad which I place on the table. These two small pieces of kit hold the key to nine million in funds. I grin and brake into song, "Money, money, money, it's a rich man's world!"

Further inside the bag are the final items. Two passports, and driver's licences to match. I'll give it a week, let the commotion die down then make my exit. The police will be pulled this way and that trying to find answers, and it will take forensics weeks to work out who died. Time's on my side. Standing, I survey the lavish surroundings. This will be my lifestyle from now on. Not here obviously, but any city, anywhere, I'll be with the glitterati. Floor to ceiling windows, high ceilings and understated opulence are going to be the norm for me. There's something nagging away though, what is it? How did they get my name so quickly? I didn't see that coming. O'Connor? Nah, couldn't be, he's in a coma, or he was last time I checked. But how would they have found O'Connor, in the first place? No, that side of things had gone perfectly. So, what then? What had they sussed? They'd figured out a part of the plan. That wasn't supposed to happen and has cost me millions. Bet it was that twat, Hilton. The tweets? I wonder if Hilton started to piece things together when he kept on receiving them. Okay, granted one or two had gone over the top, which could have put Hilton onto me. Don't know, maybe. Anyway, no more tweets, that game's over.

"Come on, Stu, have another glass of wine and calm down. Get the fuck out of here, head to Sydney maybe then watch from afar. Keep tracks on things, and you'll find out how they pieced it together. Then, in time, you can come back and finish the job. It's a dish best served cold, remember."

But thoughts swirl in my head. God, I'm good at this shit. The operational delivery of the plan had been perfect, of course it had, it had been years in the planning. Andy Huxton had provided the first inkling of how to make serious money when he'd gifted me some shares in the business.

The glass catches the reflection of the flames below, giving the wine a silky sheen. "I played him like a fiddle." Getting Andy to persuade his dad that shareholdings should remain in the business, for the business, not be given to family members. Genius. Didn't even known at the time why it might be important, but it turned out to be vital. Putting them in Diane's name until I need them was always part of the plan.

Wandering across the room to the window I look out over Leeds. Andy Huxton. What a knob. Always was, ever since school. All those years ago, both of us getting touched up by that disgusting old git, Murphy. Fucking perv. What made it worse, was how Andy would cosy up to Murphy afterwards. Killing the old paedo had been a foregone conclusion ever since. It was just a question of when, and how. Andy Huxton's life had remained like that. No talent, just a rich dad.

"I had to fight for everything," I whisper to the rooftops.

Getting rich had always been top of my agenda, first the shares and then the fortuitous watching of the news one night showing the report of a jewellery raid in Mayfair, and the uber-cool black guy carrying it out, not bothering about the CCTV. He'd got caught, and they'd found that he was a white guy wearing a silicone mask. I roll the Malbec around the glass. "Piss Poor Planning, if you ask me." But that had spawned the idea. I let it ferment, get some shape to it until it was ready to use. It was just too good to overlook, and boy had it worked. "Cheers Stu, you clever bastard." The wine tastes delicious. The Makarovs had been a piece of luck. A Polish recruitment consultant had said his dad had a shipment he shouldn't have, back in Warsaw and could get them across if anyone was interested. Ha! The guy thought I was a member of a shooting club and let me buy five, threaded for suppressors, plus ammo, no questions asked. Sorted.

Keeping them hidden in London was easy enough, but God it had been fun going down every so often and whacking druggies in Broadwater Farm. A bit risky but easy. Good practice, though, just like the soldiers on TV executing Bin Laden with the Mozambique drill, two to the body one to the head. Practice it and perfect it for use later when it mattered.

The neon lights of the city flicker and glow in the distance, mimicking the flames below. The industrial estate is still a hive of activity, no sign of that letting up. Wow, two months is that all it's been? Two incidents that changed everything. Finding out where Murphy was, and meeting Angie. Facebook has much to answer for, but in this instance, it worked like a dream. Some fucking do-gooder posting photos of a garden party at Ashfield Grange for residents and non-residents. And there he was, smiling at the camera like an advert for Rent a Pervert. Out of the attic came Murphy, and out of the attic came the silicone mask idea. And then there was Ange. The business meeting that Andy had arranged, but couldn't be arsed attending. Typical. To be fair it had been a bit weird when she called me Andy but it seemed rude to correct her and then became too late, too difficult to go back on. It had felt like a whirlwind. Coffees, lunch, then we'd met after work. Angie talked about her life, married to an ex-footballer, seemed idyllic, but I knew, gut instinct again, that she fancied me.

"Ah, Ange, it would have been so good."

Okay, fair enough I made most of the running, but she hadn't complained. Certainly not when we slept together. I feel a stirring in his jeans at the memory. God, she was hot. Couldn't get enough of her. I'd have fucked her morning, noon and night if I could have. Then, as quickly as it had started, she finished it. I sip my wine and feel the familiar rage beginning to rise in my stomach.

That fucking phone call. I thought she was ringing to tell me when I could see her again but no. "*My husband has found out. He saw the receipt from Malmaison and I couldn't keep up the lies,*" The gist of things being, it's only a fling, so thanks very much, fuck off. Then when I call back, I get him, Chad Hilton. Fucking softy southerner accent, saying Ange didn't want to see me again, and never to call, or try and see her.

"Fuck you Hilton. Ha, bet you regret saying that now you twat."

There had been rage, a compulsion to smash, break, kill. And that was it. That was when the plan began to form. Piece by piece, brick by brick it had taken shape. Nothing left to chance, every detail checked and re-checked. Ashfield Grange, what a fucking rats' nest. Full of paedos. I should have killed the fucking lot of them.

Down below the two other units are now ablaze. I've done it all for Ange, and now she was dead. I swallow a mouthful of Malbec and let the wine warm me. Still, on the upside I'm a millionaire. Impressive work, Stu. An earworm starts playing, I smile, then in the solitary splendour of John Huxton's apartment I raise my voice to the heavens and sing, "So fucking easy, that was so fucking easy."

CHAPTER 92

Tuesday 9:30 p.m.

Chad thought he'd heard his phone ring. Or maybe he dreamed it. The sleeping pill the nurse had given him made reality a difficult concept. No messages, no calls. The drugs had worked and the discomfort from his knee had lessened. Acupuncture tomorrow, he remembered that, and counselling. What time, he thought? No idea, he'd have to check his phone. He couldn't be late that was certain, Angie would go mad. What would they talk about? He didn't know that either. Day one tomorrow. New start. No drugs, he thought, well reduced quantity anyway, and they'd begin to rebuild what they had. Maybe. He dropped his head onto the pillow and closed his eyes. There was a noise in the distance but he couldn't make it out until his eyes caught the TV, attached by some sort of arm from the ceiling. The news was on. He blinked, and tried to read the text scrolling at the bottom of the screen. He saw the word 'Breaking' but it looked like it said a terrorist attack. In Leeds? Without his glasses, it could have said anything, and he wouldn't know. He couldn't be bothered to turn up the sound, so he let the noise drift over him. Hope they're all okay, he thought, if there'd been a terrorist attack it explained why no-one had rung. He lay back.

"Sleep, fella, tomorrow's the start of a new chapter," he muttered.

* * *

The morning light streamed into the room. Chad sat up as the news came on the TV. "Jesus, what the hell has happened here?"

"*The explosion happened at 8:30 p.m. yesterday, at a unit on the industrial estate you can see in the distance.*" The reporter pointed behind a cordon of high-vis clad officers. "*The estate would have been quiet at that time, with workers having finished for the day. We have no confirmed fatalities thus far, but a police spokesman told us that the situation may change when firemen and forensic experts begin the task of sifting through the rubble. First reports indicated that this may have been a terror attack, but this was dismissed as the night progressed. It now seems as if the explosion was created by some form of a gas leak. As you can see, the whole area is still being dampened down by fire-crews from all over Yorkshire. It may be some time before we understand what happened here last night.*"

Chad turned away from the TV and checked his phone for the thousandth time.

"I don't get this. I thought one of them would have bothered to ring or text, bloody hell, talk about out of sight out of mind."

The nurse had told him she needed to complete some paperwork to send to his GP, and get his prescription made up, then he could go. Easier said than done, he'd been banking on a lift from someone. He tried each of the four again in turn. Ange, Freddie, Lee, and Jas. Ange's line, was dead, and straight to voicemail for the other three. "For fuck's sake." He scrolled through his calls and clicked on Mainline Taxis. He had to hold for an operator, as he wasn't at home or the Fat badger. Ten minutes to wait.

* * *

The clock on the surgery wall said 9:45 a.m. Chad punched his number into the card machine. The needles hadn't hurt too much. Doctor Woo had inserted them with meticulous precision. Although the sensation was weird, he'd felt a type of electricity running between the needles. Probably psychosomatic. Nonetheless, the positivity of the doctor, and the simple act of taking steps to help himself, made the cost seem good value.

He stepped outside, ready to flag a cab and the spring sunlight matched his mood. On the driveway to the surgery was a familiar silver-and-black roller, and Chad smiled as he saw Freddie with his arms folded sitting on the bonnet.

The expression on Freddie's face was the same as he remembered his aunt wore when he saw her leaving his mum's bedroom as she lay dying. Chad did not attempt to move, but waited, needing the last few moments of not knowing. He wanted to hold them close. Knowledge would change everything.

Freddie couldn't look at him but instead, held his focus on the ground, a few feet away. Then like a massive bear aroused from hibernation, Freddie seemed to unfold himself from the bonnet and stand straight.

Chad at last caught his eye, and he knew. No words were needed. He knew. Ange, something had happened to Ange. My beautiful girl. No, please, please.

Freddie took three long strides towards him and he felt the hug, reminiscent of so many good times, now the portent of pain and grief. He felt Freddie kiss the top of his head, and his tears began to fall.

"It's Ange, isn't it?" Chad stepped back and looked at his friend. Tears were falling down the big man's cheeks, and his mouth was distorted. Freddie nodded and Chad's legs turned to jelly. He heard his cane clatter to the floor. Freddie leaned in and held him. He allowed himself to be turned and helped towards the car. He couldn't see through the tears, but he sensed the door opening and Odd Job brushing past him, then he was inside, the soft leather seats sucking him in. He felt a strong arm around his shoulder, and let his head fall onto Freddie's chest. "Tell me, Freddie, I need to know. What's happened?"

* * *

Odd Job drove them to Vicar Lane. Instead of going down the fire escape to the club, Chad had let Freddie carry him up two flights to his apartment, and they'd sat opposite each other in the large modern living area. He listened in silence as Freddie told him of the afternoon spent searching for Ange, the discovery at All Bar One, and the subsequent identification of Stuart Atwell. How Freddie's boys had got to Atwell's apartment first, before Lee's team. Another young kid losing his life as Atwell escaped. Freddie had explained how they'd pieced together that the Industrial Estate would be Atwell's refuge, and how they'd raced across Leeds to get there. He'd told of Lee's arrival, and how they'd begun searching, then they'd seen smoke coming from a unit at the far end of the estate. He'd described the explosion, and how his kids on bikes had helped him to get Lee to an ambulance. Chad looked up.

Freddie shifted in his seat. "He's critical, but they think he'll be okay."

"What happened to Ange, where was she?"

"Bro, we're ninety-nine per cent sure she was in the warehouse. The number plate of the car Atwell drove was found there and one of the firemen, a friend of mine, confirmed this morning that there was defo one or more people in the warehouse when it went up." He paused and sniffed. "Chad, bro. He'd given her Rohypnol, we know that. The car he took her in was in the warehouse, the firemen have found fragments of a handbag, and Angie hasn't been seen now for nearly twenty-four hours. I know you want to cling on, man, but..." Freddie's voice tapered off.

Chad sat in the same chair for two hours, aware of Freddie coming and going, he looked out of the window, on to the bustle of Vicar Lane below. People went about their daily business. A group of girls shrieked at some joke or other. Mundane, habitual, but not for him. He remembered the day his father died, and how strange it seemed that life for other people went on as normal. But how could that be? This time, it was as if he had to trudge through treacle to get from one minute to the next. If he knew anything, it was that nothing mattered, now. If only he'd had a lower tolerance to the Fentanyl, he wouldn't be here at all. Wouldn't have to go through this. Wouldn't have to know that Angie was dead, and he wouldn't have to bear the pain. It would be over. Maybe he could finish the job, he thought. The Fentanyl strip he'd kept in his jacket was gone. He looked for the methadone, enough of those would do the trick. Where the fuck were they? The fog in his head, partially cleared. Freddie. Of course. Freddie had taken them. Freddie, who knew him so well had anticipated the moment. That exit closed to him, he resumed his gaze over Vicar Lane. Unseeing, numb, alone.

CHAPTER 93

Friday Midday

He sat very still, the cane at his side as he looked out of the window over the skyline of Leeds. The nightmare would never leave, he thought, but it would fade. Twenty-four hours to confirm that human remains had been found and a further twenty-four before confirmation that Angie had been a victim. Forensics poured over the debris for further remains. Freddie had said Lee had been lucky. A blow to the head which had knocked him out, three broken ribs, a fractured wrist, and lacerations to his legs.

Jas said Freddie had saved Lee's life by grabbing him just before a sheet of molten corrugated metal landed on him before carrying him single-handed to the ambulance and giving him to the paramedics.

And Jas confirmed that they'd discovered Atwell was the beneficiary of the shares in Excelsior, which nailed the motive. They'd been so close to finding him.

Okay, he thought, get through today. One at a time. Lee was getting home this afternoon and they'd be waiting. It was time to go. The first step on a path to whatever normal was now going to be.

* * *

This was what it must be like living in another dimension, Chad thought. Helen bustled around the place, Freddie drank Peroni and entertained the kids, and he felt like he was watching it all on TV, one of those reality shows, Big Brother maybe, in which people go about their lives while others watched and then voted them out. He wished they'd vote him out. Everything went on around him but he didn't take part. He knew he'd got a smile fixed to his face, and betted he looked as dumb as hell. Every small movement by Helen, every bottle, cup, plate all triggered memories of the last time he had been there. When Angie was still alive, on a weekend away having fun with her friends. Christ, not even a week ago. None of it mattered now. Nothing mattered.

Lee hobbled into the kitchen supporting himself on NHS crutches. "Hey, Chad, how are you? What a pair we make, you with a cane me with crutches."

Chad stood, "I'm okay mate, how are you? Does any part of you work as it should? Jas tells me Freddie pulled you from the wreckage."

"I just helped out, bro, nothing to it." Said Freddie

Christ you knew things were bad when Freddie was self-deprecating, thought Chad, but he'd have been pissed if he hadn't got a mention.

Lee came close and leaned in. "I can't tell you how sorry I am, Chad. Anything you need let me know. I know you're staying with Freddie but you know you can come here any time you like."

"I know, thanks buddy. Anyway, come on sit down before you fall, and don't say anything else as I'll probably cry. I've been doing that a lot."

"Why will Uncle Chad cry? Mum, why will Uncle Chad cry?" hollered Hannah.

"Come here you little monkey and give your Dad a kiss," said Lee, distracting her from staring at Chad.

Well at least no-one was trying to jolly him along, Chad thought. He couldn't deal with that. Mind you it must have been like having the Ghost of Christmas Past for lunch.

"Anyone mind if I put the news on?" asked Lee.

"Go ahead, I don't mind," said Freddie.

Chad saw Lee raise an eyebrow towards him. He nodded. Come on fella, show a bit of interest. Poor Helen's worked her socks off and you're putting a big fuck off black cloud over the day. Nothing that's happened is their fault, at least watch the bloody news and stop staring at your shoes.

A reporter was finishing his piece to camera. Perfect frigging timing.

"It may be many days yet, before we understand fully, how and why the drama that unfolded here in Leeds on Tuesday evening came about. This is Ian White, for BBC News, in Leeds."

"What is it?" asked Lee.

Chad looked at him. "I don't know. Nothing. Just his use of the word drama struck a chord. No idea why."

CHAPTER 94

Saturday

"Explain that shit to me again, bro," said Freddie.

Lying awake for several hours during the night, the news report they'd watched earlier bothered him, but the fog of grief still enveloped him, smothered all thought, rendered clarity impossible. Then in the early hours, a chink of light began to penetrate the gloom. He'd spent the last ten minutes explaining to Freddie what he thought might have happened. It seemed he hadn't done it well.

"Okay," said Chad, "hang in there with me on this. Start with the guy on the news yesterday. He called it a drama. And that got me thinking. Atwell loves drama. Everything he does is staged. From wearing masks, wigs and make-up, to arranging scenes to look like something they're not. Andy Huxton, for example, arranged to look like a suicide, when in fact it was murder. Right?"

"Yeah, dude, I can see that. So, what?"

"So, what if the explosion was a stage. Arranged to make it look to us like he and Angie had died in it."

"Man, not that much of a stage. We know Angie did die in it, and it's only a matter of time till they find that he did too. But let's say it was a stage, bro, why would he do that, it doesn't make sense?"

"Maybe something went wrong, maybe the plan fucked up. He's not infallible, remember, he didn't manage to kill me."

"Not for want of trying, bro. What do you think his plan was?"

"Maybe he believed he had more time. If you think about it, once the police ran into a series of dead ends, and any leads they did have all led to Andy Huxton, then he was home and dry. He didn't think that the police would even look to contradict what was in front of them. Andy Huxton is an abused kid who seeks revenge. End of. Why look any further? No prints on the weapon, other than Andy Huxton's, why would anyone bother to dig? So, when Lee's team contacted the recruitment company to ask who was in charge and to get a list of staff names, he got spooked. They were too close, and he must have wondered why they were even looking? I think his plan was based on the case being closed, and once the dust had settled, he would have sold the company, got another twenty million quid, and he and Angie would run off into the sunset to spend it. It just shows he didn't know her at all."

"So, if that's the plan, what the hell went wrong? Man, so wrong, that he decides to blow the shit out of a whole industrial estate?"

"I'm not sure. I like to think that maybe Ange told him where to go. That she threw his plan back in his face, but I don't know. Had she done that, he'd have kicked off, sure, but he was holding her and she wasn't going anywhere, so I think he'd have convinced himself that she'd come around to his way of thinking. If, after several days, she hadn't, then I think we would never have found her. He'd have killed her and dumped her somewhere."

Chad allowed Freddie the time to assimilate this. Was he right? Who knew? Worth exploring? Yep, defo, he thought. He looked across at Freddie. The big man was struggling to think it through, his huge legs were crossing and uncrossing and his frown was deepening.

"Okay, but that didn't happen, and it's a big jump from there to the shit show that did happen." Said Freddie.

"Yep, it is. We'll never know, but maybe it was something so bad that he had to get out, cover his tracks and exit without anyone looking for him. Hence, blow the shit out of Leeds."

Chad stared down onto Vicar Lane, bustling with shoppers.

"Maybe Ange created the problem. Maybe she didn't come around from the Rohypnol. She'd been drinking, you said, and that's not a good mix. Maybe, he gave her more than he should have and she died." Chad paused. God, he hoped so, he hoped she was dead before it blew. "Let's just say that happened. Angie died. That changes the plan, and once it's changed, he must adapt. Atwell is nothing if not devious. He would probably have had a fallback position all along, just in case."

Chad could see from the deep furrowed frown on Freddie's brow that his mind was working overtime, but would it get to the right place? "Chad, bro, are you saying that you think that Atwell is alive somewhere?"

Chad looked at Freddie, then out of thc window. "I guess you've nailed it, Freddie, that's what I think. The question is, where?"

"The only way that dude could have gone out of there and not blown himself to shit was out the back of the warehouse. It's the only way he could have done it. My guys were on the estate half an hour before the fire, and we had the front exit covered, we'd have seen him," said Freddie. "He'd have needed somewhere to go, he knew his flat was off-limits, cos we nearly caught him there, so he must have somewhere else he can stay. Somewhere close to the industrial estate, that he could get to after he'd set the flame."

"What's out the back?" asked Chad.

Freddie reached for his phone. "Google Earth, bro. We live by it, in my line of work."

"What's it showing?"

Freddie leaned over the chair and held the phone in front of Chad. The canal ran East to West, behind the industrial estate.

"Scroll right."

Freddie's finger rolled the screen. "Not much down there.

Nowhere leaping off the page where he could lie low while this dies down. Okay, what about East?" Freddie scrolled left and parts of the city centre came into view. "The station, I suppose he could have got a train out of Leeds?"

"Nah, don't think so, he'd have stank of petrol, he'd have been dirty, and I don't think he'd have had luggage with him. I think you were right Freddie, he had to have somewhere else to stay. Keep scrolling."

Freddie rolled the screen and enlarged it. He paused, they both saw the same thing, at the same time.

"Bridgewater Place," they said.

"He's crazy, but he's not stupid," said Freddie.

"He's got Huxton's keys and fob," said Chad. "And we know he loves a bit of drama. Where's the last place we would look?"

Freddie shook his head, "I'm not sure even Napoleon would pull that stunt, but maybe, just maybe, you could be right."

CHAPTER 95

"How the seam in those jeans isn't splitting I'll never know," said Chad, standing on the towpath below the burned-out shell of Unit Five. Freddie's enormous frame squatted by the fence.

Freddie turned. "Look, bro, you can see where he's cut a hole in the fence, and there'll be one at the top of the bank but I ain't scrambling up there in these jeans, man. They're Paul Smith."

"Fair enough. How long do you reckon from here to Bridgewater Place?" asked Chad.

"Why?"

"Why cut a hole in the fence? For a shortcut. What's the only place we know close to here that it would make a shortcut?

Freddie started at the fence, then looked up. "Fuck."

"That's where he went. Huxton's apartment. He knows how to get in and out without being seen. He's got keys and access to the car park."

Freddie closed his eyes and tilted his head back. He blew out a long, slow breath, then looked down, staring at the ground for a moment, before fixing his eyes on Chad. "I'm going to eat his fucking heart."

* * *

Chad sat at the bar in the club with Freddie's team milling around him. Christ, he thought, no way would I want to get on the wrong side of this lot. Looked like prison tattooists had done a roaring trade with these punters. LOVE and HATE the knuckle adornment of choice. Freddie tapped a glass with a spoon and called his team to order.

"This is how it's going down, bros. Chad and I are going to smoke the dude out, you guys are going to cover every exit, every road and every side street within a quarter-mile of Bridgewater Place. Tony, you'll stay close to me with your boys, in case he tries to do a Butch Cassidy break for freedom and come out firing. Okay?" Freddie paused.

"Chad, anything you want to say?"

The assembled hard men stared at him. "Guys, I know you have lost two of your friends in the last few days and that this guy Atwell has shit coming to him." A murmur of agreement rose from around him. "He also killed my wife," Chad paused and swallowed, he couldn't lose it now, "and tried to top me so, believe me, I want that too. But if this ends in a shoot-out and he dies, we all lose. The police will have to make arrests, your business activities will be turned over, and a whole world of trouble will come down on all of us. I want him, as much or more than you do, but we get him alive, and we hand him over." He looked around. The eyes of Leeds's most wanted stared back at him, before turning as one for confirmation, to Freddie. Chad turned to Freddie.

"That's right, boys, we take him and we hand him over," he held Chad's eyes. "If possible."

That was the best he was going to get from Freddie, Chad thought. He nodded at Freddie. "There's a couple of calls I need to make before we go."

CHAPTER 96

Chad walked slowly down the ramp at the entrance to the car park at Bridgewater Place. George Hampsthwaite, or Inspector Frost as Chad now thought of him, was standing outside his wooden cabin. "Hello, Mister Hilton, nice to see you again," said George "And, well, blow me, it's Freddie Jackson, isn't it? Partners in crime, back in the day, so to speak."

"Hello, George, nice to see you too, and yes this is my old mate Freddie," said Chad, nodding in Freddie's direction. Chad smiled, as Freddie shook George's hand, and patted him on the shoulder as if he'd just discovered they were long lost brothers. Freddie could do that shit, in an instant, make a friend of someone he'd never met. Freddie was chattering away and Chad could feel the nerves in his stomach. It had been like this in the pre-match dressing room. Freddie talking ten to the dozen as he was now.

Freddie was insisting, "George, you must come for dinner at my club, and bring your lovely wife. On me, of course. Tell him, Chad, tell him how good the food is."

Chad began to mutter, but Freddie took over, giving George a business card and not taking no for an answer. "George," said Chad, "I'm still helping the police on Mister Huxton's disappearance and murder, and Freddie is kindly assisting me. I wondered if you'd seen anyone coming and going recently from the flats, someone you're not familiar with? To be specific, whether anyone is using Mister Huxton's apartment?"

"I wouldn't know unless they had a car," said George. "And no-one has come in or out that I didn't recognise. You'd be better to ask security, they should know if the fob to the top floors has been used."

Chad recalled the last brush he'd had with the security guard and hoped another guard was on duty. "George, they can be a bit sniffy. Computer says no, types. Not as helpful as you. Would you mind coming with us and having a quick word, it might be better coming from you."

"Of course, Mister Hilton, happy to help."

Freddie kept a monologue going, walking in stride with George. Chad's knee twinged a little as he climbed the steps to the front entrance, and then eased again as he walked through the swing doors into the foyer. He needn't have worried, he thought. Freddie knew the security guard. Of course, he did. More back-slapping and shoulder pumping, along with a variety of handshakes. "Thanks, George, we can manage from here," said Chad.

"Hey George, I expect you at the club next Saturday, at 7:30 p.m. Table for two reserved. Okay?" Freddie called as George walked away. George turned and waved. He looked like he's just been knighted.

Chad was introduced to the security guard. "Great, nice to meet you," he said. "Look, I'm working with the police." He held up his temporary ID. "And we've been tipped off that someone may be using Mister Huxton's apartment. Are you aware of this, or have you seen anyone?"

"To be honest, there are hundreds of people come and go, all the time, so I can't say I've seen anyone. But I did notice the penthouse lights on the lift have lit up recently, and no-one is occupying the top two floors. Didn't think much of it, to be honest, they sell and rent these all the time."

"No, I understand. Listen, I need you to help us here. Could you call up to the apartment, and tell whoever answers that the police need to gain access to Mister Huxton's apartment, that's all, whatever he says, tell him you don't know what it's about, you've just been told to ask. Can you do that for us?"

The guard looked from Chad to Freddie. "This is straight-up, right? I'm not going to get in any trouble?"

"No, you're not, it's fine. Oh, and can you give us access to the car park?"

* * *

The lift doors closed behind Chad. Standing still, he let his eyes adjust to the gloom, then followed Freddie through the door into the car park, noting a gun-shaped bulge in his waistband. "Freddie, if he's here, he'll have to make his way across the car park to the side door, over there," said Chad, pointing to an illuminated green exit sign.

"Right bro, you wait behind one of the pillars just there, where you're standing, so that when the lift doors open, you'll see him in the light. I'll wait in your sightline, nearer the exit door. Give me the thumbs up if it's him."

Freddie whispered into a lapel mic but Chad couldn't make out what was said. Shit, if we're right this bastard will be here in a minute, he thought. His stomach rumbled and his legs felt like dead weights. He hadn't felt like this since he'd been in the tunnel waiting to go out and play, hearing the noise of the crowd fuelling the anticipation. But he knew what he was doing then, he was in his comfort zone. Not today. The cane felt flimsy and lightweight and his skin smelled of fear. Come on. He pictured lying on his back looking at a water bottle being put to his lips. He pictured Angie, beautiful Angie. The scent of her perfume in his nostrils. Then the lift doors opened.

CHAPTER 97

I replace the phone in its holder by the door and take three swift paces to the windows. There are no coppers down there. If they wanted to come and inspect the flat, there should be a squad car, at least. What does that mean? "It means that the time has come to say goodbye," I murmur.

No more second-guessing, time to move on, and anyway it's all part of the plan, just a day early. I'll book a room at the Radisson at Manchester Airport and stay there tonight, a nice meal, then Emirates First Class tomorrow to Sydney. I walk into the bedroom and collect my suitcase and backpack.

I'll go out the side door of the car park, they'll pick me up on CCTV in the foyer, but they haven't repaired it in the car park. Typical. Useless bastards. Two minutes to the station, then gone. I open the backpack and check the pistol is inside. Better be on the safe side, I'll ditch it later. I take a final look around Huxton's apartment, smile, open the door, then pick up my luggage. "Onwards and upwards." I press the button for the lift.

CHAPTER 98

Chad exhaled slowly. He recognised the taste in his mouth from years ago. It was the taste of apprehension, of fear and of excitement. But he also felt a rage bubble inside him. Angie, what had that bastard done to Angie? Payback, he thought. At whatever cost. He looked through the darkness to where Freddie's shape hid in the shadow. Like old times, the two of them bearing the weight of expectation. They'd always delivered. They'd deliver now. In his mind's eye he could see the words on the dressing room wall: "Control the rage. Harness the anger. Lead the line." Bring it on, he thought. He heard the lift arrive and holding his breath he peered around the pillar. Peeking through the glass panel in the car park door, he saw a man emerge from the lift, carrying a suitcase and with a backpack over his shoulder. He was tall, over six feet. Stuart Atwell.

Chad pressed his body into the hard, cold concrete of the pillar as the door to the car park opened. He raised his arm so that Freddie could see. Atwell was through the door and in two paces past the pillar, striding across the car park floor towards the exit sign. Then shit happened.

"Yo, Stu, bro, how ya doing?" said Freddie, emerging from the darkness. "Let's hope you're not going to do anything stupid. And, bro, when I say stupid, you've got lots of previous, haven't you, man? Wasting two young dudes who never did you a minute's harm. Stupid. Trying to waste my best friend. Stupid. But, blowing the shit out of a warehouse, cos you'd overdosed Angie, man, that's a whole new level of stupid. That's batshit fucking crazy."

Atwell's left hand started to peel the backpack from his shoulder.

Chad stepped from behind the pillar as Freddie kept on talking.

"You can't have thought you'd get away with it, man. Did you?" Silence. "You did? Fuck, man, you're dumber than you look."

Atwell was reaching into his backpack and something black and metallic was edging its way out.

"Atwell!" Chad swung his cane like a baseball bat and the silver skull-head caught Atwell on the elbow and the Makarov clattered to the floor. Chad's momentum spun him around and he felt the air whoosh as he narrowly dodged a punch. Atwell dropped the suitcase and dived for the gun, but before he could get to his feet Freddie was on him. Like a goalkeeper's worst nightmare, he appeared out of the darkness and launched a flying kick. The sound of bone crunching filled the car park followed by a howl of pain. The connection sent Atwell spinning across the floor. No way he's getting up from that, thought Chad. A Jackson right boot, through the laces. Not a chance. Light flooded the garage as the side door to the car park opened, and then the door behind Chad, near the lift. Through the first came Jas with Joe Schmidt. Through the other came Tony and his team. Job done. Chad made to get up, but his knee locked solid, and a bolt of pain shot up his leg and along his spine. He rolled onto his hip and pulled himself along to see Freddie was leaning over Atwell. He slumped against the wheel of a car as Freddie knelt beside Atwell's head.

Atwell's eyes were open, staring up.

Freddie's voice was low. "You're going down bro, the cops are here and your little game's over. But don't you worry, my friend, you're still going to pay. Two of my brothers dead. That's a heavy price. So, here's how it plays out. You go down, dude, and wherever they send you, I'll let you stew, let you do some time, get lazy. Then, when I'm ready I'll give the word. It won't matter which nick you're in, we'll get to you. It won't matter if you're in solitary, we'll get to you, we own the screws. And when I say the word, bro, you'll remember me, you'll remember my boys, and you'll remember Angie. And you'll wish I'd killed you right now." Freddie stood. "All yours, DS Carter."

Chad grabbed the wheel and bonnet to haul himself up, but two hands came from behind and under his arms, and lifted him to his feet. The hint of perfume, and then a hand resting on the side of his neck, and her lips brushing his ear.

"C'mon, Hopalong, I need you in one piece."

He turned to face Jas.

That smile.

CHAPTER 99

Chad sat on a rickety bench in the cemetery looking out across the solemn rows of tombstones. The sky was vast and early summer clouds drifted high above Yorkshire. Would he continue to come as time passed, he thought? It had been three months since Angie's death and he'd come to sit and talk to her most days. But would that last? Was it guilt that made him come? But why guilt? What more could he have done? He'd talked to her more in death than he had in life. At least that's how it seemed. And he'd been honest in his dialogue with her, he hadn't sugar-coated things. He'd told her that he was unsure if they'd have made things work again, because once trust had gone it was tough to get back. He'd told her that he was off the Fentanyl and that the acupuncture was working, so that might have made a difference. He'd seen Jas once or twice in the intervening weeks and had told Ange about those meetings. Nothing had happened, he'd said, but he thought it might. What did Ange think? But as with all the questions he wanted to ask her, they would never be answered. Still, he found the cemetery cathartic and his conversations with Ange therapeutic.

The sun flickered through the leaves of a massive oak tree and Chad felt his phone vibrate in his pocket. He hated that phone. A text from Freddie.

Yo, bro you okay? Look, I've been invited to play in a Rest of the World eleven against a team of Aussie celebs over in Sydney for their equivalent of Soccer Aid. I said yeah it will be cool. They asked about you and I said you couldn't play but you could coach. How about it bro? It'll be cool. Expenses paid and a bit of cash as well. Take you out of yourself, just what you need.

He replied. *I'll let you know buddy. Not sure.*

Chad's phone pinged again. *Too late bro, I told them you'll do it. We fly Friday, Emirates First Class from Manchester. I'll send details through.*

Chad looked across the peaceful landscape, the flowers at the gravesides a blush of colour. He smiled. "For fuck's sake, Freddie."

The End

Printed in Great Britain
by Amazon

36912540R00212